MARY McAFFERTY

MARY McAFFERTY

Lyndon Berry

The Book Guild Ltd
Sussex, England

The Book Guild Ltd
25 High Street,
Lewes, Sussex

First published 1999
© Lyndon Berry 1999
Set in Baskerville
Typesetting by Keyboard Services, Luton, Beds

Printed in Great Britain by
Bookcraft (Bath) Ltd, Avon

A catalogue record for this book is
available from the British Library

ISBN 1 85776 359 9

*This book is dedicated to
E.T. and J.E.M. who, together,
gave me a reason for being.*

Lyndon Berry, March, 1999.

1

Light snow had fallen overnight and the dawn mist which hung low on the clifftop path made further hazard, causing the priest to pick his way with care. Yet there was a certain urgency about his going. Hundreds of feet below, giant waves spumed onto the rugged coastline, their dull roar blending with the cries of the seabirds, but the priest was oblivious to the wild beauty of it all.

Father Eamonn Coughlan was a man tormented with ambition. He had prayed many times for it to be otherwise, but it lay like a black beast, waiting impatiently for him on his every waking. His faith was not all it might have been and he had not easily entered the priesthood. Now he was in regret at not having selected another way of life, for the award of this bleak parish on the west coast of Ireland had become a daily running sore of aggravation to his very soul. Inniscourt was little more than a poverty-stricken hamlet which represented failure, a desert of despair, ignorance and illiteracy. God had surely forsaken it. Dublin's bright lights and sparkling conversation would have much better suited his academic abilities and aspirations. There he could more ably commune with the true grandeur of the Church, achieve promotion and a comfortable living. Fate had now brought him that chance, and this very morning he would be taking steps to bring the chance to reality.

He paused for breath as he reached the top of the headland. Inniscourt lay sprawled below him, stone hovels jutting through the snow and reflecting the pale light of the rising sun. He turned his gaze away to look out over the grey Atlantic.

1

Somewhere out there beyond the distant point where the sky blurred with the ocean was America. The talk in Dublin had been that America was a land flowing with milk and honey, enough to feed the whole wide world a million times over and more. The dream in which every man was equal, a great and powerful place where a body could make a new start. He would tell his flock all of this, but of course he would not be going with them. It was not at all in his scheme of things. Yet it was his priestly duty to get his people there, away from the nightmare of starvation and disease that had come on the land.

The great hunger was upon Ireland in this year of 1847, and its people were dying in their thousands of starvation. The potato crop had failed for the third year in succession, this time on a disastrous scale to leave unprecedented famine and disease in its wake. Ireland was a place to leave, and the panic-stricken exodus to Europe and North America was already well under way. It had been the lack of money for the villagers' ship passage which had held up Father Coughlan's plans. Now that problem had been resolved, and his fervent prayers for release had been seemingly answered. But in the doing of it he had joined hands with the devil incarnate.

In normal circumstances the McAffertys were not a family he would so much as have passed the time of day with. They lived some distance from his parish, and their Saturday night visits to Jimmy O'Dea's tavern were drunken, brawling affairs barely endured by the villagers. But that was as nothing when compared with their black reputation as moneylenders and extortionists. Even the act of murder had been laid at their doorstep. Yet if the priest played his part in their scheme of things they would furnish the passage money to Boston. Every last man, woman and child in the village would be included. He had Liam McAfferty's firm promise on it. But it would come at an awful price.

The priest turned away from his brief contemplation and headed downhill towards Inniscourt, his long strides covering the ground with added urgency. This was going to be a difficult day and he had much work to do but short time allowed to him. Only one real problem remained. Mary Whelan had a strong mind to go her own way in life and might yet thwart his carefully laid plans. He frowned deeply. She could not be allowed to become the stumbling block that would bar his way to Dublin... The girl would have to be made to see the way it was. In any matter of it did not the McAffertys have the grand plan for her future? It would not be what she wanted, oh no, she considered herself too grand altogether. But this was no time for her to be having fanciful thoughts. For God's sake! Why all this torment in him? There was simply a responsibility, yes that was it, a responsibility to see the girl settled.

He had made a solemn vow to her parents that he would do that. But after today the weight of it would be off his back, and he would be free of the shackles of this place. Then it would be off to Dublin, where he would surely be given a civilised parish. Was it not his right for all the years he had wasted here? In just five days' time he would be thirty years old, and nothing but poverty and misery to show for it. The priest wrestled once more with his conscience and his steps slackened as he walked into the village, for despite all the reassurances he had fed himself he knew that this was not a godly thing he was about to do.

2

Pale sunshine filtered through a small window, bringing relief to the dark corners of a modestly furnished room. The sweet smell of unseasoned timber hung in the air, vying with occasional bursts of pungent smoke which escaped from a glowing peat fire. Dominating the chimney recess, a rolltop desk stood below neatly varnished shelves which carried a goodly number of books, their titles denoting impressive works of learning.

The sound of hammering seemed everywhere, and there was no escape from its invasion as it echoed off the stone walls. In the centre of the room two coffins lay sprawled at opposing angles on the kitchen table.

Intent on his task Sean Dolan, tongue protruding in grim concentration, drove crude iron nails into the lid of the larger one. His emaciated body was weary with hunger, and only stubborn spirit kept him on his feet. Sometimes the hammer hit its target and sometimes it splintered the wood. But there was no annoyance, simply an expression of purpose.

Mary Whelan sat and watched the man at his work, the runners of her rocking chair biting sharply into the stone floor to create a soft counterpoint against the flat beat of the hammer. Mary was a true west coast beauty. Her hair, holding the softest of waves, was deep chestnut, its sheen evoking the magic of an autumn morning. It cascaded over her shawl, almost down to the waist.

The eyes would hold a man riveted, mysteriously green as the ocean, and keenly searching in their bright intelligence. Her nose was at once impudent and noble, and when the nostrils flared in anger above the stubborn chin it was a brave fellow who would stand his ground. The full soft lips were a warm promise, as yet not made in love. There was neither youth nor man in the village of Inniscourt who had gone to his bed without dreams of her.

The rosary hung from long slim fingers to lie loosely in her lap. A mourning dress of dense black cotton was ill-fitting, but it could not hide the beauty of her slim figure. She had been crying, but now seemed to have reached an inner peace as she looked once more at the coffins.

Fond memories flooded her mind. Joseph Whelan had been a caring and loyal father. A schoolteacher with strong political convictions and a simple belief in God. A man who might have gone on to better things.

The offer of a teaching post and more comfortable life in Dublin was set aside, then set aside again. Instead, his self-imposed task had been to bring education to the illiterate and world-ignorant people of this remote corner of Ireland.

'They must be taught that life is not to wonder where the next bowl of potatoes is coming from,' he told Mary. 'We have to produce educated men who will one day sit in our own parliament and free us from the yoke of England.'

His salary came from a Sligo charity fund, but it was small and often obliged him to dip into his life savings. Years of patient teaching became his reason for being. Yet all his efforts had cut precious few inroads into the dreadful lethargy of his students. Now he was dead.

Mary's mother had not been totally devoted to her husband's ideals. A learned woman, Helen gave up much to sustain the man in his cause, but would have preferred the life in Dublin.

'You waste yourself on these bog-Irish,' she said, 'they do not have it in them to amount to anything.'

But Joseph always managed to avoid a direct confrontation. 'It is what God wants me to do,' he had said.

Helen was not comfortable with religion. She did not believe in the homily of suffer now and sit in heaven later.

Joseph affected compromise to placate her.

5

'We will go to Dublin, one day,' he said. 'I have some promising scholars to guide, a year or so will do it. Be patient.'

They had met when Joseph was a rather more ambitious teacher in a private school. Helen fell in love with the man of ideals, and they were soon married.

Helen Whelan had come from an upper-class background in Castlebar, County Mayo. A gentlewoman once used to drinking the finest Madeira wine from the thinnest of glasses, with the longest of stems, she had been patient. Now she was dead.

Mary was born the day after Helen's forty-second birthday. It proved a difficult confinement, and although the couple were in raptures over their baby daughter, the act of giving birth at this advanced age was not without cost.

Helen was quite often ill, and Mary had quickly to learn a great deal of self-sufficiency. A willing and capable girl with a sharply intelligent mind, she was doted upon by her father. Receiving what was in reality a private education, Mary could read and write by the age of five, and her nose was seldom out of a book. With great eagerness she soaked up her father's teachings and philosophy.

She was just eighteen when the great hunger struck Ireland. There had been crop failures in the preceding two years, but nothing on the scale of this one. Food of any kind was at a premium. But there had been a gentle, if somewhat mysterious, trickle of sustenance into the Whelan home. Regular visits from Father Coughlan left behind potatoes, bread, apples, seed cake and even sometimes eggs.

Joseph Whelan would not have it questioned where this food came from. The Holy Father brought it, and it would be wrong to enquire into its origins.

Helen, who did not believe in miracles, often wondered about the source, though she said nothing. The amount of food was little, but properly rationed it might have been enough to keep the three alive. However, within a close family, matters are dealt with from the heart rather than the head.

Helen loved her daughter almost beyond reason and saw that most of her meagre share went that way. She would say

6

she had eaten. It did not matter that she was starving slowly to death, but Mary must not.

The worst winter in living memory came to aggravate Ireland's terrible situation, and Helen became ill with influenza. Weakened by starvation, she quickly succumbed to the illness and died in her sleep.

Joseph caught the disease, and his health deteriorated. But it was not really the illness, nor the lack of food which eventually claimed him. He simply lacked the will to live without Helen, and died within a few days of her.

Mary lifted her gaze away from the coffins to look at a picture of the Madonna and Child which hung over the bookshelves.

Who was this God who had taken her parents from her? Why did he allow the people to die in their thousands, stricken by hunger and disease?

There had to be a reason. It must be the work of the devil, that's what it was, and already putting wicked thoughts in her head to doubt the Almighty. Her thoughts strayed and a cold panic came. She was alone for the first time in her life. What would she do? Her heartbeat suddenly grew faster, pounding in her ears along with the sound of the incessant hammering.

She bit on her lower lip. These bad thoughts must be stopped at once, or they would surely take her over. Her mind raced to seek comfort. Why not go to Dublin and take a job with a grand family as a children's governess? Her father had talked of such things. For a while she felt better, but the bad thoughts crept back again.

Dublin was a far-off giant of a place, full of the rich and grand city folk who would laugh at her. They held a low opinion of the western folk. Bog-Irish they called them. That's what her mother had said. A governess indeed? . . . And who would give her such a post? She would be the most fortunate person to be taken on as a scullery-maid. And what of the money to travel there? The pounding in her head started once more, and the hammering on the coffins seemed to come louder.

7

Her jumbled thoughts were interrupted by the click of the door latch. She looked enquiringly towards the sound, and with a squealing protest the door opened to reveal the parish priest.

Father Coughlan nodded towards Mary as he bent to go under the low wooden transom of the door. His cloak was wet, and the mist had placed a large dewdrop on the end of his nose. It swung there precariously.

'Good mornin' to you, Mary Whelan, and God bless you.'

She stood up, hands clasped before her as the rocking chair groaned its way to a slow halt. She was fascinated by the dewdrop. It twinkled brightly in the light from the open door, just like a chandelier in some great house. She wanted to laugh, but the laughter would not come.

'Good mornin', holy Father,' she answered soberly.

The priest looked beyond Mary to take in the back of Sean Dolan. Hammering away without pause, Dolan was unaware of the priest's arrival.

'Would y'stop that a while, Sean?'

Dolan turned slowly, and wearily regarded the priest for a few moments. Putting down the hammer, he touched his forehead in salute.

'I did not hear y'come in, Father... I'm done with the nailin' up an' all.'

'You're a good man, Sean, y'can go now. There are other dear souls for your work. God bless you.'

'An' bless you, Father.'

He scratched together the nails which lay strewn on the table and put them in his pocket, then picked up the hammer. With a wry smile he looked at Mary and shrugged his shoulders in embarrassment of the occasion.

'God bless an' keep y', Mary, they are in heaven now.'

The latch fell into place as the door closed softly behind him, and there was a brief silence before the priest walked over to her. His embrace of sympathy was short.

'I know how it is with you, Mary, but we must all pull together if we are to survive this terrible time.'

She looked up into his gaunt face.

8

'Yes, Father, would y' pray with me for the souls of my dear mother an' father?'

'In a while... First there are things I must say to you. This very morning I met with the McAfferty family. Even though he says it himself, Liam McAfferty is without doubt a man of great notions...'

He paused as he saw the look of sudden disgust on her face, then his voice came stronger.

'Liam has the grand plans to go t'America within three days, takin' with him the dear souls who have been spared.' The priest hesitated slightly before going on. 'He has made the agreement with me that y'should go with the family and...'

Her interruption was full of fear. 'America, Father? What would I be wanting to go t'America for?'

'There are t'be no arguments about it, child. The Almighty in His great wisdom has made this the time of leavin'.'

'Surely the crop will come again, Father... Why can we not stay an' get help from Cloncarrig with the food? We can return it when we make our own way.'

He shook his head. 'The land is sorely diseased and we would all die in the waiting for it t'be otherwise. The only souls left in Cloncarrig are Patrick Duffy an' his family.'

'I could stay with them.'

'No y'could not. They take ship for Liverpool this day.'

She looked in appeal at him. 'But America is so far away, a stranger's land... Father, I am so afraid of it!'

'Child, child, child ... do not be afraid, the Lord is with you. America is a grand an' glorious place with food enough t'feed the whole wide world, an' you will be goin' there with your own people.'

Her expression became stubborn.

'Forgive me for speaking ill, Father, but I have not a great fondness for the McAffertys.'

The priest's former kindly tone took on a hard edge of admonishment.

'May God forgive you for such an utterance!... Was it not Donal McAfferty himself who has been sendin' you the food t'keep body and soul together?'

Her eyes opened wide with surprise, and her voice was full of passionate disbelief.

'Surely not, Father! I thought it t'be a blessin' from the church... Tell me, please!... Tell me it was what you were doin' for everyone!'

'Donal did not want it known. He wanted to tell you himself. He has a great love for you, and would make a powerful husband for your new life in America.'

The disgust and loathing grew more obvious on her face.

'But I have not a great love for him, Father! If I had known the food was from the McAffertys it would have stuck in my throat, so it would ... they are wicked people!'

Anger came into the priest's eyes.

'On your knees, child!... On your knees at once an' beg the Lord's forgiveness for these terrible things you say.'

Mary sank dutifully to her knees under the onslaught and put her hands together in prayer. The priest looked down with sudden compassion, then knelt beside her on the stone floor.

'Great and merciful Father in heaven. This is but a child who knows not the ways of the world. Help her to walk the path that leads to a full and righteous life as she now asks for your blessing.'

He turned his head slightly to glance at Mary, and noted the look of defiance.

'Mary Whelan!... Ask for God's guidance on the way to your new life in America.'

She closed her eyes tightly. 'Dear Lord, help me find my way through this terrible time, and bless my dear parents who are now surely with you.'

There was silence as the priest waited for more, but Mary was without further words. His voice had a brittle patience in it.

'And what about blessin' the McAffertys, without whose food you would now be surely dead?'

With a contemptuous twist to her mouth she bent again to prayer, but there was no conviction in her voice.

'An' bless the McAffertys without whose food I would be dead.'

10

'Now bless them for takin' you to America!'

Mary's voice took on a new pleading.

'But I do not want to be goin' with them, Father, please don't make me ... please, Father.'

Conscience came again to haunt the priest. He prayed softly for guidance. But the state of holiness was breached with urgent and insidious thought.

The McAffertys had presented him with the key to escape. If he spurned the chance he would surely remain here forever. It did not bear thinking about.

And was he not saving the lives of his flock? Further delay would mean the end for them. But his conscience was not so readily salved, for this girl plagued him.

Her parents had given him food for the mind. He would have been alone and lost in this wilderness but for their intelligent conversation and deep understanding. Did he not now have a duty to their daughter?

His mind was in tumult. Why did the thoughts return again and again to dwell on thirty pieces of silver? Was it not because he was delivering her up to a family she hated? But she was strong in mind and body. She would survive them.

There was no more time to dwell on it. It was God's will. Yes, it was most surely God's will. With troubled eyes he broke from prayer and turned to look at Mary. His voice was firm, yet it carried distress.

'This is a time of great danger, my child. Within three days there will not be a soul left in our village. There is not a place t'go, save over the water.'

She looked hard at the priest, and her question was searching.

'Will you be going t'America, Father?'

'The Lord has decreed that I must go to Dublin.'

'Could I not go there with you, Father?'

'Indeed y'could not! I am your priest and will be reporting t'my superiors, who will grant me a new flock. The Lord's work must go on in Ireland.'

The set of Mary's chin was stubborn, but her tone became pleading. 'I would be no burden, Father. You could get me a

11

position there in one of the fine houses. I can cook and sew and do many things, so I can ... an' I can read an' write.'

'I could not think of it! Dublin is no fit place for an unmarried girl of eighteen.'

'Why is that, Father?'

'Never you mind the why of it! Now enough of this. I have much t'do, an' must settle your future or I shall have failed in my duty.'

His voice was now full of authority, the questions and the tone of them angled to force the right answers.

'You would not turn your heart away from the will of God, would you, Mary?'

'I would not do that, Father.'

The priest cleared his throat and steeled himself to deliver his kiss of treachery.

'What I am about to tell you is the Lord's wish... This morning I have been with Him in deep an' most earnest prayer. He has revealed to me His direction for your great good and happiness.'

'Yes, Father.'

'Mary, my child, before I close up the church an' go to Dublin on Sunday I am to marry you with Donal McAfferty.'

Her vision blurred as the blood of hot temper and stark disbelief at his words flooded her brain. Her spirited retort came hissing at him.

'Marry with Donal McAfferty? I will not!'

But the priest was into his set task and would now see it through.

'Mary Whelan! ... I would not have believed you were such a wilful an' rebellious soul.'

She came back hard at him, her manner pleading yet demanding reason.

'But I do not even know him, Father. How can the Lord make for me to marry a man I do not know or love?'

'Mary, my child, I think y'talk of the love you read about in your story books. Marriage is about respect for your husband and the raising of good Catholic children to serve the Lord.'

She felt the terror grow within her. This could not be.

12

Marriage with a filthy, ignorant creature who looked at her with such strange expression whenever they passed in the village. She had never as much as passed a word with him.

Desperation entered her voice.

'If I must journey t'America, why cannot I go with the rest of the people?'

'The other families have enough with their own. You must go with the McAffertys, and it is as Donal's wife y'will be going. It would not be proper for you to go with Liam an' his sons in any other way.'

'Why not, Father ... why would it not be proper?'

'You dare to question the word of God?'

'I do not! I only ask why would it not be proper to make my own way in this land of America.'

'You have to go with the McAffertys.'

'I can well look after myself.'

The priest was tired and his voice burned with irritation.

'You do not know what you say. It is a journey of thousands of miles which will take many weeks and...'

'I will not do this thing!'

'The Lord has said y'must!'

'I cannot believe that!'

'You will be quiet!... Do you know what you have said? You are putting your soul into the hands of the devil with such words!'

She became quiet, eyes downcast, still unable to grasp the enormity of the priest's intent. He regarded her for a moment, then began to speak with affected understanding.

'I will later ask the Lord t'forgive you, my child, for I know you are in the deep sorrow an' do not mean the words you say.'

She did not reply, and the priest began to speak once more.

'Mary, on this great voyage y' will be livin' close as can be with many strangers about you, a position of the gravest danger to a young Catholic woman. You must have a husband t'take care of you.'

Mary let out a deep sob as she wrung her hands together in agitation.

13

'Why should the Lord want this awful thing to be happenin' to me?'

The priest looked at her. But his eyes contained no more compassion and his self-torment was past. It was done.

'There is no other way for it. To stay would mean y'dead from the hunger, or worse, with the people driven mad and the devil abroad the land.'

Mary looked unseeingly towards the coffins, only vaguely aware of Father Coughlan's final words. They were cold and studied.

'It would also mean the end for all your neighbours ... for if you go against God's will the McAffertys would not take them ... They would surely all die.'

He turned away and went into loud prayer, but it was lost on Mary. Her thoughts were with herself and survival from this nightmare. A great millstone had been placed upon her shoulders, and there seemed no escape from it.

3

Inniscourt had the one street. It lay straight as an arrow through a litter of stone cottages, seeming to come from nowhere and going to another such place. It was called Saint Patrick's Way, but it was no more than a rutted mess of a thing. When it rained, which was more often than not, it turned into a black bog that would suck the boots off the feet. The locals had nicknamed it Paddy's Way.

There was Jimmy O'Dea's beer tavern on the one side of it, and Pat O'Hagan's one-roomed store on the other. Neither man had a drop or a crumb left to sell. Now they waited impatiently with the rest for the time of leaving.

The sombreness of the morning burials had given way to an air of optimism. It is not in the Irish character to dwell overlong on misery, since there is so much of it to go back to. And wasn't there to be a wedding anyway? More importantly, there would be food and strong drink. The McAffertys would surely see to it.

A small timber and stone structure which served as the church of Saint Patrick guarded the northern approach to Inniscourt. Father Coughlan, prayer book in hand, stood waiting outside the door of the church, eyes closed, lips moving in silent prayer.

The chilling northerly wind that had invaded the morning was slowly relenting, and a wintry sun struggled from behind the clouds to glint in the patches of snow and ice.

The sound of voices and bursts of raucous laughter broke into Father Coughlan's prayers. His long, thin nose twitched with annoyance at the interruption, and the mirror-black eyes

15

opened slowly to fix their gaze on the far end of Paddy's Way. The face creased in a frown.

A small untidy procession stumbled towards the church. At the head was Liam McAfferty, wearing a nondescript black suit which was full of creases, speckled with lint and too small for him. A wrinkled shirt of doubtful white was buttoned up to the bull neck.

His unnaturally brick-red face, and the occasional hooking of a thumb into the shirt collar, indicated that his breathing was being sorely affected. But on this day he would sooner have stood on his head in a busy pigsty than release the top button. In another place, at another time, he would have looked incongruous.

But the clothes did not diminish the swagger of the man. Just fifty years old, short in stature, and fast going to fat, Liam had been there and back in life. His ice-blue eyes were full of craft and cunning as they darted about, missing nothing.

He normally spoke with a slow, considered delivery. But today he was excited. In his mind he was a great hero. Had he not moved up in the society? Was he not the acknowledged provider who would lead these people to the promised land? It did not matter that he didn't give a tuppeny damn for them, it was the glory of the thing, to see the name of McAfferty lifted high for the first time in his life.

But his greatest prize was Mary Whelan, the teacher's daughter. She would most surely prove to be a great asset with her book learning when they reached America. For he had great plans to make his fortune.

Mary would soon be married into the family, bringing respect to the name of McAfferty. There had been a time when he might just as well have wished to go to the moon in a golden coach. His head swam with the whole occasion. Was he not even more powerful than Father Coughlan himself?

The procession came to a ragged halt outside the church and the penetrating eyes of the priest fixed hard on Liam. Only the wheeling gulls with their plaintive cries disturbed the awkward silence which had now fallen.

Liam tried painfully hard to stay the course. But the priest seemed to be able to look into a man's soul and make him feel lame and naked. The power struggle was brief, and Liam was quickly brought to sobriety.

The priest's voice came hard and accusingly.

'You forget yourself, Liam McAfferty! This is the Sabbath, and we are about a most solemn declaration.'

Liam felt his toes curl in the worn-out leather boots. He shuffled his feet in the mud after the manner of a child caught out by a parent, and his tongue flickered nervously over suddenly parched lips.

'I'm powerful sorry about the loud talkin', holy Father.'

The tone was hoarse and there was a degree of penitence. But only just. Liam was merely biding his time.

The priest was himself again. There would be no pretenders to his throne, however shaky that might be in these desperate days. He would now exert his authority by making them wait upon his time.

Father Coughlan lifted his gaze from Liam, and his eyes moved like a scythe over the small gathering. In sharp concert the heads dropped in fear and respect. All except one.

Mary Whelan returned the searching stare, her face white to the death, and in vivid contrast to the black straw bonnet pulled deep on her head. A long dark dress, tight up to the chin, finished in the mud of the road. Her expression was etched with the pain of the mind, but there was a look of stubborn resolve about her. She stood proudly with the sympathetic arm of Sean Dolan around her shoulder, Sean, eyes fixed on the road, gaining more support from her than she from him.

The priest dwelt on Mary's expression for some moments but could not stare her down. He felt a strange disquiet and moved his attention over the rest of the villagers. They were almost beaten in mind and body as they swayed gently with fatigue, and a remarkable patience. The eyes now focused on Liam McAfferty's three sons, Patrick, Brendan and Donal. They had been born one year apart from each other, Donal taking the life of his mother.

In rough corduroys and open-necked shirt, the tall, spare

17

figure of Liam's eldest son Patrick held an air of apology. Patrick had been a humourless soul from birth, and his space of 32 years on earth had only served to make that condition more severe. He held an unswerving loyalty to his father, and did as he was told. He was Liam's favourite.

Brendan was a squat man with the mind of a child. His grubby shirt lay split open, collarless and without tie. The torn jacket, left to him by his grandfather, was so tight that it threatened to burst from its buttons. The trousers had been too hastily thieved from a tinker's cart and now hung admonishingly at calf length.

Brendan had no pretensions to self-assertion, perfectly content in his shallow mind and ready to follow any mood set by the general will of the family. He was little more than a slave to Liam's whims.

Patrick and Brendan were without wives, a state not brought about by choice, rather more simply through having not a single saving grace with which to attract the opposite sex. Even the lowliest and plainest of women would look away from them. But compared with their younger brother Donal, they were pearls beyond price.

Hands clasped behind his back, the bridegroom stood with head bowed. It was a head that looked too big for the body as it sat without neck on broad sloping shoulders. Long, black, greasy hair hung uncombed, and his body stank for want of a rub of water. The eyes, reminiscent of a pig, lay deep-socketed in a broad, flat face.

Donal was not capable of smiling. Instead, a grin of chilling proportions would, without particular reason, flash nervously across thin, shapeless lips.

The dark serge suit fitted well enough. An almost white shirt, badly assembled green tie and polished black boots completed the trappings. The whole had been obtained from behind a clenched fist, the promise of a broken nose, and no place on the ship to America.

Jimmy O'Dea had been the reluctant benefactor, but the tavern keeper's agony over the enforced deal had been temporary. They had been his only decent clothes, but he didn't

18

want to be buried in them. And had he not witnessed Donal's frequent black rages in the drink, when bar chairs were splintered and the window glass lay in the road?

Somewhere near the back of the crowd a man fell down from exhaustion, and was just as rapidly hauled to his feet by a neighbour. It served to distract the priest from his musings.

'Patience is a virtue seldom seen in man. But I think you are now ready to commune with the Almighty ... Good mornin' t'you all, and the blessing of the Lord be yours.' The reply came back in a ragged and tired chorus.

'Praise be t'God, an' good mornin', holy Father.'

Father Coughlan raised his arms to summon absolute silence.

'This is a sad day, yet it is also a time to rejoice. The Almighty in His great wisdom has said we must leave our dear village. But He has given us the joining together of Donal an' Mary before they set out over the water t'serve Him in the great land of America. May the Lord bless and keep them safe.'

Contriteness behind him, Liam raised his arms and with the excitement back in his voice, shouted towards the sky.

'God bless y', Father, an' bless this day!'

With the promise of food growing ever nearer, the crowd took up the shout. The priest allowed this for a few moments before once more raising his arms for silence.

'Come, let us go into church.'

The priest strode purposefully down the short aisle with the set expression of a man who wanted to get the affair over and done with. Stopping before the altar, he gave the sign of the cross and knelt to pray.

It was cold inside the church, much colder than it had been on the dirt road. The stone pavings were like ice and seemed to cling to the feet as the congregation jostled into the rough, wooden pews, huddling together for warmth as Liam shepherded Donal towards the altar rail.

Sean Dolan appeared in the doorway with Mary on his arm, and together they walked slowly towards the altar.

As in a dream Mary heard the sound her footsteps made on the stone. It was surely not herself but a stranger taking this

19

walk. The thoughts came in a hazy tumble ... This was an ungodly thing she was about. It was not proper to be marrying this man. Had she not read about the mystery of love between a man and woman, and wondered on it? But this mockery was made by the devil.

Mary trembled slightly, and her mind fled the darkness of the church into make-believe.

She had often wondered on the man she might fall in love with. Surely handsome, good and kind. And her wedding day ... The bridal gown, white as driven snow, long as midsummer's day. The gentle smile of her proud father ... a fond kiss from mother. And there would be tea and cakes.

Sean brought Mary to a stop as they arrived at the altar rail. His restraining hand had been gentle enough, but it brought her spinning from warm daydream back to the nightmare.

Liam turned and looked at Mary. A triumphant leer spread across his face and he dug an elbow into Donal's ribs, indicating Mary's presence.

Donal turned and gazed open-mouthed at Mary. He had lusted after her for as long as he could remember. Now she was to be his wife. Under him in his own bed. His brain whirled at the thought and his mouth went bone dry.

Hard-eyed, lips clenched tightly, Mary looked back at him in fear and loathing.

Curiosity filled Donal's face. He was still in awe of the woman. She was the teacher's daughter, holding the terrible power of the reading and the writing ... a woman who knew of the worldly things from books, a great and grand creature altogether, apart from others. And she was so beautiful that it caused a sweet agony of pain in the guts and groin. The dark grin flashed across Donal's face and he turned to face the altar.

Father Coughlan extended his hands towards the congregation. His voice was soft but commanding.

'Time is short and we have much to do before we leave to go our separate ways with the Almighty. That means there'll be no Nuptial Mass as such. But it does not take away the holy meaning of the occasion. Let us pray.'

The heads dropped obediently and a deep quiet came over

the church. Into this the priest poured his prayer in loud chant which echoed thinly back off the dripping wet stone walls.

'*Respice, quaesumus, Domine, super hos famulos tuos et institutious, quibus propagationem humani generis ordinasti, benignus assiste, ut qui te auctore iunguntur, te auxiliante serventur. Per Christum Dominum Nostrum ... amen.*'

Moved by the prayer, the congregation swelled with new-found spirit as they came back with their amens.

The priest nodded briefly to Sean Dolan to bring Mary forward, and with the gentlest of movements Dolan complied, easing Mary between Liam and Donal.

Mary stood ashen-faced and almost fainting with tension, no longer able to hold back the tears.

The priest looked down at the unlikely couple, his eyes taking in Mary's deep sorrow. But his recent flirtation with compassion for her was past. His thoughts were now practical. He could already taste the sweet promise of Dublin Town, its civilisation and order. There was just this to do.

'I have known you both for many years, an' I know there is no just cause or impediment why y'should not be joined together.'

Father Coughlan looked around the congregation, his eyes scanning every face, hard expression warning on the folly of contradiction. He turned away from the silent audience and regarded Donal briefly before speaking.

'Donal ... wilt thou take Mary, here present, for thy lawful wife, according to the Rite of our Holy Mother the Church?'

In a tight choked voice Donal replied, 'I will.'

The priest paused for a moment as he looked at Mary. His formal marriage question came more as a command than a request for reply.

'Mary ... wilt thou take Donal, here present, for thy lawful husband, according to the Rite of our Holy Mother the Church?'

Mary opened her mouth to speak, then closed it again. The church was silent, and time seemed to hang suspended from the rough timber ceiling of the place.

The embarrassed shuffling of feet from within the pews

21

caused the priest's face to harden. He repeated the question in a manner that would bear no denying.

'Mary! ... Do not put Almighty God to shame in his own house. Answer in the proper manner ... wilt thou take Donal, here present, for thy lawful husband, according to the Rite of our Holy Mother the Church?'

Mary looked up at the priest. His dark eyes seemed to fill the universe and they were drowning her ... She was not here at all, but now a little girl again in summer, running along the sandy beach, ankle-deep in the foaming surf of the ocean, just for the sheer joy of life, no companion needed or wanted, save for the golden sun in a limitless sky.

But hard thought returned. There was a need to put this empty ceremony behind her, for it had no more importance other than being a means to an end. She no longer trusted the priest, but for now there was nothing for it but to play his game. Later, with God's help, she would rid herself of this creature who stood by her side. Her answer came without emotion.

'I will.'

The priest nodded in satisfaction. 'I join you in holy matrimony, in the name of the Father and of the Son, and of the Holy Ghost ... Amen.'

Relief washed over the congregation in a storming tide of chatter, while some of the women began to cry openly.

But the thoughts of all present were not concerned with the priest's sacrificial offering of the virgin Mary to the beast that was Donal. There was no feeling of guilt. It simply meant there would now be food and a new life in America.

4

Liam McAfferty was a strange mixture of a man, uneducated and uncouth on the one hand, intelligent and cunning on the other. He had been brought up in the hard school of life at the hands of a brutal father. But he held the name of McAfferty in great honour, and nursed a burning ambition to make his mark on life.

Along with his three sons he farmed land as a tenant for George Carew, an absentee English landlord. Carew was more interested in the coffee houses and gambling tables of London than farming, so his visits of inspection were rare. As a result Liam was able to run the estate in his own fashion and had, over the years, siphoned off a good deal of money.

Kildrew Farm stood eight miles out of Inniscourt, and the McAffertys visited the village two or three times a week. Liam sought popularity with the people there, but his ways were not theirs.

He would hold drunken court in Jimmy O'Dea's tavern of a Saturday night, telling tall stories about his money-making deals with the captains of merchant ships over at Sligo. Some were true, others fell short of that mark. But his almost constant theme had been the doings of his late father.

Joseph McAfferty had operated well outside the law, extorting money and goods from merchants and peasants along the west coast. Many people danced when he died. Liam wisely chose not to follow too closely in his father's footsteps. His notion was that there were easier ways to kill a pig than cut its throat ... a man could choke it to death more smoothly with a pound of butter.

Despite this seeming adherence to the law he was a feared man, for even in death his father still threw a long shadow. The people of Inniscourt may well have told the embroidered tale and unsavoury joke about Liam and his sons, but they did so quietly, and well out of their hearing.

When the famine struck Ireland, some cried and gave up, others put their faith in daily prayer. But Liam had emerged as the only man capable of engineering the grand escape to America. There was no inclination to voice questions about where the money to make it possible was coming from, least of all by Father Coughlan.

Liam's plan was simple. He would furnish the passage money for the exodus, and then get every last penny back, plus a sizeable interest, when the people found jobs. To all intents and purposes Liam now ruled the roost, and he revelled in the heady joy of it.

The wedding feast would have been considered a simple affair in other circumstances. But in these times, when many a man would have murdered to gain a crust, it was nothing short of a miracle to the twenty-eight men, women and children still left to draw breath in the stricken village.

Three tables were dragged from the nearest dwellings and placed in the middle of Paddy's Way. Nearby stood a moth-eaten donkey harnessed to the shafts of a two-wheel open cart.

Liam bossed his way around a small group of haggard women and boys as they ferried boiled potatoes, stale bread and some doubtful-looking cake from the cart to the tables. A large jug, lid tightly strapped down, protruded from a pannier on the donkey's back. With great care Liam eased the jug from its holder and carried it to a nearby chair.

The jug contained home brewed alcohol that had been hastily made up of this-that-and-the-other. It was a near-lethal mixture which held the firm promise of being able to part a fit man from his brain in quick time.

The work was swiftly completed, and now the food lay there

like some shimmering mirage. In the manner of obedient dogs the wedding throng stood silently eyeing the feast, drool coming unchecked down their chins as they awaited the nod from their new master and benefactor.

Liam was totally aware of the moment and the power. He wanted to hold this time forever, and even into eternity. He strode slowly around the tables on a tour of inspection, his boots crunching heavily in the grit now the only sound to invade the deep silence.

Patrick, Brendan and Donal lolled close by, arms folded, faces creased in grins as they enjoyed their father's glory to the full.

Mary stood some way behind them, head bowed in deep thought, eyes fixed on the road. This was only a bad dream and she would work to awaken from it. She lifted her head slowly to look at Donal. He was oblivious of her, eyes only for his father's mastery over these people who had thought themselves a score of cuts above the McAffertys.

Mary took in Donal's cruel mouth and the madness of his expression. This monstrosity was her husband, and the sudden realisation of what that meant caused a panic in her.

She wanted to flee now ... yes now, and run, and run and run. The blood ran from the corner of her mouth as she bit the soft inside of her cheek to quell the panic.

Not yet, not here. Be patient, wait for the right opportunity, the proper time and place.

Father Coughlan walked from the church and stood for a few moments, unobserved, taking in the scene. The priest knew exactly what Liam was about, and he frowned in that knowledge. His voice broke like the crack of doom across the silence, bringing an abrupt end to Liam's brief enjoyment.

'I will bless the food now, Liam! The time for leavin' is almost upon us. God's time and tide wait for no man.'

Liam turned in annoyance towards the sound, his eyes locked with the priest's for moments before giving way.

Jeez! What did it matter? Wouldn't he shortly be rid of the

interferin' man? Sure, he was still not on firm ground. But his tone would be cocky, he would not lose face.

'As y'say, Father... I have gotten the food, y'can bless it now.'

The priest walked slowly towards the tables, his eyes fixed on Liam with every step of the way. He stopped in front of his would-be usurper, and with a sardonic smile looked down on him.

'Once more you forget yourself, Liam... God provided the food, and I will now bless it.'

The priest turned and raised his hands over the tables.

'Dear Lord in heaven, in Your mercy bless this food which You have provided, and for this we humbly thank You. May these good people eat well, then go in peace to find guidance from You on their long journey. We ask this of You in the name of Your dear son Jesus Christ ... amen.'

A low rumbling amen came back from the villagers, who now lifted their bowed heads to look towards Liam. He knew they would not move until he gave the nod.

He turned in triumph towards the priest. The power was no longer with the Church. It was his.

Arms spread wide, Liam shifted his gaze over the crowd, then shouted out in a voice that was near to hysteria.

'I have gotten this food wit' the sweat of my body an' the sense of my notions ... now come an' eat it!'

The villagers fell on the tables like a pack of ravening animals, their clutching hands grabbing at everything in sight. Potatoes, bread and cake tumbled into the road, where the fingers of starving children risked pulping as they snatched at the grit-covered food under an avalanche of boots.

The priest looked coldly at Liam, then turned his gaze to take in the *mêlée* at the tables. Fighting had broken out, and any pretence at civilised conduct was gone. Men and women now rained terrible blows on each other in a desperate battle for food. Cursing and blaspheming, kicking and yelling, they rolled in the churned-up snow and mud, tables crashing down about them, spilling their contents to all four corners of Paddy's Way.

Father Coughlan slowly shook his head, and a look of contempt came to his face. He had been right. These people were wild animals, better left to their own devices. Thank God he had been delivered from them.

Peace had returned when, an hour later, a pony cart driven by a young cleric pulled up outside the church. Father Coughlan, carpet bag in hand, emerged and looked towards Paddy's Way.

Steeped in the ecstasy of full bellies and mind-numbing drink, the villagers lay sprawled in the road. The odd burst of bawdy song reached the priest's ears, and from where there had been fighting now came drunken vows of eternal friendship.

The McAffertys, arms about each other, were flat on their backs, snoring loudly and out to the world.

Mary was sat on the low stone wall outside Pat O'Hagan's shop. She had never once taken her gaze away from the church since Father Coughlan had gone in there. Now she rose slowly to her feet to look across at the priest, and he could see the painful accusation on her face.

Without a word or gesture he turned and climbed aboard the cart. A soft flick of the whip above the pony's head caused the animal to bend to its task, and the cart rumbled slowly out of Inniscourt, carrying the Father to his deliverance.

Mary watched his going until the cart disappeared in the late afternoon haze, and wondered on the man. What manner of priest was this who could break her life into pieces and then desert his people?

5

The three roads which led into Sligo Harbour were choked with people fleeing the great hunger. Farmers, traders, landlords and peasants, all rank forgotten, fought their way in a crawling nightmare towards the docks. Yet these were the lucky ones; many more could not raise the few pounds which would have afforded escape.

They could be numbered in their thousands, with pathetic bundles of possessions on their backs and tickets to America clutched tightly in hand. For many they would be tickets to oblivion. The ships were light on provisions, heavy on passengers, and a winter crossing had never before been attempted. Now three thousand miles of stormy ocean waited to do battle with ships that were in the main not fit for the fight.

The *Elizabeth* stood off the docks, waiting for the evening tide. She was a three-masted barque, normally used to bringing in timber from Canada and returning in ballast. The ballast was a necessary but unprofitable dead weight, whereas the new trade in emigrants produced instant money in the hand.

She was owned by Captain James Halloran, a privateer without an ounce of compassion or understanding for his fellow man. Like others he had seen the opportunity for a quick cash return in the transportation of emigrants, and had taken it.

There was a long-time trading relationship between Liam and Halloran, but no friendship existed between them. Neither man knew much about the other, and cared even less.

Vegetables and other provisions stolen from the farm were exchanged for money and whiskey, with few words to interfere in the process.

A deal had been struck between them for the passage to Boston. Thirty English pounds had changed hands, and the absentee English landlord would be the poorer for it.

The decks of the *Elizabeth* were swarming with emigrants. Anxious-looking fathers and mothers shepherded their children along, earnestly seeking guidance on where they should go. The more adventurous children found energy enough to climb the rigging, and in screams of excitement were just as quickly hauled down and cuffed about the ears by exhausted parents.

Ignorance ruled, and many thought that America was no more distance than where the sky met the sea. In this belief a good number of emigrants lay down and fell instantly asleep on the first available yard of decking they could find. Some climbed into longboats, while others gathered on the ship's rails and, with fearful expressions, looked out over the ocean.

A harassed crew worked like sheepdogs, their biting invective and liberal use of digging fists herding the main body of emigrants towards open hatches which led to the main hold.

Over all was the noise: a constant shouting, fearful screams, bloody curses, dire threats, and sudden loud wailings as the newly bereaved cried over those who had suddenly given up the ghost.

In the midst of this chaos was a strange oasis of calm where a large group stood in loud prayer, asking God's help in guiding them through their awful uncertainty. As if in answer, it began to snow. The large velvet flakes came spinning and tumbling from the darkening sky, here and there giving a twinkling diamond flash as they briefly flirted with the ship's riding lights.

Mary McAfferty stood at the aft rail, the snowflakes falling

29

unheeded on her face and making sharp contrast as they lay briefly in the dark sheen of her hair.

Her one thought on coming aboard had been to distance herself from the others. Drunken, spewing wretches all, and far removed from the caring people they had once been. Liam and his sons had been obliged to keep the party in tight check and were now busily sorting out space in the hold. It would be only a matter of short time before Mary's absence was noted.

She looked out towards Inniscourt, straining to catch a last glimpse of the familiar. But it had already been swallowed up in the darkness, the headland gone to imagination. The same headland where she had lain in delicious half-sleep on the short warm grass, looking up at the huge banks of cloud, so intensely white, their darkened edges making them look like a fantastic mountain range where giants strode and adventure lay. Where her true love might well spring from.

Donal McAfferty scrambled from the darkness of the hold, his fingers gripping the top of the companionway rail as he sought to lift himself for a better view over the crowded decks. He had hurriedly arranged a rough bed of straw and sacking below, grinning like a fool as those around chided him about his wedding night. Now he was looking for Mary.

Half out of his mind with drink, he mouthed obscenities at her disappearance, his over-large dome of a head moving slowly from side to side as he scanned the milling crowd. He saw her and with a loud curse dropped from his hanging perch. Punching, kicking and cursing, Donal cut a bloody swathe through the emigrants as he slowly closed the distance.

Mary was unaware of Donal's presence until the fist crashed into her back. The force of it sent her spinning into the rail and down to the deck. With a cry of pain she looked up to see Donal glowering at her.

His brutal passage had not been without cost. A bleeding nose marked the accuracy of a well-timed blow from an unforgiving passenger, the tie had been torn from his neck and one sleeve of the jacket was missing.

30

The drink had proved too much for him, and he had near spewed his guts up. Jacket and trousers glistened with thick vomit and his hair lay matted with the stuff. The eyes were bloodshot and rolled in their sockets like some crazed beast in a slaughterhouse.

'Y've led me a merry dance, so y'have, makin' me look the 'eejut ... seekin' y' all over the damt stupit boat!'

Despite her pain and fear, Mary's reply was spirited.

'You filthy creature! Get away from me!'

Growling in anger Donal reached down and grabbed Mary by the arms. With one pull she was dragged to her feet and held before him. His stinking breath came full into Mary's face, making her convulse in a spasm of retching.

He looked at her for a brief moment. The insane grin flashed across his face, then without another word he turned abruptly, pulling her behind him towards the hold.

She dragged on his arm, making his passage even more difficult as he pushed his way through the protesting mass of bodies. But he did not seem to notice the handicap as he snarled at her from time to time over his shoulder. The bursts of hate came thick and fast.

'If y'ever do this t'me again you're for a great beatin' ... y'can stop playin' the smart lady wit' me ... wandrin' off an' all ... I'm y'r husband, an' y'll do what I tell y'now.'

Breathless from their efforts, they reached the head of the hold, Donal grabbed Mary by the shoulders and thrust her towards the steps which fell away into darkness. With a sharp cry she missed her footing and went crashing full-length down the steps, to lie sprawling on the hold decking. He looked down at her, his hands gripped the top rail, and the lunatic grin flashed in brief spasm.

'Y'see what happens when y'take t'hidin' away from y'r husband ... now it's us for the bed, an' I can tell you there'll be precious little sleepin' done.'

Donal grinned once more and began a slow, shambling descent backwards into the hold.

Mary looked up as the man's bulky figure blotted out the faint lighting from the deck. Fear now came to replace hate

31

and she was transfixed, like a rabbit trapped by a weasel. She felt the shudder of the planking beneath her as the ship began to move out on the tide. They were under way, no turning back now.

Her mind raced. She had to escape ... get back into the far reaches of the hold. There would be families there. Yes, that was it ... Move now, and quickly, he was almost upon her.

Mary scrambled to her feet, and for the first time took in the horror of the overcrowded conditions. The smell was appalling and assaulted her senses as she began to move into the depths of the hold. The only light came from flickering hurricane lamps which cast bizarre moving shadows as they swung gently on their hooks with the roll of the ship.

Deeper and deeper she went into the darkness, holding a sleeve across her mouth to numb the stench. Strangers lay everywhere; some were already vomiting from seasickness, others had given way to a loud nervous chattering.

Mary did not see the figure which had ghosted behind her for some minutes. It came suddenly out of the darkness, and large powerful hands gripped her shoulders from behind. An involuntary scream came from her as she was bundled around.

Liam McAfferty had the coldest of smiles on his face, and a knowing look in his eyes. He spoke softly.

'No need for the screamin' now, daughter, y'r safe wit' the family. Y'should not take t'wandrin' away on your own.'

Mary looked back at Liam and tried to speak. But no words would come.

He eyed her questioningly. 'Are y'sick or somethin'? ...'

She shook her head. But still the words would not come.

He spoke again, his voice now harder. 'An' where is y'r husband?'

The question brought Mary into speech, her voice full of loathing.

'That he will never be!'

Before Liam could reply, Donal came lunging from the shadows to close on Mary.

'Y'bloody cow! ... I'll teach y'z t'run away!'

He hurled himself forward in an effort to seize Mary, who swayed out of his reach. The elbow went straight into Liam's nose, bursting it wide in a shower of blood. A look of horror came to Donal's face. He had struck his father, and he knew he would not be forgiven.

Liam shook his head to clear the pain, then drove his left fist into the pit of Donal's stomach, bending him forward like a tree in a high wind. The force of the blow brought fresh spew spurting from Donal's mouth, making him choke for breath. The right fist blurred in its speed to deliver a perfect uppercut. Donal's eyes glazed over and he fell slowly to the decking like a bundle of old rags.

Mary had stepped well back during the onslaught and now stood wide-eyed. Her voice came perched on the edge of unreasonable hope.

'Have y'killed him...?'

With both sleeves of his coat, Liam wiped the blood from his nose. The question had amused him, and a wry smile came.

'May the words on y'r lips fly straight t'the Almighty an' make it so, for I have this great notion that Donal was put on earth t'bring me nothin' but the blackest of trouble. I am lookin' t'you for t'make a man out of him.'

Liam turned to Donal and aimed a savage kick at him. The boot landed squarely in the belly to force a groan, and Liam smiled more grimly as he looked at Mary.

'Y'see? ... I doubt I could kill him wit' a horse pistol.'

He shrugged his shoulders in resignation and walked over to where the nearest family lay huddled together. They were a young couple with five small children, strangers to Liam and unaware of his reputation. But they had witnessed the violent beating and were plainly in fear.

The family came closer together in a frantic rustle of straw, eyes wide with apprehension, arms tightly locked about each other. Liam stood looking down at them, his narrowed eyes scanning their faces as he delighted in their terror of him.

He moved his gaze away to survey their belongings, and finally saw what he was looking for. The large wooden bucket which served as a urinal was more than half full. With a malicious grin Liam bent down and grasped the cast-iron handle, hauling the bucket to his side.

The man on the bed suddenly found courage to remonstrate with Liam, but his tone was unconvincing.

' 'Tis our piss-bucket y'r takin', mister...'

Liam looked at him with contempt, and his reply came witheringly.

'I am Liam McAfferty ... y'will come t'know the name an' then y'll thank God I did not come for more.'

Liam turned away and, heedless of the bucket's contents slopping out on to his breeches, closed on Donal. Mary watched Liam's every move, first in puzzlement then in disbelief as she suddenly became aware of his intentions.

The urine hit Donal full in the face, bringing him to choking life. He rolled about in a fit of coughing which racked his body into a shuddering mass as, eyes streaming, he fought for every breath.

Liam hurled the bucket back at its owners. It cracked against the beam above the bed before falling to hit the man across the shoulders. He cried out in pain but did not venture any rebuke.

With a whimsical expression Liam regarded Donal for a few moments, then burst into wild laughter. Hands on hips, he rocked about with malicious glee as he watched his son clamber slowly to his feet. He spoke between the gales of his merriment, and with some difficulty.

'Didja ever see such a sight?... What a great an' wonderful weddin' day you're havin' altogether.'

Liam collapsed to the decking as another fit of laughing took him over. Donal staggered upright, wiping his face on his jacket front as he tried to pull himself together.

Mary looked about her. There was nowhere to run, and surely no one who would dare help her to stand up against the McAffertys. Her thoughts grew more studied.

Could it be that she had found an unexpected ally in Liam? There was plainly no love lost between father and son. She must somehow find favour with Liam, get him on her side, then drive an even deeper wedge between the pair.

Liam clambered to his feet and chuckled softly. Hurt and bewildered, Donal sat down on a bale of rags, head in hands. From time to time his body jerked in convulsive sobs.

Mary moved alongside Liam, who laughed once more as he pointed towards Donal.

'Ain't he a beauty?... You'd better get him to his bed, but I've a notion he'll not have lovin' thoughts this night.'

Donal's eyes were filled with anger as he looked first at his father, then at Mary. His head rang with pain and the rest of him fared little better. But he was far from done.

His fretful glare switched again to Mary. No matter how much his body ached with the beating, it ached far more in its lust for this beautiful woman. He would have her this night ... he would have her even if it was with the last breath left in him.

6

The *Elizabeth* was well out of the lee of Donegal Bay and on course for Boston. But the glass was falling rapidly as a fierce north-westerly brought heavy rain lancing into the ship. Quickly but methodically, the seamen worked on deck and in the yards to meet the advancing storm. It would be on them in full fury within the hour.

If it was bad for the crew, it was worse for the hundreds of emigrants packed below decks. The holds had once held the sweet odour of new timber from the forests of North America. Now, overcrowded beyond reason, they were rapidly to become the breeding ground for all manner of diseases. There were no sanitary arrangements, other than wooden buckets, and washing or bathing was an impossibility. Some timber berths had been installed, but in the main the emigrants slept on the decking.

Liam McAfferty lay on a pile of rags and straw. Open-mouthed, he snored fitfully. On each side of him, and fast asleep, sprawled Patrick and Brendan.

A short distance away Mary sat upright, trying not to make any movement which might awaken Donal. Still dressed in his vomit-soaked wedding suit, he had fallen into the crude bed of straw and gone out like the snuffing of a candle.

The smell of the man was making her gag and she fought to keep from retching. Numb with the cramp of staying in one position, she attempted to ease further away from him.

The movement brought Donal into instant awakening. Mary's eyes were wide with fear as he eased himself up on to one elbow. The insane grin flickered and was gone.

'Would y' ever put credit to it ... a man goin' t'sleep on his weddin' night!'

Mary felt her flesh crawl, but did not fall to panic. She would use her intelligence in an attempt to keep him at bay. Her tone was soft and soothing.

'Y'are a sick man, Donal ... you've taken a terrible beatin' and may be broken inside. I have read such things in the doctor books ... you need t'sleep.'

The words were totally wasted. His evil grin twitched briefly, the voice pitched low and taunting.

'Sleep, is it? Sure, there won't be any this night.'

He leaned over to her, and the fingers of both hands spread like spiders as he lowered them on to her thighs. Grunting with pleasure, he closed them in a pincer-like grip which cut through the thick dress, making her wince with pain. His voice came thick with lust.

'Get your damned rags off ... I'm for havin' y'.'

In swift reaction Mary speared her nails deeply into the back of his hands and brought the blood. With a soft curse he released his grip, allowing her to move further away.

Her voice came with loathing. 'You're not to touch me!'

Donal grinned as he proudly examined the bloody nail marks. Brought up on a diet of violence, he was now on common ground. He understood her attack on him, and his voice held respect of a kind.

'Aren't you a little wildcat an' all?'

His manner now changed to one of wheedling as he leaned over and pawed in playful action at her shoulders.

'Come on now, 'tis our weddin' night. You're not stupit! Y'know damned well what I want.'

Mary looked away for some moments before replying. There was a need to fight for time. Her tone was soft.

'Could we not just be friends, Donal?'

Donal's face took on a look of amazement. His hands stopped their pawing and closed on Mary's shoulders in a tight grip as he wheeled her round to face him.

'Friends! ... Friends, is it? ... Y'must be stupit! Y'r my wife an' I want my rights, so I do.'

Mary stayed with reason. She had at least got him talking.

'This isn't the place, all these people watchin'...'

Donal interrupted in an outraged tone, 'T'hell wit' the people, I'm for havin' you ... it's my rights!'

Mary kept her voice low and injected a note of pleading.

'And what about my rights? ... Have y'no thought for my feelings?'

Donal was illiterate and uncouth, a man who held a deep-seated fear of book education, and on the face of it he was basically animal. Yet he had a sharp intelligence that often plagued him, and his mind now boiled in a turmoil as hot-blooded lust fought against a strange fear of this woman.

Instinct told him they were worlds apart. Yet was she not his lawful wedded wife? Like some awful bird of prey he cocked his head on one side as he looked at Mary.

Jeez! She was a beauty an' all. Would it not be great an' good for her to come willin'? Or would he have to rip the clothes off her? He would if he had to.

His previous sexual excursions had been few, and paid for. The travelling folk were not shy when it came to trading love for money. His mind fled to the memory of a tinker's daughter who had given him her very experienced best, a whole afternoon for the price of a bottle of cheap gin and half a shilling. But Mary was not that slut. She was a schoolteacher's daughter and full of the learning.

A sudden wave of hate come over him. No more of this bloody thinkin' stuff. Just grab hold of the woman an' make her have it. But he was still uncertain, and his manner sullen.

'I'm for takin' y'down a peg ... y'think cause your dar was the teacher that you're too good for me, don't y'?'

Mary was now sure that she had Donal on the run. Her tone was carefully studied.

'That is not so, Donal. 'Tis not a matter of being too good. All I ever wanted was my books and my own company. I was for the learning so I could make a better life for myself.'

Donal snorted with impatience. He was over his fear of her.

'Y'won't need any books wit' me. I'll teach y' all you need t'know ... now come on wit' you!'

He struck in fast movement, tearing open the neck of the dress to grasp her naked breasts in violent embrace. A fierce anger and revulsion swept over Mary, and she broke free to punch him full in the face.

'Get off me! ... Get away, y'dirty pig.'

The blow took Donal by surprise and knocked him off balance. It hurt, but his pride hurt more. He backed off, holding his smarting face.

'A dirty pig I am, is it? I'm your husband, that's who I am, and y'll give me my rights!'

All pretence and patience had gone. They glared at each other eyes narrowed, mouths tensed in snarls like wildcats before a fight. Back arched, Mary thrust her head in threat towards Donal as she hissed back her reply.

'You have no rights with me! 'Twas the priest's doing that we be married, not mine!'

Donal writhed with fury. This bloody-minded woman was making him look the idiot. The veins throbbed in his temples and his bared teeth opened only enough to allow a choked accusation.

'Y'made your vows before the Holy Father ... y'said the words before the Almighty, so y'did. I heard y' ... I heard y'with me own ears!'

'It was an evil mockery of God. I want nothin' of you!'

Donal moved with the instinct of a predator. His giant hands swallowed up Mary's small fists, and in the same momentum he forced her back into the straw. His full weight was now on Mary, and her closeness drove him into a frenzy of desire. His mind raced in anticipation ... begod! He was going to have the teacher's daughter!

'No more of the bloody talkin' ... I'm goin' t'give you a babby, so I am.'

Mary grew weak with fear as his face, red-bloated in lust, came down on her. The breath of the creature was in her mouth, and she gagged at the stench of it as he spoke.

'If y'struggle any more I'll punch y'black an' blue.'

The man now had but one thought in mind. He eased himself away and laboured two-handed as he ripped frenziedly to undo the tough leather buttons at the front of his breeches.

39

Mary looked up with new-found hate. She would not allow this awful thing to happen. With an almost aching slowness she gathered the fingers of both hands together into a combined fist, and with a deep indraw of breath, launched herself forward.

The blow landed full square on Donal's already battered nose, and blood squirted like a fountain over man and woman. He fell away under the force of the attack, his loud cry of anger and pain echoing round the hold.

With some alarm, those who had been looking on shrank away into the shadows, but fascination brought them slowly back like moths to a candle.

Liam broke from sleep and sat bolt upright, rubbing his eyes. Donal and Mary had begun to struggle afresh, voices intermeshed in such a fury of frustration and hatred that it was impossible to make sense of the words.

Liam glanced round the hold at the pale, watching faces of those who saw him as their leader. Face dark with anger and shame, he jumped from his bed and was on Donal and Mary in a second. Gripping both by the hair, he glared at his son with an expression that made the blood run cold.

The voice was pitched low but full of terrible promise.

'Y'are bringin' black shame an' ridicule on the name of McAfferty ... What are you about?'

Donal's reply came in a pleading flow.

'It is not me causin' the shame, dar.'

Donal struggled to turn his head and point an accusing finger at Mary.

'She will not let me have her!'

Chin thrust out in defiance, he turned again to Liam.

''Tis my rights as her husband, an' she called me a pig, so she did!'

Liam's voice was flat with hate.

'She's right ... y'are a pig ... I've allus had it in the mind that you're a pig. Now y'show me you are in front of the whole village. I oughta kill you here an' now with me bare hands.'

Donal swallowed deeply, eyes downcast as he wisely decided to ride out his father's storm.

Mary looked at Liam and wondered. Could this be the miracle she had prayed for?

Donal did not dare face his father's eyes as he spoke. The tone was humble and penitent.

'I have not it in mind to bring the shame, dar. I am only doin' what any man would on his weddin' night, so I am...'

Liam's hand moved like lightning to change its grip from hair to throat, choking off any further words. With a vicious tug, he yanked Donal towards him. They were now inches away from each other, and Donal blinked furiously under the terrible stare of his father.

'I will not have our name dirtied! Would y' behave like a pig mountin' a sow in the public market ... an' before all these people?'

He tightened his grip on Donal's throat until the eyes ran bloodshot under the pressure of suffocation. Liam's voice came louder.

'Would y'do that? Would you?...'

He released his grip to allow Donal a gulp of air and chance of reply. Donal's voice came back thickly.

'I'm only doin' what is my rights, dar.'

Liam shook his head slowly as he looked with pity at Donal. The voice was cold, emotion gone.

'The trouble with you, Donal, is y'haven't a single, solitary brain in your thick skull.'

Liam twisted his mouth in contempt, then forced Donal's head round, making him look into the darkest corner of the hold. It housed the shadowy forms of a small family, who dropped their gaze away at this sudden attention.

'Take her yonder an' do it.'

Mary stared with horror at Liam. He could not mean this. He would surely not be party to such a thing.

Her voice came full of pleading.

'You cannot do this ... for pity's sake ... before God.'

Both men were totally oblivious to her plea or presence. It was simply a matter to be settled between them, and she was not in the reckoning of it.

41

Donal forced his head back to look with a puzzled expression at his father.

'But there's people there as well, dar.'

Liam wondered on Donal's stupidity. The laugh was short and without humour.

'Tell them to move, you bloody eejut! Tell them I would look on it as a great and wonderful kindness to remember ... or I will move them with the buckle of me belt.'

Mary, unable to get away from the tight grip of Liam, closed her eyes and began to pray softly. 'Dear Father in heaven, help me...' The prayer dropped away into a silent movement of her lips.

Donal had now regained some confidence.

'An' how am I t'get her over there? She'll kick over the traces, shoutin' and screamin', showin' us up an' all.'

'You go an' have a word wit' the good people ... I'll get her over.'

Liam pushed him away towards the hold corner. Donal grinned with the air of a conspirator.

'Right, dar, right y'are.'

Shambling to his feet, Donal moved to where the family now sat huddled in fear at his approach.

Liam's expression was set in grim fashion as Mary's eyes filled with pleading.

Releasing his grip on her hair, he put an arm round her shoulder. He spoke softly, but there was no denying the menace which lay behind every word.

'I am not lookin' for the trouble from you, Mary. But if y'give me the cause of it I'll beat you, so I will.'

Liam paused for a few moments as he sought the words which would afford the least problems. His tone softened even more.

'Lookit ... I know how it is with you, but I cannot keep your man at bay all the long night that lies ahead. Better get it over an' done with ... quiet-like, over there.'

The family had scuttled away on Donal's approach, and he now lay on his belly in the hold corner, the straw crackling under him as he wriggled his body in delight. Chin cupped in hands, he regarded Liam and Mary as they talked. The distance between would not allow him to hear any of the conversation, but he tried hard to follow the drift. The eyes narrowed into slits of concentration as they flitted from one face to the other. His gaze came to rest on Mary, and he licked his dry lips in anticipation. Dar would make her shut up and do as she was told.

Donal wriggled again in his excitement. She would soon be under him in this very straw. He would make her pay for all the trouble she had caused.

Liam had gone as far as he was going with what he considered a reasonable approach. He attempted what he thought to be a comforting smile.

'Shall I take you over there now?'

Mary had defiance in her eyes.

'I won't do it. I won't go to him, and y'cannot make me.'

The smile went from Liam's face, but his reply came quietly.

'I can, I will, an' you know it. I won't bandy words with you any longer ... I have t'keep the respect of these people, watchin' at this very moment t'see what happens.'

Mary shook her head.

'I will not do it.'

Liam turned his head towards Patrick and Brendan. They had been awake for some time, but had summoned up enough sense to keep clear when they saw their father was into making bother.

With an imperious wave Liam beckoned them towards him. Both men were up from their beds and by his side within seconds. Liam addressed them in formal tones.

'Mary is a shy bride, an' her husband is waitin' for her.'

Patrick whipped his right hand round Mary's waist, his left pulling the shawl across her mouth to deny her any sound. Brendan closed from the other side to grab her legs. With one effortless heave she was hoisted into the air, and in the same movement carried towards the waiting Donal.

Liam turned with a smile, holding up his arms to the other occupants of the hold. His voice was loud.

'Just a little shyness on the part of the bride is all.'

He spread his hands wide in appeal.

'Y'all know how it is, weddin' night worries an' all.'

Liam burst into raucous laughter, looking around him in a manner which clearly demanded everyone must do the same. The emigrants nodded and smiled back at him. Some even managed a laugh. But the humour was inspired by fear as Liam's inquiring gaze swept over their faces.

A terrible scream rang through the hold as Mary wrenched the shawl away from her mouth, and her plea cut to the heart.

'Help me, please! Somebody help me...'

The plea was suddenly cut off as Patrick put his hand across her mouth, smothering out any further cries.

It would not have mattered if she had called out a thousand times for help. It was not a wise thing to cross the McAffertys in their business, and already the villagers she had once called friends were turning away to merge with the dark shadows of the hold.

7

Ranelagh Harbour lay a mile inland from the Solent, just short of the River Hamble, and the scene was in sharp contrast to the spartan huddle of Southampton Docks which fretted like a grey mirage in the far distance. Nature had been good to Ranelagh, bestowing upon it a deep-water harbour and an easily navigable route to the sea. Smartly painted offices and warehouses stood on its broad quayside which was, at this early morning hour, already swept clear of overnight snow. A flagpole on the central quay flew the Bramwell Line company colours of blue and gold, and looked down on a cluster of merchant ships in various stages of loading and unloading.

Behind the massive stone seawalls the ground rose sharply before giving way to a wooded plateau; dominating this was Ranelagh House, an imposing Georgian manor with well-kept lawns and gardens. In summer these were a burst of colour, spilling forth heady perfumes from exotic flowers, the products of many voyages around the world. But even in this month of January the gardens were a delight, the lofty trees highlighted by their covering of frost and snow.

From this setting Frederick Bramwell ruled the fortunes of the Bramwell Shipping Line, a successful company which had been built on merchant adventuring over a quarter of a century. Frederick was a man with a rare sense of world commerce, gleaned from a lifetime in the business. As a boy he had run away to sea, and over the years moved the hard way from deckhand to captain.

During that period he observed that captains may come and

go but trade goes on forever. For him there would be no retirement cottage in which to eke out a pension; he would instead learn the profession of international trading and work hard to gain his own shipping line. With backing from the DeVilliers Merchant Bank, and his own savings, he bought Ranelagh House and its natural harbour for a fair enough price from the bankrupt James Wilbur, a man of weak character who had suffered the consequences of bad investment and dependence on advice from doubtful sources.

There was no such flaw in Frederick: his great appetite for work had seen the company grow from one small ship into a six-strong fleet and the building of golden relationships with traders round the globe. He had refused to consider marriage until his company was on a secure footing, an astute decision since his social ambitions, and the choosing of a wife who would further them, were tempered by the gulf which still existed between the landed gentry and those in trade. He reasonably assumed that the gulf could be spanned with an acceptable blend of carefully acquired background and a great deal of money, and in the event was proved right in that assumption. His shrewd attention was focused on Georgina, daughter of the impoverished James Wilbur. She had been little more than a schoolgirl when Frederick first arrived on the scene, but from their first meeting she was impressed by the handsome and dynamic sailor, so different in every way from her imprudent father.

Georgina's mother had died of consumption some years before, a fact which left the girl much to her own devices, for she had neither brother nor sister to consult in the way of family advice, and was shrewd enough never to discuss her misgivings with friends. Her maxim was that today's friends could so easily become tomorrow's enemies, and one should not provide them with spears to throw later. There was little in the way of counsel from her father, especially in the year or so preceding the enforced sale of Ranelagh. During that period, James Wilbur spent much time away, pursuing one frantic deal after another in an effort to save the property, but Georgina had placed no faith in his capabilities to work the necessary miracle.

Hardened to life's realities and mature beyond her years, she had moved smoothly to attach herself more closely to Frederick when it became evident that he would be the purchaser of the home and estate she adored. At almost eighteen she was fully blossomed into beautiful womanhood, and was already scheming ways on how she could hold on to Ranelagh, for she held no illusions as to her fate if she were parted from it. Poverty was an unforgivable sin, and many of her acquaintances even thought it to be contagious. The life she knew and enjoyed would go like snow off a ditch, and inevitably she would become an outcast. But as Frederick's wife she could reign as mistress of Ranelagh, and in the event he was flattered when she agreed to become his wife, for it greatly suited his business purposes and social aspirations.

Georgina had been privately educated, and was a most capable young woman who held all the social graces and who mixed naturally within the leading county set. Not least of all, as Frederick saw it, she was privy to the social and commercial gossip of those who ruled the Hampshire roost. There were powerful people here who could make or break a fellow's expectations, and it was as well to nurture profitable relationships. He had also noted that Georgina's father was strong in this sphere, and despite Wilbur's glaring business inadequacies he was a much liked man, his droll wit and intimate knowledge of horse racing seeing him welcome at any society gathering.

Astutely, Frederick made a private financial arrangement with Wilbur, one which enabled the man to keep afloat where it mattered, and at the age of thirty-five was married to Georgina on her eighteenth birthday in the year of 1823. Once more secured at Ranelagh, she had early laid down the law on the production of offspring. She would have no more than two children. Jonathan was born within ten months of the marriage, Ann a year later. Brother and sister adored each other and through their childhood years became joyful conspirators against their parents' strong discipline, and at the age of sixteen Jonathan had been apprenticed to serve before the mast. For many years it had been a reasonably close and happy family, but this new year of 1847 had dawned to signal change and the distinct promise of upset.

With the advent of steam power at sea growing stronger, the glorious age of sail was coming slowly to an end, a fact brought home to Frederick almost daily by Georgina. The talk among the well informed was much on the shape of things to come, and Georgina was determined that the Bramwell Line would not be left behind in the race to re-equip. She was a most ambitious woman, but it was a dark ambition fired by a deep fear which had never left her since the enforced sale of Ranelagh. Of late the fears had grown into the beginning of obsession, because she could see the spectre of history repeating itself. Frederick was not of a mind to make change and refused to be panicked, opining that sail would last for many years to come, and had told her that in any case they could not, overnight, afford to turn to steam power. But she was not content with this, and was too sharply reminded of the grim parallel in her father, a man who had closed his mind to advice and stubbornly persisted in canal investment while others grew fat on the railway boom.

Georgina was never a person guilty of masking herself to the grimmer side of reality. Had Frederick not married her it would almost certainly have meant the workhouse, or at best a tenuous charity arrangement with the soon-counted friends she and her father might muster. Luck had played a great part in her survival, and she was not of a mind to ride on it. The act of regaining Ranelagh once had been fortuitous, to do it twice would take a miracle, and Georgina did not believe in miracles.

She was painfully aware that Frederick held the reins of power, a man careful to delegate only the most menial of administrative tasks, and she saw this as the main weakness of the company's structure, for it was virtually a one-man organisation. However, over the past few months she had made certain inroads into Frederick's stubbornness. Now fifty-nine, Frederick was slowly being made to face up to the fact that certain changes had to be made, the primary one being to take their son, Jonathan, more into his confidence and set about the task of schooling him into the eventual takeover of the company.

48

Despite Frederick's assertions that lack of money blocked the way to change, Georgina had not been idle in scheming an alternative route to her desired target, and Jonathan would figure largely in it. This cold winter morning would see the practical start of her plan.

The vast library of Ranelagh House served also as Frederick's private office, the inner sanctum where few were called, and only then on the most important business. Hundreds of books lined the shelves which climbed high into a white-corniced ceiling. Indian carpeting covered most of the maple floor, and the furnishings were the best money could buy. Five large windows, with royal blue velvet drapes spilling to the carpet, ran the length of the wall, each affording a spectacular view of Ranelagh Harbour and beyond to the haze of Southampton.

Frederick was well over six feet tall and had the bulk to complement it. A full head of iron-grey hair framed his tanned face, and the hazel-flecked green eyes, so sharply inquisitive, could summon up the attitude of a cat watching a mouse. It was an ability he was very aware of and which he used to some effect when the occasion warranted.

He was always impeccably dressed for business, and this day had chosen a clerical grey suit, high wing collar with bottle-green cravat and black leather boots which bore the result of much polishing. Despite his age he still held a youthful look, and moved easily for such a big man.

The leather chair creaked softly under his weight as he read the morning correspondence, chin on hands, elbows resting easily on an enormous oak desk littered with shipping charts and files. The only sounds to disturb the silence were the crackle of burning logs in the stone fireplace, and the comforting rasp of the clock's pendulum. From time to time he glanced up from his reading to peer over gold-rimmed spectacles and take in the figure of his son, but his expression did nothing to indicate his thoughts.

Jonathan stood looking out of the far window at the docks as he patiently awaited his father's pleasure. He smiled easily as he watched one of the seamen chase a galley boy who had been cheekily making faces from what had seemed a safe distance. A sharp crack of the rope's end gave the lad incentive for speed, and the seaman was left quickly behind, arms waving, lips moving in silent threat.

Jonathan was strikingly handsome. Slightly taller than his father, he was an erect figure carrying the gold-braided uniform with style and a certain panache. His hair, light brown and tinged with the faintest auburn, held soft waves and had grown rather longer than his father would have liked. Bleached by the suns of many voyages, it bore evidence of a life above decks, for he was essentially a sailor and spent as little time as possible in chart rooms or offices. He had the soft blue eyes of a dreamer, yet the firm set of his mouth and a rugged jawline indicated it could be otherwise. He had served a tough apprenticeship in his father's service, during which he neither asked for nor received any favours. As heir apparent to the shipping line he might well have had an easier passage, but it had been quite the opposite and he would not have enjoyed it any other way. His sense of humour was well known, and his willingness for work was legendary. Often he would labour with the cargo alongside the crews, with whom he joked and mixed freely.

Frederick pushed aside the pile of letters and now looked fixedly at Jonathan. He had much to say, and none of it would please his son, least of all that which he planned to leave until last.

'My congratulations on your achieving a master's ticket, Jonathan. You have done well in your studies.'

Jonathan turned from the window, his reply cautious, apprehensive of how his request for a command would be met.

'Thank you, sir.'

Frederick glanced at the papers on the desk. 'However, you may be classed as a ship's captain within these documents, but you have yet to prove your worth in commerce.'

Jonathan's face clouded. It did not promise to be nearly as

comfortable an interview as his mother had predicted. 'I agree, father, but I cannot progress further without my own ship.'

There was an awkward silence before Frederick spoke again. 'Do you then think yourself ready to shoulder all the demands which go with that office?'

The reply came hurriedly, and with anxiety.

'I do, I have proved myself over many years at sea, and...'

Frederick interrupted him in mid-flow. 'You wander from the point of contention.'

Jonathan walked slowly over to the desk, and looked down at his father. 'What point of contention, father?'

'Your inexperience.'

A sudden anger welled in Jonathan.

'I am the best damned navigator in your fleet, sir!'

They eyed each other like prizefighters, and Frederick half rose from his chair as he hurled back his reply.

'Do not bring your alehouse language in here! My stars! Is this how you would conduct yourself in commerce?'

Jonathan was at once contrite, and ashamed at losing his temper.

'I am sorry, father, and I beg your understanding ... it was in my anxiety to prove my worth to you that I lapsed into such a statement.'

With a glare, Frederick eased himself back in his seat.

'I accept your apology, but would be obliged if you conducted yourself more properly during the remainder of this interview.'

'As you say, sir.'

'Very well. Now let us return to the subject... I find no fault with your abilities as a seagoing officer. But such talents as you have there prove little about your competence to do business.'

'What would you have me do then?'

'You need to learn the markets.'

'I agree, sir, and have come to seek your blessing to remedy such fault I may have in that direction.' He moved smartly to attention, tone now formal. 'May it please you, sir, Captain

51

Jonathan Bramwell respectfully asks your commission to command a ship of the line, and do business as you would decree in any of the world's oceans.'

'I think not.'

The bald reply hit Jonathan like a fist driven hard to the stomach, but he remained rigidly at attention as Frederick continued.

'You may in time prove able to command a merchant ship, but you are quite plainly not yet at that point.'

Jonathan steadied the tremble of anger and disappointment.

'May I ask how you have arrived at that decision, sir?'

'You may, sir. Observe how you have conducted yourself in this interview. You have displayed little tact, a propensity to lose your temper, arrogance and a self-confessed anxiety. Are these the qualities I should embrace in a merchant captain?'

Jonathan's reply was formal. 'May I speak in my defence, sir?'

Frederick was equally formal. 'I should be pleased to hear how you see yourself.'

There was a plea for understanding in Jonathan's voice.

'If I display anxiety, then I think it natural in the circumstances. I have worked hard for my master's ticket and am most anxious to prove myself to you in that capacity.'

Frederick shook his head.

'An anxious captain is not a good thing. Calmness and a decisive manner are called for in that office. You really must acknowledge that from the outset.'

Jonathan forced himself into a more reasonable approach.

'I do, sir. But I fear you mistake me. I am set on having my own ship, and in such mind allowed my feelings to surface... I would be calm and deliberate in command since it would be me in charge with no one to gainsay my orders.'

Frederick's fingers drummed the desk in brittle impatience.

'Would the rest of your defence be in like manner? That concerning your arrogance, your impatience and inability to put a bridle on your temper?'

Jonathan swallowed deeply, the heat from the burning logs forcing beads of sweat on to his brow.

'With respect, sir, I feel you mistake me... I do not feel that I am arrogant. My patience I have proved, both at sea and in the many years of study which this very week have gained me my ticket. As for my temper, I have witnessed this to be no bad thing in a captain.'

Frederick leaned back in his chair.

'That is your defence concluded, then?'

Jonathan nodded curtly. 'It is, sir.'

There was silence for some time before Frederick spoke.

'You claim I mistake you, I assure you I do not. You are my only son, and I have great hopes for your future. One day you will sit at this desk with no counsel save your own, and it is because of that coming responsibility that I must be hard on you.'

A log rolled off the fire and landed with a clatter in the hearth. He gave it a cursory glance before continuing.

'A year as second-in-command to Captain Anstruther on the *Pelican* will do much to prepare you for your own ship.'

Jonathan's mouth twisted in disappointment.

'Is that your final word, father?'

Frederick relaxed his expression and his tone became kinder.

'Not quite. I am looking on this year with Anstruther as a proving time for you, Jonathan. He will teach you the art of international commerce. I would now have you learn to mature, to grasp the nettle of business acumen ... to be more worldly.'

Jonathan was puzzled.

'More worldly? I do not think I understand you, father.'

'Then let me enlighten you. My findings indicate that you are somewhat naive of life's more demanding responsibilities.'

Jonathan prickled. 'You have the advantage, sir.'

'Very well, let me put it straightly to you. I am told that you are much too close to the crews over which you are supposed to hold command. You mix with them far too freely.'

'I do not see that, sir!'

'Obviously not, but others do. You are not only heir to this shipping line, but also a serving officer of that line.'

'I am aware of that, sir, and believe that I have the respect of the crews which I deal with.'

53

'You would enjoy more respect if you did not work along-side them like a common labourer, and cavort with them in alehouses and the like.'

Jonathan was astonished at the accusation. He had never before been criticised on such matters by his father. But he was not to know that his mother's housekeeper had picked up such gossip from talkative crew members and fed it on to Georgina, who quickly acquainted her husband with the facts. A stickler for discipline, Frederick had resolved to bring his son to closer order within the business, exactly what Georgina had hoped for.

'Cavort? That is harsh, sir. I simply join them in a drink from time to time, the better to understand them and their attitudes. That is why I also share their labour, for there will be times at sea when I must know upon whom I can rely, and for what task.'

'My dear fellow! ... Such revolutionary thinking. They are sailors, not statesmen. You give orders and they obey, for they are conditioned to their tasks.'

He paused and shook his head in wonderment at his son.

'You had better dismiss any such attitudes from your mind, for these are simple men you deal with and know their station in life. You apparently do not.'

Jonathan's reply was reasoned and sincere.

'I do not see that I have done harm, father.'

There was a distinct reddening of Frederick's face. He was angry that Georgina had been the one to tell him of Jonathan's deviations from the straight and narrow, for she was invading his territory more with every passing day. But he was angrier that his captains had apparently not steered Jonathan on a tighter course. Was he indeed losing touch with his son? It might be that Georgina was right, that Jonathan should be schooled without delay in the administration of the company.

'Do not talk nonsense, sir! What you are doing will confuse them, and to your peril. Mark well the proverb which says that familiarity breeds contempt.' He paused to take breath, and his voice came through gritted teeth as he continued. 'In future be more discreet in the company you keep. I will not tolerate lax

54

discipline, and have this company come tumbling down about my head. Do I make myself clear?'

Jonathan writhed under the telling-off, but checked his quickly rising temper. 'You do, sir.'

Frederick's anger shifted to embarrassment as he considered his next move, for he was far from comfortable in what he now had to say.

But despite his best intentions the words came bluntly.

'Your mother and I believe it is high time you were settled down.'

'Settled down?'

Frederick cleared his throat in some discomfort.

'I will not beat about the bush. Your mother's wish, and mine also, is that you become engaged to be married to Charlotte.'

Jonathan was shocked and dismayed. 'I beg your pardon, sir?'

'I believe you heard me clearly enough.'

A profound frustration welled in Jonathan. He had come to this meeting in hope of being given his first command, but there would be no such appointment, only another long year to endure as first officer, and no surety in the probation ending there. Very well, so be it, he would prove himself in that task. But he would not be instructed on the conduct of his private life. His voice was firm.

'With respect, father, I have no intention of becoming engaged, or married, to anyone at this stage in my career.'

A scowl of annoyance came to Frederick, for he was under great pressure from Georgina to implement the proposed union.

Charlotte Bingham-West was a jewel in Hampshire society and her ageing parents were most powerful within that clique. Charlotte had been born late in the marriage and was an only child. As such she would inherit the Bingham-West Shipping Company, a rival of the Bramwell Line.

The marriage of Jonathan and Charlotte was eagerly sought by Georgina as an integral part of her plan, for she saw it locking the two companies into a most formidable enterprise,

55

and in this she had the complete backing of Charlotte's parents, who had expressed a desire to see an alliance of the respective shipping lines. Frederick could see the merit in such a move, yet he was proud of the company he had built from virtually nothing, and was at first suspicious of what amalgamation might bring. However, he had been sweetened by the promise of being made chairman of the enterprise, should it come to be.

He growled, 'You are impudent, sir!'

'I regret your opinion of me, father, but I will not have a wife chosen for me.'

Frederick hesitated, but he was under strong orders from Georgina to pursue the matter to the bitter end. He would try another tack. His tone now came laced with sweet reason, as he pointed to a chair which stood in front of the desk.

'Please sit down, Jonathan. Our formal business is done, and this is a family matter.'

'As you wish, father, but my mind will not be changed.'

He sat stiffly upright in the chair.

Frederick steepled his fingers and looked over them at his son. A tight smile flickered as he glimpsed his own youth and short temper in him.

'Your mother tells me that Charlotte has more than a great fondness for you, Jonathan.'

Jonathan looked squarely back into his father's eyes. What exactly was afoot in this attempt at an arranged marriage? Whatever it might be, he was determined not to come into line. His reply came in a balanced, even tone.

'And I am fond of Charlotte, but that is as far as it goes.'

Frederick was suddenly beginning to enjoy the duel with his son, sure in the winning of it, and his counter was delivered purringly.

'I am sorry to hear you say that, for she would make a most excellent wife.'

'I do not doubt it. But it will be for some other man.'

'Then you puzzle me. Why do you keep her company so closely? I know you seek the girl out frequently when you are ashore.'

56

'Because she does not bore me, as so many of the others do. We find much in common to laugh at within this snobbish society.'

Frederick dropped the purring tone, and his reply was caustic.

'A snobbish society? You are an odd fellow ... it may be you would be happier ragged in the parish workhouse.'

'I believe there is a middle road through life, father.'

Frederick moved to thought. He was straying from the point. In any case, did not all young men have a rebellious streak, a fire within to change the face of society and a desire for social reform? He had gone through all those growing pains, but emerged with the knowledge that a man cannot forever carry the world's causes on his back, and so it would be with Jonathan.

However, the bridle of responsibility must be placed on him with great care. Frederick unsteepled his fingers and leaned back in the chair. He would have to fish for information so that he might be more informative when he was later closeted with Georgina and under barrage from her tireless questioning.

'Do you have someone else in mind? After all, you are of an age to be thinking about marriage, and it would be quite understandable if there were another who attracted you more.'

Jonathan was finding the interview tiresome. He had been denied his own ship, and was now being forced to endure what in other circumstances would be laughable. He was never at a loss for female company, and freely enjoyed the favours of many women. Certainly he was in no mind to exchange that delicious freedom of choice for the prison of a society marriage ... Damn it all, this was his mother's doing for sure, and no ship to boot. Why could he not escape the lot of them and go to another shipping line? He had his master's ticket, and was certain to get a command. His frustration made him want to strike back.

'Why this sudden haste to have me married to Charlotte?'

'There is someone else, then?'

57

'No there is not! Nor likely to be. I do not want for a wife.'

Frederick's ebullience waned slightly as he realised his lack of headway. He would try to prick the conscience of his son.

'I find myself rather disturbed that you should have encouraged Charlotte to think otherwise.'

Plainly stung with the accusation, Jonathan almost shouted his reply. 'I have done no such thing!'

Frederick smiled inside at his success, but his expression was inscrutable.

'Such a statement confirms your naivete ... Good Lord in heaven, boy! What do you suppose an eligible young woman thinks when a man regularly seeks her company? Do you really imagine that what she has in mind is making daisy chains with you?'

Jonathan looked perturbed.

'This has come as a sorry surprise to me, father. I did not appreciate that Charlotte may be entertaining thoughts of marriage.'

Frederick slowly shook his head.

'Indeed, you have much to learn about women and life.'

'I see I appear at fault, sir. But I assure you that I would never do harm to Charlotte, for she is a dear friend to me.'

The words caused Frederick new hope. 'I am pleased to hear it. Now take my advice, proper marriages are built on foundations of friendship and understanding, rather than doubtful emotions. Both you and Charlotte have great responsibilities before you. One day, in the not-too-distant future, each of you will inherit important shipping companies, giving much-needed work and sustenance to many families in Southampton. Your alliance in marriage would be a most proper undertaking.'

Jonathan smothered his true feelings into a polite reply. 'I do respect your counsel, father, but I am not yet ready to consider marriage.'

Hopeful of making further inroads, Frederick pressed on in his endeavour, his voice pitched in an encouraging tone.

'I appreciate what you say, Jonathan, but you are twenty-three ... rather time to be thinking of putting roots down.'

'With respect, father, you plainly did not think that when you were my age.'

Frederick's jawline visibly tightened.

'Have a care that you do not anger me with further impudence.'

'But it is true, father, is it not? You were thirty-five before you were married. Why should it be different for me?'

'Because I was in no position to think of marriage. I was fully engaged in the building of this company, whereas your future is assured.' He dangled the carrot of a half-promise. 'Having the responsibilities of a wife and children, and the maturity that station naturally brings, would make you an altogether different proposition in the selection of officers for command ... Anstruther will soon be retired, which would see the company flagship in need of a responsible captain.'

Jonathan grimaced. 'Really, father. With the greatest respect, if you were to make me the Lord High Admiral of all the fleets in the world, getting married to achieve that post would be the very last thing I should do.'

Frederick lifted the front of the documents folder and slammed it shut on the papers containing Jonathan's certificates. He became sharp and businesslike once more.

'This interview is at an end. Captain Anstruther is waiting outside. Show him in, then away about your business. Oh, yes ... your mother wishes to speak with you. Kindly save me the task of explaining your feelings, and do not forget today is her birthday, she will expect you at this evening's dinner party, and mark well my earlier comments, for we shall discuss this matter further.'

Jonathan stood up and came to attention before speaking.

'On the matter of our formal business, sir, I should like to record my disappointment. I had hoped that you might...'

Frederick interrupted with a dismissive gesture.

'Your disappointment is duly noted. Now show Anstruther in!'

59

Jonathan gave a stiff bow of salute from the neck. 'Yes, sir.' With a tight about turn he walked to the door, then paused. 'I hope, sir, to change your opinion of me.'

Frederick had already busied himself in writing, and replied without looking up. 'And I, sir, look forward to that time.'

The door closed behind Jonathan, Frederick gazed at it reflectively before turning once more to his correspondence. A few minutes later, there was a light knock on the door.

'Come in, Captain Anstruther.'

An air of quiet authority cloaked Joseph Anstruther. He was a tough man well into middle age, widely experienced in commercial shipping. Short and stocky, with a face the colour of teak, he sported a beard with more than a little grey in it.

Anstruther was fair in his dealings with crew and traders alike. A keen disciplinarian who drew respect from all those with whom he came into contact, he had sailed with Frederick almost from the beginning of their respective careers, and when Frederick started his own shipping line Anstruther joined him as a seagoing captain. He took no advantage of their long relationship, and it was for him, strictly employer and employee.

He walked over to the desk and saluted smartly before taking off his cap.

'Good day to you, sir.'

'And to you, Captain. You are no doubt aware that Jonathan has gained his ticket.'

'I am. It is already the talk of the crews.'

'He wants a ship.'

Anstruther stroked his beard nervously.

'Which one will you be giving him?'

The question made Frederick smile. 'Not yours, Joseph. In any case, I am of the mind that he's not yet ready. Do you have any thoughts on the subject?'

Anstruther was embarrassed.

'He's a good lad, and we've put in many sea hours together. There's no better sailor or navigator in the company, but your mind seems made up and I've no wish to put my oar in to complicate matters.'

'You think he is ready, then?'

'With respect, Mr Frederick, I did not say that.'

Frederick eased himself away from the desk and spread back in the chair.

'We will stop playing cat and mouse, Joseph, we have known each other too long for that. The times we've had, eh!' The two men smiled at each other. 'Sit down, we'll have a pipe and a yarn on the matter.'

Anstruther sat on the edge of the chair vacated by Jonathan, and Frederick dragged a pipe from his jacket, then slowly filled it with tobacco from an elegant humidor which stood on the desk.

'Take your fill, Joseph, this is from your last voyage.'

With pipes lit, both men were more relaxed as they regarded each other through the rising blue plumes of smoke. Frederick gently sniffed the air. 'Interesting blend, and much in demand on the London market. You secured a good piece of business at the right price.' He regarded Anstruther carefully before continuing. 'But would Jonathan have been so astute?'

Anstruther shook his head reprovingly. 'You cannot put blame on him for that. He has not my experience.'

A triumphant smile appeared on Frederick's face.

'Exactly my point! You are the best merchant captain in my fleet, Joseph. That is why I have decided to put Jonathan under your wing.'

Anstruther drew on his pipe and looked uncertain.

'What would you have me do with him? For I can teach the lad no more about sailoring.'

'He will be your first officer for at least a year. You will teach him every aspect of commerce, and introduce him to our best contacts around the world. That is your charge.'

Anstruther nodded. 'I see. When will he join me?'

'At once. He will sail with you to Boston at the end of the month. Meanwhile you can take him around the Southampton agents and the like.'

The look of embarrassment returned to Anstruther.

'Does he know of this arrangement?'

'He does.'

'And how has he taken it? I know he wanted his own ship.'

'With a fight, but he has accepted my decision.'

Anstruther was plainly relieved.

'I am glad for that at least. I would not have wished myself a first officer with a grudge in his heart.'

'Jonathan does not bear grudges. He has spirit and resolve. But let us not get sentimental, Joseph, this is business we are about.' He stood up, right hand extended towards Anstruther. 'I wish you good luck in the venture.'

They shook hands. Anstruther stood back from the desk, put on his cap and saluted.

'I will make a grand time of it ... as we used to.'

Frederick had a glint of emotion in his eye, and the hardness had gone from his voice.

'Make a real man of him, Joseph. Make him more worldly.'

'There's little wrong with him, as I've found, and with God's help I'll make you proud of the lad.'

Anstruther had gone, and Frederick was left to his thoughts. He dipped into his coat pocket and pulled out a handkerchief, then blew hard into it. Clearing his throat, he muttered aloud, 'Damn the weather. I must be getting a cold.'

The dining room of Ranelagh House was large and elegant, and had an easterly aspect. Its tall, Georgian-paned windows, draped in red velvet, afforded a panoramic view of the gardens to the rear of the house. At the end of the room, twin French windows provided access to an expanse of stone-paved terracing. The ceiling was a soft white, embossed with angel illustrations, and boasted a magnificent chandelier which held fifty candles. The blue and gold wall-covering ended on white splashboards which gave way to deep gold carpeting, patterned to match the ceiling angels. A display of mahogany sideboards flanked the room, which was dominated by an impressively long dining table, the high-backed chairs indicating a capacity of forty place settings.

Georgina Bramwell seemed to float through the haze of pale

morning sunshine which filled the room as she inspected the various arrangements of evergreens and dried flowers on the sideboards, moving majestically from one to another like some fastidious butterfly. At her side, hovering silently in black dress, white collar and high-buttoned boots was Sarah Hawkins, housekeeper to Ranelagh.

Sarah had been in service at Ranelagh House for thirty years, working assiduously through the ranks from scullery maid to her present position as head of a small army of servants. She had been sad when James Wilbur was forced to sell the estate, thinking herself out of home and employment. But at the time of sale, Georgina had been skilful in encouraging Frederick to retain Sarah and the rest of the staff.

As children, and oblivious of their stations in life, the two women had played together, enjoying a friendship which had continued into adulthood. Yet from the very first day of her new beginning as mistress of Ranelagh, Georgina had engineered a respectful distance between them. It would not do at all to be close to a domestic. However, Sarah remained devoted to her, keeping her closely informed of all talk below stairs, and facts carefully gleaned from table talk by visiting guests, a useful intelligence service to Georgina, who affected little interest but made no attempt to dissuade her loyal servant from eavesdropping.

Today was Georgina's forty-second birthday, although she had not chosen publicly to announce that precise number of years. A tall, desirably proportioned woman, she did not look nearly her age and was aware of the fact and her beauty. The still-youthful figure and perfect carriage enhanced her aristocratic symmetry of face, the high cheekbones giving a certain haughtiness. The possessor of a sumptuous wardrobe, she invariably dressed the part of lady of the manor without ever overdoing the role.

Now suited in a tailored riding habit preparatory to her daily outing on the downs, she was in an edgy mood, her mind on what course Frederick's meeting with Jonathan might be taking. Honey-blonde hair swept tightly up into a severe black hat, riding crop in hand, her ice-blue eyes missed nothing as she inspected the flowers. She paused at one of the arrangements and poked the crop into its midst.

'Rather tight I think, Sarah, and I believe that applies to the other displays. I would like them more open, more flowing.' She smiled in a patronising fashion. 'I am sure you know what I mean.'

'Yes, ma'am. I will see to it at once.'

'Thank you, Sarah, but before you do so, tell cook to come and see me without delay, and to bring up the menu cards. I am thinking of making changes in the desserts.'

'Yes, ma'am.' She hesitated a moment. 'May I wish you a happy birthday?' She handed her mistress a small package, but Georgina made no attempt to open it, and the patronising smile returned. 'How sweet.'

'I hope, ma'am, it will be a grand party for you.'

'Thank you. Now run along and get cook, or I shall be at sixes and sevens all day if I am delayed for my ride.'

Sarah bustled away down the room. As she approached the door it swung open and Jonathan entered. His smile was brief, for it was less than an hour since he had gone through the torrid interview with his father. But his tone was civil enough.

'Good morning, Sarah. You are well?'

'Good morning, Mr Jonathan, I am well enough, thank you. And yourself, sir, do you fare well?'

He wrinkled his brow. 'I often wonder on it, Sarah, and too often fail to arrive with an answer.'

She smiled at his reply without understanding it. Georgina's voice boomed out imperiously from the other end of the room.

'Sarah! At this rate of progress it will be moonlight before I am able to take my ride!'

Jonathan interrupted with sarcastic humour.

'What a novel idea, mother ... why not wait upon its rising?'

Sarah was quick to cut in and save the embarrassment.

'Sorry, ma'am. I will go at once.'

She bustled from the room and Jonathan smiled knowingly at her quick retreat, then turned to regard his mother. The

64

smile was gone and his delivery reflected a brittle mood.

'Good morning, mother, my compliments upon your birthday. Many happy returns.'

Georgina's smile was polite, but her reply bristled with ill-concealed displeasure 'Thank you, Jonathan.' She drew herself more erect. 'I would greatly appreciate your not addressing me in such a vulgar manner before the servants.'

He shrugged. 'The moonlight ride? Sorry, mother, but there was no vulgarity intended ... I simply thought it humorous.'

'It was not, and I perceive from your attitude that you are not in a proper mood for discussion. We shall meet later.'

'With respect, mother, a postponement will not be necessary, for what I have to say will be brief enough.'

'I take it that you have seen your father this morning?'

'Yes, we have spoken.'

'Thank goodness for that small mercy, then.'

'I have a message from him.'

'A message?'

'Yes. I am to tell you that I shall not become engaged, married or in any way fastened in arrangement with anyone.'

Georgina's expression hardened, but she remained calm.

'What an extraordinary statement to make.'

'I am merely carrying out my father's orders.'

'Am I to understand that your father was the author of these words?'

'No, mother, I was. He declined to deliver them himself and instructed that I should do so.'

'Then I should be obliged if you would explain yourself.'

'With pleasure, mother. I will tell you what I have already told my father. I have absolutely no intention of marrying Charlotte Bingham-West. What is more, I believe I know what prompted such a preposterous idea, and I do not even care to discuss it. However, when the time comes for me to take a wife, I shall do the choosing.'

She gripped the riding crop firmly with both hands.

'I cannot believe my ears. To think that I should have to endure such insolence from my only son ... and on my birthday!'

65

'I regret your upset, mother. But I was not the architect of the plot.'

There was a small silence as she wondered on what ham-fisted approach Frederick must have made to achieve this mood in her son. Evidently the meeting had not gone as they had planned. She would need to find time in order to think of what her own approach would be ... Damn Frederick for a bumbler, she might as well have done the job herself in the first place.

'I find no excuse for such an outburst, Jonathan, but I will accept your apology. Now please leave me, I am expecting cook at any moment ... We shall resume this conversation later.'

Jonathan sighed deeply.

'Mother, there is no point in the prolonging of this farce. My father left me in no doubt on the matter you wish to discuss, and I have given you my answer.'

Her face tightened, and for the first time her composure was in danger of slipping away.

'You are an arrogant young man, Jonathan. Do not have the impertinence to assume that you know all I have to say.'

Before he could reply they were interrupted by the cook, who immediately sensed the mood. She now stood awkwardly, half in, half out of the room, nervously fidgeting with the menu cards.

'Sorry, ma'am, I did not know you were busy ... Sarah said as how you wanted to see me directly. I can come back later.'

Georgina was relieved by the interruption, and became suddenly composed.

'That will not be necessary, cook, Mr Jonathan is just about to leave.'

'Yes, ma'am ... shall I wait outside?'

The reply came tightly, 'If you would.'

The cook withdrew, quietly closing the door behind her, and Georgina now pitched her voice in a more gracious tone.

'Let us put this unpleasantness behind us, Jonathan. We have not had the opportunity for talk since your return from Africa. I suggest afternoon tea together ... shall we say four o'clock in my sitting room?'

He smiled in grim admiration at her resolve and fixity of purpose, but he would not be churlish.

'Very well, mother ... four o'clock in your sitting room.'

She wondered at his smile but found herself unable to guess what lay behind it. Yet she was now more sure of her ground, and attempted some degree of warmth as she smiled back.

'Please ask cook to come in, and do try to be on time for our *tête-à-tête* ... I would not want the tea to become cold.'

'I shall not keep you waiting, mother. By the way, are you able to tell me the whereabouts of my sister? I have spent the better part of an hour trying to find her.'

'I believe she has repaired to the schoolroom.'

He gave a little bow. 'I am indebted, mother.'

Georgina looked vaguely annoyed as she watched him walk from the room. Such stubbornness in the boy, and too like his father. But she would make him see the great benefits which marriage to Charlotte would bring to them all, both in business and society ... And if he wanted a separate life outside his marriage, well, these things could be discreetly arranged.

67

8

The schoolroom held a comforting atmosphere, made more real by the dancing flames of a coal fire which glowed in the grate of an iron range. A pleasant odour of oil paints and spirit blended to fill the air as Ann Bramwell, dressed in a long smock of white cotton, busied herself before a canvas which lay stretched across a much-used easel.

Ann did not have the regal stature or the well-favoured looks of her mother, and was handsome rather than beautiful. She had inherited the stronger features of her father; the wide inquiring hazel eyes, so uncannily like his, and the rare ability to raise one eyebrow higher than the other in question of any doubtful statement. But in pleasant contradiction, the generous mouth and an engagingly warm smile suggested that friendships properly forged with her could be lasting. She moved about the painting, her softly waved auburn hair shimmering like burnished copper in the glow of the fire. The artist's green velvet cap sat at a rakish angle, pushed into that attitude by a regular scratching of the forehead as she intently studied the book of illustrations from which she copied.

The schoolroom held many fond memories for Ann, and she found happy retreat there. Jonathan and she had undergone their early education within its walls, and countless winter evenings had been spent in the making and telling of ghost stories while chestnuts hissed and roasted on the fire and tales gave way to great plans for the future.

Jonathan paused at the open door and for a few moments fondly watched her at work. 'What masterpiece are you about now?'

She turned from the painting and smiled in greeting as he walked into the room and halted by her side. 'I am attempting a Canaletto, though I fear without a deal of success.'

He kissed her on the cheek, then gently squeezed her shoulders in encouragement as they both regarded the painting. He grinned, 'Do you suppose they called him Canaletto because he was always painting canals?'

Her laughter was warm and appreciative of his humour. 'Always the wit, Jonathan. I had never thought on that.' She looked once more at her work. 'What do you think of my labours, then?'

'Good, very good. St Mark's Square, is it not?'

'At least you recognise it.'

'Of course.'

'I thought I should concentrate on buildings since I find water so difficult to convey.'

'It can also be difficult to sail upon.'

His smile was rueful, and she noted the expression.

'What is it, Jonathan? Father?'

He nodded. 'I am newly from a rather difficult meeting with him ... he has refused me a command.'

Her eyes showed the disappointment she felt for him. It had been in this very room, just the evening before, that together they had celebrated the news of his master's ticket. In echoes of times past, they had talked about the future, enjoying the simple delights of hot chocolate and biscuits ... but to them it had been like a grand party.

'Oh, Jonathan, I am so very sorry.'

'He thinks me immature, and gave me to understand that mother shares his opinion.'

'Immature? What an unfair thing to say ... you are the finest sailor and navigator in his fleet!'

He smiled at her vehemence. 'Ever to my rescue, dear sister. But do cheer up, for I told him as much as you have just said, and got him hopping mad.' He laughed and picked up a paintbrush, twirling it in circles as though agitating the contents of a cooking pot. 'But I did add a curse for the seasoning of it.'

69

She grinned conspiratorially. 'You actually swore at father? What did you say?'

'I told him I was the best damned navigator he had.'

'How brave you are. He would not like to be told that, and sworn at into the bargain, true as it is.'

'You are right, but true or not I should have held my temper in check. Whenever I meet with father I seem to attract more the sting of bees rather than their honey.'

'In what way does he think you immature?' She looked at him inquiringly as he put the brush back on its palette.

'It would be easier to state the things he finds me mature in.'

'I see, and how did the meeting conclude?'

'I am to become apprentice to the tricks of world trade under Anstruther's probation for the period of one year.'

'And then he will give you a ship?'

'He intimated as much, but who knows with father?' His face clouded. 'Ann ... has Charlotte Bingham-West spent much time at Ranelagh during my time away?'

She was curious at the sudden question, more so in that he had referred to Charlotte in full name and so formally.

'No more than is usual, but why do you ask?'

'You will see by and by, but first answer me this. Have I ever given Charlotte cause to think that my feelings towards her were other than in the normal course of friendship?'

'I would not know that, Jonathan, since I am not privy to all that goes between you. But she is a sweet enough creature and would make a fine wife. Do you think along such lines?'

He frowned and walked over to the window, gazing out over the gardens for some time before replying, the while she waited patiently for his answer.

'I do not think of her in such a way. Charlotte is, as you say, a sweet creature, but we go no further in our relationship other than being good friends.' He became silent, thoughtfully tweaking his chin between thumb and forefinger as he continued to gaze through the window.

Ann's face was filled with curiosity. 'Well?'

70

His reply was brusque. 'Well what?'

'For goodness' sake, Jonathan, you take me halfway along the path only to abandon me there. What is this about?'

'I will tell you, and undoubtedly shock you in the telling, for it shocked me ... Father calmly announced that mother wishes me to become engaged to be married to Charlotte.'

'Engaged to be married! ... To Charlotte?'

'There, did I not tell you that you would be shocked?'

'I am not shocked, Jonathan, but rather taken by surprise.'

'I see. Not shocked by your brother being press-ganged, merely surprised.' He walked slowly towards her and halted by the painting to look down into her eyes. 'In what context, surprised?'

'In that I had never really matched the pair of you as man and wife.' She smiled wickedly. 'But it is an interesting thought, Jonathan, and she is very pretty.'

'Now you make jest of me.'

Her smile broadened. 'Do not be so stuffy, dear brother. The two of you are well suited, and she is very wealthy, or will be so; what is modernly referred to as a good catch.'

'Do not joke about this, Ann, for I have no wish to catch her. What is more, I have said as much to both father and mother.'

'I doubt that father conceived the idea.' Her expression grew more serious. 'This is undoubtedly mother's doing.'

He nodded in agreement. 'I believe mother is attempting to engineer father into a union with the Bingham-West Line ... for what reason I cannot fathom.' He placed his hands behind his back and began to pace back and forth in front of the fireplace. 'But I do not think he has yet completely swallowed the hook of her scheme, whatever it may be. I find myself further puzzled by father's sudden decision that I should speedily learn the business ... he has always brushed aside my interest and ideas for the future.' He stopped his pacing. 'However, it would appear that I am set to be the sacrificial goat in the proposed binding. I simply will not have it, Ann!'

'That is your prerogative, Jonathan, but let me assure you that whatever may be afoot has been kept secret from me.'

Once more he began to pace angrily.

'The whole affair is quite outrageous! I feel myself being hemmed in from all sides ... father is attempting to bribe me with the captaincy of the *Pelican* if I settle down, as he puts it, and mother has attempted to move on me from another direction. She wishes again to talk with me this very afternoon, hoping no doubt to change my mind.'

Ann walked over to him and put a restraining hand upon his arm to bring his pacing to a halt.

'There will be opportunity this evening for talk with Charlotte. Mother has invited her to the dinner party. But be gentle in your questioning, for she is most likely innocent of the affair.'

He took her hand and squeezed it in gentle affection as he bent to kiss her forehead.

'Very well, Ann, for I do value your counsel in this matter.'

'Have a care now, Jonathan. You must learn to play well the games of others, the better to beat them at their tricks.'

'I shall take care.'

She nodded. 'Good, and remember that I am with you in this. You only need to ask.'

'God bless you, Ann, I must go now. I will see you at dinner.'

He strode purposefully from the room, leaving her to gaze reflectively at the painting. Could her mother really be scheming an arranged marriage? Lately, Georgina had been spending an unusual amount of time with Samuel Bingham-West, a man whose personal fortune was of legendary proportions ... Could it be that there was a financial crisis? These were increasingly hard times, and the competition grew ever stronger.

She picked up the fine sable brush and put detail to the painting as her thoughts deepened. If the two companies were to come together they would undoubtedly present a formidable force to others. But who would steer such an alliance? Samuel was well into his seventies, with no son to take over from him, and Charlotte would not even be considered in the reckoning of it, therefore it would have to be Frederick. An alliance did promise mutual benefit, and with the marriage of Jonathan to Charlotte children must surely follow, providing a natural progression. After all, Frederick would not live for ever, and Georgina had to secure her future. It could be that in the interim Georgina saw herself as queen mother and adviser to Jonathan when he eventually inherited the company.

Ann smiled knowingly as she carefully draped a dustcover over the painting then began to clean the brushes, watching the spirit become a lurid crimson under the discharge of the bristles. Georgina was like a tigress with cubs when it came to matters which might affect the security of Ranelagh, and she would not be afraid to draw blood in the protection of her interests. Ann picked up a rag and wiped the ochre from her fingers as her thoughts turned to Charlotte... She might well be in love with Jonathan and want in any case to marry him. However, such a feeling was plainly not shared by her brother. The three of them had been close-knit from childhood, sharing secrets, pains and pleasures, while Ann had always championed the shy and reserved Charlotte in the sometime divisions within the trio. A bond of close friendship had grown therein and she had no wish to break it, but if events were to lead to the barricades she would ally herself with her brother. There was no doubt of that.

Resplendent in dress uniform, with gold braid denoting his rank of captain, Jonathan stood at the top of the staircase which swept grandly into the front hall of Ranelagh House. The soothing notes of Beethoven's *Pastoral Symphony* floated up from a string ensemble which played discreetly within a roped-off alcove as Frederick and Georgina, with Ann, welcomed the first of the dinner guests. Unobserved, Jonathan regarded his mother and thought once more on their afternoon meeting.

Georgina had been completely frank, and the full content of her revelations had placed him in a state of mixed emotions. He remained thoughtful on his mother's disclosures as he made his way down the stairs. The guests were arriving in more steady numbers as he crossed to where the alcove offered a

73

degree of anonymity. Arms folded, he leaned against the wall and awaited the arrival of Charlotte, for there was a need to speak with her before he became lost in his inevitable dinner duties.

The meeting between Jonathan and his mother had not taken long, and she had quickly got to the heart of the matter.

'Your father will be heavily engaged in business over the next few days, so he has requested that I speak with you.'

He had lounged in the leather sofa as he sipped tea from a delicate china cup and warily awaited his mother's onslaught.

'You are no longer a boy, Jonathan, and should be acquainted with the facts concerning the company which gives you your livelihood. Your father's wish is that you take closer order of the running of the business.'

She paused to pour herself more tea, then looked over the laden cake stand which stood on the small table dividing them. Her expression was one of interrogation.

'Tell me ... what do you know of its administration?'

He was already not happy with the interview, and straightened up to place his cup firmly on the table.

'With all respect due to you, mother, should it not be father to ask such questions?'

She placed the teapot heavily on to its stand. 'I have already told you that I have his *carte blanche* on this matter.'

'Even so, mother, and once more with respect, this is the business of men.' He smiled without humour. 'I was under the impression that our subject would be quite another.'

'The business of men?' Her smile in return was icy cold. 'You have much to learn on that score, Jonathan. As for the other matter, we shall discuss that presently. Now kindly do me the courtesy of answering my question. What do you know of the company's administration?'

'I believe you must already know the answer ... little or nothing!' His tone grew angry. 'But I do not see myself at fault in that, for until this very morning my father apparently wanted it no other way. Yet out of the blue my part in it has seemingly become the most important thing in the world.'

'No one seeks to lay blame upon you, rather do I wish to make good the error. There is need in all for a change of attitude.'

'Why has it come so suddenly, and in such a heavy-handed way?'

She smoothed the neck of her flowered dress which had been so carefully selected to give a maternal appearance, and her voice came cooingly.

'I regret that you should think me heavy-handed, Jonathan, for I do not intend it to be so. I am your mother and desire only your future welfare in what are changing times.'

'What changing times do you speak of?'

'Most probably you see this company as wealthy and success-ful. Is that not so?'

'Are you telling me it is not?'

'At the moment it is comfortably off, but we are in grave danger of it being otherwise.'

He was suddenly concerned.

'You alarm me. How can it be so?'

'Steam power is the threat, Jonathan. A number of our rivals are already making the change, and unless we address the matter with urgency we shall soon begin to lose our markets.'

'I have told father as much, but my time was wasted. He assumes that sail will rule until at least the end of the century, and that steam is presently an unreliable toy.'

She put down her cup. 'I am aware of his assumptions, but he is now more ready to make the necessary changes. During your recent time away there have been impressive new times recorded by steamships plying between England and America... Traders and manufacturers want faster conclusion to their dealings and are already being attracted away from sail.'

'You seem remarkably well informed.'

'I make it my business to be so.'

'I see. Very well ... if we are indeed to make the change, when will it be implemented?'

Georgina did not answer at once, for she was faced with the

necessity for good timing. If her bombshell was delivered on Jonathan too soon the interview would collapse. She decided to proceed with caution. Better first to make him see his responsibilities.

'We do not have the capital necessary to effect the change.'

'Then we must ask the DeVilliers Bank to furnish us with a loan. After all, they assisted father to found the company.'

'Jonathan, I have told you these are changing times. The new board are not willing to venture capital on such a change... They are old men with no vision.'

'You have doubtless tried other banks?'

She sipped her tea as she regarded him.

'I have. Their required interest rate is exorbitant, and would also entail us in pledging Ranelagh House as guarantee. I have to tell you now that I would never agree to that, nor would your father.'

'We could equip for part-steam, part-sail.'

'No, Jonathan. That would involve us in wasted expenditure, for we should be faced with total change within a year at the most.' She looked at him very carefully before delivering her next words with a degree of drama. 'We must go all the way, or do nothing and perish slowly.'

'Then we would seem to be in something of a cleft stick ... what does my father intend to do?'

She placed the teacup back in its saucer with infinite care. It was a time to watch one's step, but it was also time for the kill.

'Your father and I have had a number of meetings with Samuel Bingham-West. He has agreed a merger. The alliance would afford the immediate building of a steamship fleet, and there would be capital to spare.'

Jonathan knew what was coming but he would play it out to the end. After all, why should he make it easy for her?

'You have taken me on a rather circuitous voyage to tell me that, mother, for your problems would seem to be settled.'

'They are also your problems, Jonathan.'

'Very well, our problems would seem to be settled.' There was a ragged note in his voice.

'Not quite, Jonathan.' In spite of her determination, she

found difficulty in choosing her next words. 'I would ask that you listen most carefully to what I finally have to say. Samuel Bingham-West has strongly intimated that he would not be opposed to your becoming engaged to be married to Charlotte.'

Jonathan smacked a hand across his knee as he laughed in bitter interruption.

'I'll wager he wouldn't! It is as I suspected, then, I am indeed intended as the human offering.'

Her claws were now fully extended. She had lost Ranelagh once, if she were to lose it again it would be forever. Men had no real foresight nor sense of value in these things. Jonathan would have to be made to come to heel or else all would be lost. But again, her words must be well chosen.

'There would be nothing wrong in such a marriage. Charlotte is a fine girl and would make a good wife ... she is much liked in society and would do nothing to hamper your personal freedom or predilections in any other avenues you may wish to follow.'

Jonathan pursed his mouth and gave a slow shake of the head.

'My God, mother, can you not hear yourself? I am to be thrust before the altar with *affaires* already afforded me. You are the limit.'

'You mistake me, sir! I spoke only of the personal freedoms you presently enjoy.'

His look was naked of any pretence.

'Mother, mother, mother! Do not insult my intelligence. Is Charlotte privy to the plot?'

'You would oblige me by not using the word, plot, for there is none ... Charlotte has not been consulted. We thought it better in the circumstances that you should approach her.'

'I see! I am not only to act as the pawn, but also to effect the checkmate.' He was silent for some moments. 'Let us now get to the dry bones of it. Does the proposed company alliance depend on my marrying Charlotte?'

She smoothed at her lap and, affecting sadness, looked away to the window.

'Samuel has implied as much.'

'I see ... he wants rid of his daughter and sees this as the ideal time for such a ridding. I have to salute his gall.'

Georgina replied softly, continuing to avert her gaze from him.

'You are harsh, Jonathan. He desires only to see his daughter married within a proper station of society.'

He stood up and flicked the cake crumbs from his jacket.

'What utterly delightful words you use, mother. I will go now and think on the matter. As you say, I am no longer a boy but a man with responsibilities. I must bear in mind that even Christ had to go to the cross for the greater good.'

He strode from the room, leaving Georgina in a more certain frame of mind than she had previously enjoyed. She poured more tea, then studiously selected a fruit biscuit from the cakestand.

Jonathan had been raised in the proper manner and, despite his blusterings, he was loyal to the family. Indeed, he had often proved to be self-sacrificing in its cause. He would assuredly come to accept what must be done.

The ensemble was playing Handel's *Water Music* as Charlotte, wearing an off-the-shoulder ball gown of the richest dark green, entered the hall with her parents. Jonathan made no attempt to move from his position in the alcove as he watched her walk slowly forward within the knot of guests waiting to meet their hosts. His appraisal of her was now through quite different eyes, for he had never thought on her as a wife.

She was indeed beautiful. How strange that he had never before seen that, or noticed the rich brown darkness of her hair, or the depth of smile which now lit her face as she talked with fellow guests. He was once more reminded of her knife-sharp wit and shrewdness. A smile twisted slowly across his mouth as he recalled his mother's words ... 'She would do nothing to hamper your personal freedom or predilections in any other avenues you may wish to follow.' The smile grew tighter. He would not care to wager his life on that ... yet she

78

would make a good and caring wife, for they had much in common and were rarely at fault with each other, and as his father had said, good marriages were based on strong friendships rather than doubtful emotions. Was love then a doubtful emotion?

He had heard people talk of love; how it ruthlessly blotted out all other emotions, how nothing else mattered on God's earth but that one person ... a person without whom you were no more than a pale shadow, were willing to die for, and be dead without. If that were love, then he felt no such emotion for Charlotte. He became suddenly aware that she had seen him, her expression one of puzzlement. No doubt she wondered why he had not chosen to be with the welcoming group. He conjured up a smile, then with a quick wave of the hand rapidly closed the distance between them, noting with relief that she had become some yards detached from her parents. His kiss was light on her cheek.

'Good evening, Charlotte ... you are well?'

'Good evening, Jonathan. I am well enough, thank you.'

'I am pleased to hear it, for we have need of serious talk, and I would as soon say my part of it before we become embroiled in idle chatter with these people.'

Charlotte looked perturbed at his sudden announcement.

'What serious talk is this, Jonathan? And why are you not with your parents and Ann to greet the guests?'

'Do not worry your head about that, for they manage quite well without me.' He looked about him, seeking a suitable place where they might talk in private, then took her firmly by the hand. 'Come along, Charlotte.'

She pulled in protest as Jonathan drew her in his wake towards the conservatory.

'But I have not yet given my salutations to your parents.'

Jonathan smiled reassuringly as he indicated a wrought-iron lovers' seat.

'Please sit down, Charlotte. You may give your salutations later, with me if you wish.'

'Very well, Jonathan.'

She had never liked the conservatory, and on this winter

79

evening its steamy dark interior of foreign floriculture seemed especially claustrophobic. She was reminded of the time, when as a child, she had thought tigers to be lurking in its midst. She sat down on the very edge of the seat and carefully arranged her gown, its cleverly tailored folds falling in neat array to the terrazzo-tiled floor. She smiled indulgently at him as he remained standing, looking down at her. 'Why all the mystery?' Her smile broadened. 'I know, you plan a jape and naturally require my help in it ... what is it, Jonathan? Do tell!'

He smiled at her enthusiasm and willingness to take these boring society people down a peg. What a dear friend she was, and what joyous rogues they were together in full cry against the common enemy. His pulse quickened at the memory of their many conspiracies, and now the delicate smell of her perfume insidiously heightened his animal senses as for the first time he saw not the joker but the woman. The wide blue eyes regarding him in patient question, that impudent little nose and full warm lips ... the firm breasts which thrust so defiantly against the strictures of a discreet cleavage ... whatever it was that now heated his blood and stirred his loins, it was not the love contained within fairy stories.

He felt at once surprised and ashamed. Surprised that Charlotte could have aroused such feelings in him, and ashamed at the darkness of his sudden and arrogant desire. What base thoughts were these that now came unbidden to him? He flushed at the realisation. The plotters had lain Charlotte vulnerable before him, and now he felt a sense of power over her. God help him, he was no better in selfish intention than they ... in fact worse, for a part of him had become animal, wanting to take her here and now as he might use a street woman, to defile her, a woman who trusted him and called him friend. Was it then that he wanted to humiliate her in revenge for the web which the plotters had spun about him? Her lovely smile, as she patiently awaited his reply, humbled him. She was as much a victim as he, and there was a clear duty to acquaint her with the facts.

Gently, he took her hands in his.

'I regret there will be no japes on this occasion, Charlotte.'
He tried to smile, but it was an effort which did not reach his
eyes. 'My dear, sweet friend ... there is no easy way to set
before you the things I must say.'

He faltered, and she looked at him once more in puzzlement.

'Are you not well, Jonathan?'

'I suffer only embarrassment.' He squeezed her hands in
gentle reassurance. 'Now please hear me out and then give me
your thoughts.' She nodded her assent, and he continued in
firmer tone. 'Firstly, do you know anything of recent discus-
sions between our respective parents on matters concerning
us?'

Her eyes opened wide in question, and the innocence was
plain for him to see.

'Matters concerning us? You have me at complete disadvantage, Jonathan.'

'Very well, Charlotte, I shall tell you ... they wish us to
become engaged to be married.'

A myriad of expressions chased across her face as she rose
from the seat and stood before him, then stumbled slightly
with the dizzying effects of shock which his blunt statement
had caused. In concern he took hold of her. 'You had better sit
down.' Her face was pale as he helped her back into the seat. 'I
regret the suddenness of my telling, Charlotte, but there was
no other way. Shall I bring you smelling salts?'

Despite herself she smiled. How like a man to think that a
whiff of smelling salts would serve as answer to such a bald
announcement! 'Thank you, that will not be necessary, Jonathan.
I have no intention of fainting.'

He looked relieved and nodded approvingly, 'You are very
brave.'

'At this moment I am shocked rather than brave, Jonathan.'

With scant regard of her condition at his revelation, he
thoughtlessly pressed on.

'They would have had me approach you in deceit ... playing
the part of the ardent lover to achieve their ends.'

A strange emotion took her. She had loved him for as long
as she could remember, and her constant hope had been that

81

he would one day return that love. Laughter born of irony came unbidden from her ... that he should at last speak of love, but in such a callous manner.

She felt the tears start behind her eyes at his words. His protest had been so petulant, like the pitiful appeal of a little boy who thought himself wronged. Yet she could not allow him to see her true feelings, and instead her voice affected banter.

'I see. They would have you act the lover, and me the fool. I wonder, how did they expect to succeed?'

'I do not even pretend to know.'

'Do you then know what lies behind this plot?'

'They wish to merge the two companies and make the binding more solid through our marriage.'

'You are telling me that my parents conspired with yours to hatch this strange scheme?'

'I have my mother's word on it.' He brushed away a lazy gnat which had emerged from a palm plant and now attempted to land on his face. 'Charlotte, I must know your thoughts on this.'

She lowered her gaze, vaguely conscious of the swirling patterns within the tiled floor. Her mind whirled in a like way, made hurt and angry by his matter-of-fact tone. He spoke of love and marriage in the manner of a kitchen porter ordering so many cabbages from the greengrocer. The proposed marriage scheme he spoke of might well only be one of arrangement, yet he should have been more caring, more tender in his delivery.

She looked up at him, the smile tight on her lips.

'So, you wish to know my thoughts. What if I said in reply that I must first know yours? What then would you say?'

He sensed her hostile attitude and became suddenly resentful.

Most certainly he had not expected such a reaction. On the contrary, it was to have been a simple discussion ... Great heavens! Could she not see what turmoil he was in at having had this thrust upon him? What possessed her to make such heavy going of it? If anything, she ought to have been flattered

82

that he was in a mind to even talk of such a marriage. Foolishly he chose to reply in a sarcastic tone, 'I had thought my feelings plain to see. But it would seem that my powers of communication are at fault.'

She rose from the seat, self-discipline bringing a degree of control to her raging mind as she bravely searched his eyes.

'I see you in a new light, Jonathan, for I had never before imagined you to be so clumsy in expression. Now you will please excuse me, since I must apologise to your parents for my bad manners.'

Head erect, she swept from the conservatory. There had been an impulse to smack him hard across the face and run from the agony he caused, but perversely her mind dwelt more on the pitifully tiny steps forced upon her under the imprisoning hold of the gown, and with each laboured stride she trembled in a frustration that weakened her limbs.

He stood locked in indecision, wanting to go after her, yet wanting not to. There was no conscious intention in him to speak, yet he was suddenly calling out her name. She heard the appeal in his tone, and wanted so much to yield, to turn and see his beloved face, to return and embrace him, to tell him of the unending love she felt for him. But she would not; much rather would she endure the purgatory of hurt pride.

He watched as she walked up to his mother, saw them speak with each other, and noted the disapproving look which Georgina now levelled at him ... would that he were afloat in some distant ocean, five thousand and more leagues away from it all.

The dining room was alive with the buzz of chatter, while the many servants, severe in starched white dress and bearing large silver tureens of steaming roast goose, threaded in and around the seated guests. Jonathan, flanked by two matronly women who were complete strangers to him, had been placed so that if he chose he had only peripheral vision of Georgina, a happening for which he silently thanked God. Yet he noted that only so much mercy had been extended to him, for

Charlotte was sat immediately opposite, and short of engrossing himself with his plate for the duration of the meal he had, perforce, to exchange glances with her. In the main these were uncharitable, since neither was in a mood to proffer the olive branch.

'May I be allowed to congratulate you on your promotion, Captain Bramwell?' Jonathan started at the enquiry, and turned his attention to a guest placed a little way down the table.

'You may, sir, thank you.'

The man heaped vegetables on to his plate from the tureen held by a hovering waiter, then waved the servant away as he once more addressed Jonathan.

'I regret we have not been formally introduced, but you were pointed out to me on my arrival ... Trevelyan, Hugh Trevelyan, for my sins a civil adviser to Sir James Graham, the Home Secretary.'

Jonathan nodded graciously before refusing the offer of vegetables from the waiter, the large portion of goose which lay on his plate already diminishing his jaded appetite.

'Mr Trevelyan, my compliments and apologies to you, sir. I was otherwise engaged and not able to join my parents in welcome.'

'I understand. Who better than myself to appreciate the burdens of duty?' He did not say it pompously, but rather in sympathy, the food now being forked enthusiastically into a mouth which lay almost secreted within grey-bewhiskered features. He paused to smile engagingly at Jonathan. 'And only the Lord knows the half of it, eh, Captain?'

Jonathan stifled a yawn. The very last thing he wanted was to be drawn into a boring conversation, but at least it meant he would not have to exchange stares with Charlotte for the duration of this wretched meal.

'You are busy then in the matter of government, Mr Trevelyan?'

'Indeed I am, Captain Bramwell, indeed I am.' His liberally laden fork came to a stop between table and mouth. 'The curse of the Irish is giving us cause for many long days of work, and sleepless nights.' The fork delivered its contents to his mouth, and Jonathan watched amused as Trevelyan chomped heartily on the food. The man might be enduring sleepless nights, but it had plainly not affected his capacity for eating.

'What then is this curse of the Irish, Mr Trevelyan?' He toyed with his fork at the leg of goose, not really caring to know the answer to his question, then glanced across at Charlotte.

She had been looking at him but now quickly averted her gaze. He smirked in pity for her as she openly flirted with George Maddocks, a local landowner for whom he knew she did not give a fig. Trevelyan speared a potato and held it towards Jonathan, who regarded it with silent curiosity. Trevelyan made loud his announcement. 'These things, sir! Potatoes. Their crop has failed for the third year in succession, and large sections of the population are starving to death.'

The woman who sat between them joined the conversation.

'Then why do they not eat something else? Pork is very good. I like pork.' She began to eat in a greedy manner.

Trevelyan's reply was terse. 'My dear madam, there is no pork, nor hardly any other food to be had in the land. The humble potato is, in the main, the staple diet of the Irish people. Without it they die in their many thousands.'

The woman reflectively sipped her wine.

'What an extremely odd country it must be.'

Before Trevelyan could answer, further interruption came from Jonathan's left. An elderly gentleman, sporting a great number of military campaign medals, leaned forward to address Trevelyan. 'The Irish, sir, are a confounded nuisance! Just why you should concern yourself over whether or not they have enough potatoes I cannot imagine. I would have thought you people at the Home Office had better things to do with your time.' He bristled. 'And our money, sir, our money!'

Trevelyan smiled indulgently.

'With respect, sir, we talk of a great famine, the like of which has never been known.'

Jonathan became suddenly bored with the conversation.

85

Trevelyan did ramble on so, thank goodness the man now had his hands full with these two old buffers, and praise be that the woman on his left was content in silent assault on the meal, eating as though she had never before seen food. Wherever did his mother get these people from? He stole another glance at Charlotte. How silly she was to flirt with Maddocks, more so since she had said that she found the fellow a bore. He grew petulant and stabbed his fork at the goose. Why had she taken on this way? Damned if women weren't the oddest creatures on God's earth. All he had tried to do was to explain the situation ... and damned if he didn't miss her. They could now be having so much fun, their secret code across the table, as at so many other stultifying dinners when they had made jest by imitating the manner of stuffier guests. Instead she chose virtually to ignore him. How stupid.

He became aware of Trevelyan addressing him, and realised that he had missed some of what had already been said. His apology came stiffly.

'I do beg your pardon, Mr Trevelyan. I am afraid my attention was elsewhere.'

Trevelyan was expert in summoning up smiles of indulgence.

'I understand, Captain, you have other guests to attend to. I merely stated that the great exodus from Ireland is already under way, and many thousands of its people are taking ship in emigration to North America.'

He was rudely interrupted by the elderly gentleman.

'Good riddance, say I! Let them go and persecute the damned Americans for a change.'

The women went on eating. Trevelyan pointedly ignored the man's interruption and continued talking to Jonathan.

'I am given to understand, from official sources of course, that a great deal of money is to be made in their conveyance. Perhaps you would be interested ... I could give you guidance.'

'That is something you would have to discuss with my father, Mr Trevelyan. I have little to do with selection of cargo, but I seriously doubt we are equipped for passengers.'

Trevelyan persisted, 'They are not passengers as such, Captain. Their requirement is merely hold space, with a little

86

food and water. They furnish such trappings as they might need for the voyage.'

Jonathan's expression was polite but plainly dismissive. Devil take the man, would he never stop talking? A dinner table was not the place to discuss business, and in any case he was in no mood for it.

'As I have already told you, Mr Trevelyan, it is a matter you would do better to discuss with my father.'

Trevelyan noted the expression. 'Thank you, Captain Bramwell, I will take it up with him when the ladies retire.' He turned to begin a conversation with the woman who had proclaimed the Irish to be an odd people.

Jonathan sighed aloud with relief and looked once more across at Charlotte. This time she did not avert her eyes, but there was a cold and studied look about her expression. Well, if she could not be friendly, the devil take her also. What desperate pity there was not some way he might disconcert her ... why was there not a beautiful woman at his side with whom he might flirt?

He dropped his gaze to the cold, untouched portion of goose which lay in a greasy pool upon his plate, aware that Charlotte was still looking at him. But whatever, he would not be the first to make the peace.

9

The *Elizabeth* was thirty-five days out from Sligo and still a full eight hundred miles from Boston. Fierce winter storms harried the ship without let, and the tempers of an overworked captain and crew were badly frayed. In the holds conditions had worsened dramatically, and for the past three days the emigrants had seen no food other than mouldy bread, with a water ration barely enough to support life.

Ship fever had persisted for some time. The malady went under such a name but was in fact typhus, and the disease thrived within the filth, human excrement and complete lack of any sanitary conditions. It was becoming an everyday occurrence for the dead to be dragged from the hold and dumped overboard. Prayers had been said over the first victims, but now even a brief word was rare. Rather, minds were more concentrated on the hunger and thirst which tortured the sick and healthy alike. Many of the wretches lay unmoving in their beds to conserve energy, while others prowled the shadows like hyenas, looking to steal from the weak and defenceless, even the dying. However, there was better order in the Inniscourt section of the holds, although its occupants shared the same agony as the rest.

Liam McAfferty was still very much in charge and determined to get his people alive to America. Yet it was not a determination caused by any stirring of conscience; they represented an investment to him, and even he could not make profit from dead bodies. He had carefully segregated the sick from the healthy, but despite his efforts things were running against him. The bribing of a crew member to bring in food and water was an astute move, but the money budgeted for such a contingency was now almost exhausted and he was aware of the need to hold on to some dollars in order to survive the first few weeks in America.

There was a further setback for him in that Donal and Brendan were ill with the fever, Brendan the more seriously. Now, as the *Elizabeth* battled with yet another storm, Brendan lay flushed and still in his bed of filthy straw with Donal alongside him in agitated sleep. Free from Donal's attentions, Mary had helped to nurse the sick and dying for many days and nights, but it was nursing of the most basic kind since there was no medicine nor ship's doctor to advise. A damp cloth to mop fevered brows, and a small jug of water to moisten dried lips were her only earthly help. But to the suffering she brought relief and some peace of mind with her gentle touch and sympathetic manner. She had become almost expert in following the course of the disease which had struck down so many of the people, and now, as she looked at Brendan she doubted he would last the day.

Her gaze switched to Donal. He was certainly ill, but his iron constitution would see him through. Of that Mary had no doubt. She quietly observed the fat red face of the man, and the dribble running from the corner of his mouth. Formerly devout in the faith, she had begun to grow ever more cynical in the torment of these terrible days and nights ... If God existed, then did He not move in mysterious ways indeed? And what of the priest? Believer or not, he was no fool to have taken the pony cart to Dublin. What pious prayer was he mouthing now? What prayer might he have said in this place of hopelessness and evil? Her musings were distracted by the sound of Liam waking Patrick from sleep.

'I'll shortly be needin' you. I am about t'speak with Halloran, for we're done if we don't get the food an' water.'

Patrick sat up, rubbing his eyes.

'How will y'do that? Us nailed up an' all since the fever came.'

'I talked with the mate at first light. He's away to fix up the meetin' with me and Halloran.' He swaggered away to the centre of the hold and shouted for attention. 'Listen t'me now!' His audience stared at him with stony-faced expressions. 'Lookit! We have been sorely tried, but I am still lookin' after yez, an' by God or the devil I will get us justice!' Puffing up his chest in ridiculous pride, he curled his hands into fists. 'I am just after talkin' to an officer from the ship, an' told him I want t'talk to the captain about our grievances.' He paused to clear his parched throat.

'The waitin' will be over soon, for 'tis my notion that your man Halloran cannot know what is happenin' to us.'

Silence greeted this statement, and for the first time Liam McAfferty found it hard to stare his people down.

Under darkening skies the *Elizabeth* shuddered her way through a mountainous sea which threatened with every fresh onslaught to engulf her. Captain James Dominic Halloran was many things he should not have been, but there was no doubting his expert seamanship and experience. His climb from seaman to captain had been spread over thirty years and most of the world's oceans, a long and demanding lifetime which might have tempered him to a more philosophical outlook. Instead, he nursed a doubtful view of mankind and the world in general, and was cursed with bouts of acute clinical depression, an illness aggravated by much hard drinking. Physically a big man, he looked much older than his forty-five years, and the brooding dark brown eyes held a lost and staring look about them.

He surveyed the quarterdeck where the helmsman, aided by two seamen, hung on to the wheel as the ship ran fully reefed before the storm. Hands cupped, he shouted through the howling wind, 'Keep her tight!'

The helmsman shouted in acknowledgement, 'Aye Cap'n, but she's takin' some holdin'.'

Halloran scowled, his hate piercing the gale. 'If y'can't do it I'll find some bugger who can!' The helmsman gripped the wheel tighter and stared grimly ahead into the kindness of the storm.

Halloran's attention was drawn away by a movement along the deck to where a seaman was slowly making his way towards the quarterdeck. Gripping every affordable means of support, the man fought his way forward to arrive wheezing and badly out of breath. Halloran looked at him with contempt. First mate Daniel Blake was an Englishman of good education who had fallen on hard times. His failings were drink, women, gambling and other people's money, yet he was weak rather than bad, and further hampered by having a too-strong sense of compassion – not a wise trait in an officer on a doubtful merchant ship.

This was his first voyage on a tramper, and he had formerly been used to a better class of passenger ship. He had floated out of that good berth on a tide of cheap whisky and light fingers, suffering a jail sentence and confiscation of mate's papers for taking a single guinea from the cabin of a passenger. Halloran had met him in a tavern and, short of a first mate had coldly weighed up Blake as good for one voyage. By then the man's gratitude at having been rescued from the beach would have worn thin, and he would become as slipshod as the many others had been. But for now he was a cheap bargain.

Blake had recovered his breath.

'I need to talk with you urgently, sir.'

'Then talk, man!'

'Not here, sir.' He gave a warning glance at the wheel crew, then indicated the captain's cabin,

Halloran nodded his assent. 'Go on ahead.'

Pushing open the cabin door Blake stood aside, but his attempt at politeness saw him shoved fiercely to his knees in front of the chart desk. 'Don't you stand on bloody ceremony with me!' Halloran closed the door. 'Well, what is it?'

'We have trouble, Captain.' Blake wiped the rain from his face and clambered to his feet. 'It's the passengers, they are seeking...'

The interruption was heavy with scorn.

'You aren't on your fancy-Dan ships now, Blake. We don't have any bloody passengers. Y'mean you've dragged me away from the wheel t'talk about that scum below? Is that what y'r tellin' me?'

'They have been almost without water for two days, and are down to a handful of bread, rotten at that.'

'Well, and aren't you the hard man now?'

Blake shrugged his shoulders at the sarcasm.

'They have a deputation, and they demand to see you.'

He was pushed aside as Halloran made for the chart desk and took out a bottle of whisky. With a look of hatred he tore off the metal-topped cork and threw it hard at Blake. Its jagged edge scored his cheek to bring a trickle of blood before spinning away with a sharp rattle on the decking. Blake winced in pain but stood his ground while Halloran swigged deeply on the whisky, lowering the bottle to his side as he looked with vague curiosity at the wound. He grinned and belched.

'Well, jailbird, y'haven't got the royal blue blood in you at all.' The grin went. 'So, they demand t'see me? Demand is it?' He swung the bottle back to his mouth and drank as a man might drink water, pausing to continue his attack.

'Lookit, thief! I saved you from the beach t'do a job for me, not to play Holy Mother ... get back there now an' tell them any more trouble an' I'll hang every bastard one of 'em for mutiny.'

Blake's reply lacked conviction, for he was rapidly losing whatever edge he had first mustered.

'They surely cannot be charged with mutiny, Captain. They are passengers.'

Halloran swayed slightly as the rough alcohol bit into his brain.

'One more word, thief, an' I'll have you locked in there with 'em.'

Blake wheeled about and strode quickly for the door. There was no use served in further pleading, the man was the very devil, anyway, he had done his best. Halloran took another drink, then grinned at Blake's retreating back, 'Don't forget t'tuck your passengers in f'r the night, you old woman! Tell 'em a fairy story, y'r good for nothin' else.'

He burst into a fit of drunken laughter and fell back into a chair as the door banged shut. But the laughter was not long and his mood swung from humour to dark depression as the drink claimed him. In gradual movements he tilted forward in a stupor, staring unblinkingly at the whisky as it hypnotically changed its angle of level under the steep rise and fall of the ship.

'God help any man who makes trouble f'me.' The slurred whisper tailed off and he slumped head down to the desk, already asleep.

Arms folded, Liam sat patiently at the foot of the steps which led up to the main deck. With the instinct of a dog awaiting its master's return, he sensed that Blake would shortly appear, an instinct soundly backed up by the fact that he had promised the man a half-dollar for his efforts. The sound of movement on deck caused him to look up as the hatch cover groaned open to give a clear view of the grey sky, and with it came the roar of the storm. Fresh air tumbled down into the rotten atmosphere of the hold, and he clambered to his feet, breathing in greedily.

Blake peered over the edge of the cover and caught the full blast of foulness which rushed from the hold. 'Sweet Jesus!' He pulled his head back sharply, dragging out a sweat rag which he clamped to his mouth. The two seamen he had ordered to accompany him grinned at his discomfiture, waving their heavy clubs in mocking fashion to indicate that he should lead the way. Pressing the rag close to his face he clambered one-handed down the steps, the seamen close behind and almost stepping on his fingers.

Liam backed away slightly as the party arrived in the hold.

'God be praised, sir, have y'brought the captain?'

Blake steeled himself to pull the rag from his face and retched briefly.

'No, Mr McAfferty, he has given me the matter to deal with.'

Liam's expression moved to disappointment.

'What's this you're tellin' me?'

Blake shuddered as he reluctantly took breath.

'The captain is busy with the storm. I will do what I can for you.'

Liam screamed back at him, 'You can do nothin'! I have t'see the man or I promise there'll be trouble!'

A group of men moved forward to stand alongside Liam. Blake took in their wild faces, in no doubt that they would break for the deck if given the word. There was menace in Liam's tone as he squared up to Blake.

'They're after murderin' anybody who keeps the food an' water from their women an' kids!'

Blake glanced at the seamen who were edging away to the steps, and a fear began to crawl over him.

'Keep the peace, Mr McAfferty, and I will do what I can for you.'

The reply was instant and threatening.

'We're not for keepin' the peace, we're for comin' up wit' you t'see Halloran!' Liam turned to the gathering mob. 'Are y'with me?' A ragged roar of approval went up. 'Come on then! Grab a skull-buster an' we'll show the bastards!'

They had rid themselves of quiet acceptance, and all but those too ill to move began to smash up anything that could be made into a weapon. As Blake turned to flee, the seamen had already begun a swift retreat up to the deck, and he hurled himself in panic after them. They arrived on deck in a sprawling heap, Blake yelling out in hysteria, 'Batten the hatch! I'm away to get the captain.' He lurched away into the storm, leaving the seamen in a frantic securing of the hatch, and sobbing with fear he made for the cabin, sure that Halloran would now have him hanged.

The assembly was armed with weapons of all descriptions, and a rare hatred burned in every man within its ranks. Liam called for silence and the mutterings fell away as all eyes came to rest on the man who would lead them.

'We have t'get to the captain, t'wont be easy, for the crew will try to stop us.'

He paused and looked around the sea of faces. Everywhere

he saw respect and determination. 'Patrick an' me will go on ahead, the rest of yez beat off any man tryin' t'stop us gettin' to Halloran.' The rebels shouted encouragement, and in return Liam urged them on once more. 'Are y'for it then? Are y'for gettin' the food an' the water?'

A roar of approval washed over Liam and galvanised him into action. Turning away, he loped towards a baulk of timber, fully sixteen feet in length. 'Come on wit' you!' They surged forward and the timber rose easily in their hands to thud against the hatch cover.

From the shadows of the sick quarter Mary had been a silent witness throughout. She was against violence, but her sympathies were with the rebels. They had not sought this way to right the wrongs against them, but they now had to succeed or more of the people would surely die. With this thought she returned to tend the sick, leaving behind her the sound of splintering timber as the makeshift battering ram crashed again and again on to its target.

Halloran awakened with a groan as the cabin door burst wide open. Wet to the skin, and fighting for breath, Blake stood in the doorway, panic all about him.

'Did I not tell you? They won't listen ... they're breaking out...'

Halloran staggered to his feet.

'What the bloody hell?'

Blake screamed out, 'We cannot hold them ... break out the arms, or they'll take the ship!'

Through blurred vision Halloran saw Blake slam the door shut and ram home the bolts. 'Damn y' for the idiot y'are!' In the manner of alcoholics, Halloran had suddenly come from stone-cold drunk to stone-cold sober. Cursing wildly, he dragged the arms chest from under the desk and viciously shook the padlock and chain.

'Key?'

'In the chart drawer.'

'Get it!'

95

In panic, Blake yanked the drawer from its liners for it to go crashing on the decking, the contents hurtling about the cabin. With a moan of frustration he fell to his knees, clawing frantically through the jumble in search of the key.

'You stupid bastard!'

Halloran lurched forward and swung a wild punch which missed the back of Blake's head by inches. A noise from outside caused Halloran to break off his cursing and there came a muffled outburst of shouts, followed by loud banging on the door. Blake stopped his search and looked anxiously towards the sound. The voice of Liam McAfferty came clearly to them.

'Can you hear me in there?'

Sweating with fear, Blake went back to his search, and his probing fingers suddenly closed on the key. Within seconds the chest lay open to reveal five pistols, a musket and naval cutlass. Halloran swiftly checked the musket before handing it to Blake.

'Go stand by the door.'

Blake moved soft-footed to take up a position a yard inside the cabin while Halloran calmly selected a brace of pistols as more loud banging shook the door.

Liam spoke again.

'Captain! Let us in! We only want to talk t'you ... do y'hear me now?'

Halloran cocked both pistols. 'Open the bolts, then move away an' leave all the talkin' to me ... shoot if there's any trouble.' He noticed the look of doubt that crossed Blake's face. 'Don't go soft on me, Englishman, or they'll do for the both of us.'

The sweat of fear glowed on Blake as he slid away the bolts and stepped back. Halloran aligned both pistols on the door. The ensuing silence had an unreal quality about it and Blake shook visibly, the musket unsteady in his grasp. With a suddenness that made him cry out the door swung open and the howling of the storm tore into the cabin.

Flanked by Patrick and Sean Dolan, Liam stood boldly in the entrance. Behind them moved a seething mass of chanting rebels, all wielding heavy pieces of timber. Liam grimaced as he looked into the barrel of the musket then at the pistols aimed at him. In appeal he spread his arms wide to show empty hands.

'What's this? Great God Almighty, are we for the murderin' of innocent men who seek only the food an' water?'

Halloran ignored the question.

'McAfferty! So it's you causin' the trouble.'

'I want no trouble, Captain.'

'Then speak your piece.'

'Do y'need to point the pistols at me, Captain?'

His tone was carefully weighted, hoping to shame Halloran, and he was very aware of Blake's trembling fear.

'It's powerful hard t'talk wit' the thought in my poor old head that I might any minute meet the maker.'

The pistols did not move a degree.

'Don't try my patience, McAfferty, get on with what y'came about!'

Liam shrugged and came on another tack.

'You an' me made the deal for the food an' water for which my people are dyin', an a terrible sickness has come down on us...'

Halloran interrupted viciously.

'You've used up all y'paid for, now get below before I hang the lot of you!'

Liam stood his ground and shouted back at Halloran, 'For God's sake, man, give us somethin' t'take back or we shall all surely die!'

'I'll give you lead in the belly if y'don't obey my orders!' With this threat Halloran thrust the pistols menacingly forward and Liam grabbed Patrick's arm, backing away to leave Sean Dolan just inside the cabin. Halloran now directed his aim at Dolan. 'Get below!'

Dolan did not move. He was some distance beyond being half out of his mind, and well past caring whether he lived or died. His hands closed more tightly on the rough wooden club, and a crazed look became etched on his face as he spoke in a voice that crackled with hatred.

97

'I'm not for the goin' back without the food an' water ... my little sweet innocent girl is dead, an' my wife is dyin', y'bloody divvil!'

Dolan moved forward in a half-crouch, fanning the club left to right, his breath raspingly uneven as he approached Halloran.

Liam stood in open-mouthed fascination, for he had not thought Dolan capable of such nerve. Behind him the mob had retreated into a wondering silence and all eyes were now on Dolan.

Halloran's fingers tightened visibly on the triggers.

'One more step an' I'll kill y' stone dead.'

Dolan stopped and glanced over his shoulder at Liam.

'They're for givin' us nothin', we have t'take it. D'you hear me? We have t'take it!'

Then, without waiting for reply, he let out a scream of fury which made every man's blood run cold as he launched himself on a run towards Halloran. He had almost reached him before the deafening report of a single pistol shot rolled and crashed about the cabin. The round hit Dolan in the centre of his forehead, ripping his skull wide open in a gusher of blood that splattered over Halloran's face. The body trembled for a moment before sliding down the desk front to fall spread-eagled on the decking.

In the shocked silence which followed, Blake looked across at Halloran in disbelief but found no remorse there. Liam broke the spell as he padded forward and looked down at Dolan. His gaze lifted to take in Halloran.

'There was no need for the killin' at all, he was half out his mind wit' worry for his family.'

Halloran's reply was dispassionate for he knew the crisis was past.

'He was in the whole mind t'club my brains out.'

Liam sighed and made the sign of the cross.

'May God forgive y', Captain.'

'Take your people below, McAfferty. I'll send down a barrel of water an' some bread ... go now, before I change my mind.'

Liam's thoughts whirled like a straw in a mill race. Things had looked black and the initiative surely lost before Dolan stepped in ... He must move quickly to grasp the victory now presented to him, yet the withdrawal would have to be done with some show or he would surely lose face.

'I have y'r word then, Captain? You will send the water an' the food?'

'You heard me! Now get below before I hang the lot of y' from the yards!'

But Liam was still about the business of saving face.

'Thank you, Captain.' He pointed at Dolan's body. 'Would y'see he gets a Christian burial, we have no priest an' Sean was a good soul.'

There was menace in Halloran's reply. 'Don't ride on your luck, McAfferty. Go now!'

Some of the rebels had flooded into the cabin while others stood at the door. All had bemused expressions. Liam addressed them with a feigned dignity.

'Listen t'me now ... Sean is with his maker an' I shall look upon it that he died for us.' He looked briefly at Halloran before continuing. 'I have done the business an' the captain has promised fresh water an' bread, so we will go below ... come on now.'

In silence, and with Liam at their head, they shuffled from the cabin. Blake lowered the musket and took in a shuddering breath.

'We shall both surely go to the gallows for this day's work.'

'It is your doin' Blake, y'failed to show authority!'

'I warned you about their mood.'

'Shut y'r bloody mouth! And keep it shut when we make land, or I promise y'will not have to wait for the gallows.'

'What of the others? Will you kill them all to shut their mouths?'

The reply came softly as Halloran pushed the loaded pistol into Blake's face. ''Tis not the mouthin' of the rabble that concerns me...' He left the threat unfinished and moved the pistol to point at the corpse. 'Get this overboard an' then make sure that scum below is secure.' He saw the expression of hate and smiled without humour. 'Don't say it, Englishman, for y' have not the guts to back it up.'

Blake slowly lowered his gaze and without further word grabbed the feet of the dead man and dragged him towards the cabin door. Halloran watched in grim fascination as the head of the corpse repeatedly caught the edges of the decking, leaving behind a shining bloody trail.

There was nothing to fear. He had shot in self-defence, and at the height of a mutiny. Still, he would think very deeply about what to do with Blake once Boston was reached. He scrubbed a boot into the congealing blood. The man was a damned Jonah, and he talked too much after a drink. A careless word from him could lead to the gallows. He was dangerous.

10

An early morning frost sparkled across the downs, reflecting a low sun in a clear blue sky, its soft golden light bathing the two riders who galloped their bay hunters at near full stretch across the short tussocky grass. It was a day to be alive.

Charlotte urged her mount into a slight lead, face glowing with an impudent grin as she hurled out a breathless challenge to Jonathan.

'Slowcoach! Race you to the point for a guinea ... if you dare!

He grinned back and put his horse to better effort.

'Competitive harlot! You have a wager!'

They went at breakneck speed over the mile to the point, splinters of frost glinting like sparks under the flying hooves, wild bursts of laughter invading the still air with clouds of breath. Charlotte reined in at the point, her mare blowing hard as she pulled it round to view Jonathan, fully a hundred yards in arrears. He arrived with a rueful smile.

'I am handicapped for playing the gentleman, for I gave you the better mare.'

She laughed in friendly disbelief at his words.

'Nonsense! I have always been the better rider, and you know it! Now it will cost you yet another golden guinea.'

'I content myself in knowing you had a good head start.'

His face was alive with happiness as he pulled a coin from the riding jacket and flicked it spinning towards her. Smiling, she caught it expertly in her gloved hand.

'I thank you, kind sir. We should do this more often, for I like nothing better than the amassing of easy wealth.'

'Hardly amassing, you devil. You have only beaten me the twice before.'

'Three times is nearer.'

'Wretch!'

He dismounted and helped her from the saddle, the Solent shimmering in glorious backdrop as he held her close and searched her eyes.

'I am so glad we are together once more.'

Her look was deliberately coquettish.

'I was not aware we had been apart.'

He pursed his mouth in mock admonition.

'Really?'

With reluctance she wriggled free of his arms, attempting a smile.

'We must not allow the horses to become chilled.'

She had enjoyed the intimacy of the embrace but felt at some disadvantage in conducting the new angle of conversation at such close quarters. There was a need in her for freedom of movement, not entrapment, if she were to hold her corner.

Picking up the reins, she thoughtfully walked the mare along the cliff edge. There would have to be frank talk before they rode back, but he must not be allowed to get the upper hand in it. She loved him; however, he would have to do the running, for her stubborn pride would not have it otherwise. She paused to look out over the misty sea and heard his boots rasp against the frosted grass as he came alongside her.

'Is not the Solent looking benign today?'

He would make his approach with niceties. They began to walk once more, the mares shambling behind on long reins.

'Yes, Jonathan, benign indeed.'

He grimaced. This was stilted stuff and would serve no real purpose. Better get it done with.

'I have missed you most terribly.'

There was reflection in him that a lonely week had elapsed since the dreadful dinner party. Surely to goodness she must feel as alone as he. But her reply was short.

'And I you.'

102

He frowned. For pity's sake, must he make all of the going?

'I regret our upset, Charlotte, and will try to make up for it, for I dearly love you and our times together.'

She stopped and took his arm in check.

'Jonathan, will you tell me what you mean by love?'

He was openly flustered as he looked into the honesty of her expression.

'What I mean by love? Well, there is nothing I would not do for you.'

Her reply came softly and on the instant.

'Would you then wish to marry me of your own free will, truly, and without duress?'

The horses nuzzled vainly into the frozen grass and only the muted roar of the sea held against the sudden silence. He had not expected such a bold question, but he was more surprised at the calmness in his reply.

'You wish the truth?'

'What else would better serve?'

'Then I have to tell you, at this moment I do not know.'

'I am obliged to you for your honesty.'

'What of you, Charlotte? How would you answer me the same question?'

She smiled bitterly at the cold, empty feeling which now lodged in her stomach.

'Like you, Jonathan, at this moment I do not know.'

He saw the hurt in her and became angry. What right had their parents to put them to so much embarrassment and pain? It not fair. 'They have come between us!' The assertion was hissed from between clenched teeth. She felt calmer now, although the empty feeling was still there.

'Only we can do that, Jonathan.' A cold breeze ruffled her hair causing her to shudder. 'We had better return, the weather is becoming uncharitable ... will you help me mount, please?'

The ride back was in sorry contrast to their earlier joy and good feeling, for they both shared the same sense of isolation. The first mile was covered in silence as each went over what had been said. Jonathan had never before felt so lost and bewildered. She looked grimly ahead, straight-backed, lips pressed tightly together, and he knew she was bravely holding back the tears.

A flush of self-hate rose in him. Why could he not have been more caring and tender in approach? He had gone to the matter in the way of a village clodhopper ... how could he deserve her friendship when he treated her so? There was need to redress the wrong, with honour, and like a man ought. His father was right. Good marriages were built on sound and lasting friendships. He should be so fortunate that this lovely woman would have him as husband and they were so close in all they did, their joy in each other boundless ... Who had ever made him laugh so? Who had more made him feel glad to be alive? Who had ever been such a good comrade?

He pulled alongside, reaching across to check her mount.

'May we speak a moment?'

Her look was straight ahead.

'If you wish.'

The horses snorted, bits jangling as they shook their heads in annoyance at the halt.

'I desire to ask you that which should not wait.' She remained silent, eyes unmoving from the horizon as he continued, 'This constant circling around our problem is driving me mad and...'

Her voice came sharply in its interruption.

'Problem? If you see it as a problem then you should get shot of it!'

'Do not be so damned pedantic! Call it what you will, it does not matter what name you give it, but please give me a chance to speak.'

'Very well, how do you see the resolving of this ... whatever you choose to name it?'

'I only know that in the week which has passed I have never known such misery, and I cannot imagine what life would be without you.' He paused, searching for the right words. She now looked at him with new curiosity. Could he really after all be in love with her? And had it been the hard events of the past eight days which had brought him to realise it? Was he now about to tell her so? Yet she could not fail to see the vague look of uncertainty in his expression as he spoke once more.

'Therefore, I believe we should become engaged to be married.'

A fury boiled within her as his words echoed mockingly around and around in her brain. Not a word of love, nor even endearment, no solace offered, no understanding. Just this indifferent offer, for it was no more than an offer of repair, little different in feeling from that of a farrier in regard to a loose shoe.

He grew disquieted at her prolonged silence. Why did she look so strange? Why did she not answer? Surely now their problem must be over? Cautiously, he ventured further words.

'Well, Charlotte, what do you think?'

Even in her wretchedness she could not contain the bitter imp of laughter at his temerity. But it was short.

'What then of love, Jonathan?'

'Well of course, I love you dearly.'

'There is no "of course" in love.'

'I do not understand you.'

'For the first time, I am deeply aware of that, Jonathan.'

Despite her best endeavours the tears rolled freely down her cheeks, and he looked wonderingly at them.

'Please, Charlotte, do not cry ... this has been hard on both of us, and now may not be the time to give answer to my proposal.'

She scrubbed away the tears with the back of a glove and regarded him from within the eye of the hurricane which whirled in her mind. Why did she still love him in spite of his intransigence? But love him or not, she could not hold back her bitterness of frustration.

'There is no need of time to consider your...' Her voice almost choked on the words. 'Your proposal! For I sincerely believe your need is not of a wife to love and care for, but rather a constant playmate to ease you of boredom!'

In the wild gallop away from him her mind was seared with one thought. She had surely lost him forever, for he would never come back to her after this. The thought cleared as the freezing air cut into her tears and a panic rose within her. There must be a way to make him return that love, or her life would no longer be worth the living.

He watched her headlong flight and wondered on it. What had he said to cause this? For they were friends and there was no more a problem. He had been the perfect gentleman, considerate in every way, yes, and with proper proposal, even giving her time to reflect on the answer. Carefully taking up the reins, he pressed the mare into a gentle walk as his expression hardened. If she thought for a single moment that he would go in pursuit of her then she was sadly mistaken. Never mind what she may think, he would be at sea within the three weeks, bound for Boston and evidently the better for the parting.

11

Like a grey ghost the barque *Elizabeth* lay at anchor a discreet distance off Boston harbour as the dawn fog came and went at the caprice of a March breeze, at one time blotting the whole of the vessel from sight, at another, revealing her storm-battered appearance. The *Elizabeth* had fought her way across the winter Atlantic, covering near four thousand miles over fifty-six days. But she would not enter the harbour. Instead, she would lie hiding in the fog as her captain discharged his human cargo from what he considered to be a safe position. Then he would run for it, out to the open ocean.

Halloran was a man who put his own business and welfare first. He knew that with typhus aboard he should have shown the fever flag and put in at Deer Island quarantine station, but the grim prospect of a mandatory twenty days' isolation did not fit his plans. He had a profitable cargo of timber waiting up the St Lawrence River, an appointment he intended to keep, and there was also the matter of Sean Dolan's death to concentrate his mind.

Halloran's voice boomed eerily in the fog as he addressed the crew assembled on deck.

'Listen well t'me now. I want these bloody peasants off my ship afore this fret clears. Mind y'keep well away from the harbour, put 'em down on the mud or any damned spit y' come across! God help you if y'buckle on me, now get to it!'

Below, in the fever-ridden holds Mary was helping to tend the sick and dying. But the urgent activity from the decks caused her to pause, and glance up towards the noise.

'Did y'hear the anchor go, Mary?' The young man was very

ill, but he had a gleam of hope about his eyes. Mary had been looking after him for most of the night.

'I did, Jimmy.'

'Is it America we're at?'

'I think it must be.'

He nodded, and his eyes closed as he surrendered to sleep. Mary swayed with sudden fatigue. Was it really the end of this desperate journey? She had grown used to the ceaseless moaning and screaming, the indescribable smell, the daily catalogue of death, the hunger, the thirst, the hopelessness. Less than half of the four hundred and eighty emigrants who set sail were still alive. Brendan had died of typhus and Donal was still suffering from the disease, but Liam and Patrick, quartered well away up the hold, were free of illness. She had held on to reason through looking after the less fortunate.

The nursing was a crude and basic affair, but under the guidance of one Molly O'Rourke it proved to be a light in the darkness. Molly was a woman tempered by hardship, and made cunning in that process, wheedling bread and water from the crew when no one thought it possible, and in the doing had saved many lives. Well past middle age, she had brought up a family of five boys and three girls in a tiny hovel just outside Inniscourt, and that on little more than ingenuity and wit. With her blessing they had all since gone to Liverpool and other parts in search of a better life.

Her husband Peter had been a wild, romantic fellow, a man with dreams of building castles in the sun. That was when his belly was full of whisky. His dreams ended when he drowned, trying to steal fish from a boat in Sligo harbour. Mary had hardly been on nodding terms with Molly, for even in the remoteness of Inniscourt there had existed a class structure of a kind, and within that pattern there had been no cause for them to meet socially. But the exodus dismantled social barriers and Mary soon learned to respect the character and determination of this formidable woman.

A friendship was slowly forged as they talked during the night hours, Mary confiding her determination to run away when the opportunity presented itself. In common with most of the villagers Molly had no love for the McAffertys, but held great sympathy for Mary. Her voice came softly, 'I'm thinkin' we're there ... what'll y' do now?'

There was a loud bang as the hatch cover was lifted off to go crashing on the deck. Light flooded into the hold and both women shielded their eyes from the unaccustomed glare. A seaman poked his head into the opening. 'Get on deck! You're going ashore.'

Mary took a deep breath of the cold air which swept down, and a feeling of hope came to her.

'I'm for going my own way, Molly. I will find work, for I can do any number of things.'

'Sure y'will.'

Some of the more hardy were already on their way up to the deck. With a soft kiss on Mary's cheek the old woman gently pushed her towards the hold steps. 'Fly little bird, God bless y'now.'

A few faltering paces and Mary was at the foot of the steps which led to freedom, and within seconds was outside, swallowed up in what had become a thickening fog.

There was no finesse employed in the business of landing those who had thus far survived the outrage of the voyage. Healthy, sick or dying, all received the same uncaring treatment, and in their fresh-found agony wondered why they had left Ireland at all. The three longboats shuttled busily between the *Elizabeth* and the fog-shrouded mudbanks, the seamen cursing in their furtive haste as they herded the ashen-faced, trembling wretches over the sides. The screams of terror and protest at being landed on the forbidding wastes were swiftly dealt with, well-aimed fists and boots ensuring rapid settlement of the issue as many tried to clamber back into the boat. Men, women, children and babies, bloodied and broken, too weak to move, bodies upon bodies, and a great number beneath choking to their death in the suck of the clinging mud.

Made late with the work of evacuating Donal from the hold,

Liam had quickly given up the search for Mary, dismissing her from mind in his certainty that he would find her ashore. In any case there were more urgent priorities, for he had shrewdly guessed what Halloran would do once landfall was made, and the slipping of a dollar to the leading hand of his longboat had served as incentive to make for shore.

In the event, the man proved willing to go only as far as a wood jetty which jutted out from derelict workings into the mud flats.

Liam and Patrick lay on the planking, gasping for breath after carrying Donal to the upper reaches of the jetty, where he now sprawled fast asleep. Others who had come ashore with them littered the jetty, dozing where they had fallen. Liam wiped the mud from his eyes, blaspheming in breathless protest.

'Jesus, Mary an' Joseph ... Halloran is a bloody divvil altogether.'

Patrick eased himself up on his elbows.

'Are we for tellin' the law about him killin' Sean an' all?'

'We want no trouble with the law, I have troubles enough ... that bastard has killt near half my workin' gang, for which I put up the passage money ... ruined is what I am!'

He sat more upright in a listening attitude, signalling Patrick to be quiet. 'Somebody's comin', keep still!'

The sound of oars groaning in their locks gave way to a grinding of wood against shingle as a boat bit into the shore below the jetty. Agitated voices came muffled through the fog, and within minutes vague figures appeared, cursing and moaning as they hauled themselves on to the jetty. Then came heated discussion as they argued their next move. One voice was clear above the others. 'I will say how 'tis to be ... 'twas me paid the bloody man t'bring us t'dry land!'

Liam peered through the fog as others of the party joined in the argument.

'Jimmy O'Dea, so it is, who owes me the passage money, an' him wantin' to take over, thinkin' me dead.' His grin was chilling. 'Jimmy O'Dea! ... Can y'hear me?'

'An' who's that askin'?' The query was full of hesitancy and suspicion. Liam stood up and swaggered towards the group, his voice holding a cockiness about it.

'Liam McAfferty himself, that's who!'

O'Dea scrambled to his feet, hands outstretched.

'The saints be praised, we were after mullin' over what t'do.'

Liam looked at the fog-blanketed figures along the planking.

'Is Mary wit' you?'

'She is not.'

'Have y'seen her?'

'Not the hide nor the hair.'

'Never mind, I will find her with the liftin' of the fog ... How many do y'have from Inniscourt?'

O'Dea scratched his head.

'Wait'll I see now ... about eight, I'm thinkin'.'

'Good.' There was menace in Liam's stare. 'Did my ears play the fool with me, for I am near sure I heard y'say somethin' about being the leader an' all?'

'Not me, Liam!' He trembled more from fear than cold.

'I am glad t'hear that ... well now, your troubles are over, for I'm back in the brains of it.'

12

Mary had been in the first longboat to leave the *Elizabeth*. Unable to see more than fifty yards in the conditions she supposed they were only a short distance from the harbour, but the reality was starkly different. Yet it might have been far worse if the crew of the longboat had not overshot the outer ring of mudbanks. Missing their intended target in the dense fog, they pushed on before coming across a small group of sandbars much further inland. Barefoot in the icy grip of the wet sand, she watched in quiet despair as the boat disappeared into the gloom, and all around her was the wailing and cursing of the abandoned.

Not able to tell in which direction lay sea or shore, there followed many long hours of waiting before the fog began to lift. In that endless time she struggled to keep awake, aware of the peril which awaited those in sleep at the turning of the tide, vaguely aware of the anguished cries from those who had begun to wander away in delirium and were now drowning. Others simply gave up the struggle and died where they lay. Only a grim determination to outwit the McAffertys kept the will to live inside her, and in reward the sun came to pierce the fog, revealing the shoreline a quarter-mile away.

Mary's surviving companion proved to be an old man. Not a word or gesture passed between them as they struggled inland. Together at first, they crawled across the chain of sandbars which led the way to shore, wading and swimming the many dividing channels.

But youth soon outpaced age on a grim journey that was opposed to anything but selfish survival. She stumbled on to the beach and looked round for the old man, but there was only the muted roar of sea on sand and the wild cries of the seabirds. Then all about her spun in a sickening kaleidoscope of vivid colour and she fell in a faint.

The fog was lifting, reluctantly giving way to pale sunshine which reflected off the distant buildings of Boston. With Patrick by his side Liam strutted around the jetty, rubbing his hands in a businesslike fashion as he mouthed encouragement among the small groups of immigrants. Of those who had survived the landings to the jetty, only twelve were from Inniscourt. Skilfully dividing them from the others, Liam coaxed and herded his charges some fifty yards away from the rest. 'Sit now an' rest while I talk t'yez.'

His tone was sympathetic, and obediently they slumped to the planking and waited in silence for their leader to speak. With a full sense of theatre Liam looked out to sea before turning slowly towards the group, noting the absence of any children. His mind went into swift calculation. Eight men and four women. Much less than half his original workforce; those left would have to work so much the harder. He conjured up an expression of the deepest sympathy.

'All of us have had the desperate sufferin' ... my dear son Brendan, dead of the sickness, an' Donal fighting for his very life.'

He paused, and dramatically pointed out to sea.

'An' I fear Donal's blessed an' beautiful new bride Mary is drownt out yonder.'

There was a soft low sigh from the gathering, and Jimmy O'Dea spoke up.

'A terrible business altogether ... I saw Mary's dear friend, Molly O'Rourke, drown before my very eyes, God help me if I did not!'

Annoyed at the interruption, Liam looked peevishly at O'Dea.

'That is desperate bad t'hear. But we have t'go on living.' His ending was abrupt. 'Now I'm away t'seek the fella in charge.'

113

Taking Patrick by the arm, he walked him some yards away. 'Stay on the jitty an' keep an eye open. Don't be for lettin' anyone of 'em wander away.'

Not waiting for a reply, he swaggered away and headed inland as the seagulls whirled about him, their raucous cries seeming to jeer his already leaden-footed progress through the shingle.

In the mid-morning haze the *Elizabeth* was almost lost to view from the shoreline, her decks alive with a frenetic activity in preparation for hasty departure. Pressed by creditors, Halloran badly needed the money from the Canadian timber deal. If he were to be arrested for the illegal landing in Boston his ship would likely be impounded, and prison would follow. At best it would mean an enforced twenty-day quarantine period eight miles down the coast on Deer Island, and there was still a danger of being held for the death of Sean Dolan. Either way would surely see him ruined. In deep depression, he stood at the aft rail looking towards the distant mudbanks.

Some minutes passed before a longboat emerged from the haze, its oars threshing up a phosphorescent spume as it sped towards the ship. It had landed the last of the immigrants and was now wasting no time in getting back. Halloran turned sharply from the rail. 'Do y'hear me, thief?'

Blake looked up from where he was coiling rope.

'I hear you, Captain!'

'The last cutter's comin', get the crew aboard, leave the boat in the water!'

Blake dropped the rope and stood up, his question coming hesitantly.

'Leave the cutter in the water?'

'Are y' deaf or what? We have to get outa here, or we're all for prison!'

'Prison! What's going on?'

'We should've docked at the fever station.'

'Why didn't we?'

Halloran ignored the question, eyes fixed on the longboat,

still a good two hundred yards away. He gripped the rail in renewed anger and shouted in a vain attempt to reach the crew. 'Pull harder, y'bastards!'

Blake tugged on Halloran's sleeve, voice shaking with agitation.

'Why didn't we dock at the fever station?'

Halloran punched Blake's hand away as he snarled a reply.

'Because there's a bloody twenty-day quarantine!' He regarded Blake's shocked look. 'Don't act the goat wit' me! Y'knew we had the typhus aboard.'

'Oh my God! I did not know that. I thought it to be fever.'

Halloran turned away to look once more on the progress of the longboat.

'It's me y'have to worry about, not God. Now get about an' make ready, they'll be alongside directly.'

Liam trudged from the shingle and laboured up the stone steps which led to the harbour yard. Despite the cold breeze he sweated freely and his body shook with fatigue, for it had been a long haul from the jetty and much of his former cockiness had been spent on it. He looked suddenly a much older man; the rags which had once been clothing hung damply from his emaciated body, stockingless feet holding tight to boots which had split to ribbons under the milling of the pebbles, wild eyes staring from a bearded, dirt-ingrained face splashed with numerous bird droppings. The effort of the two-mile walk had aggravated his desperate thirst, but it was the hunger which plagued him more. His distended belly, shot with burning needles of pain, griped and rumbled, and with almost every step wind broke stinking from him in a steady ripple. An involuntary moan came through cracked lips. 'Christ Almighty ... I'm that hungry.'

He became aware of a figure standing in his path some thirty yards ahead, but the mist blurred his vision, making it difficult to hold focus. He stopped and forced his knuckles to rub hard into his rheumy eyes, then stared ahead once more, the thoughts coming thick and fast to pummel his exhausted brain. What's this now? The man must be at least an admiral, never had he seen so many gold buttons, nor such a fine uniform.

There must be proper respect shown. He crabbed swiftly towards the man, shoulders bent in humble attitude, right hand reaching for his forelock.

'Good day to Your Honour, God bless you for the gentleman y'rightly are!'

'If you don't want trouble stay where you are!'

The command forced Liam to a halt.

'I mean no wrong, sir, lookin' for the man in charge is all.'

'Then you've found him. I am Senior Port Warden Demarest. Who are you?'

'Liam McAfferty, sir.' His attempted salute was clumsy.

Lips curling in disgust, Demarest surveyed Liam from top to toe. A third-generation Bostonian, he had been a leading port official for the better part of ten years. It was easy employment before the great influx from Ireland, but now his task had been made tiresome and difficult with these people who arrived on every day that dawned. He moved his gaze away from Liam, shielding his eyes as he looked out towards the *Elizabeth*.

'You are from that ship?'

'I am, sir.'

'What is her name, and who is her captain?'

Liam cleared his throat noisily.

'We have just now landed from that very ship and...'

The interruption was harsh.

'Idiot! I can guess that much! Now, ship's name and captain!'

''Tis the *Elizabet*', Y'r Honour, an' the captain is a divvil of a creature called Halloran.'

'Why did the ship not dock in normal manner?'

'Y'd do better t'ask Halloran that, Y'r Honour.'

'Do not be insolent! It is you I am asking.'

Liam hung his head and the reply was full of contrition. 'I'm desperate sorry, I don't know that, sir.'

Demarest looked away to the *Elizabeth* once more, then turned again to Liam.

116

'There has quite obviously been an illegal landing. You could well be shipped back to where you came from.'

Liam felt a new terror. Holy Christ!... To be shipped back to Ireland after all he had been through. He fell to his knees, voice breaking with emotion.

'Please t'God, sir, we've suffered the terrible agonies t'get here ... for pity's sake don't be after sending us back.'

Demarest felt embarrassed. 'Get up off your knees, man!'

Liam clambered slowly upright, moving to untidy attention as he looked with appeal at his tormentor. The next question came with less hostility.

'Are there others ashore with you?'

Liam seized eagerly on this softer approach. 'I have 'em on the jitty ... told 'em not t'move till I got the nod to come into the town, sir.'

'How many?'

'Twenty, maybe thirty, Y'r Honour.'

'Are you their leader?'

'I am that, sir!'

'Very well, tell me the truth now or it will go hard with you. Do you have the fever aboard?'

'We do, sir, an' right badly.'

'Right, McAfferty, do exactly as I say or you'll finish up in prison. You wouldn't want that, would you?'

A tremble of fear ran through Liam. 'I would not, sir.'

'Good. Now go back to the jetty and make sure no one leaves. Do you understand me?'

'I do, rightly enough, sir.'

'On your way then, I will be along to talk to you all.'

In a pathetic desire to please, Liam bowed in ungainly fashion. 'I'll keep 'em on the jitty, my life on it, sir.'

Demarest watched Liam trudge away over the shingle. Then with a shrug of the shoulders he headed for the dock immigration buildings.

The cobbled dockyard gave way to a number of red-brick offices. Dominating the centre of the yard was an imposing

117

building of two storeys, painted overall in gleaming white. From its centre tower flew the flag of the stars and stripes.

Mary clambered over the low wall into the yard, pausing for a few moments to take breath. The sodden rag of a dress clung to her body in a clammy embrace and the once-beautiful hair hung like muddy rats' tails round her shoulders. Dry, cracked lips trembled in a face that was almost black with dirt, and only the gentle eyes gave hint of the woman within. The dockyard cobbles felt like ice and struck without pity through bare feet. She lifted first one leg, then the other in an impossible attempt to avoid direct contact, her tired mind uncertain of the next move.

She must seek help, but which building ought she to make for? Her gaze fixed on the flag. She had seen it before, but only in books, now it flew grandly before her in reality, making her heart beat faster, she was in America and free... The McAffertys were a thing of the past.

'Hey! You there!' She turned to see a trooper running from one of the buildings. The man stopped almost on top of her and she could feel his hot breath on her forehead as he grasped her by the shoulders. 'How in hell did you get in this yard?'

She swayed, almost on the point of fainting again, and in her uncertain vision the man's face blurred, his loud voice making her head ring with pain. Unable to frame words she waited for him to speak again.

'Do you understand me? Can you speak English?'

With a deep breath she fought off the nausea and her senses began to clear, but she sought her words with care. 'I am come from Ireland on the *Elizabeth.*'

'Has your ship been wrecked?'

'No ... no it has not.'

'Then where did it dock?'

She defiantly pushed the hair away from her eyes as the trooper's voice probed again. 'Where is the ship now?'

The question was never answered. Fresh from his encounter with Liam, Demarest strode into the yard.

'What are you about there, Davison?'

118

The trooper released his hold on Mary and sprang to attention.

'I caught this woman trespassing, sir, says she's off a ship called the *Elizabeth*.'

'Keep away from her, you Goddamned idiot! She most probably has the typhus.' The trooper stared in horror at Mary, then broke away into a trot to stand before Demarest.

'What will we do with her, sir?'

Demarest looked with mild curiosity at Mary. What strange people these bog-Irish were. He could claim Dublin roots and Gentile grandparents who had crossed the Atlantic in proper fashion before settling in America. But these creatures who came in cattle boats and coffin ships were surely from another world.

'There are more on the jetty at Connor's Point. Get a party of troopers to march her back, tell them to stay on guard, the wretches are straying all over the place.' A touch of humanity moved him. 'Get bread and water to them. Move quickly now!'

The man doubled away, leaving him to gaze at Mary from the safety of thirty yards. Great heavens, was this filthy being really a woman? He spoke with an attempt at compassion.

'Stay where you are now. You will soon be back with your own people.'

A wave of nausea swept over Mary, and the dockyard seemed to sway... Back to her own people. Back to Donal, to Liam, to Patrick. For as surely as night follows day, they would be there. But maybe if the man knew she was without the fever, and ready to work, he might relent. She would first seek God's help in prayer ... yet within the evils of the ship had she not denied His being and vilely forsaken Him? But He would surely forgive her in this moment of persecution.

Her lips moved in silent prayer. 'I am truly sorry, Lord, and ask forgiveness for my wrong to you. Please help me at this time, Lord ... please make him let me go.'

She glanced up to take in Demarest's penetrating gaze and became painfully aware of her appearance. Instinctively she attempted to smooth down her skirt, hands coming away heavy with mud, and knew how utterly wretched she must look to him. But her voice was firm.

'I am without the fever, sir, an' able to work. I can read an' write and would be harm to no one.' She paused, trying to gauge Demarest's reaction. His eyes were difficult to read at such a distance. But he was plainly listening. Her heart began to beat faster, and the words now came in a rush. 'I'm askin' that you let me go into the town and find work to keep body an' soul together, sir.'

'There is no chance of that. You have made an illegal landing, and face being sent back to Ireland. Now be quiet, I do not want to hear another word from you.'

His words had come like a heavy fist to her face and she rocked under the blow, biting back the tears of anger and disappointment ... was this then the way God answered so fervent a prayer? Maybe her mother had been right all along. Maybe, as she had said, there was no one out there, and in the end it was devil take the hindmost. The wind blew colder, and in pitiful defence she put her arms about herself in tight embrace, rocking slightly as an indescribable exhaustion closed upon her. But she was determined not to go down before the man's probing stare.

Head erect, eyes blazing, she looked defiantly back at him. Her mind was clear now, and a new resolution came. This was not the end of it. She would surely find another way to escape.

13

Liam half fell on to the jetty, eyes wild with panic, the breath rasping from him in painful bursts as he fought for speech. When his voice came it was little more than a croak.

'We have trouble, so we have. Trouble enough for a hundred.'

A loud murmur of concern came from the gathering, and Patrick steeled himself to the question. 'Trouble, dar?'

'Prison! ... Prison or worse!'

The peasants turned away to each other in shocked discussion, but Jimmy O'Dea's voice cut loud and clear through the babble. 'Shut up! For Christ's sake let's hear what he has t'say.'

In the silence which followed, all eyes were firmly on Liam.

'I'm just after meetin' the man in charge. He's in a mind t'send us back t'Ireland.'

A woman began to cry softly. O'Dea scratched at his nose and looked carefully at Liam. 'Back t'Ireland, is it? Surely t'Christ they would not go t'all that bother ... an' y'must have it wrong about the prison.'

Liam looked warningly at him.

'We're t'stay on the jitty, or it's the lock-up.'

O'Dea persisted. 'And why would your man make the trouble like this?'

Liam's answer came with cold finality. 'I'm tellin' y' what the man said. He's after comin' soon, an' you can shut up, O'Dea. I'll be doin' the bloody talkin'!'

Patrick watched in silence as the troopers brought Mary in,

121

waiting with pained impatience until they marched away to take up guard at the shore end of the jetty, then walked slowly to where she was sitting alone on the planking.

There was no love lost between them. Patrick simply tolerated his sister-in-law for the sake of what his father called family unity, but to him she was no more nor less than a chattel, and he had no respect for the woman or her book learning.

She looked up at his approach, and a new hate arose in her. This was the man who had brutally carried out his father's orders on that awful night. This was the creature who had held her down while Donal forced his bestial way into her. This was the man who had shouted obscenities, laughing and joking as he urged his brother on to rape her again and again through the endless night hours.

She shuddered at the pictures in her mind ... the flickering lamps of the hold ... the people she had once called friends, who now turned their backs on her screams ... the savage blows to her face, the helplessness, arms stretched wide and near broken ... Brendan standing, staring, watching, giggling hysterically as his brother made entry into her ... the pain, the indignity, the immeasurable shame ... Brendan's sudden, open-mouthed curiosity, like that of a child as his brother howled in climax, like a mad dog, then began his fearful, grunting invasion anew ... poor Brendan, a pitiful creature and no more than a halfwit, who now lay dead at the bottom of the ocean ... why was this vile animal not rotting there with him?

Patrick poked the toe of his boot into her stomach. 'I'm thinkin' y'tried t'run away, y'bloody slut! Get over t'Donal, he's sick an' needs t'be looked after.'

She had never before felt the urge to kill, but the desire came now. Yet she knew the rage was impotent, knew that any resistance would fetch a beating. She would wait her time, for it would surely come.

Donal lay on a pile of damp rags, alternately shuddering and sweating. He watched her approach, his face growing more sullen with her every step, fevered brain wrestling to frame words that would wound. But nothing evil enough would come to him. Why was it not her with the sickness instead of himself? Her voice carried to him in a cold monotone.

'I see you are over the worst of it.'

'I'm dyin', so I am.' The reply had come with difficulty for he was parched for lack of water, but she felt no compassion.

'I doubt that ... I doubt that very much.'

'Y'wish I was dead.'

'I wish only to be done with you.'

He whimpered in self-pity. 'God love us, aren't I sufferin' the terrible sickness, an' you not here t'care for me as a wife rightly should.'

She looked away in revulsion.

'Do not even think on me as your wife, for that I shall never be.'

His face contorted in a slow fury. 'Y'bloody bitch ... get me water.'

What few provisions the troopers had brought were long since gone. But pretending to seek some would get her away from the sight of the animal. He watched her walk away down the jetty, and despite his illness the lust grew strong within him. The drool ran unchecked down his chin at the thought of it. Soon he would be cured of the fever, and this terrible weakness which would not allow him even to stand. Then he would take her many times ... as many times as he wanted. His eyes closed slowly and he drifted into a deep sleep.

14

In perfect step the three men strode towards the jetty, the shingle rasping in military rhythm beneath their boots, an air of determination in their bearing. They were a hundred yards short of the jetty when the unmistakable odour of unwashed human beings hit them. It grew stronger to lodge in their mouths and throats, and was not merely the want of water to the body, but a rottenness which beggared description. There was a perceptible slowing down in the two men who walked slightly behind the senior port warden, and their steps went into a shamble before coming to a sudden halt. Demarest had walked on some yards before he became aware of his companions' halt.

'Is there something wrong, gentlemen?'

'That awful odour, Demarest, is it coming from those people on the jetty?'

Demarest tried not to smile. He had grown so used to the smells which invariably accompanied immigrants that he no longer noticed them. But for these councillors who served the city fathers of Boston it was a new experience, and he enjoyed their discomfort. Their visit was totally unnecessary, for he could have easily dealt with the situation, but he had contrived the outing that they might see at first hand what he was up against. Josiah P. Hobson and Silas Golding were pompous men who worshipped at the shrine of bureaucracy, more at home in the lobbies of council chambers than mingling with the proletariat.

Hobson nastily repeated his question. 'Is that smell coming from the jetty? Answer me, Demarest!'

'I am sorry, Mr Hobson, my mind was elsewhere for a moment. Yes, they do smell somewhat, but one gets used to it after a short time.'

Golding wrinkled his nose in distaste. He was the lesser in rank to Hobson, and totally subservient to him.

'Demarest, is there really need to subject Mr Hobson to this awful business?'

'I'm afraid so, sir.' The lie came easily and was laced with flattery. 'Normally, I can handle port affairs, but this is a blatantly illegal landing. It needs a senior official like Mr Hobson to personally judge the situation.'

'Quite right, Demarest.' Hobson puffed up his heavy jowls in self-importance. 'These terrible people need to know who they are dealing with. I will not flinch from my duty. Lead on!'

Liam jumped down from his perch on the jetty rail. He had been watching the approach of the three men since they left the harbour. Now, as they mounted the jetty he walked slowly towards the front of his people. The trio of officials stopped a good ten yards from the immigrants, and Demarest stepped a pace forward. He was determined to get full value from the charade.

'Pay attention! ... These gentlemen with me are officers from the city of Boston. Senior Councillor Hobson will address you on the seriousness of your illegal landing in this port.' He glanced at Hobson. 'If you please, sir.'

The survivors gazed in awe at Hobson. His clothes were immaculate: doeskin trousers, polished boots, velvet jacket, and a cream waistcoat from which hung a gold watch and chain. A beaverskin stovepipe hat sat squarely on his head.

'My name is Josiah P. Hobson, a senior councillor for the city of Boston, Massachusetts, in the United States of America. I have been summoned here in great haste to deal with your most criminal act of illegal landing, and...'

He was interrupted by Liam.

'Your Great Honour! We are honest, God-fearin' souls, an' paid the passage money. We've done nothin' t'hurt a body.'

125

'Silence, you impudent creature!' Golding glared at him. 'No more interruptions during Mr Hobson's address to you!'

Liam cringed under the verbal lashing and Hobson surveyed him with open curiosity. He had never before seen new immigrants at such close quarters. What frightening people they were.

'As I was saying ... you people have landed illegally in the United States of America, and as such you should be transported back whence you came.' Hobson paused, and looked around the sea of faces. 'Do not look innocent about the matter! Mr Demarest has heard a confession from the very lips of your leader, a man named, er...' He turned away to Demarest. 'Who is this man?'

'He calls himself Liam McAfferty, sir.'

Liam winced, but stayed silent as Hobson continued.

'This man, McAfferty, has confessed a most terrible crime in that a great number of you have ship fever.'

In a horror of realisation, Hobson plucked out a perfumed handkerchief, pushed it hard to his nose and stood back a pace. With frequent dabs around the mouth he continued, but in some distress.

'This is in violation of an ordinance passed by Boston City Council, sitting in chamber on the sixteenth of March, in this year of eighteen hundred and forty-seven.' He made the mistake of taking in a deep breath to go on, and the stench made his head reel. He retched, then beckoned Golding to him. 'Explain what that means, Golding, I am feeling unwell.'

'Of course, Mr Hobson.'

Hidden behind a lavender-sprinkled handkerchief, Golding had been relatively safe from the smell. He now obediently stepped forward, but without enthusiasm for the task, eyeing the restless crowd with distaste.

'You cannot just land as you please, orders are there to be obeyed. You should have disembarked at the quarantine station, and there spent twenty days before being allowed on the mainland.' He became growingly aware of his elevation to spokesman. These people were silent before him, hanging on his every word, and he warmed to this newly found power.

126

'You vagrants are landing in hordes, making the fair city of Boston into the moral cesspool of the civilised world ... you bring no trades with you, other than the doubtful ability to grow potatoes, of which we have a surfeit.' The crowd shifted uneasily, unable to understand many of the words being hurled at them.

'Many of you are drunken lawbreakers, and only the Lord knows what we have done to deserve your presence. You should be sent back to the filth you came from, or at least serve a period of hard labour in imprisonment.' There was a loud murmur of fear. They had clearly understood the latter offering, and he smirked at their terror. 'If, and when, you are admitted to Boston, take note of this ... we have stern justice and strong prisons.'

He would have gone on, but the glory of the situation was being rapidly outweighed by the smell, and he was feeling sick. Pale-faced, he nodded towards the port official. 'Demarest, explain to these wretched people what they must now do to comply with the laws of this city.' Demarest nodded acknowledgment.

'Listen! You will be taken to Deer Island and remain there for the prescribed time ordered by the port physician. After that period you will be allowed on to the mainland. Now a warning. I am leaving two troopers on guard. Stay here until the boat comes for you. If you disobey this order you will fare badly ... I promise you!'

A look of profound relief came to Hobson's face.

'Well done, Demarest, let us return at once to our separate and various duties.'

With a pace that sacrificed dignity, Hobson and Golding marched off the jetty and away over the shingle. Smiling in satisfaction, Demarest followed in more leisurely stride. Maybe now he would receive a deal less interference and criticism from that particular quarter.

A babble of conversation broke out among the crowd, but Liam chose to ignore it as he whispered to Patrick.

'I am not for goin' to this Deer Island place.'

A loud shout interrupted him. 'Look yonder! 'Tis the ship makin' off.' O'Dea pointed to where the *Elizabeth*, in full sail, was heading for the open ocean.

'I cannot say I blame the rogue, he'd be sure for the gallows.'

'The bastard!' Patrick's angry voice bellowed. 'An' would it not be right for the murderin' of Sean?'

A hard punch in the back cut off further words as Liam warned.

'Shut up! I want no trouble ... we're for runnin'.'

A look of disbelief crossed Patrick's face.

'Runnin'?' His gaze moved away to take in the crowd, then came slowly back on his father. 'Wit' all these?'

'They will not be comin' with us.'

'But, dar, they owe y' the money.'

'I will be back t'round them up when they land from the fever place.' He glanced furtively over his shoulder to make sure they were not overheard. ''Tis fortunate what has happened, for I now have time t'prepare the work for them.' With a sly look he tapped at his breeches pocket. 'I have here the name of a man of great business who will give us the work.'

'An' is this man of great business here?'

'Not at all! I was told this Boston place is full to the brim wit' the likes of us, scratchin' for work and bein' kicked up the arse for the pain of it.'

'Y'know an awful lot of powerful things, dar.'

'I know if we get taken t' Deer Island the jobs will be gone, an' us out in the cold.'

He glanced around once more before continuing.

'We are t'make our way to a place called Clarkstown, just aways up the coast. I have some dollars t'make the goin' easier.'

'How are we for gettin' away wit' your man already sendin' the boat t'take us to the sick place?'

Liam grinned knowingly. 'Demarest has done his little jig, an' won't be back.' He looked away up the beach where Demarest was talking to the troopers. 'I have been watchin' the soldier boys. They make sure to stay a good distance from us, for they are frightened to death of gettin' the fever. They will not be a trouble.' He returned his gaze to Patrick. 'It will soon be dark, when it is we get under the jitty. I have seen just the place.' He smiled. 'We lay low 'til the ship leaves, then we're off.' The smile disappeared as he looked across to where Donal lay asleep on the planking. 'Your brother is a desperate burden t'me, Patrick, a weak man, fallin' to the sickness like that. 'Tis you should have married Mary, like I said in the first place.'

Patrick flushed scarlet at the thought, and changed the subject. 'Surely we're takin' him with us, dar?'

Liam's voice held a resigned note.

'We are. But first we have t'get him under the jitty without anyone seein' what we are about.'

'I'll get him there, dar.'

Liam glanced away to where the sun was already setting.

'Get Mary to me, for I have t'tell her the way of it. We will soon have need of the woman's book-learnin'.'

The pitch blackness of the night was only faintly pierced by the troopers' oil lamps, and their fire was a poor affair, affording no more than five paces of light. It sputtered and hissed in its reluctance to flame, the damp driftwood cracking out huge sparks of burning timber which seemed maliciously to seek them out as targets. They were neither of them yet twenty, both new to the service and nervous of their task. The younger of the two had just returned from a patrol. He put down the musket and knelt in front of the fire trying to warm his hands, now and again coughing as the acrid smoke curled about his head. His companion lay nearby, half-closed eyes regarding the man at the fire. The voice was taunting.

'Sammy boy, you ain't trodden your good old boots no place near that jetty, have ya now?'

'You tellin' me you did, Dan?'

'Not tellin' you nothin' 'cept I was left in charge here.'

'I know y'didn't.'

'Smart as you then, ain't I though?'

129

'Have to be loco t'go pokin' 'round them critters in the dark, have my musket off me quicker'n shit.'

'Sure as hell, Sammy, shoot y' stone dead with it too.'

'Surely would. Anyways, don't get paid enough to go gettin' the fever an' all ... an' they ain't goin' no place, 'cept on the boat.'

'You ain't wrong there.' He peered towards the sound of the soft hiss of breaking waves on shingle, but there was only a deep blackness beyond the fire circle. 'Gotta be here soon.'

'Why in hell couldn't they come in daylight?' Sammy's tone was peevish. 'An' how come we get all the shit jobs t'do?'

'New boys is why.'

'We ain't that new, six months an' more.' His mind moved to other matters. 'You do a head count like Demarest said to?'

Dan lazily scratched his stubble. 'Tried, tried like hell, but they just kept on movin' around.'

'You can't count no more'n up to your twennies, anyways.'

'Can too!'

'What comes after twennies then? Tell me that.'

'Fifties.'

'Fifties shit! How in hell you ever get in the army?'

Dan sat up and shook his head. 'Don't rightly know, boy.' Then with an oath he scrambled to his feet and pointed out to sea where a signal light flashed. 'Hell! ... The goddamned boat's here.' Picking up both lamps he handed one to Sammy. 'Swing it one side to t'other, make 'em see us.'

Beneath the jetty, eyes already accustomed to the darkness, Liam placed his hand in a tight grip across Mary's mouth as the cutters ground ashore. But she had no intention of crying out, instead she would wait until they reached the town of which Liam had told her. Better then to plot her way free of them rather than endure their presence for the better part of a month within a fever station. Muffled shouts and the shuffling of feet came from overhead. Then, clearly, a voice full of irritation.

'Why in hellfire couldn't you get here in daylight?'

'Watch your mouth, soldier! We've been picking these wretches up since morning. How many do you have?'

'Twenny-five.'

'Seems like more to me.'

'They keep damn' well movin' around is why!'

'Get them down to the cutters.'

Within a half-hour the last cutter had departed for the fever ship, but Liam waited to make his move long after the final splash of oars had sounded. 'Wake your brother, Patrick. Sick or not, he has a deal of walkin' t'do now.'

They emerged into the starlit night and in silence looked over at the fire where the troopers were making ready to move off. Liam grinned as he watched them walk towards the main harbour, their oil lamps gradually fading into the darkness. 'Follow me now, an' mind y'keep close together.'

The light from the dock tavern illuminated the quayside where a number of small craft lay at anchor. A pony, tethered beside a stone trough, turned in curiosity as Liam stood listening to the sounds of conversation which drifted from the bar.

Satisfied that the place presented no danger, he whispered to Patrick, 'The three of yez sit down over there.' He indicated where a pile of ropes lay coiled on the quay. 'I will not be long about my business.' Silently they made off while Liam knelt beside the trough and plunged his head and shoulders deep into the water, snorting clear to run stubby fingers through his hair in the manner of a comb.

The bar was dimly lit by oil lamps, their fitful glow falling on a handful of drinkers talking at various tables. They looked up in mild interest at Liam's entry, but almost immediately resumed their desultory chatter. In confident manner he approached the bar as the tavern keeper nodded in greeting. 'You're pretty wet lookin', fella.'

'I am, an' there's a sorry tale to it. Will y'take a drink wit' me, landlord?'

'Right kind.' With the drinks on the bar they fell into easy conversation. 'Can't recall seein' you in these parts before.'

Liam smiled reassuringly. 'Y'would not have, I'm from up the coast, been visitin' the relatives here.'

131

'What place would that be?'

'Y'would not know it, a scatterin' of cottages is all.' He carefully weighed the man up. ''Tis a place I'd like t'be gettin' back to, if I can get the use of a boat.'

'How'd you get here, then?'

Liam took a drink before answering. 'Boat, just now lost it.'

'Lost it?'

'A terrible business altogether.'

'How'd it happen?'

'Hit a rock.'

'Where would that be?'

'I could not rightly say. 'Twas black as all hell out there.'

'You'll be wanting a bed for the night, then?'

Damn the bloody man, questions, questions, questions. But there was a need for patience. Liam forced a polite smile.

'I would like nothin' better in all this world, but we have t'be gettin' back.'

'Who else is with you, then?'

'My two sons, and daughter.'

'Where are they?'

'On the quay.'

'Well for Chrissakes bring 'em in!'

'They are not for comin' in ... one of my boys is sick an' needs t'be quiet, he is bein' kept company by the others. Can y' help me with the boat now?'

'I can try.' He shouted towards the far end of the bar. 'Zeb, Jesse, get over here.'

The two men shambled over.

'What's the trouble, Henry?'

'Zeb, this poor fella lost his boat, has kids outside and needs to get home. Can you take 'em?'

'Don't know 'bout that, Henry ... have t'be up at dawn t'get in the catch.'

'Zeb, this is a Christian act you're being asked to do.'

'We gotta make a living, Henry.' He looked at Liam. 'Where you from then, fella?'

Liam's thoughts moved furiously. If he were to tell them it was Clarkstown it would be leaving an open trail. But to hang

132

about this place for much longer was only inviting trouble. Damn it all to hell!

'Clarkstown so it is.'

'Clarkstown! That's more'n twenty miles ... sorry, fella, if we're not off with the fleet come dawn it'll cost us a couple of dollars apiece. We gotta eat, you know.'

Liam drank the rest of his porter down in one mouthful, then gazed with sadness at the empty glass.

'I cannot have y'out of pocket on my account. I will give each of y' three dollars for the job of gettin' us there safely.'

'You must wanna get there mighty badly.' They were now openly curious.

Liam feigned tears and rubbed hard at his eyes.

'God help me ... 'Tis a most desperate time, my dear old mother is alone back there an' likely thinkin' us drownt t'death.'

Zeb was embarrassed. 'Well now, that ain't right, ain't right nohow.' In a gesture of comfort he put his hand on Liam's shoulder. 'Hey, old-timer, don't go getting yourself upset like that ... what the hell, we'll do it.'

15

The small fishing boat took less than eight hours to reach landfall at Clarkstown, and it was not long after dawn when the runaways emerged from the beach to make their way across the quayside. Dressed in a miscellany of clothing wrangled from the fishermen, they caused little curiosity from the dockers who were loading timber aboard a gaggle of ships. Clarkstown had been no more than a fishing village, but was now growing apace within a thriving timber industry, its many lumber mills working round the clock to satisfy domestic and overseas orders.

Liam glanced about the quay and nodded approvingly at the bustle.

'A fine place indeed... Listen t'me, no strayin' now, I have to go find our man.'

'Will we stay here, dar?' Patrick's question expressed concern as he eased Donal to a sitting position on a bale of rags.

'An' where else would y'be goin'?'

'I was thinkin' the law might come nosin'.'

Liam considered the matter for a moment.

'Find the town eatin' house, I'll get t'you there.'

'Can y'give us the money, dar?'

'I'll want t'see change from this.' He shoved 50 cents into Patrick's hand, then fabricating a look of sympathy he walked over to Mary, who had distanced herself some yards away. Bitterly aware of his illiteracy, he resented the power which this slip of a girl now held over him. But there was an urgent need to know the contents of the note given to him in Sligo.

The resentment changed to doubt as he approached her.

She had not fared well at his hands and now might turn on him, yet he dare not risk the help of strangers. His cunning overture was carefully weighted.

'Mary, I am before God powerful sorry about your hurtin' an' all the happenin's. I will have the strong words wit' Donal when we are settled, an' I ...'

Her gaze was steady upon him as he faltered. What new game was he playing? For game it must be since the man had not a spark of sympathy in his body. She remained silent, allowing him time to continue.

'He will harm you no more, my word on it.' Awkwardly, he fished out the grubby paper and held it within a few inches of her face. 'Y'have the sharper eyes than myself. Will y'tell me what it says? ... For the work, y'see.'

She took in his anxious expression, then looked beyond him to where Patrick sat huddled with Donal on the rag bale. A grim satisfaction dawned in her ... they were all helpless as babes, for not a one of them could read or write. This was not Inniscourt in which they once bullied and blustered, and where the written word was akin to the riddle of the universe. This was America, a vast country of great wealth and many opportunities, even for the very poor. Yet the illiterate would find the going so much the harder, and the only tasks on offer would be the most menial. In silence she read the note which contained a name and address with information on where work might be obtained. Lifting her gaze over the top of the paper, she feasted herself on his confused expression and halting words.

'Well now ... daughter ... what does it say?'

She would make him wait and suffer doubt. Why not say that the name on the note was Connor, or Riley or whatever? Give a wrong address and have him running about the town like a fool. He would not know the difference, nor would he dare ask anyone else for help, or surely he would not have asked her. But would it not be better if they were found work? That way meant she would be free of them for most of the day, time in which to plan a more sure escape. His voice came in irritation to cut short her thoughts.

135

'Can y'not read it?'

'I can.' Her tone was clipped and precise.

'What does it say?'

'A number of things.'

'For Christ's sake! Tell me what!'

'Do not take the Lord's name in vain, Mr McAfferty.'

'Are you tryin' t'make the goat of me?' She did not reply, her look of contempt making him writhe in his ignorance. 'Alright, I know what you're at.' His tone became stronger. 'But I warn you, if we don't find the work there'll be no food or shelter.' She accepted the oblique acknowledgment of her victory, and decided not to ride further on this first success.

'Y'need to find the Meredith Lumber Company on River Street. The man to speak with is Mr John Meredith.'

'Meredith, River Street.' He repeated the words a number of times, committing them to memory. 'Nothin' more?'

Mary shook her head, and without thanks or further words he headed towards the town. She trembled in the cold air. Why not simply walk away here and now? . . . Liam would be gone for hours, and he was surely the only one with will and energy to pursue her. Vaguely she saw the timber stacks which towered about the road into town. Once into them she would be lost to view . . . but would Patrick come after her? His voice drifted across as he urged Donal to stand up, then he called out in a vicious tone, 'Come on, y'bitch! We're for gettin' somethin' to eat.'

For a moment their eyes met in mutual hate as he turned away, and with Donal hanging on to him for support moved slowly from the quay. Now there was no obstacle to flight . . . run! Run now! Her legs trembled violently as the pains of hunger came to rack her body. Run? There was hardly the strength in her to walk, for she was near starving to death. Hazily, she recalled Donal's haggard face and tottering steps. He would be no threat for some time to come. She needed food, and they had the means to obtain it. There would be time enough later to think of escape. Uncertainly, she stood up and, as in a dream, followed in their wake.

The sweet smell of newly cut timber was everywhere. Eyes wide

136

in childlike wonderment, Liam watched as the giant circular saws ripped noisily into their work, sending fountains of yellow sawdust hurtling into the still morning air.

Shaking his head in admiration, he reluctantly moved his attention from the scream of the saws to where a team of horses was being backed into the shafts of a flat cart. Urging the labourers to better effort was a tall, ruddy-featured man, cropped red hair alive with sweat which ran freely down his face. Liam flinched as the man's gaze fell on him. The eyes were hawklike, golden, flecked with hazel and deeply inquiring.

'What's your business?' The voice came in a cultured New England accent. Liam took a deep breath and crossed the few yards which separated them.

'I am just after lookin' for Mr Meredith, sir.'

'You're talking to him.'

'Beggin' your pardon, sir... McAfferty. I am understandin' there is work t'be had wit' you, sir.'

'What do you do?' Meredith pulled out a neckerchief and rubbed hard at the sweat on his face. 'What kinda work?'

'Anythin', sir, anythin' under the sun.'

'Who sent you?'

Liam dragged the note from a jacket which stank of fish, and proffered it to Meredith, who wrinkled his nose in disgust.

'You tell me what it says.'

'I am just over the water, sir, 'tis your name on the note, a sailor gave it me.'

'So, you can do anythin', eh McAfferty?' He stuffed the neckerchief back into blue cotton coveralls.

Liam beamed. 'I can, sir, an' I have the two sons wit' me.'

'Know anything about the lumber trade?'

'I can learn fast as the lightnin', sir.'

Meredith smiled at the enthusiasm. 'Daresay you could, but I have enough labourers. Can you measure?'

'Measure is it, sir?' Liam's face took on a blank look.

'It is, McAfferty, with rulers, tapes an' all.'

In embarrassment, Liam rubbed grimy hands across his face as he swayed with fatigue and frustration, for he had not the

137

remotest idea what the man was talking about. 'No, sir, I cannot do the measure.'

Meredith was sympathetic. 'Sorry, fella, you'll have to try elsewhere. It's brains I'm looking for, not broad backs.'

Liam nodded and shuffled away towards the yard gate. Meredith watched him go before a sudden idea came.

'Hey, McAfferty, get over here!'

Inspired by new hope, Liam found the energy to trot back.

'Y'have the work for me, sir?'

'What did you do for a living in Ireland?'

'Farmer, sir, I was a farmer ... taties an' the like, an' I put much t'market in Castlebar an' Sligo. I have the brains wit' me there, sir.'

'I got a spread needs looking after. You and your boys hard workers? Trustworthy? Godfearing?'

Liam's eyes lit up with greed at the prospect of easy pickings.

'Indeed we are, sir!'

'This farm you had, did it make any money?'

'It did, sir.'

'Why'd you leave it, then?'

'The great hunger came, an' all Ireland is diseased, sir.'

Meredith nodded understandingly.

'Heard tell something on that score ... wiped you out then, did it?'

Liam rubbed wearily at his brow.

'It did, sir, an' many a thousand other poor souls.'

'Must've been hell.'

'The divvil's hand was surely on it, sir.'

'How many field hands you run?'

'Me, an' my boys, an' six or seven of the labourers, sir.'

'You have references?'

'References, sir?' Liam looked nonplussed.

'Sure, letters stating your character and background.'

'We left in a powerful hurry, so as not t'miss the catchin' of the boat, an' left the many things behind, sir.'

'Can anybody speak for you then?'

Liam's mind spun like a top. If he failed to come up with something convincing, and quickly at that, he was going to lose

138

whatever chance was on offer. 'There was the holy priest, sir, Father Coughlan.'

He lowered his gaze to the wood chippings which scattered the yard, and pitched his voice low. 'We were close as could be. But, God rest him ... taken from us.' He looked up to meet the unblinking stare of Meredith and knew the man was not convinced.

'A dead priest ... nobody else?'

Liam started to sweat as he saw the chance slipping away. He would have to play his last card, a dangerous one at that.

'There is my daughter, sir.'

'So, you have a daughter?'

'Mary, sir, a truly blessed an' beautiful child, married to my dear son, Donal.'

'That makes her your daughter-in-law.'

'She is closer t'me than that, sir, for I love her as my own.'

'I'm sure that's a fact, McAfferty. But you got me lost ... how can she speak up for you?'

'Mary is knowin' of the readin' an' the writin', sir, an' the schoolteacher's girl. She has the brains of it, sir.'

'You saying she's a schoolteacher's daughter?'

'I am, sir, a great man indeed at the big school in Ireland.'

Meredith was more impressed. A second-generation American, he had made good in Clarkstown, and not only ran a thriving business but was also the leading town father. His numerous offices included stipendiary chief of police and chairman of the school governors. He deeply respected the values of education, and now reasoned that a schoolteacher would hardly marry off his daughter to an untrustworthy family. Yet he still had doubts, for he was a man who had come up the hard way.

'Where's your family now?'

'Havin' a meal in the town, sir.'

'I'm of a mind to give you a chance, McAfferty, but God help you if you let me down.'

'Not me, sir ... May all the divvils in hell tear me t'pieces if I do.'

But there was no longer tolerant humour in Meredith's

139

expression. 'Wouldn't need all the devils in hell, fella, I'd be there to do it myself!' Liam looked into the man's eyes and saw the promise there. Meredith gently patted the horse which nuzzled at his shoulder but his gaze never left Liam. 'How'd you fetch up in Clarkstown?'

'The sailors brought us from Boston, sir.'

'You handy with your fists, licking field hands together an' all? This is a tough job, needs a hard man.'

'I c'n get the work done, no fear of that, sir.'

'McAfferty, listen to me good now. The last man to manage my farm was carried over the County Line last night.

'Carried?' Liam swallowed deeply.

'Carried.' Meredith's voice held a deceptive softness as he rubbed at the neck of the horse. 'Somehow or another he got his money all mixed up with mine. When I'd finished with him he just couldn't walk. When he's mended, which I figure will take some time, he'll pass the message about me one helluva sight better than any jail sentence could.'

Liam sagged under the trembling which shook his backside. 'I see how it is, sir.'

'Hope for your sake you can.' Meredith pushed hard against the lead-horse, skilfully easing the cart into the loading bay.

'Talking about money, I'll pay you fifty cents a day apiece, you get your keep, logs for the fire, oil for the lamps. There's always plenty vegetables and the like, plus you get a good sound cabin with four rooms and a kitchen.' He finished his labour and shouted for the yardmen to begin loading, then turned to face Liam. 'You settle for that?'

'I will, sir.'

'Right, give you a month's trial. Come up to scratch and you get to keep the job. Now away for your folks and I'll take you over to the place.'

Liam scurried from the yard, pleased at having landed work but fearful of Meredith as an employer. There had been hope of rich pickings when Meredith first mentioned the farm tenancy. But the cocksureness now fled before his intelligence, for there was no absentee English landlord here to rob and blarney ... only the certain promise of a swift and bloody end

140

if he moved so much as an inch from the straight and narrow. The scheme for fame and fortune, so carefully laid with the priest, continued to slide through his fingers like the very finest sand.

16

The overnight snowfall gave a cold luminosity to the morning darkness as the first faint rays of dawn vaguely fingered the horizon, and from somewhere far out in the estuary a navigation bell rang out its mournful warning. In defiant contrast the quayside of Ranelagh Harbour was alive with the bustle and urgency which accompanies the final minutes before a ship puts to sea, dockers and seamen labouring in the glow of blazing torches, their shadows thrown dancing long and crooked across the broad side of the flagship *Pelican*. Up on the quarterdeck Jonathan talked with Anstruther as they waited to cast off, but the conversation was stilted and a degree of embarrassment hung between the gaps of it.

'I know your disappointment, lad, but a year will pass quickly enough.' Anstruther's delivery was awkward, yet there had been no other way he could think of to broach the subject.

'I am sure you are right, Joseph.'

There was little conviction in Jonathan's voice as he watched the toiling seamen, his thoughts returning to the events of the month just past. This was hard fortune indeed, no ship to command and a twelve-month probation into the bargain. What a changed man his father had become of late... Poked and prodded like a sheep into mother's doing, and it was she who was responsible for the added burden of Charlotte. Damn it all, why could not women stay at home and leave the matter of business to men? Anstruther's voice interrupted his self-pity.

'What say now we buckle to and make you a master of

commerce?' Jonathan lifted his gaze from the quay to meet Anstruther's broad smile. 'What say then, lad? If only to confound your father.' Sudden memory came to Jonathan of the day he had first met Anstruther, no more than a raw youth, sent by his father to begin a seaman apprenticeship, wincing under the powerful grip of the man's handshake. They had been hard and demanding years, but he had come away from them master of his trade, and as a man. Now he was acting like a child. He blushed with shame as they shook hands.

'Forgive my sulking, Joseph. I have allowed my personal difficulties to cloud our long friendship.'

'Your father wants only that you should succeed in the business.'

'I shall do that, if only to put him about.' They laughed easily. 'Now, with your permission, Captain, I shall make the rounds and report on the ship's readiness for sea.'

'Permission granted, Mr Bramwell.'

Calling out the final orders for sailing, Jonathan strode from the quarterdeck. Anstruther carefully watched his progress along the lower decks, and the easy but firm way he dealt with the crew. He nodded in satisfaction. The lad was over the sulks and sound as a bell, and would in due course of time be a good master.

Eight hours out from the last sighting at Lizard Point the weather worsened considerably and within the chart cabin, Jonathan took a final reading of the glass as he pulled on his oilskin.

'Falling like a stone. I'm aloft to relieve Grant.'

Anstruther looked up from his study of the cargo manifest. 'We have much heavy machinery aboard. Engine parts, looms and the like . . . I had best take a look.'

'You think they may shift?'

'It's as well to make sure. You know where I shall be if you need me. If not, I will relieve you at eight bells.'

A wall of darkness ran the full stretch of the south-west

143

horizon, closing rapidly on the *Pelican* as Jonathan took over the watch, and within minutes the ship was ploughing through a heavy gale. A sudden feeling of elation welled in him as he felt the deck shudder beneath his feet and saw the waters crash over the bow to spume and swirl about the planking. There was escape for him here in this vast, grey waste of ocean, a world away from the nagging of scheming parents and the problem of Charlotte. He was at last in his element, and in this moment, the master of a great ship, taking on the more bearable hostility of a winter Atlantic. Yet insidiously, thoughts of Charlotte returned to harass and haunt him. Why could it not be as before, when they had been friends? Marriage between them would in all certainty grow to be empty and worthless. Had he not witnessed as much in so many arranged alliances? In an uneasiness of thought he moistened lips which had become dry, and tasted the bitter tang of salt upon his tongue.

Doubt came to replace his elation as the ship ran before the storm. They would be many leagues off-course before it blew itself out, yet there was nothing to be done for it, nothing. His thoughts wandered. Was he not so much like the ship? Did he not run in like manner, unable to face head-on the storm which raged in his mind? Sheet lightning flickered persistently about the rigging and darkened decks, its ghostly blue light playing across the faces of the helmsman and mate as they clung to the wheel. Irritably he wiped away the rain which dripped from his face.

It was unfair, this pressure on him to marry Charlotte, wrong of his mother and father to accuse him of dalliance and the compromising of her reputation, when all they desired was their own securement. How stupid he had been that day when he had ridden with her on the downs. Whatever had possessed him to offer hope of his yielding to the situation? He recalled how she had galloped away after hurling the words back at him, yet on the night before he sailed she had said she loved him.

Memory of that final hour with her now came to mock him. He had felt confusion and anxiety in what to say. But was there not a responsibility on him for the future of the company? The

144

rain lashed his face as an involuntary shout broke from him, 'Excuses! Bloody excuses!' The words were ripped away on the howling wind, but the shame persisted. He had not been forthright, vaguely hoping for some miracle in the way of other investment to save the day ... then for Christ Almighty's sake, why had he not said as much?

They were lifelong friends. She would surely have understood his predicament. Instead he had told her that they would talk more upon the subject when he returned from America. She had seemed content on that, but he saw again the pain in her eyes and knew the agony which lay ahead for them both.

His sweat of confusion became heightened by the tight constriction of the oilskins. With an oath he tore away the top buttons, shuddering as the freezing rain began to soak through into his vest. Surely to God there was finance available somewhere to ensure the company's future ... if not, he would have to decide between making the proposal that would please his parents and Charlotte, or end the relationship.

17

High Pines farm was a very different affair from the small estate in Ireland which the McAffertys had bled dry, and within the two weeks they had spent as working tenants there came a reluctant acceptance that there was no absentee landlord here to rob and make a fool of, for John Meredith was a most regular attender, a hard master to serve, and a man gifted with an experienced ear for tall tales of accountancy.

The farm commanded well over a hundred acres of land, on which the main crop was Indian maize for market; vegetables and the like went into Clarkstown for sale to the timbermill workers. The livestock was secondary, made up of a few cows, chickens and goats, intended for use by the tenants and fieldhands. All in all, High Pines represented backbreaking toil from dawn to dusk, six days a week and God give Sunday. The hands numbered around a dozen, mainly negroes who had somehow or another found their way up from the south. Chargehand Ben Ambrose referred to the rest as white trash, drifters out of Boston, and only imagination could figure where else. However, Liam's fists and well directed kicks produced more than a fair day's work from them all, and for something less than the allotted twenty-five cents, since he had already begun his payday extortion, yet there was not a body who would dream of educating John Meredith on the fact.

Mary had determined that her escape would be more carefully planned than the pitiful attempt she had made in Boston. To this end she encouraged the overtures of friendship from Ambrose's wife, Rebecca, a petite, half-breed woman, and in return for lessons given to their three children had received a number of cotton dresses, a coat and a stout pair of button-up boots. From time to time Ambrose had given her a few cents for the extra eggs she brought to their home, and she enjoyed the renewal of family company. Nevertheless she was wary of taking anyone into her confidence and revealed nothing of her personal misery or intention to flee.

It was closing on evening when Mary got back to the cabin following a day's teaching of the children, and first making sure there was no one about, she retrieved a rag bundle from beneath a flagstone. Pushing aside various pieces of clothing she emptied the contents of a purse on the scullery table, where a careful count made a total of thirty-five cents. She frowned at the small heap of coins. Little enough for such a journey as she now intended, but it would have to suffice. Donal grew better from illness with every day that passed, and only his exhaustion from work in the fields and her desperate struggles had so far kept him from her. But it could not last. A shudder of revulsion ran through her at the thought as she wrapped the coins tightly into a strip of paper to keep them soundless, then placed the bundle back under the stone. Detachedly, she mused on the fourteen days and nights which had passed since their arrival at the cabin.

Why had she not run from the quay on that first day? What a nonsense of mind. How far could she have travelled in such condition? Starving near to death and without coin to obtain a crust. No, she had done the right thing and would look passably presentable when she sought for work in Boston ... passably presentable? Her distorted reflection in the panes of the window denied the thought as gentle fingers examined the heavy bruising about her face. What matter? There was nothing to be done for it now.

She was suddenly aware of the growing darkness. They would soon be back from the fields and there must be no arousal of suspicion, all must look normal. Crossing to the range, where a low fire flickered beneath a cauldron of stew, she took a spill and lit the lamp. It was not long before she heard the bang of the door and clatter of boots across the stone slabs. She took a deep breath and remained silent within the scullery, listening as Patrick's voice sounded in protest.

'Jeez! 'Tis terrible hard work this place, dar. Will y' look at it! I have blisters the size of turnips.'

Then Liam, 'Patience, son, America is full of the money for a man wit' brains, an' we shall have our own place soon enough.'

Mary winced as Donal growled into the conversation.

'The sooner the better then, crowded here like hens in a pen.' Then Liam again.

'Sure I know what's bitin' you, boyo! Your love life is goin' down a bumpy old road, an' no mistake at all.'

She felt the heavy, brooding silence which followed. Better to take the stew in now before they fell to fighting and disrupted her plan.

Filthy, bearded and dishevelled, they lay sprawled about the table, and Liam glanced up at her as she ladled the meal on to tin plates. His manner was teasing.

'Y'have a face like sour stout, woman.' He winked at Patrick then taunted her once more. 'Why don't y'let the man have a bit of the pussy? Maybe then we would hear less of the shoutin' an' screamin'.'

'Y'are makin' me look the gossoon!' Donal's scream of protest brought an instant punch in the face from Patrick.

'Don't y'dare talk to our dar like that!'

'Calm yourself, Patrick, I'll take care of it.' Liam's voice was pitched low and menacing, but Donal took no heed of it.

'I have me bloody rights!' His voice faded as he saw the fist before his face.

Liam growled. 'Do y'see that?'

''Tis her y'should be wantin' t'thump.' But the protest was no more than a whine as he felt the fist crush hard against his mouth, making the already cracked lips split and bleed.

'I will ask y'just the once more ... do y'see that?'

'I see it, dar.' There was fear in his bowels as Liam glared at him.

'Right! Y'useless article. When y'next get the urge to shag the woman take her to the barn, or the fields, or any bloody where away from here ... I'm warnin' y'for the last time, if y'keep me awake one more night wit' your shenanigans I'll give you a hidin' y'll never forget!' He opened the fist into a flat hand, cracking it hard against the side of Donal's head to bring a soft whimper.

'I will do as y'say, dar.'

'I know it! Now get your damned supper, the lot of y', an' let that be an end to it.'

Mary had distanced herself to the far end of the table and watched in a horror of fascination as they tore into the meal. Plates quickly emptied, they grabbed at the stew-filled cauldron, and the division which had so recently existed between father and sons faded into animal equality as they fought like wild dogs over the bigger scraps of meat.

With the meal done all enmity became forgotten, and flurries of coarse laughter filled the cabin as they downed their home-made alcohol and discussed the sexual merits of the field women. Her gaze moved unobserved over them as she took in their degradation and filth, bodies stinking for want of water, hands almost black with the dirt of many days, beards matted in the juice of stew which showered upon the table with every raucous laugh. They were evil incarnate, and the priest who had delivered her into their hands, was he not the devil himself? Yet she no longer felt any great emotion, only regret that she had waited so long to make her escape.

18

The bedroom was austere. Rough wood planking served as floor, the many gaps in its uncovered surface inviting a plague of draughts which howled in soft mournfulness about the place and sustained the biting cold within. The deep blackness of night hung on the panes of one small window, situated at the end of the room, which was dominated by a brass bedstead. Mary stood fully dressed in the farmost corner, slim fingers tightly rolled into fists, her gaze fixed on Donal's every move as he kicked off his boots and breeches in the dim light of an oil lamp. He dragged a metal chamber pot from beneath the bed, grunting contentedly as he used it in noisy fashion, and she retched with the stench which crept over to wrap itself about her.

When they had arrived at High Pines she had begged Liam to allow her to sleep in the kitchen; instead he had damned her to the nightly encounters with this creature. But despite the many brutal beatings she had never shared his bed, choosing to sleep on the bare boards. His presence was just bearable at first, for he was still too weak from illness to overcome her fight, but over the past few nights he had grown stronger in effort.

The smell made her head swim, and defensively she tightened her fists. There must be no fainting nor giving way now, not on this final time she would ever be in his loathsome presence. He stood up and swayed drunkenly, looking somehow ridiculous in the rumpled folds of soiled long johns. The smell of him came again to make her gag.

'If you touch me you'll regret it!'

He looked at her without reply and scratched his backside as he weighed up the situation in his tired mind. The cow was set for bothermaking and his dar would be in to thump the head off him long before he could mount her... Holy Christ, she was a beauty though. He lowered a hand to caress the hardness beneath the long johns, and in his imagination felt himself slide within her as he had done on the ship... Jesus, but that was a long time past and he had the horn on him fit to burst. But it was not worth a beating. The maniac grin came and went... Sunday was only a day away. He would wait for her in the yard when she went to draw water from the pump, then drag her off into the barn. No one, not even his dar, would stop him. He grinned once more and without a backward glance clambered under the blankets and fell instantly into sleep.

Mary was brought awake by the numbing cold which precedes first light. Immediately alert, she got up from the board floor and listened to Donal's steady snoring. It was time to go. Now, and quickly, before he stirred. For pity's sake, where had she put the boots? Searching fingers closed on them ... thank God. But her heart beat so fiercely he must hear it at any moment. She took a deep breath to clear the mixture of fear and excitement, and with a painful slowness began to pick her way barefoot to the door. She was alongside the bed when one of the boots slipped from her grasp and fell to rattle the boards. Donal snorted and turned in sleep to face her, but there was no other movement from him.

Yet she could not move, as in a bad dream when pursued by monsters, unable to turn from the man and flee, limbs heavy in leaden disobedience to the scream within her mind. In spasm, she dug the broken fingernails into her bruised face, and the agony of it brought her to sense. Mechanically she picked up the boot and was gone from the bedroom within seconds. She left the cabin with nothing other than the clothes she wore, fearful of the noise she would make in raising the flagstone to obtain her bundle and the few cents in the purse. It did not matter, nothing mattered other than getting far away from the horror of the McAffertys, never to see them again. Softly she closed the latch and slipped on the boots then ran towards the dirt road which led to Boston. There was nothing surer than that they would try to hunt her down. But no matter what trials or pain she might yet have to endure, there would be no going back.

It was breaking day as Mary struggled up the wooded bank and clambered out on to a broad, timbered road. Far below in the valley, about five miles distant, she made out the smudged buildings of Clarkstown and a sob of frustration broke from her, for she had hoped to be much further away before full daylight. Anxiously she glanced up and down the road which led from the high timber line. It would make for easier walking but invited the danger of meeting up with loggers, who must soon be starting work.

She took in the formidable heights of the alternative route before deciding on the road which more gently skirted the mountain. It was slow going but the sun grew warmer, and the morning chorus of birdsong brought a smile to her bruised face. She felt a sudden, painful longing for her father and mother. How she wished them to be with her now. The thought and smile went as suddenly as they had come. Wishing and praying counted for nothing. There would be no more foolishness, this track beneath her feet was the only reality. It would take her to Boston and freedom more ably than wishes and prayers.

The neighing of horses and heavy rumble of a waggon drifted through the trees, causing her to stop and look for means of leaving the road, but there was no escape. On the one side was an almost vertical climb, on the other a sharp decline to the valley floor. A calm determination came upon her. If it were them, she would fight and die here on the road rather than go back. Head erect, she waited as the waggon approached and pulled up alongside her in a cloud of billowing dust. Praise be, it was not them, just a lone man about his

152

business. Shielding her eyes against the sun she looked up at him and decided to brave it out.

'Good morning, Mister. It is a fine day we have.'

He touched the brim of his broad floppy hat. 'Good day to you, Mrs McAfferty, you're up and about early.'

She swayed under the wave of shock. How did the man know her name? Had they sent him to bring her back?

'Ma'am, you seem not to know me.'

'Indeed I do not.'

She was aware of the shaking in her voice.

'Let me remedy that. I'm John Meredith, I own the farm you tenant.'

The strength ebbed from her, and she sank slowly to her knees. It was true, then. They had sent him, and he was now merely playing with her as a cat would with a mouse. Meredith jumped down from the waggon, concern in his voice.

'Hey now, you alright?' He knelt beside her, and for the first time saw the heavy bruising. 'You're hurt bad! How did you come by such injuries?'

She must not tell him the truth.

'I fell down, sir.'

'Not in this world you didn't.'

She must get away from him. 'I was without care and fell.'

'Ma'am, I've been around the lumber yards long enough to know a fist-beating when I see it. Now suppose you tell me who did it? An' how come you're alone? Don't you know there's bear and wildcat up here?'

They had not sent him at all then. She trembled in relief.

'I thank you for your concern, Mr Meredith, but I have much t'do an' must get to Boston.'

He was plainly surprised. 'Boston? Do you know how far that is, for goodness' sake? Thirty miles overland, and I reckon the way you are, one mile would be one too many.'

She did not reply, a weariness overcoming her under the burden of questioning. Why could he not leave her alone and be on his way? Impatient at being disturbed from their routine the horses snorted and stamped, hauling-chains jangling about them as their flanks quivered under the irritation of a swarm of flies. Meredith had been on his way up to the timber line and was not sure what his next move should now be, but whatever, he could not leave her here.

Devil take it, just when he seemed to have chosen hardworking tenants who wouldn't give him trouble. Well, plain enough to see there was trouble here. What in hell was the woman doing so far from the cabin? And who had given her such a beating? Only one thing made sense of it.

'You're running away ... isn't that the truth of it?'

Despite her fatigue, the reply was spirited. 'Indeed it is not! I am on my way to visit friends.' She saw the disbelief in his eyes.

'Mrs McAfferty, you don't even know the way to Boston.'

There was a pleading note in her voice. 'Please, sir, put me on the right road then an' leave me to make my way.'

His expression tightened in resolve. 'Sorry, but I just can't frame to do that, you're all in. I'm taking you to Mrs Meredith. She'll 'tend to your face, then we'll see.'

She sank once more to the road, almost all fight gone. Meredith's powerful arms closed gently about her, and with one hoist she was lifted into the waggon, where he carefully arranged sacking under her head. She wanted so much to sleep, and be done with it all, but the vital spark of resistance still burned.

'Please, Mr Meredith, please let me go. I do not want to be trouble to anyone.'

His smile held genuine admiration. 'You're a real fighter, little lady, an' no mistake.' Climbing into the driving seat, he released the brake and glanced back. 'You'll be fine when you've had food an' rest.' With a crack of the reins, Meredith turned the team about and thought over the encounter as he headed the waggon back to Clarkstown.

During the short time the McAffertys had held sway at the farm crop production had improved, and the last thing he wanted to do was disturb that trend. There was no doubting Liam McAfferty was a good farmer, but for all that, undeniably brutal in his ways with the fieldhands. They feared and respected the man for good reason. Was he at the back of this trouble with the woman? Had she been thieving or playing around? Meredith flicked the reins hard in agitation. He had a position to hold in Clarkstown, and come election time next month tales of women being beaten up on his property would do him no good at all. The woman's injuries were pretty heavy, and if Liam had done the inflicting, chances were he'd do it again and who knows where it would end?

Meredith frowned. He might not be able to get the truth from her, but for sure his wife would, and as the waggon rumbled on he contented himself in that thought. Bright rays of sunlight pierced the overhanging trees to dapple gentle, moving patterns across Mary's face, but in her mind was the nagging realisation that yet another attempt to escape the McAffertys had come to naught. Yet she was too tired to think any more, and soon the steady sway of the waggon lulled her into the velvet of sleep.

'What is it, John? Has there been an accident?'

Meredith lifted Mary, still sleeping, from the waggon. 'Calm yourself, Agnes, this is Mrs McAfferty from off the farm, found her way up on the timber road, needs medication, taking her indoors.'

Carrying Mary as if she were light as thistledown, he strode away across an expanse of paved yard towards an impressive colonial-style house, its white stucco walls and small-paned windows reflecting the hard morning light. Hampered with her heavy skirt, Agnes Meredith tried to keep pace with him as he climbed the broad verandah steps and passed through the open door. He paused.

'Needs to be in bed a while, which one will I put her in?'

Breathing heavily, face flushed with indignation, she approached him. 'A bed? Have you gone out of your mind, John? If the woman is hurt, why did you not take her to the doctor?' The accent was Boston, high-class and educated.

'Couldn't do that, Agnes. I need you to talk to her.'

'You are not making sense, John. Now will you please tell me what all this is about?'

'I will, when you tell me what bedroom she can go in... I

155

can't carry her around forever.' With a snort of impatience, Agnes swept away over the thick, scarlet carpeting of the living room.

'Daisy is off today, you can use that bed, but I do not want tenant-women anywhere near Braganza a moment longer than necessary!'

Meredith smiled broadly as he followed her up the staircase... Braganza! The name she had given to the house never failed to amuse him. Where she'd got it from he could only wonder, probably one of those European books she always had her nose into. But hell, she was nowhere near as stuffy and high-faluting as she made out, and he adored the woman.

Underneath the hard shell was a very warm-blooded lady, and passionate, as he knew, and sympathetic. He wouldn't change her for the world, and now as she opened the door to the maid's room he knew he needed her wise counsel. Carefully, he laid Mary on top of the bed. With a sigh of concern, Agnes looked at the bruised face and blackened eyes.

'Why, she's no more than a girl, poor little thing, and so thin. However did she come by such injuries?'

Meredith eased the muddy boots from Mary's badly cut and bleeding feet. 'Agnes, that's what I want you to help me find out.'

'Did she not give you any explanation when you found her?'

'Said she'd had a fall, but I've a feeling she was beat-up by Liam or that creature she's married to. My bet is she was running away for some reason or another.'

'This man she's married to, I don't recall him.'

'Name of Donal, McAfferty's youngest boy. Moody, insolent fella. Never liked him from the moment I clapped eyes ... a real bad hat, if I ever saw one.'

'Leave it to me, John, I'll get the truth of it when she wakens.'

'I'm counting on it, Agnes. We've had enough trouble with High Pines already. Thought we had settled tenants this time. Take care though, she could have been thieving from them, or playing around, even.' The chimes of the clock filtered up from the living room to startle him into movement.

156

'I'm late for the timber run. Say nothing to the McAffertys if they come nosing around, I'll need to get their side of it before we send her back. See you around noon.'

He was gone, leaving Agnes to her musings. No matter what the girl had done she had not deserved this, and whoever was responsible should be punished. She walked thoughtfully from the bedroom, and there was no doubting her look of determination.

19

Stripped to the waist, Liam and Patrick shivered in the dawn breeze as they washed sparingly in the pump trough. Patrick rubbed himself dry with a cotton shirt, then pulled it over his shoulders, where it lay steaming from the heat of his body.

'Did y'sleep well, dar?'

'An' about time.'

A sudden, unearthly howl made them turn about to face the cabin, where Donal came stumbling from the doorway. Wild-eyed he ran towards them, babbling without sense or reason.

'Have y'gone stark ravin' mad?' Liam grabbed at him as he started to run towards the road, but Donal struggled to free himself.

'The bloody bitch has run off!'

'Get hold of y'self, man!'

'I'm tellin' y' ... she's run off.'

'Have y'searched the place?'

'I did! I am away t'find her!'

'You? Find her? Y'could not find your prick in y'r drawers!' The flat of Liam's hand landed with stunning force. Donal snivelled and rubbed his aching jaw.

'She has made me look the eejut.'

'Y'need no help in that direction!'

Patrick had discreetly stood some yards away during the short altercation. 'Shall I go after her, dar?'

'No y'won't. I will do that, an' God help it when I find her.'

Donal freed himself as Liam's grip relaxed. 'Will I come with y', dar?'

'Shut y'r friggin' mouth! Our livin' is hangin' on this place. We would be thrown out on to the road if the man knew, scourin' the land for a runaway woman. Off t'the fields wit' Patrick, an' y'd best work bloody hard, for y'will have t'make up for me.' Grabbing his shirt off the trough, he strode away across the fields, cursing with every step of the way.

Mary awoke, and her mind raced in anxiety to make sense. How had she come to be in this place? In this bed? The subtle smell of lavender brought some calmness, and she became more aware of her surroundings. It surely could be nothing to do with the McAffertys. Her eyes moved slowly over the ceiling of the small room and down the patterned wallpaper, then on to a shimmering haze of freshly cut spring flowers, nestling in a tall vase atop a pine dressing table. Patterned curtains framed a little window which admitted strong sunlight, and she felt the warmth of it upon her face.

She lifted her head to take in more of her surroundings. A large black cat lay sprawled in a cane chair, and at Mary's sudden movement it stopped its washing to regard her through hazel-green eyes. Wearily she sank back into the comforting warmth of the bed, to become aware of the nightdress and the strong smell of ointment about her face. Her heart missed a beat as she saw the woman standing in the doorway.

Tall and straight-backed, dark hair piled-high above a tanned face, the woman smiled reassuringly, a kind expression in the dark blue eyes as she advanced into the room.

'You are awake, then?'

Mary cowered back into the pillows as Agnes Meredith walked over to the bed.

'There is no cause to be afraid, nothing will harm you here.'

Mary clutched tightly on the sheets around her chin. Had this woman come to take her back to the McAffertys?

Agnes saw the terror which held the girl. The approach must be made with great care if the truth were to be obtained. 'You look much better. How do you feel?'

Mary did not reply, her gaze fixed on the open door, sure

159

that Donal would appear through it at any moment, and this woman would deliver her up to him.

Agnes guessed the thoughts. 'There is no one in the house but us, nor shall I allow anyone to intrude upon our talk. I want you to believe that ... will you?'

Mary felt a little more assured, but still on guard as she nodded assent, only her eyes showing above the raised sheets.

'Good, for I want us to be friends, and the first step to that is knowing each other's name. I am Mrs Meredith, it was my husband who found you on Timber Road and...'

The interruption was almost inaudible. 'I must go now. I have people to visit.' Agnes rode smoothly over it.

'Yes, my dear, later when you feel stronger.'

Mary thought on her next move. The woman might be sympathetic now, but in the end she would summon the McAffertys to take her back.

'You are most kind, Mrs Meredith. But I must go now. I would be obliged for my clothes an' boots, please.'

Agnes was surprised at the articulate delivery. She had supposed herself to be dealing with a simple, peasant girl, but there was no such person here. So much the better for it then, now she would be able to conduct her questioning at a more intelligent level. Mary pulled away the covers and stepped from the bed, but her legs buckled and the room seemed to spin about her. Weakly, she fell back on the bed.

'I regret my nuisance to you, Mrs Meredith.'

'What nonsense, you are not well.' Agnes tucked in the covers. 'Is that more comfortable?'

'Thank you, I will be more able in a while.'

'You need something warm to eat. There is chicken soup ready prepared. Will you have some?'

Mary shook her head. 'I am not hungry, but thank you for your kindness.'

'Later then, you will need to eat if you are to get better.'

Mary did not reply, her thoughts concentrated on how best she could get away from the house.

Agnes regarded her with renewed interest. There was undoubtedly good breeding in the girl; the proud set of the

160

mouth, and intelligent, wide green eyes. She was also very beautiful; even the bruising could not hide that. In what circumstances then had she come upon such lowlife company as the McAffertys?

'Will you tell me your name?'

Mary closed her eyes. Why did not the woman leave her in peace? But she would not, and the questioning would go on until she was satisfied. Better to get it done with, then leave when she was gone.

Her eyes slowly opened, and Agnes felt slightly uncomfortable under the unblinking gaze. 'Mary ... my given name is Mary.'

'Did you go to school in Ireland, Mary?'

'My father was the schoolteacher. He taught me.' She was taken by a sudden fear. This woman might not be friendly at all. She had most probably already sent for Liam and was now simply distracting her attention as she awaited their arrival.

'I am much better now.' She tried to contain the panic. 'Please give me my clothes and boots, an' I will no longer trouble you.'

Agnes felt the unease. 'Calm yourself, child, you are safe here. Whom do you fear so? Have you done wrong? Taken something which did not belong to you?'

'Is that what they have told y'then? That I am a thief?'

'I have not spoken to anyone other than Mr Meredith. I wish only to find out why you are running away.'

''Tis they who are thieves, an' worse. Sooner I would die than go back to them.'

'Do you mean Liam McAfferty?'

Mary's mouth twisted in hatred. 'I mean all of them.'

'What of your husband?'

'Husband? He will never be that. I hate the creature!'

'Was it he who beat you?'

Mary could not bring herself to give words in answer. Instead she gave the ghost of a nod, then closed her eyes to force back the tears. Agnes paused. The girl was exhausted.

'You must eat. I will bring the soup, and afterwards you can tell me the how and why of it.'

161

Agnes had sat by the bedside for a full hour, offering no interruption as Mary recounted her meeting with the priest and the horror of all that had happened since leaving Ireland. But Meredith's reaction to the story was not at all what she had expected.

'If she's telling the truth, then it sounds like the girl's been through hell. But how do we know she's not lying?'

'John, I believe she is telling the truth. We surely cannot let her go back there.'

'Well, we can't keep her here.'

'We must, John. If she goes back they will surely beat her for trying to run away. Maybe even injure the girl, or worse. Then where would you be?'

'I'll go talk with McAfferty, get his side of it. Then we'll see what's best to do.'

'Take care then. You have told me the man is cunning.'

'I can handle him. But we don't know the truth of it yet. Can't go blundering between man an' wife without good reason. Now I have to get the barnhands started on the afternoon work. We'll talk about it later.' He had gone before she could say another word.

20

Liam stood on the ridgeway which overlooked the Meredith homestead and took in a deep breath of the still air. His short, stocky legs ached from the climb out of Clarkstown and his mood was sullen. He had spent the morning hours searching for Mary among the fields and back roads, then the town, before deciding to approach Meredith. The man would surely have noted his absence by now, and there was need to conjure up a tale to suit the occasion. But Liam did not relish such an encounter. What tale would it be then? The man was not stupid, he would see through any lies. Best tell him the truth, or near to it as he could. Why not say there had been a family squabble and that she had just up and left? Yes, that was it. Tell him he was near worried from his mind, wanting to find her and bring her home to the safe bosom of her husband's care, for it had been nothing but a small misunderstanding.

Christ, but he would give her a thrashing when he had her alone. The bloody bitch she was to give him this trouble. Yet did he not need her for the times which lay ahead? Having a schoolteacher's daughter in the family was a great notion and had already earned its salt. Without her, there would have been neither shelter nor work. Picking his way down the slope, he made for the homestead.

Liam's expression was uncertain as he walked up to face Agnes. She had followed his approach across the fields and was already waiting for him on the verandah.

163

They had met only briefly when the McAffertys took over the tenancy of High Pines. The meeting had been cursory, Meredith effecting the distant introduction as she sat with him in the carriage during a round of property inspection. But she remembered the face well enough.

'Whom do you seek?'

Liam framed apology as he touched his forehead. 'Good day t'you, ma'am, sorry t'be the trouble, I'm McAfferty from over the farm, an' I...'

'I know who you are. What do you want?'

'I am after speakin' wit' Mr Meredith, if he's home.'

'On what business?'

'If y'please, ma'am, I'm wantin' the words wit' him to ease my troubled head.'

'You are ill then, Mr McAfferty?'

'Ill, ma'am? Me? Not at all! Sure, I've never been sick a day in my life.'

'But you say you have a troubled head.'

'Family squabbles, ma'am, as himself will likely as not tell y'later. Would I not dearly love rather t'have the same sweet path through life as the cut of the plough through the good earth. But as God knows, ma'am, 'tis not often the way of it.'

'Mr Meredith is in the barn. You had best go find him.'

'Thank y' right kindly, ma'am.' He touched his forehead then trudged away to disappear into the darkness of the barn. Agnes shuddered at the encounter. There was an evil about the man.

Meredith was saddling up a horse as Liam came into the barn.

'You've saved me a journey, McAfferty.'

'Good day t'you, sir, I'm desperate sorry not t'be in the fields, sir, but I'm sore in need of the guidance.'

'Don't beat about the bush, McAfferty, I'm a busy man.'

''Tis the girl, sir, she's up an' gone. I was wonderin', sir, if I could be spared the rest of the day t'find her. I will work Sunday to make it up, sir.'

'Up and gone? What does that mean?'

164

'Well, sir, I'm of the mind she's run away … women are queer cattle, sir.'

'What do you suppose made her want to do that, McAfferty?'

''Tis a powerful mystery t'me, sir. Does she not have every mortal thing a woman could ask for? A roof over her head, an' the food in her belly.'

Meredith carefully cinched the reins round the pommel of the saddle.

'Know what I think, McAfferty?' Menace had entered his voice and Liam's blood chilled at it.

'No sir, that I don't.'

'I think you take me for a fool.'

Liam blustered, 'Not me, sir! I would sooner chop off my right arm so I would, it's the truth of…'

'McAfferty, you are a natural-born liar. I found the girl up along Timber Road at first light.'

'The saints be praised for it, sir, an' God bless…'

'You lying weasel! Interrupt me once more and I'll have you tarred an' feathered and ridden out of town on a rail.' Liam lowered his gaze to the barn floor. 'McAfferty, you are one helluva lucky man you're not in jail… Christ, her face is bad enough, but Mrs Meredith says the girl is black and blue all over her body. Was it you did the beating?'

Head down, Liam sweated in terror.

'No sir, I swear t'was not me, sir.'

'I don't hold with beating women, it's the work of a coward and bully. If you want to keep the hide on your back you'd best tell me who did it.'

Liam swallowed deeply as he looked up to meet Meredith's anger. There was to be no hiding the matter with any fancy tales here.

''Twas my son, Donal, sir.'

'That the one married to the girl?'

'It is, sir.'

'Why would he want to beat her?'

'She is not settled t'bein' a wife, sir.'

'That's it all? Nothing else? Thieving or the like?'

'The truth of it, sir.'

Meredith looked hard and long at him. 'It had best be so, or you're in big trouble. I can promise you that much.' Liam wisely remained silent. 'McAfferty, you're a slippery enough fella, but you're a hard worker, and you've done middling well on the farm. Do you want to keep the job?'

Liam's eyes filled with sudden hope.

'I do indeed, sir!'

Meredith paused for a few moments. He would much rather have rid himself of them all. But harvest time was not far off.

'Right, I've just now talked with Mrs Meredith. She's for keeping the girl here 'til she's better, then we'll see.'

Liam writhed at the statement. He would lose face with his sons and the fieldhands when he returned without her. But at least they were not to be thrown out, and she must be returned to them in a while. He would tell them it had been at the cost of much hard bargaining.

Meredith kicked gently at the straw which littered the floor, the boot swinging back and forth like a clock pendulum as the words came with slow consideration. 'I've a mind to take a chance on you this once, McAfferty, but you'll have to get your house in order, show who's the boss-man ... else if you don't you'll all end up being thrown clear out of Clarkstown. Now get back out there and give the boy a bloody good hiding.'

'I will make him see the way of it, sir, an' thank y'right kindly, sir.'

'It's not over yet, fella. If you're lying to me I'll find out. Now get to hell out of here and back to work!'

With a touch to the forehead, Liam crabbed away, seething at the indignity. Jesus Holy Christ, but he would make Donal pay for this day.

166

21

The sun's morning promise had disappeared behind a lowering sky and a dense fog crept down from the nearby hills, already choking the horizons of the maize workings. Stretched out in a slowly moving line the fieldhands hacked out the weeds, their odd bursts of conversation muffled in the still air.

'Dar will find her, bring her back! You'll see!' Donal's wild shout brought no reaction from the men, but Patrick lifted his hoe in a threatening gesture.

'Shut y'r mouth! Y've given us trouble enough wit' the woman.'

''Tis her caused the bother!'

'Dar's missed a day's work through y'. If Meredith gets t'know there'll be a right old ruckus, an' you'll be for it, boyo!'

Donal gave a sullen look and began thrashing once more at the weeds. Patrick glanced briefly away over the field to check the progress of the fieldhands, and in the same instance saw Liam bearing down on them. 'God help you now.'

Donal blinked in a sudden fear. 'What is it?'

'Dar's comin' an' he has the divvil on his back.'

There was a rigidity about Liam, the quick, impatient strides kicking up small clouds of dust in his rapid approach. He came to a halt in front of Donal, head going back like a snake about to strike.

'Y'bloody, useless article! Am I not scarlet wit' the shame an' you the blame of it!'

Cowering almost to the ground, Donal whined in terror.

167

'Don't be hittin' me, dar, 'tis her the blame. An' am I not workin' the arse offen me t'please you?'

'How dare y' open y'r mouth when I'm speakin', y'spineless pig? Not t'blame is it?'

Donal whined again. 'I'm sorry, dar.'

Liam had recovered his breath, but lost none of his rage. 'I'll tell y'what y've done! Y'have got us within an ace of bein' tarred an' feathered, an' thrown out on the road.'

With considerable bravery Patrick tried to ease the situation. 'Did y'find her, dar?'

Liam did not take his gaze from Donal. 'I did right enough. The bloody woman is at the Meredith house.'

'How was she there, dar?'

Liam blinked wildly in his fury. 'Y'r man found her on the run is how.' An oddly wistful appeal entered his voice. 'He shamed me, Patrick … shamed me, 'tis a miracle I was able t'keep the roof over our heads.'

'You were always a powerful man wit' the words, dar.'

Donal looked witheringly at his brother, jealous of the fact that Patrick could talk so freely with their father, while he was never allowed to state grievance. Foolishly, he could contain himself no longer, and thinking the issue closed, stood up and mockingly confronted Patrick.

'Cluck, cluck, cluck! Aren't you the white hen's chicken? Never takin' a wrong turn in the road, suckin' up to dar, an' me told t'keep quiet. Me, who wants only the rights of it.'

Before Patrick could reply, Liam had Donal by the neck, choking off further speech. 'Your rights, is it? I'll give you rights!' He indicated the nearby plough. 'Patrick, get cord an' tie him t'that.'

Patrick hesitated. 'Can y'not forgive him, dar?'

The plea was sincere, but Liam had moved from fury to cold resolve. 'Do as I tell y', son, an' do it now … or so help me, I'll beat the both of you senseless.'

Reluctantly, Patrick lifted a length of baling cord from his breeches pocket and took hold of Donal. The fight was pathetically short and within a half-minute Donal lay tied and spreadeagled, face down across the plough. Liam's smile was tight. 'Patrick, y'are a good son, an' I thank God for it.'

Donal listened in hate and gritted his teeth in silent preparation for the onslaught to come. The fog had closed in to create a small arena about them, and it was as if the rest of the world did not exist. Almost lost to view, the fieldhands stopped work and stood nervously unsure of what to do as Liam unshackled the broad leather belt from round his trousers. 'Stop work an' get over here! Now!' Obediently, they shambled forward to form an untidy circle around the plough.

'This is my son!' Liam pointed at Donal. 'He has brought shame on the house of McAfferty.' Squaring off the brass buckle, he lifted the belt and whirled it in whooshing circles above his head as he cried out, 'If I can do this t'my own flesh an' blood, I c'n do it t'you a thousand times over. Don't ever give me cause!'

Without further preamble he swung about in full fury to bring the buckle of the belt whistling down on Donal's back. The agonised screams echoed eerily off the fog as the buckle fell again and again on to its target, cutting the thin shirt into ribbons and leaving furrows of blood in its wake.

The fieldhands watched in satisfaction. Their boss-man, who robbed them every payday, and his goddamned sons, likely as not to kick the shit out of them at the drop of a hat, had fallen out. Hallelujah to it then, and saints be praised. With head bowed, Patrick stared away into the fog, wincing with every blow that fell on his brother's back. Donal was unconscious long before the violent act of madness was spent. And when it was done, Liam walked away without a word, only one thought consuming him. The humiliation which his son had brought on the name of McAfferty had been well purged.

22

The *Pelican* wallowed in a flat calm, the currents gently pulling her north by west on an ocean almost smooth as glass. In the near distance, stretching west to east as far as the eye could see, a bank of fog towered hundreds of feet into the silent sky. Jonathan had just left the cabin to relieve Anstruther's watch, and now stood beside him on the quarterdeck.

'What do you make of it, Joseph?'

'Not good, Jonathan, not good at all.'

'How long before it is on us?'

'At the rate it's coming, less than five minutes. Let us hope the drags will hold us until it clears.'

'We ride it out, then?'

'Aye, and pray.'

'I am not good at praying, Joseph.' He smiled. 'But there is hot cocoa below and I am ready to take over the watch.'

'No, Jonathan, we will stay it together, at least a while.'

'As you wish, sir. What is our position?'

'I have been unable to take a sighting since noon.' Anstruther pulled a pocket watch from his sea-jacket. 'It is now just after four. I had hoped for sight of the mainland an hour ago.'

'But we had not reckoned on this.'

'No, it is down from the Grand Banks.' He frowned. 'Never known it be so far south this late in the year.'

'The drags will hold us until it passes.'

'I trust so, but the drift has been steady for some time. This is a treacherous coastline.' As he spoke the fog closed about the ship, swallowing it up in a grey darkness, and visibility was down to a few yards. The drift had been insidiously faster than

170

Anstruther had reckoned, and the *Pelican* was off course, well to the north of Boston. Now, less than a hundred yards away lay the mile-long rock archipelago known locally as the Blackstone Edge.

Jonathan peered through the gloom. 'With your permission, Joseph, I should go to the for'ard watch.' Anstruther nodded assent.

'Aye, urge the rest to keep eyes an' ears open. Tell them to call loud if they see or hear anything ... anything at all.'

Jonathan made his way for'ard, shouting encouragement to the crew on watch at the rails. A sudden cry made him halt.

'Rocks! I can see rocks!'

'Where away?'

'Port! Midships!'

'I hear it, Jonathan!' Anstruther was calm in his order.

'Hard o'starboard.'

'Hard o'starboard it is, sir!' The helmsman frantically spun the wheel over, and the aft end of the ship moved slowly to port as the sound of sea on rocks came clearly. Jonathan scrambled back towards the quarterdeck. 'We are going abaft on to the rocks, Joseph!'

'Stay with the wheel, I'll see for myself.'

Visibility was down to little more than a yard as Anstruther arrived at the rail and peered out into grey darkness. The *Pelican* hit the rocks stern-on, the force of collision swinging her bow in compensation to heel the ship in a steep angle. Taken by surprise, Anstruther lost his grip on the rail, his cry muffled in the roar of splintering timbers as he went head first to the Blackstone.

'Man overboard! Man overboard!' The shouts brought Jonathan running from the quarterdeck to where ropes had been lowered.

'Who is it, Grant?'

The mate's face was ashen with shock. 'It's the master, sir!'

A numbed disbelief hit Jonathan. 'Are you sure?'

'I saw him go over!'

'What action have you taken?'

'I have lowered Wilkins and...'

171

Jonathan turned away and ran to the rail as seamen hauled Wilkins back on board. 'What do you report?' The man grabbed for breath.

'Nothing there, sir ... I fear the captain is gone.'

'It cannot be!' Jonathan shook in a rage of despair then leaned out over the rail. 'Joseph! Answer me, Joseph!' But his wild repeated shouts were deadened to impotence against the wall of fog. The crew stood in silence. Most had sailed with Anstruther over many years, but if they felt emotion they were impassive in it, concerned only with their own safety. They had a new master, the owner's son. How would he prove to be? And why was he not giving orders to abandon ship before they all followed Anstruther to the ocean bottom?

Jonathan grabbed up the discarded rope and lashed it expertly about his shoulders.

'Grant, lower me over the side. I shall find him.'

A loud murmur of disapproval came from the crew and Grant was quick to join it. 'We may go down any moment! You should give the order to abandon ship, without delay.' Some of the crew were already moving to the longboats.

'Do you dare to invite mutiny by questioning my order?' Jonathan's voice was pitched quietly away from the crew's hearing. 'If you disobey me, I shall have you hanged in the first harbour we chance upon.'

With a scowl, Grant turned away to one of the seamen. 'Johnson, smartly now, help me with the master!'

In the second before he was lowered, Jonathan thumped Grant in the chest. It was not a hard blow, but contained meaning. 'God help you if the crew are not full assembled upon the deck when I return!'

The sea was numbingly cold, and Jonathan went waist-deep before his feet found purchase. Through a gap in the drifting fog he saw the rising mass of the Blackstone directly above him and waded towards it. This was where Joseph had gone over. Perhaps he had crawled higher. A dangerous quarter-hour was spent clambering about the rocks in a fruitless, shouting search, before Jonathan returned to his starting point. In frustration he looked into the greyness where the keel hid below a dark sea, and instinct told him that Anstruther lay somewhere below. For one mad moment he felt the urge to dive under the keel and find him. But reason prevailed. It was too late for a grand gesture.

For the first time he became aware of the biting cold. He shivered violently, blaming himself for his friend's death and the loss of the ship. Savagely he tugged on the rope in signal to be brought back aboard. Sat huddled together for warmth, the crew looked at their new captain with sullen reproach as he was hauled back aboard by Wilkins. Grant stood up, mouthing an oath. 'Thank Christ! Maybe now the stupid young bugger will give the order to abandon ship.'

'Get on your damned feet!' They were not prepared for the sudden command, but heard the threat in it and quickly obeyed. A fury took Jonathan as he heard the murmurs of discontent. His father had been right. Familiarity did indeed bring contempt. Very well, he would show them the obverse side of the coin.

Grant hurried forward. 'You find him, sir?'

'Are you imbecile as well as coward?' Jonathan gripped the man's sea jersey about the throat. 'Would he not be with me now if I had found him?'

Grant hung unmoving in the tight hold as he looked into the rage of Jonathan's eyes. 'I am sorry, sir, I thought that...'

Jonathan released his grip and pushed Grant roughly away. 'Line up the crew! Then stand with them!' Like a caged tiger he paced up and down the deck while Grant hurriedly assembled the seamen into disciplined lines.

Some moments passed before Jonathan spoke, but when he did the words came to wound. 'Surely you must all die of shame at your conduct!' One by one their heads lowered under his penetrating stare. 'You are not seamen, but old women afraid of your own shadows!'

His voice shook with rare passion. 'Not for one instant did any one of you think of your captain ... that he might be lying injured on the rocks!' His tone changed to one of cold scathing. 'Instead you wanted to flee your ship like rats, thinking only of your own worthless skins, and to hell with the master.'

He looked pointedly at the first mate. 'Mr Grant, I shall note in the log that your attempt at immediate search was worthless, sir! A dereliction of duty, unbecoming of an officer!' Grant quivered under the lash but remained silent. 'Had you pursued the rescue more thoroughly within that first minute we might well have found Mr Anstruther. But now he is dead!'

A heavy silence followed the outburst, only the gentle lap of the sea against the ship's side daring to disturb it. His tone was calmer when he resumed, but had lost none of its edge. 'If your search had been less perfunctory, Mr Grant, you would also have found there is no immediate danger of sinking.' He brought a hand cracking down against his side, causing Grant to flinch.

'We are tight wedged on the rocks, sir, and only the most violent storm will alter that situation.' His voice rose again. 'Does that not make you feel stupid, Mr Grant?'

The reply was shaky. 'I regret I was in error, sir.'

Jonathan nodded. 'You were indeed, sir.' His anger receded under the awareness of his new office and immediate responsibilities. But he must finally make them all aware of his command. 'Circumstances have made me your captain, and I will be obeyed. So mark my words well, for I shall not repeat them.'

He walked slowly along the ranks, never missing a man's eye. 'In the past I have tried to deal with you as comrades. I regret I was gravely wrong in such conduct. Now I give you but one golden promise.' He paused in stride. 'If any man should step the slightest from duty at this time of great danger I shall have that man flogged in such manner that he will never forget to his dying day. Do I make myself understood?' There was an immediate murmur of acquiescence.

He turned away to the first mate. 'The situation is plain, Mr Grant. We are not able to lower the boats, but cannot be far from the mainland. Start firing distress rockets, and repeat at one-minute intervals.'

174

23

Mary started from sleep and called out in a sudden panic as Agnes Meredith entered the bedroom, 'Have they come for me?'

Agnes walked over to the window, meaning to close the drapes, but instead looked out at the growing darkness. 'The weather is worsening by the minute. I have never before seen such a fog.'

Mary lifted her head from the pillows. 'Was it Liam McAfferty?'

Agnes did not move her gaze from the window. 'He was sent away.'

'I thought it would not be Donal, he has not the courage.' Wearily, she sank back. 'They will try again. I must leave before they do.' Too tired to pursue the issue she drifted back into uneasy sleep, her long black curls in a tumble about the pillows, slim fingers stretched out across the pink coverlet.

Agnes regarded the sleeping girl. What innocence there was in the beautiful face. But there was no doubting the stubbornness and fight there. Josie would have been about the same age, had she lived. Agnes sighed. What a long and lonely time she had spent in this backwoods place.

Her thoughts went to when she had first met Meredith. He had come to Boston in an attempt to raise capital for his venture into the timber business. She was eighteen, had recently finished college, and courtesy of her father's influence worked as a junior clerk at the bank which Meredith had approached for a loan. Five years her senior, he was nevertheless largely unsophisticated and wide-eyed on his first ever visit to the big city.

175

She had been impressed with his determination and ambition to make something of himself, and during his week-long stay in Boston they saw a great deal of each other. On the evening he was due to return home he had proposed marriage, and they were wed in Clarkstown within a month of their meeting. But the whirlwind romance did not go down well with many of the townsfolk, opinion being that Meredith should have chosen a local girl rather than bring a city woman into their midst. Her outspokenness on many issues affecting the town had tended to further isolate her from the women, but the more enlightened of the leading males held her in great respect. Meredith was a considerate husband yet was ignorant of a woman's special needs, and Agnes missed the intimacy of talk with other women.

The arrival of Mary had stirred her dormant maternal instincts and, despite the first feelings of caution and reserve, she was now enjoying the unexpected role of foster mother. Yet she knew that the circumstances surrounding the girl's arrival were bound to bring trouble. There was a volatile Irish faction in the town and they would not take kindly to one of their own being held against the wishes of a family.

Her thoughts were interrupted as Mary awoke. 'Sorry, ma'am. I did not mean t'doze off when you were talkin'.' Her voice was huskily soft with sleep.

Agnes dismissed the apology. 'I was not speaking, rather thinking. Tell me, what is your age, my dear?'

Mary sat up. 'I shall be nineteen on the ninth of April, ma'am.'

Agnes smiled at the precise delivery. 'Will you now? That is not far away.'

Shyly, Mary returned the smile, but it went as quickly as it had appeared. 'Mrs Meredith . . .' She sought for the right words. 'The McAffertys are evil, cunning people, an' will bring great danger on this house. I must leave first thing in the morning.'

The reply was scornful. 'Liam McAfferty is a bully, that is all. Now stop making speeches. You are to stay here.'

Mary gave a shake of the head. 'I know how it will be. They

will wear down Mr Meredith an' he will send me back, for he must keep the peace. Sure, he has business t'care for an' I will not be allowed to get in the way of it.'

'Nonsense, and in any case after what you have told me I would never agree to it.'

Mary had grown unused to kindness. 'Mrs Meredith, I am given t'wonder ... why are y'doin' this for me?'

Agnes had not expected such directness. Why indeed? Was it simple conscience? Or that she was childless and almost fifty? 'Anyone would have done the same.' But she knew it was not so.

'Ma'am, I doubt they would. The McAffertys are the devil made flesh, an' most able t'bring the great misfortune down on any who stand in their way.'

Agnes smiled. 'This is not Ireland, child. They hold no sway here, and I am quite capable of handling them.' Mary noted that the woman had not once mentioned Meredith's attitude, but spoke only of her own.

'I must not be the cause of bad feelin' between husband an' wife. Mr Meredith cannot be happy with it.'

Agnes chuckled at Mary's vehemence. 'Now and again it does no harm to test a husband's love and mettle in a stride over the bigger hurdles.'

But Mary was not placated. 'You are desperate kind, ma'am, but I will go anyway.'

The reply was firm. 'I have told you what I intend. You are safe here for the meanwhile, let that be an end to it.'

A dull glow suddenly illuminated the window then grew stronger before fading away. Mary became agitated. Had the McAffertys come back and set fire to the house? 'What is it?' The glow came again to reflect redly off the fog and light up the room.

'Oh my God!' Agnes made rapidly for the door. 'Those are rockets, there's a ship in trouble.'

'What will y'do?'

'I must help with blankets and hot soup.'

'Please, let me come with you, I dare not stay here alone. They will come, I know it!'

177

Agnes stopped at the doorway and saw the look of fear. 'I would not put it past them.' She was troubled. 'But I must go, it will be expected of me.'

'Please, ma'am, please let me go with you.'

Agnes hesitated. 'Do you feel well enough?'

'I am not sick!'

'Very well, I will get you a warm coat and shawl. But you are to stay indoors when we get there. Do you understand me now?'

Relief flooded over Mary. 'I will do as you say.'

She dressed quickly, alive with excitement. There was a ship out there, maybe it was from Ireland and there would be good people on it with better news of the old country.

The fog had brought the working day to an early finish, and Murphy's bar on Main Street was full of drinkers. Liam sat with Patrick and Donal at a centre table. He had downed a deal of drink and was in loud voice. 'Nothin' beats a glass of porter, eh, Patrick?' He winked. 'I think y'r brother is still sulkin'.'

Donal glowered. 'My back is broke.'

Liam banged his glass on the table. 'Y'got what y'deserved! 'Twill do y'good t'be without wife for a while.'

'An' when is she after comin' back?'

'When the man Meredith says, an' not a single minute sooner.'

''Tis not right, not right at all!'

'Is it another beatin' you're after?' Donal looked sullenly into his beer glass. The pain was still with him and he must not invite more.

'Hey, McAfferty! For Chrissakes hold it down, we're tryin' t'play cards here!' The shout came from a nearby table where one of the town's leading lights, Bert Johnson, was playing poker. The room went expectantly quiet, and all eyes were on Liam.

'This is family business y'r buttin' into, Johnson!' Liam's tone promised there would be no retreat, but Johnson could not back off with half the town as witness.

178

'Is that a fact now? Well this is a saloon, McAfferty, we come here t'get away from family matters. For Chrissakes! Folk can hear you clear out on the boardwalk!'

Primed with drink, Liam jutted out his jaw in threat. 'Bein' a grand fella on the city council gives y'no right t'boss me, Johnson!'

A gruff interruption came from one of the other poker players. 'You have a big mouth, McAfferty.' David Sullivan ran a boat-building company in the town and was normally a quiet man. 'What Johnson says goes for all of us. Keep it down!' He turned away. 'Let's get on with the game. Whose deal is it?'

Liam's face darkened at being dismissed in such fashion. 'Y'bastard, Sullivan! Y'strut aroun' the town like you're God Almighty, an all y'are is nothin'!'

Sullivan turned from the game. 'McAfferty, you're like a damned horse-fly ... you want swatting.'

Liam clambered up, swaying drunkenly. 'On your feet, Sullivan!' Patrick and Donal rose silently behind him, fists clenched. The occupants of the poker table exchanged glances, then without a word stood up from the table. Sullivan was about to roll up his sleeves when the saloon door burst wide open and a young boy fell headlong into the bar, knocking over a chair in his wild panic.

'Mr Sullivan! ... I need to find Mr Sullivan!'

'Over here, Peter! What ails you, boy?'

'My dad sent me runnin', sir, there's a ship in trouble off the Blackstone!'

Sullivan raised his arms for quiet in the ensuing uproar. 'I need six men, only the strongest of you now! It's a long pull to the Edge. I'm away to the yard, get there quick as you can.' He left on the run.

Now ignored, Liam gulped down his drink as pandemonium broke out. 'Lucky for him or I'd have broken his skull!' He grinned in triumph. 'Get more drinks in, Patrick. We shall make a real night of it now.'

A vast crowd stood in the harbour yard as the evening darkness formed alliance with the swirling fog, the yellow light from Mulligan's dining rooms adding a ghostly atmosphere as it spilled out over the wet cobblestones. Having done her stint in preparation for the survivors, Agnes had allowed Mary to accompany her to the harbour but was already uncomfortable in that decision. News of Mary having run away from the McAffertys would already be abroad in the town, and it was not wise to aggravate the situation.

'Keep close by me, and if you see anything of the McAffertys say nothing.' Fearfully, Mary looked about the crowd. They might be out there somewhere, maybe even now watching her every movement.

Delayed by arrears of work at the lumber mill, Meredith was not happy in finding that he had arrived too late to man the rescue boat. He could have used the glory to some effect within the forthcoming re-election of officials. It was a mood exacerbated when he eventually located Agnes and saw that she had allowed Mary to leave the house. But before they could exchange words a wild roar of cheering broke across the harbour yard. Two cutters packed with seamen had emerged from the gloom and, amidst more cheers, Sullivan and his crewmen began helping them ashore.

Agnes called out excitedly, 'God bless you, David!'

He grinned his delight and waved. 'Agnes, John, we have them safe!'

Meredith waved back. 'Good work, David ... sorry I was too late to join you.'

Agnes interrupted, 'We have hot soup at Mulligan's, bring the poor creatures over.'

Her attention switched to Meredith. 'John, I know what you think, but I had no choice. The girl could not be left alone.'

He nodded in brief acknowledgement. 'We shall discuss it later.' But he was more concerned at having missed the glory. 'I had better do my duty and welcome these people ashore.'

'Very well, but it would be better to wait for them indoors.'

Concerned at his disappointment, and unwittingly careless

of Mary in this moment, she took Meredith by the arm and led the way to Mulligan's. The crowd surged noisily behind, urging the survivors forward, and Mary became cut off from Agnes. Calmly, she waited until the shouting, milling throng had passed to leave the yard in silence. She was about to follow when she became aware of a man standing near the harbour steps, head bowed, hands together in an attitude of prayer.

Curiosity filled her. Why did he not immediately join the others? The fog which eddied about him lifted slightly and she was able to make out the gold braid of his uniform. He must be off the ship. Such a grand-looking fellow, yet there was a lost look about him which tinged her with compassion. Should she not go over to greet him? He had been left quite alone and maybe would not know the way. She might also ask if the ship had come from Ireland. But while she hesitated he had already begun to walk towards the dining rooms and the moment had gone. Not wishing to startle him, she remained perfectly still as he passed within a few yards of her, and an odd disappointment stabbed as he disappeared into the fog.

There came the faint click of a door being opened, a burst of voices, the creak of hinges, then silence. Thoughtfully, she lifted the hem of her dress clear of the wet cobbles and walked slowly to where the lights shone from Mulligan's.

The dining rooms were warm and alive with chatter. A large fire of logs burned in the open grate while the smell of tobacco smoke vied with the more delicate aroma of chicken broth as a bonneted group of women served food to the seamen. Jonathan sat alone in a far corner, face pale with shock, his mind in a misery at losing his friend and mentor. A bowl of soup lay before him on the table, untouched.

Mary entered quietly and unnoticed, standing near the door as she tried to catch sight of Agnes, but the room was filled with people. She raised up on tiptoe for a better view, then started in recognition. It was the man who had been in prayer on the quay. How drawn and pale he looked ... but so handsome, the long waves of sun-bleached hair in boyish disarray about his face. Yet he looked desperate lonely, set apart from the others. It was a feeling she knew well and she

181

was drawn to him in his misery. Then suddenly he was looking directly at her.

A fierce blush burned her face and in confusion she averted her gaze, falling back awkwardly to her heels as she glanced about in the opposite direction. Part of her mind told her that she was looking for Agnes, but another denied it, for all she could see was his face. Agnes blurred into vision. 'Mary! I have searched all over for you.' The tone scolded. 'Come with me directly. I need more help with the serving of food. These poor men are starving.'

Agnes prompted her to where steaming dishes lay on wooden tables, yet with every step Mary felt a desire to turn and look back to see if he still watched after her. But dutifully she picked up a knife and began cutting thick slices of bread.

Meredith and Sullivan, who were touring the room to chat with the seamen, stopped at Jonathan's table. 'Your soup grows cold, Captain.'

Jonathan stood and attempted a smile. 'I apologise for my bad manners, gentlemen, but I am without appetite.'

'Don't worry yourself. I can figure how it is ... the name's John Meredith, peace officer and leader of the town council.'

'My compliments, sir. Bramwell ... Jonathan Bramwell.' They shook hands as Meredith nodded towards Sullivan.

'You two will have met up already.'

'Indeed we have.' Jonathan had been impressed by the swift efficiency of Sullivan during the rescue. 'Sir, I am most deeply in your debt.'

There was modesty in Sullivan's reply. 'I am glad I was able. A master should not have to suffer such misfortune.'

'Forgive me, Mr Sullivan. I should have explained at once. I did not command the ship.' They looked at him enquiringly. 'I am indeed a master, but on this voyage I was first officer to Captain Anstruther. I regret he was lost overboard when we struck the rocks.' Murmurs of condolence came from both men, then Meredith smiled in sympathy.

'Maybe you and your men would appreciate us holding a service for Mr Anstruther, next Sunday. Saint Andrew's is a fine little church, and a man should not go unmarked to his grave.'

'You are most generous and thoughtful, sir.'

'Good, just you leave it all in my hands now.' Meredith was nothing if not first a politician. He had been late for the rescue, but he would save face in the town with a church service.

Sullivan looked thoughtful. 'I have an idea, Captain.' Picking up two plates from the table he lodged the soup bowl between, locking the plates in shallow angle. He smiled at Jonathan's quizzical look. 'Don't worry, I haven't gone crazy.' He tapped the soup bowl. 'Say this is your ship, the plates are the Blackstone ... what has happened is the ship has lodged herself on the flat plates of the Edge. Some repairs at low water, and I reckon we just might ease her off on the tide, and back to the yard for a proper going over... What do you say to that?'

The offer took Jonathan by surprise. 'Is it possible you could work such a miracle?'

Sullivan grinned. 'Only God works miracles, Captain, but now and again I try to give Him a hand ... would you like me to attempt it?'

Jonathan tried to answer, but could not find immediate words. The *Pelican* was the very first ship of the line, and his father had sailed her over most of the world's oceans. She had seemed lost, but now she might be saved and he could yet sail her home to Southampton. It was difficult to grasp at such a fantastic possibility.

'Mr Sullivan. I am unable to give proper words to my thoughts, but when we came ashore I heard a lady cry out a blessing upon you, and I cannot better it.'

Sullivan was a modest man, not used to compliments, and there was an awkwardness about him. He shrugged his shoulders. 'We'll see.' He chuckled. 'By the way, the lady you speak of was Agnes, John's wife. She made the soup you're not eating!'

Meredith joined in the ensuing laughter. 'You could be in real trouble for that, Captain!'

Agnes glanced up from her work. 'It sounds as if they are having a high old time over there.'

Mary intended only a brief glance, but she was held by the

183

change in Jonathan's face. How young he now looked. His laughter filled her with warmth, and the room seemed alive with colour. She wanted to laugh out loud, and suddenly the feeling bubbled from her in a joyous, infectious ripple, causing Agnes to join in. 'There must be brandy in the soup!'

Jonathan looked towards the sound of merriment, and again his eyes met with Mary's. How very beautiful she was, and what warmth of feeling there was about her expression. The laughter faded and for long moments they were locked in wondering gaze at each other. Somewhere in the room a plate fell to the floor, and the spell was broken. Blushing furiously, she turned away and began stacking the dishes, unable to understand her feelings. Agnes was speaking, but Mary was unaware of it. Then again, more sharply, 'Mary, are you ready?'

'Ready?'

'You are in another world. Ready for home!'

'Oh yes ... yes, I am ready.' Absentmindedly she pulled the shawl about her shoulders as Agnes spoke again.

'We must let Mr Meredith know we are going. If I am not mistaken, the man with him must be the captain of that poor ship ... my, but he is a handsome fellow!'

Mary was thrown into confusion at the prospect. 'Oh no! I cannot ... I will bide here, ma'am.'

'What nonsense!'

Agnes took her tightly by the hand, steering a swift course between the tables to arrive in a rustle of skirts. Mary felt her face burn with shyness as she looked up at Jonathan. He was so tall. She had never before seen anyone so tall. His eyes were blue, then ... blue as the sea, and so tender in their look upon her. Her heart began to beat faster, and she barely heard Meredith speak.

'Captain, my wife, Agnes ... Agnes, this young man is Captain Bramwell.'

With reluctance, Jonathan moved his attention from Mary to meet a smile of sympathy from Agnes.

'Captain, I am sorry on the occasion which brings you to us, but most glad to meet you.'

'Mrs Meredith, the pleasure is mine.' He gave a slight bow

184

before returning his gaze to Mary. God in heaven, but she was the most beautiful woman he had ever seen ... and such eyes, so green and compelling. His gentle gaze dwelt on the bruising about her face. It did not diminish her true beauty, but what had caused such a state? It seemed to Mary an eternity before he spoke.

'And this elegant young lady is your daughter, so like her mother.'

Agnes cut across Meredith's attempted reply.

'How charming of you, Captain Bramwell. But I am afraid not. This is Mary, she is staying with us for a while.'

He felt foolish at his presumption. 'I am sorry, do please forgive me, Mrs Meredith.' Not allowing time for reply, he turned once more to Mary. 'Will you also forgive me ... Mary?' His voice was caring, and she thrilled at hearing him speak her name.

'There is nothing t'forgive, sir.'

Discreetly, she lowered her eyes, unable to hold his look any longer. There was a short embarrassed silence, broken by Agnes.

'We must leave you now, gentlemen.' She took Mary by the hand. 'There has been quite enough excitement for one day, and you will wish to discuss arrangements of accommodation.'

Jonathan watched after Mary until she and Agnes had left the room. Even then his look was intent on the door, almost as if he expected her to return.

'Shall we resume, Captain?' Meredith's question was weighted with admonishment. Broken from trance, Jonathan slowly turned and faced his hosts. There was a roguish look on Sullivan's face.

'At least you got to be introduced, Captain. Maybe I will be as lucky next time.'

But Jonathan failed to appreciate the humour.

'My apologies, gentlemen, I was distracted ... Mary is a most charming and beautiful young lady.'

Meredith frowned. 'Take care on what you say, Captain. The girl is married.'

A profound disappointment swept over Jonathan, and he was unable to think clearly as Meredith continued.

'There's the matter of housing your crew. I have a large cabin near my house, plenty of room, furnished. As for yourself, I am sure that my wife would want you to be our personal guest.'

'Thank you, Mr Meredith, I appreciate what you do for us.' Yet Jonathan's tone was distant, his thoughts still with Mary. If she indeed had a husband, why was he not here to escort her in such perilous circumstances? And what of the marks of injury on her face? They had been caused by fists. He had been in too many fights to doubt it.

'We should be moving off, Captain.' Meredith's flat tone irritated Jonathan. He felt suddenly exhausted, and his reply came wearily.

'Very well, sir, I shall assemble the crew.'

24

After breakfast on the morning following the shipwreck, Mary was asked by Agnes to attend her in the study. A coal fire burned newly in the grate and the evocative smell of books greeted Mary's entry, bringing an acute memory of her father and the years she had spent under his teaching. Nostalgia swept over her but fear was the stronger emotion.

'Please, they have not come for me?' If it were so, she would not go gently.

'Of course not. Nor would they dare.'

Agnes indicated a writing desk bearing pen, ink and paper. 'You tell me you can write. I want you to put something down of your home and family.' She nodded in reassurance at Mary's puzzled look. 'It is with your wellbeing in mind ... do you feel able to do as I ask?'

'I will try, ma'am.'

'Good, now make yourself comfortable at the desk.' Her smile was brief. 'As I recall, an examiner at one's shoulder is not conducive to a writer's best work. I shall return in an hour or so.' She bustled from the study, leaving Mary in a whirl of mind. Why had she been asked to write of her home and family? Was it merely to find out if she had been lying about her ability? Indignation met the thought, and with a flourish of temper, Mary pulled a sheet of paper from the neat stack. She would show this woman. But uncertainty came as she regarded the pristine whiteness of the parchment, and her fingers moved over it to smooth out the wrinkles which were not there.

How would her hand behave within this agitation? Round

and clear as her father had taught? Or a scrawl, with ink blots to further disfigure it? Despite the misgivings, she felt a thrill of anticipation as her fingers closed about the pen. This must be the best work she had ever done.

An hour passed before Agnes returned to the study and began to read the finished work. Mary sat patiently awaiting the verdict, now and again searching Agnes's face for reaction, but there was none evident. She began to fidget and her attention wandered to the mantelshelf where a marble clock sombrely ticked away slow minutes. In competition, the faint moan of a foghorn invaded the room, its compelling note dragging her gaze to the window, where the fog clung like a ghostly apparition against the panes.

Was it really only yesterday that the ship had come to grief? It seemed longer. He was a handsome man, the captain, so charming and considerate. She felt the heat of the blush on her cheeks, but delighted in it and again saw his face, heard his laughter. Such gentle eyes for a man, and his smile was shy. But he had not been the slightest put about when corrected on his mistake. Her expression softened at the remembered words. 'And this is your daughter, how like her charming mother.' He had asked forgiveness, her forgiveness also. How polite and correct he was, and with a manliness about him she had never before experienced. From which land had he sailed? Where was he bound before the ship-wreck?

'You have a good hand, Mary.' She jumped at Agnes's voice. 'How refreshing to see such correctness in spelling.' Agnes placed the sheets of paper on the writing desk. 'I am most impressed.'

Mary was still half in daydream, not wanting to be brought so sharply back to reality. The desk seemed large, and her companion distant.

'You are kind, ma'am, but it has been a while since I last put pen t'paper. I was not sure of myself.'

'I understand. Well, you have certainly passed my little test with flying colours. How do you fare at ciphering?'

It had been a test, then. But for what reason?

'I am able to do division, an' more.' Her answer held a tone of query, but Agnes ignored it.

'That is good. What of the rest of your education?'

'My father taught me much of history an' geography.' She could no longer contain her curiosity. 'Ma'am, why do y'want to know these things?'

Agnes rose thoughtfully from her chair and crossed to the fireplace, where she took up a poker to nudge the slumbering cobbles into blazing life. 'There, that's much better. It gets chilly, do you not agree, my dear?'

'It does, ma'am.'

Was the delay in explanation caused by something too fearful to tell? She was illegally in this country, and maybe the Boston official people were asking about her. Running from the fever quarantine and all. Was that why she had been asked to write about her home? So that she might be sent back to Ireland?

'Mr Meredith and I have given a great deal of thought to your future.' Agnes stowed away the poker and slowly walked over to Mary.

'We believe what you have told us and, if it is against your will, you should not return to the McAffertys.'

They were not for sending her back then. The relief was almost choking. Yet Liam would not give up as easily as that, and what chance would she or they have if he arrived to claim her? Surely none. Her gaze went again to the window. She must not wait upon the moment but flee the place this very day under cover of the fog.

It was as if Agnes had read her thoughts. 'However, before I explain what I have in mind I must have your promise that you will not try to run away again.'

Mary shivered with apprehension. 'I am in great fear they will come t'get me...' Her voice trembled to a stop at the touch of Agnes's hand on her shoulder.

'They shall not. My dear, I do understand your fears after what you have suffered at their hands, but I must have your promise.'

Mary hesitated, uncertain of what to say. How could she give

189

such a promise? But perhaps the test had been for employ-ment, for a wage. She could save money then later make her own way if things should go badly. 'You would not let them take me?'

'You have my word.'

Mary considered her choices only briefly. How far would she get if she did choose this time to escape? She had not a penny in her pocket, and at least it would not harm to hear the woman out.

'Very well, ma'am. I will not run away.'

'Good, for I think I have found a way from your troubles. I have a friend in Boston who may be able to place you as a governess. Would you agree to accept such a position?'

'A governess, ma'am?' She was shaken by the offer. 'I should be more fitted a maid in such a great city.'

Her modesty made Agnes smile. 'Nonsense, all you lack is confidence, and we shall soon cure that.'

It was more than Mary had ever dared imagine. She did not doubt her ability to teach, but as Agnes had said, she was lacking in confidence. 'I am not sure on it, ma'am ... you truly think me able?'

Agnes pointed to the written pages which lay on the desk. 'My dear young lady, your ability is plainly there to see, and I have never been more sure of anything. You will make a fine governess.'

The words brought sudden elation to Mary. She must take this chance, and in the doing free herself from the McAffertys. Impulsively, she reached out and touched Agnes.

'I know not how t'properly thank you for your kindness, Mrs Meredith ... but I will try desperate hard in the work an' shall never bring you shame.'

Agnes clasped Mary's hand in comfort. 'I am sure of that, my dear, but keep in mind that nothing is yet certain. Leave me now, I must write the letter without delay.'

During the next few days the fog retreated north, giving way to warm spring weather, and within a week of its going the Blackstone surrendered the *Pelican* to Sullivan's expert use of winch and pontoon. The ship now stood dry-berthed under

190

repair in Clarkstown harbour, with the expectation that she would be ready for sea within a month. In the meantime the crew had been housed on the Meredith estate, and in return for lodgings, plus a small wage, worked variously in the forest and lumber mill.

Jonathan had accepted Meredith's invitation to become a personal guest of the family, and journeyed daily from the house to work long hours helping with repairs on the ship. During his first days at Braganza he sometimes chanced upon Mary but their conversations were limited, his early departures and late homecomings denying other than the mundane. Yet even such brief encounters were eagerly anticipated and soon happened by design rather than chance, for the couple grew daily more attracted to each other.

Their rendezvous were innocent enough in intent, yet in other circumstances both might well have considered their conduct indiscreet. He was a trusted guest, and although Mary did not care to recognise the fact, she was nonetheless married and only in this house under duress. Servants are invariably the first to note anything even slightly untoward within a household, and the early morning trysts had not escaped notice. Yet all Mary now knew or cared about was that in Jonathan's presence she felt newly alive, her doubts and fears melting away like the late spring snow before the sun.

25

It was Sunday morning, marking the sixth day since the sending of the letter to Boston and, as on previous days, Mary watched from her bedroom window for sight of the mail coach. At first she had waited in the realisation that it was too soon to expect reply. But now almost a week had passed, surely enough time for response. Yet did she now want it ever to happen?

During the past few days a delicious limbo had settled upon her, and she feared to be drawn from it. Her mind wandered as she fondly recalled the snatched meetings with Jonathan, upon the stairway, in the hall, at the door, and then remembered the emptiness within her each time he left for the ship. How then would she feel when it was repaired and ready for sea? Her fingers whitened in their grip on the curtains ... he would surely sail away and a boundless distance come between them ... never again to look upon his face or hear his voice.

A strange weakness filled her as she saw the coach ease into view over the ridge and begin its rapid descent into the valley. It would be here directly, the letter opened and she packed away to Boston within hours. Not daring to move, she looked down on the foam-flecked horses as they raced towards the house at full gallop, the coach almost lost in the dust kicked up by their flying hooves, heard the driver's shout and the crack of his whip, then her own sigh of relief as the blurred impression disappeared down the trail.

Slowly she released her grip on the curtains. Maybe the grand people in Boston did not want an Irish peasant girl as governess and would never send for her. But what then? And for how long would the Merediths continue to tolerate her presence in this house? If the appointment were to be offered, then she must accept it, any other course would be futile. As in a dream she began to dress.

Jonathan was taking a mid-morning stroll through the yard when he saw Mary collecting eggs in the chicken sheds. He stopped and leaned inside the door, watching her at work. How beautiful she was, and how gently she went about her task.

'May I help?'

She turned quickly, blushing scarlet as she saw his tall figure dwarfing the doorway. Her fingers relaxed their hold on the basket, and a number of eggs tumbled to the straw-littered floor.

'I am sorry, I did not mean to startle you.' He stepped into the shed and bent to inspect the damage, his hair falling softly about his face, causing a sudden longing in her to reach out and brush it from his eyes.

'Not a one broken! I hope they will not prove as hard in the eating.' There was a boyish good humour in his eyes as he straightened up, and she was unable to break her gaze from him. But the challenging crow of a cockerel which had strutted in to investigate made them both jump, and their spontaneous laughter melted the moment.

'I am glad to see you, Captain.'

'And I to see you.'

She was aware of the feeling in his words. But a sudden imp in her mind made her answer cool, even though she felt otherwise. 'Mrs Meredith bid me find you. She has invited you to the midday meal ... it being Sunday an' all.'

'Oh. I see.' He was disappointed at having mistaken the meaning of her greeting. 'May I ask if you will be there?'

Coquettishly, she smiled. 'I shall.'

He smiled in return and gave a little bow. 'Then I should be honoured.'

She began to gather eggs from the nest boxes, feeling remorse at allowing the imp. 'Y'will please to excuse me, but I must finish my work.'

He moved purposefully alongside her. 'I have delayed you in that task, therefore I must make amends.' A thrill ran through her as his hands brushed against hers in the straw. But in a sweet agony of shyness and reserve she moved to the next box, yet his touch still lingered on her, and the warmth of the shed and the soft clucking of the hens held together the gossamer thread of intimacy.

From time to time he glanced at her as they worked, and thought on their previous meetings. They had seemed to be so full of words, but in fact nothing of any personal moment had been discussed.

'I have just returned from morning service at Saint Andrew's. The whole town seemed to be there. I thought to see you.'

She frowned. 'Y'would not.'

He had been about to say that the service was for Anstruther. But there was a flatness in her tone which made him change the subject.

'Mrs Meredith tells me she is from Boston. Are you also from there?'

'No, I am newly from Ireland.' Her eyes became wide and enquiring. 'I have been wonderin' ... is your ship from Ireland?' She felt wrong at having asked. He might think it none of her business.

'No, I have never done other than sail past it on my way to the Americas. A great pity I think, for I am given to believe it is most beautiful.'

She was aware of the meaning in his words, but her reply was calm. 'It is so.'

With affected care he placed an egg in the basket. 'The ship is out of Southampton. We were bound for Boston until encountering the fog. Thank God, at least she can be repaired.' He moved closer. Reluctantly she edged away.

'Have y'always been a sailor?'

His eyes shone with mischief. 'No, I was once a highwayman with a great black horse and silver pistols and held up coaches

194

... your gold or your life!' Her laughter made his senses swim, and suddenly he wanted to hold her. To kiss her.

She smiled up at him. 'An' is that how you got the money to buy the grand ship?'

She was agonisingly close, the scent of her hair about his mouth, in his throat, the deep green of her eyes drowning his senses. He must keep control of himself or she would fly from him.

'Once I robbed a Duchess, and made away with gold enough to buy a thousand ships.' He said it in the manner of a theatre villain, hoping to make her laugh again, and she responded to his play-acting.

'I know what happened then ... y'became sorry an' took back the gold, she wed you in reward and y'became the Grand Duke!'

They laughed and exchanged shy glances of enjoyment in the making of their story.

'You are almost right. She did beg of me to become the Grand Duke, but I refused.' His expression grew serious as he looked again into her eyes. 'And in this moment I am glad of it ... I am not married.' The image of Charlotte's face flashed into mind, only to be as instantly dismissed. Mary felt a breathless joy at his words. He was without wife, then.

'When did you become a sailor?'

'When I left my school. I was sixteen, and went to sea the very next day.'

'An' now you are a captain, sailing all the oceans of the world.' A wistful look came and went. 'Do y'like being a captain?'

He shrugged. 'I have not had time to think on it, for I have only now taken command, and that by ill-fortune.'

'I am sorry about your friend. Mrs Meredith told me of what happened.' She paused. 'Sometimes it makes a soul feel better to talk. If y'wish, I will listen.' He saw in her eyes the willingness to share his sorrow.

'His name was Joseph Anstruther. I sailed with him from being a boy, and he taught me all I know about the sea ... I already miss him very much.'

195

Mary sighed in sympathy. 'I know the way of it, for I have not long lost my dear parents.'

'My thoughts are with you in that loss … may I ask how you fare now?'

Her reply was resigned. 'I fare well enough.'

'You are married, I believe?'

'I regret that is so.' There was a harshness in her answer that made him wish he had not asked the question.

Yet how else could he learn of this man and the circumstances which plainly caused her so much pain? 'I fear my questions bring you distress.'

She went quietly about her work. 'Y'do not cause me distress.'

He wanted to ask about the cause of the bruising to her face, but did not dare.

'I, in my turn, would listen.'

'And what would y'have me say?'

'That which comes from your heart.'

'My heart has no part of it. I am given t'understand it is a common enough tale … a woman given in arranged marriage.'

'You do not care for him?'

'I do not!' The fury in her denial made his heart beat faster.

'Is your husband here with you?'

'Please not t'call him husband, for I do not see him as such.'

'Forgive me.'

'There is nothing t'forgive. He is not with me, but lives with his father and brother at High Pines.'

'Where is that?'

'Some miles from here. It is a farm belongin' to Mr Meredith, they are tenants, an' work the land.'

'Will you return there?'

'I shall never return.' He felt delight at her words, but before he could reply she was already moving towards the door.

'I must go now, or Mrs Meredith will think me lost.'

He took the basket from her, and in that rare beauty of mind where new love begins to take its first tentative steps, they left the shed and made towards the house. But their going was not without notice. Unseen by either, Ben Ambrose stood watching from the shadow of the barn. The High Pines foreman had ridden the cart over for provisions, and now searched Mary's expression as she chatted animatedly with Jonathan.

The couple disappeared into the house, and Ambrose's look became one of calculation, for during his comings and goings he had heard snatches of gossip from the servants and stable hands. Now he had seen it with his own eyes. The English captain and Donal's wife were indeed getting closer to each other than was seemly. Ambrose scratched reflectively at the heavy stubble on his chin as he thought on the matter. Had to be worth at least a silver dollar from the wronged husband.

Justification for such treachery sat easily in his mind. To hell with her. Hadn't she done him down anyways? Skedaddling off from the teaching of his kids, just when they were starting up to read and write. He climbed to the driving seat of the laden waggon and with a loud click of tongue against tobacco-stained teeth headed the team out of the yard and on to the road for High Pines.

There was an air of pleasant feeling in the table chatter, yet Meredith held a certain reserve about him as he carved the joint of beef. He had lately become aware of the gossip and now saw the increasing closeness between Mary and Jonathan.

If it were allowed to blossom, more complications would develop, and he had enough to contend with already. It had to be nipped in the bud carefully, however. With the carving completed he passed around the meat-filled plates. 'You must be a happy man Captain, your ship off the Blackstone.'

'I am, Mr Meredith. It is little short of a miracle.' Unaware of her husband's observations, Agnes joined the conversation as the move for vegetables ensued.

'I have heard the good news, Captain, how long will the repairs take to complete?'

'David thinks it will be about five weeks.'

'He is a sound man, you can rely on him.' Meredith spoke

between mouthfuls. 'You've let your people know of the progress?'

'Yes, by the steam packet from Boston. David had one of his men take my letter. I expect to hear from my father by return.'

Meredith was gratified. 'Good. I've no doubt he'll want the ship back lickety-split.'

Agnes reproved him. 'John! I think Mr Bramwell would be more in joy at his son's deliverance than getting a ship back.'

He brushed away the reproval. 'That goes without saying, Agnes, but I'm sure he'll want to see both back, soon as possible.' His glance went pointedly to Mary, then returned to Jonathan. 'Wouldn't you say so, Captain?'

'I am sure you are right, sir.'

Mary watched Jonathan with growing fondness. How polite and manly he was under the badgering. She had become unused to such good manners. A delight filled her and a shy smile formed on recalling his jest when the eggs had fallen from the basket.

'Not a one broken! I hope they will not prove so hard in the eating.' She wanted to reach out and take his hand, to be alone with him and talk of many things. Suddenly aware that Meredith's eyes were on her, she blushed deeply. Every secret thought must have been mirrored on her face, and he had plainly read her expressions as he might an open book.

Meredith stood up, the scrape of his chair cutting into her thoughts. 'If you'll all excuse me I have visits to attend, but please don't disturb yourselves.' His smile was amiable enough, but she was conscious of the edge to his voice. 'A fine meal, Agnes, I shall be back around seven.'

Mary felt only slightly more composed when he had gone. Her presence in this house was not that of an invited guest, but one brought about by unsavoury circumstance. She was nothing more than a runaway, both from the law and the McAffertys. Meredith would only tolerate her as long as she caused him no further trouble. He was kind enough, and well-meaning, but his personal standing in the town was shadowed by her being at Braganza, and she sensed that he awaited the letter from Boston with eagerness.

Her train of thought was interrupted by Jonathan. 'A meal fit for a king, Mrs Meredith, and I thank you for inviting me to join such pleasant company, the better to enjoy it.'

'My pleasure, Captain.' Agnes basked in the praise, for she had grown fond of his presence in the house and the gentlemanly breeding which he brought with it. 'I hope you will find the time to join us more regularly in future.'

He smiled. 'Indeed I shall try, Mrs Meredith, and thank you once more.' He paused. 'I wonder if you would allow me to return the compliment by inviting you both to look over the ship?' There was mischievous appeal in his eyes as he glanced at Mary. 'I thought you curious enough to see what I obtained with the Duchess's gold.'

Meredith's unspoken warning came to her mind but was dismissed on the instant, and she looked in silent appeal to Agnes, who smiled assent. 'What a wonderful thought. We should adore to see the ship.'

26

The sound of hammering came from the far side of the ship as Mary and Jonathan stood near the gangplank while Agnes chatted nearby with Sullivan. Mary looked up at the bow and read aloud the name there.

'The *Pelican*! How grand and jolly. Why did y'name her so?'

He laughed at her eagerness. 'I cannot tell you that, for I was hardly born when she was named, and since then have not thought to ask.'

She pursued the question. 'Then why d'you suppose?'

His eyes shone in merriment. 'Could it be because she waddles in the water?'

'She does not!'

'She has her moments.'

They laughed, then a wistfulness took Mary as she looked up into the top rigging. 'Makes a body want t'sail away from all the cares an' troubles. She is a beautiful ship.'

Protectively, he took her by the hand. 'Not nearly as beautiful as you.'

Pleased with his attention, but uneasy of the advance in this public place, she gently disengaged her hand. His manner became defensively formal. 'I am sorry. I forget myself. Shall we go aboard?'

Aware of his hurt, she tried to reassure him. 'It would please me greatly.'

'May I then be allowed to help you up the gangplank?'

'I would find it terrible hard t'make my way without your help and understanding.' The meaning conveyed in her words made him ashamed of his childishness. Tenderly she slid her hand into the crook of his arm and smiled away his look of contrition.

They had begun to climb the gangplank when Agnes called out, 'I will join you within the hour. There are matters I must discuss with David.' Jonathan waved acknowledgement as he helped Mary on to the deck, glad that for at least a short time they would be alone.

As they entered the cabin, painful memory came to him of the afternoon when he had gone on deck to relieve Anstruther's watch. Even now, he expected to see him appear from the inner quarters.

'And is this where y'steer the great ship from?'

Her question dragged him from thought. 'Steer the ship? Oh no, that is done by the helmsman.' He pointed to the open door. 'Out there, on the quarterdeck.'

'But it is surely you tells him where t'go.'

He smiled at her childlike interest. 'That is so. I plot the course from here.'

'An' how do y'do that?'

'I look at the stars and the sun.'

'The stars an' the sun? They tell you the way?'

'They do.'

She gazed around the cabin, then pointed at the charts. 'And what are all those papers with the strange cyphers upon them?'

'They are the charts of the oceans. I write upon them that which the sun and stars direct.'

In awe, Mary shook her head. 'The wonder of it.'

He echoed the softness of her voice. 'Indeed ... the wonder of it.'

They stood only a touch apart, each in a longing to embrace the other but fearful of making even the suggestion of a movement. 'We must see the rest of the ship.' His words were unsteady, and her reply came equally so.

'We shall do as you say ... Captain.'

Gently he took her by the hand. 'Please then, not Captain, but Jonathan.'

His touch sent a tremor through her. 'Jonathan...'

He smiled in delight. 'My name has been spoken many times, but I have never before known its sound.'

Both searched for further words but wished to find none, wanting only to remain wrapped about in this new closeness. Yet one thought nagged at Mary, and wondering on it would be harder to bear than the knowing. 'When will the ship...' She faltered, afraid to ask the direct question. 'Will you be glad t'return to England?'

'I thought I should, but no longer.' In irritation at the thought he glanced away over the deck. 'I have presently little say in the matter. But my father will require me to return as soon as I am able.' The words brought disappointment, but she understood his position.

'Your mother also, she will have been desperate worried.'

'I am more sure of that than anything.'

She heard the sarcasm, but did not question what might lie behind it. 'Do you have brothers an' sisters?'

'I have a sister, Ann. You would adore to meet her, and she you.' He smiled in memory. 'She is a terrible rogue, and together we lead father a merry dance.'

'You tease him?'

'He is stuffy, and has need to be taken down a peg in the cause of making him tolerably human.'

It was strange, this feeling she had on hearing him talk of his family. The family he would soon return to, which she would never know or see. But they were a part of him and she felt a longing to know more about them so that she might hold him close in memory when he had gone from her. 'Would y'tell me about him?'

A rueful smile twisted Jonathan's mouth. 'He is hard, but fair I suppose. He founded the line, and we now have eight ships.'

'Do y'love your father?'

'Do I love him?'

'I ask because y'tell me of lines an' ships, but not about the man.'

He was unprepared for such directness, but respected her

for it. 'I like him well enough, but he can be a stickler for convention and the careful road of commerce.'

'What fault is there in that?'

'We do not always see eye-to-eye.'

'It is the same with all families. But always there must be love an' trust to bind up the wounds.'

'He would like you for such words. I do believe the pair of you would get along together like a ship and her sails.'

'And why do y'say that now?'

He chuckled, forcing away the solemnity which had invaded their conversation. 'You both have the same stubborn chin.'

She caught his mood and smilingly fashioned defiance. 'Stubborn I am not!'

He regarded her with new-found admiration. 'Whatever you might be, I would not by one degree change the way of you.'

There was a dankness about the hold, made worse by the strong odour of trapped sea water and oily machinery. Jonathan had not wanted Mary to accompany him during his check on the cargo, but in a spirit of bravado she had insisted and now waited at the foot of the stairway as he went forward to bring a lantern. Her gaze wandered into the blackness of the hold, and a sickness came to her stomach as memories of the *Elizabeth* returned. The dark corners held silent menace, as if Donal lay there waiting still. She tried to fight down the thought but it would not be stayed, and again she suffered the terror and degradation of that night without end.

In panic she swung about to flee, but her hand missed its grab for the rail and she fell heavily against the stairway. Her cry of pain brought Jonathan running, the lantern held high, its disjointed movement causing the shadows to dance frantically about the place. Every shadow became a face of the sick and the dying, and it was not Jonathan behind the glow of the lantern, but Liam, coming to take her back. In terror, she huddled against the steps and felt the scream rise within her but could not stop it.

'Mary! What is it? Are you ill?'

His distraught expression brought her to reason. 'I am not ill, Jonathan, this place frightens me.' A sob broke from her. 'Please, oh please, let us leave it.'

Pausing only to hang the lantern on the bulkhead he lifted her from the stairs, thrilling suddenly in the soft warmth of her body as she clung to him in fear, her heart beating wildly against his chest. 'Take breath a moment ... nothing shall harm you.' She pressed her head tightly against his shoulder, breathing in the musky smell of his uniform, its cold metal buttons growing warm under the heat of her cheek, feeling secure in his embrace yet excited by it.

'Mary, what caused your fear?' He felt the shudder which ran through her.

'I have bad memories of this place.'

'How can it be? You have never before stepped foot here.'

''Tis the same as the ship we sailed on.'

'The one which brought you to America?'

'Yes.' She burrowed more deeply against him as he caressed her hair.

His voice was soft with concern. 'I have heard terrible things of those crossings, men, women and children crushed into the holds with little food or water. I am angry that you should have suffered so.'

She did not want to speak of it, but the words came in honesty. ''Twas not that which brought the fear.'

'Then tell me the cause so I may rid you of it.'

Instinctively she thrust closer to him in a pitiful attempt to hide from reply, and some moments passed before she found the courage to speak. 'It brings great shame on me.' Tenderly, he eased her from him and touched her face.

'I could not ever imagine that you would bring shame upon yourself.'

Her gaze went towards the darkest corner of the hold which mocked beyond the circle of light, and her reply was almost a whisper. 'If I should tell of it y'would not ever again want to see even the shadow of me.'

There was a firmness in his hands as he brought her to meet his eyes. 'If I were never again to see you, then I would surely

204

die ... do you not already know that I love you? Adore you with all my heart and soul ... Tell me I am right in my hope. That it is the same for you.'

She had only daydreamed on the words, and the realisation of them made her catch her breath. 'It is so, Jonathan ... I have loved you from first sight but there is ...' She felt the sweet warmth of his breath on her mouth then was lost to all else but the glory of their first kiss. His lips moved to kiss her face, her neck, and she began to return his passion, only suddenly to break away.

'We must not do this, please, Jonathan, for pity's sake. I have not the right.' She pushed free of his arms. 'I love you an' shall always, but there is no hope for it.'

He was embarrassed at the suddenness of change in her. 'If you love me as you say, how can that be?'

'I am married, an' can do nothing t'change it. That is why.'

'What nonsense! We shall seek an annulment at once.' He took tight hold of her hands to give reassurance but, feeling no response, released them in fretful impatience. 'You do not love the man, I know that ... know it in your words, in your kiss. Why do you do this to me? To us?' She felt an infinite sadness.

'It is so, what y'say. But there can be no breakin' of the holy Catholic vows.'

'You would let the Catholic faith come between our love? Is that what you are saying?' There was hurt in his shout. 'I cannot believe it!'

She flared back, eyes blazing. 'How can y'say such terrible things? Do y'not know? Do y'not care that my soul will go to eternal damnation if I break the vows?'

He became incensed. 'Damn these Catholic priests! They lead you about like so many goats on a chain ... making you believe such ridiculous tales as even a child would not swallow on. It is drivel!'

'Drivel, is it?' Her face shook in anger. 'You cannot mean t'say such words!'

The hurt and disbelief on her face brought his fury to turn inwards. What had possessed him to utter such bullying and profane words? Was this how little he loved her? 'Damn my soul to hell!' He swung about in a madness of self-hate to punch his fist hard into the bulkhead, causing the lantern to quiver, the blood glistening in its light as it pulsed freely from torn knuckles.

With a cry of concern Mary took hold of the injured hand and kissed it, then tore away a piece of her petticoat and wrapped it about the wound. He stood silently compliant as a small boy might while she tied the knot on the makeshift bandage. 'What made y'do such a thing?' Her voice was quiet, all anger spent. 'And y'cursed your dear soul to the devil.'

He fumbled out a handkerchief and gently dabbed it on her face. 'The devil would get the worst of the bargain!... You have blood on your stubborn chin.'

She tried to smile, but it ended crookedly on her lips. 'What shall we do, Jonathan?'

He stared unseeingly at the bandage as the blood began to seep slowly through its thin cover. 'Will you return to him?'

'Never so long as there is breath in my body.'

'For what reason? I must at least know that.'

'There are many reasons.'

'Tell me again that you do not care for him.'

'I have never cared for him.'

'Then why in God's name did you marry the man?'

The random drips of sea water which fell from the cargo seemed loud in the long silence. She must tell him without further delay. What difference would it now make? He would be gone from her within a few short weeks, and they would never again see each other. Yet she was not prepared for the sudden pain which took her breath at the thought.

27

There was a subdued air between Mary and Jonathan as they journeyed back to Braganza, for both had much to think about. Yet they were at least alone to meditate on their shared troubles. Agnes was to return later with David Sullivan, having decided to visit a mutual friend who had been taken ill.

Mary's graphic revelations on board the ship had wounded Jonathan, and the instinct to seek wild justice for her was still there, urging him to go to High Pines and wreak a bloody vengeance on the McAffertys. Again and again in his mind's eye he saw himself take pistols and shoot the family dead where they stood, without care of the consequences.

A mile distant from Braganza, he stopped the carriage and turned towards Mary. She looked defenceless, her face pale and drawn as he lowered the reins into his lap and took her by the hand. 'Mary, I have not yet fashioned the way but I shall deliver you from this evil, no matter the price.'

There was no denying the warmth and sincerity of his words, but they did little to lift the misery she had felt since leaving the ship. Brave words would not dissolve her marriage vows, nor defeat the McAffertys. Gently, he kissed her hands. 'What you have told me changes the whole issue. I cannot see the Church giving difficulty to ending this unholy marriage.'

She looked away over the fields, resignation in her voice. 'They will say the truth of it. That 'twas a vow made before God in the Holy Church.' He bristled with barely controlled anger.

'That may be, but it was also one of trickery and convenience to suit the priest.'

'To my eternal shame for the Church, I know that.'

'It is the priest who should be ashamed!'

'He will never be ... an' I know the Church will not agree t'end the marriage.'

There was a brittle impatience about his reply. 'They are not God Almighty, but merely serve Him, and badly at that. If we were in England the marriage would be annulled within days of application.' He paused and slapped his knee in impatience at himself. 'Of course! Why did I not think of it before? My family has the best lawyers in the world.' He smiled in new-found confidence, sure that he had found a perfect answer to the problem, confident that she must agree with the plan that was already forming in his mind.

The *Pelican* would soon be ready for sea. Mary would return with him to England, and while the lawyers went about their business she would stay at Ranelagh with Ann as chaperone. He smiled again, revelling in his cleverness, then tenderly closed his hands about her face. 'My darling, I have the grandest plan.' He was suddenly shy. 'I had pictured a better setting in which to ask this question, but I can wait no longer ... when you are free and able, would you do me the great honour of becoming my wife?'

His wife? He wanted her to become his wife. She had been sure he would be repelled by her story but it was not so, neither was it pity in his eyes as he patiently awaited her answer. Never had she loved him more than at this moment.

'Y'do me great honour, Jonathan, an' for as long as I live I will never forget this moment ... but I fear t'go against the vows.'

In disappointment he slowly lowered his hands from her face. 'I am at loss to understand this Catholic dogma. You are educated, and intelligent of the modern world. How can you then believe that a just God would place your soul in eternal damnation when you only seek to redress the wrong brought upon you?'

She pleaded for his understanding. 'Please, Jonathan, it is not t'do with education, or such. It is the faith I was brought up with.'

The words were on his lips to damn the Church once more, but he checked himself to a more persuasive approach.

'Mary, when we first talked on this I was at fault in my insult to the Catholic Church, and there is no excuse for that.' In agitation he picked up the reins, wrapping and unwrapping them around his fingers. 'But what you later told me brought me again to question the wisdom of this faith... You have the very strongest grounds for the Church to dissolve this quite ridiculous marriage.'

Anger welled in Mary. Why would he not try to understand this great torment she suffered? 'Y'do not listen to me, Jonathan. We go round and round in circles on it and bring nothin' but argument an' pain to the both of us.'

'If that is indeed so, then you must provide answer to this... What happens to our love from this moment?' A rising wind moaned through the branches of a nearby copse.

'I do not know, Jonathan.'

In sadness at her reply he looked towards the tall grass of the distant meadows which rippled in surging waves. How like the ocean it was. Why was he not standing on the quarterdeck with Anstruther? And if not that, alongside him, dead in the sea. He broke from self-pity and turned to look at Mary. She had taken off the pale straw bonnet, and now the wind pulled playfully at her long dark hair, sending it in shining wisps across her face.

'Mary ... I love you so much it drives me to unreason.' He hesitated. 'Maybe it would serve you better if I were to go away and leave you in peace.'

Her reply was almost a whisper. 'There would be no peace in that... I love you.' He looked at her in adoration, then gently took her in his arms, and with an infinite tenderness he kissed her.

28

It was just after ten in the morning when the stagecoach from Clarkstown arrived at the Boston harbour staging post. Wearily, its few passengers clambered down and began to retrieve their luggage. Liam McAfferty remained hunched in the corner seat. Cautious as a fox on the run, he surveyed the quiet streets. It would not do to rush things. If he were to run into Demarest it would mean prison without a doubt. He glanced down at his polished boots then carefully picked at some flecks of lint which lay on the black serge suit, and his old cockiness returned. For Christ's sake, the man would never recognise him in this get-up, and anyroad, he would surely not be about on a Sunday morning. Pausing only to arrange the felt hat at what he thought to be a rakish angle, he emerged from the coach and strode confidently towards the harbour bar, sure that his mission would prove successful.

From his vantage point behind a stack of cotton bales, Liam scanned the faces of the immigrants as they trooped down the gangplank of the quarantine ship. At first sight he did not recognise Jimmy O'Dea. The man had lost a deal of weight and his clothes hung from him as they might from a coat-peg. Liam stayed his ground a moment, looking up and down the quayside for officials, then with a grin of triumph he closed on his quarry.

'Jimmy O'Dea! ... I have been countin' the days.'

O'Dea looked at him in disbelief. 'Jesus! Am I taken wit' the madness or is it really you, McAfferty?' He had not expected

Liam to meet the boat, nor did he want other than to be done with him for he had plans of his own. But he quickly recovered his composure. 'Y'went on the run, then?'

The reply was filled with contempt. 'I was for findin' work, so y'could all come out to jobs, not idlin' about a fever place.'

O'Dea's smile was sardonic. 'You were always the thoughtful man, McAfferty.' His gaze dropped to Liam's polished boots, then travelled up the suit, noting the new shirt and badly tied cravat. 'Would y'look at you, so grand an' all. Have y' become a millionaire already?'

'Y'can say I am settled, but there's room for it t'be better.' His tone changed. 'Well now, an' where are the others?'

O'Dea shrugged. 'There is just meself.'

A frown of annoyance crept over Liam's face. 'How is that, now?'

'We started out eight of us.' O'Dea hawked up phlegm from the back of his throat and spat it on to the cobbles. 'Sooner would I be in hell with a broken back than return t'that place ... Connor, McIlroy an' Yeates dead an' buried in it.'

'What of the rest?' Anger broke in Liam's voice. 'They cannot all be bloody dead!'

'They chose t'go on the Canada boat.'

'The treacherous bastards! An' what of the passage money they owe me?'

O'Dea shrugged again. 'Unless y'follow them to Canada, I'm thinkin' y'll have to whistle for it.'

He saw the fist coming but could not avoid it, his teeth jarring together under the blow and trapping the tongue to bring blood. Liam followed up the assault, grabbing O'Dea by the collar to keep him from falling into the dock. 'Y'would dare talk t'me in such fashion?'

Fear filled O'Dea as he looked into the crazed eyes. The man was stark raving and likely to kill him before he had taken another step from the docks. 'I meant no harm in it.' But Liam's grip tightened.

'Y'were not so bloody lippy when y'were starvin' t'death, an' me forkin' out the many pounds to save your miserable bloody lives.' O'Dea screwed his head about looking for help but his former companions hurried past, eyes averted. He would have to use his own wits to save himself from this deadly encounter.

'You are right as rain, McAfferty, an' I am sorry for it.'

Liam released his grip. 'That's better now. Do y'have any belongin's wit' you?'

'I have not.'

'Right, we're for the coach t'Clarkstown. I have work there.'

'What work is that?' The question trembled from his lips.

'Farmin' an' the like.'

'But I know nothin' of farmin'.'

'Y'will not have to.'

O'Dea's thoughts came quickly. There would be no escape if he went along with McAfferty's scheme, only backbreaking toil in the fields and the swift parting from any wage he might be paid. It was a time for cunning. 'I have the better notion.'

'An' what would that be now?' There was suspicion in every word of Liam's question, and O'Dea did not fail to recognise it.

'A fella told me of a job here in Boston.'

'What fella?'

'An official fella, back there in the queer place.'

'Y'will not have need of it.' Liam turned away towards the staging post. 'Come on now, we've wasted enough of the time.'

In desperation, O'Dea grabbed him by the arm. 'Will y'look at me, McAfferty? If I was wet to the skin I would not weigh the eight stone ... I'm not up to the farmin' work.' His tone grew in urgent appeal. 'Christ! I'd be more sick on your hands than workin', then where would y'be for the payin' back of the money?'

Liam grew doubtful. The last thing he needed was a sick man at High Pines. He was already in enough trouble with Meredith. 'What is it y'are tryin' to tell me?'

O'Dea sensed he would be allowed only one further attempt to put his point. 'The truth of it is y'do not want me, but the money ... is that not so?'

Liam sniggered. 'An' just how would a raggy-arsed little bastard like you get a job for money?'

O'Dea dragged a folded note from his jacket. 'Here y'are ... the letter for t'introduce me. Five dollars a week. Y'could not

212

match that with the farmin' work.' He saw the greed appear in Liam's eyes. Now was the time to tell a grand tale. ''Tis in a brewery, an' you know me, McAfferty, I could fiddle another ten an' more with the clever loadin' of the drays. Think of it now, fifteen, maybe twenty dollars a week.' He held the note tightly.

Liam licked at lips which had gone dry at the thought. 'Do y'know how much y'owe me?'

'I do not exactly.'

Liam decided to treble the figure. 'Six pounds, an' four more for the trouble of it.'

O'Dea feigned a quick calculation. 'Will we say fifty dollars?' It would not matter if he said one hundred and fifty, since he had no intention of ever paying back a single penny.

Liam pretended to consider the offer. 'It is not enough for the great trouble I have been caused.' He delighted at O'Dea's frantic look and would have liked to torture the man further, but there was danger in dallying too long in this place. 'However, we shall say eighty. When do I get it?'

O'Dea almost cried in relief. 'Give me the name of the place y'live an' I shall send it by the mail coach, ten dollars a week.'

'Is it a fool y'take me for?'

'I do not!'

Liam moved closer to him. 'Now listen t'me well, O'Dea. I shall be back here on this very spot, at the same time, four Sundays from now. Y'will then have forty dollars for me. Do y'understand that?'

O'Dea nodded in vigorous agreement. 'I do indeed.'

'Good. I shall allow y' another month on top t'find the rest.'

'Y'are a generous man, McAfferty.' Nervously, he cleared his throat. 'Well, I had better be off then. The sooner I start the work the sooner I get your money.'

Liam squeezed O'Dea's hand very tightly. 'Where is this brewery?'

O'Dea had not expected the question. 'The brewery, y'say?' His voice shook.

Liam squeezed tighter. 'Where is it?' Sweat broke out on O'Dea's forehead as he strived for imagination.

213

'It is, er, it is McGuire's. I believe it t'be not far from the docks.'

Liam frowned. 'Y'do not seem sure of it.' O'Dea gave a cry of pain as he felt the bones crunch in his fingers.

'Christ! Y'll break my hand.'

'I'll break your bloody neck if you are moonshinin' me.'

'I would not do that!' In a wild gamble that Liam would not be able to read, he wrenched free and thrust the crumpled note forward. 'See for yourself if it is not the truth.'

Liam scanned the writing and felt the hate rise in him at his inability to make sense of it. But it looked right, and there were the official stamps on it. He moved his gaze from the note and frowned at O'Dea. 'Y'have rumpled it so much that I cannot read it. But take warnin', O'Dea, if y'should cross me I will surely find you, an' break every bone in your body.' He kicked O'Dea up the backside. 'Now get off wit' you!' Grinning, he watched the man shamble away. There were rich pickings here. He would take the eighty dollars, and when that was done return again and again for more.

O'Dea paused on the corner of the dock road and looked briefly back at Liam, congratulating himself on a lucky escape. Boston had seemed to be the natural place to get a start in work, just a hop, skip and jump from the quarantine island. But it was now a place to get out of. Come nightfall he would make very sure he was shipboard for New York, for he had been told work was in plenty there.

He screwed the note up into a tight ball and dropped it into the gutter, then smiled at the irony. It had served one use if not another, for he had been told that the quarantine discharge certificate was the only way he would be allowed to go free, ashore. He turned away from the docks and within seconds was swallowed up in the busying streets of the city.

Aching from the effects of the bumpy stage ride and already nursing doubts over his decision to leave O'Dea behind, Liam was in a foul mood when he arrived back at High Pines. The

214

cabin, once neat and orderly under Mary's care, was now in neglect. The food lay unlardered and prey to the many flies which buzzed incessantly about the place. Empty whisky bottles littered the floor, and the place reeked of filth.

Donal's attempt at making the evening meal aggravated Liam's worsening mood, and his expression was malevolent as he spat a mouthful of food on to the table. 'An' what's this y'r after poisonin' our guts wit'?'

Donal's answer was defensive. 'Rabbit stew, dar, so it is.'

Liam mimicked his son's voice. 'Rabbit stew, dar, so it is.'

Patrick stopped eating, aware of impending trouble. He looked down at his plate but Liam's penetrating gaze ferreted out his attention, and when their eyes met the question came finely balanced just this side of hell about to break loose.

'What d'you make of it, Patrick?'

'It is not good, dar.'

'Not good? 'Tis half bloody raw is what it is!' In fury he rounded on Donal, who was noisily shovelling the stew into his mouth. 'Y'bloody pig! Y'd eat shit, so y'would!' Donal winced, his eating brought to a choking stop. But he wisely kept from speaking. 'Y'll finish up poisonin' the lot of us! Well? What have y' t'say?' Donal picked his way into speech with the care of a man walking barefoot on broken glass.

'I'm desperate sorry, dar ... y'allus told us cookin' was a woman's job, an' I do not know the way of it.'

'An' why is not the woman here t'do it? Because y'cannot control yourself is why!'

Donal threw away caution. 'I was only after seekin' my rights!' Patrick looked in pity at him.

'Did I ever know a man more able t'talk himself into a bog of trouble. There's no peace wit' you, Donal.'

Liam nodded in agreement. 'Patrick is right, y'have nothin' t'offer save a big mouth.'

Donal buried his face in grimy hands, then looked up at each man in turn, tears of anger running down his cheeks. 'Sure, an' am I not allus in the wrong of it?'

Liam winked at Patrick. 'Oh dear, would y'look at that. God help us, for we have upset the poor boy.'

215

Donal angrily wiped the tears away. 'Y'call me the eejut, but I know a wife should be wit' her husband.'

'Well now, an' is that so?' Liam's voice was mocking. 'Away wit' y' then, big boy, an' bring her back, why don't you?'

Donal stood abruptly, accidentally knocking the remains of his stew over the table. 'I will then! I'll away now an' drag her back every inch of the bloody way!' Liam smiled, but there was no humour in it and his tone was deceptively mild.

'Sit down before I knock y'down. Y'already have us in enough trouble t'last a hundred years.' Donal sat and glared at his father.

'They have no right to be keepin' her!'

Liam spat at him. 'Y'have only yourself t'blame for that!'

In the silence which followed, Patrick regarded Donal with curiosity. His brother was risking a beating over a matter which was out of their control. Why had he shown fight when there was no apparent reward to be gained? 'What's got into y', Donal? You're in a queer old state altogether.' Donal did not reply.

Liam thumped hard on the table. 'Answer your brother!'

'I'll tell y'what ails me!' Donal shouted the words. 'Dar, y'told me from a boy that the McAffertys allus stuck together ... was not that the way of it?'

'I dearly hope t'Jesus you are not after mockin' me, boy!'

'I would not do that, dar.'

'Then say what y'have to.'

'I have been hearin' the bad things.'

'What bad things?'

'The English sailors is what.'

'Make sense now or shut up!'

'They are stayin' in a cabin at the Merediths.'

'An' what of it?'

Donal looked sullen, unsure of an answer which would convince his father that he had a point to make, then spoke in a rush. 'Ben Ambrose told me as how the English captain an' Mary was holdin' hands makin' the lovin' talk an' all, an' she my wife!'

'Ben Ambrose told y'this?' Liam was barely convinced.

'He did!'

'Sure, he's a fat windbag of a nobody. How would he know anythin' worth the tellin'?'

Patrick interrupted. 'Dar is right. Ben Ambrose is an old woman sellin' you a pig in a poke.'

But Donal would not be moved. 'Ben an' me are good friends, he has no reason for t'be tellin' me the moonshine.'

Liam pushed away his plate, and leaned heavily on the table. 'What was the man after sayin', now?'

'Ben was over collectin' things from the Merediths an' he saw Mary an' this captain fella talkin' close t'gether in the yard.'

'Is that it, then? Talkin' close t'gether?'

'No! There is more of it.'

'Jesus Christ Almighty! Will y'get the tale told? 'Tis like drawin' out the teeth of a bloody mule!'

'The pair of them was in the chicken sheds a long time, t'have him thinkin' the bad things ... Ben hoped t'die if not. They came out laughin', so they did, an' went into the house.'

There was venom in Liam's voice. 'Is it the truth y'r tellin' me?'

Patrick looked alarmed. 'Please t'God, dar, it will be nothin' but a wild tale.'

Donal interrupted with glee. 'It is the truth, dar ... what'll y'do t'him?'

'Nothin' till I find the way of it myself. But if this bloody sailor boy is cavortin' wit' your wife I'll kill the bastard!'

'God bless y', dar!'

Liam motioned for quiet, incensed at Donal's revelation, yet his instincts did not doubt the truth of it and his mind writhed in new-found fury. Would things never go right for him? He had once ruled the roost but it had now become shaky. Even his sons were beginning to question his authority. And was not the why of it plain for even a fool to see? No more easy pickings, no clever notions to outwit Meredith. The man was cocking a snook at him by holding Mary, making him eat the dirt for all to witness. On top of it the bloody English had again come to haunt him. They were to blame for his leaving of

Ireland in the first place, creating the havoc and hunger which had tipped him out from the comfortable little carry-on he had enjoyed at the farm. Now this bloody English captain threatened to tear the family apart, to steal Mary from them, and how then would they make their way without her book learning? It was time to right the wrongs.

'I will show y' what happens t'anyone who shames the name of McAfferty!'

Patrick looked anxiously at his father. 'I am wit' y', dar, to my dyin' day, but the blame for any harm to the man will surely bring us to standin' on the gallows.' But Liam was already scheming a plot.

'Do not worry y'r sweet head, Patrick, have I not told y' these many times, there are more ways of killin' a pig than chokin' it with butter.' He turned away to Donal. 'Get the whisky an' let me swill down the bloody rubbish you tried to poison me wit'.' The assurance did nothing to abate Patrick's concern.

His father was not without brains, and there was no denying he had often rescued the family from situations where many another might have been lost. But for all that he was a violent man and with whisky in his belly well capable of bringing the whole world crashing about their heads. He must do what he could to talk him away from it, now, before it festered.

'Y'have not told us about Boston, dar. Did y'bring them back?' The subject of Liam's excursion had so far not been touched upon.

'What business would that be of yours?' Liam's face twitched in anger.

'I was only after wonderin', dar.'

'You leave the bloody wonderin' t'me.' He was angry at being reminded of his failure. 'I had the great hopes of you, Patrick, but your mouth is gettin' as big as your brother's. I would not like it to be so.'

Patrick lowered his gaze. 'I am sorry, dar.' He had never before suffered such words from his father. It was Donal's doing. Damn him to bloody hell for it.

218

29

The letter from Boston had arrived. Agnes carried it before her like she might a shield as she left the study and headed purposefully towards the kitchen. An hour before, Meredith had told her of his concern at the growing relationship between Mary and Jonathan. It had come as no real surprise to Agnes, for she had already begun to guess at the truth and was considering what the best approach might be. However, Meredith was in no mood for niceties and she was left in no doubt that he wanted the matter resolved before he returned from work. Subsequently the letter was delivered, its contents seeming to Agnes to afford an immediate solution in what was threatening to become a difficult situation.

Warm sunshine lit the window alcove where Mary sat darning a petticoat, a wicker basket at her feet spilling over with freshly washed linen. Deep in a misery of thought on the previous day's visit to the ship and all that had followed, she was nevertheless aware of Agnes's quiet entry, and sensed an air of trouble in the way the woman paused just inside the door.

Whatever she had come to say was not good. It had to be the McAffertys. What else? They had made Mr Meredith agree to send her back. That was it. So much for all the talk of keeping her in safety and finding her employment as governess. She should have run that day in the fog. Well, it may be they had it all cosily arranged, but she would be gone from this place before any such happening.

'You look busy, my dear.' Agnes's voice was tight.

Mary looked up from her work, the smile forced. 'The mendin' is always with us.'

'It is, and those who make the holes.' Agnes crossed to the alcove. 'I missed you at breakfast. Is something wrong that you did not join us?' Mary stopped darning the petticoat and gave polite attention.

'I was not hungry, ma'am.'

'Are you not well?'

'Thank you, I am well enough, but have not the appetite.'

'I see. I hope you are not sickening for some ailment.'

'I am not, ma'am.' Mary resumed the darning as she chafed with an irritable impatience. What was really on the woman's mind? Why were not the upper classes more straight to the point? She had witnessed it when the gentry called on her father in an effort to lure him away to private teaching. He had called it a painful overture. They did go on so. Maybe if she asked her to sit down? 'Will y'bide a while, Mrs Meredith?' Agnes sat down, then gently stayed Mary's hand from the darning.

'My dear, there is something of an intimate nature I must ask. Please do not be afraid to tell me the truth. Is there a liaison between yourself and Captain Bramwell?' Mary dropped the needle in shock at the unexpected question. They knew then. It was not the McAffertys at all.

'We have done nothing wrong, Mrs Meredith.'

'I did not suggest you had. Nor do I think it. I want only to resolve the issue.'

'We did not seek t'fall in love, ma'am.'

'Mary! You disappoint me. Can you not see the complications in this matter? You are already married.'

'I wish not t'be rude, ma'am. I meant there was nothin' mean nor underhand in it ... 'twas an innocent happenin' to the both of us.' She neatly folded the petticoat and placed it in the basket, surprised at her own calmness. 'But you are right.' A resigned note entered her voice. 'There is no help for it.'

Her forthrightness took the edge from Agnes. 'I am glad you agree.' There was an awkward silence before Agnes continued. 'These things happen, and we must learn to understand them... Captain Bramwell cuts a most romantic figure and

220

was no doubt persuasive ... you were lonely and unhappy. It is painful now, but it will pass.'

Mary found it difficult to control her temper at this oblique attack on Jonathan and the patronising way it had been delivered. Instantly, she struck back, her tone coldly formal. 'With respect, ma'am, it is not like that at all. Captain Bramwell is the most honourable man. He wishes me t'seek an end to my marriage at once an' return with him to England as his wife.' She could not have delivered a more stunning bombshell.

'His wife?' There was disbelief in Agnes's question. 'Are you saying that Captain Bramwell has proposed marriage?'

Mary nodded briefly. 'It is so, Mrs Meredith.'

'I wonder at you both... Under what circumstances did this proposal take place?'

'When we visited on the ship.'

'It was wrong of me to have left you alone together.'

'Y'have no blame in that, ma'am. If not there 'twould have happened in some other place.' Mary's retort was firm, almost matter of fact. Agnes had not expected such a stand, expecting the girl to crumple at the very first words of accusation.

'But, child, you have hardly had time to know each other.'

'Mrs Meredith,' her smile was paper-thin, 'I have come t'know that time has nothing t'do with love.'

Agnes gave a slow shake of the head.

'Mary, if it were only so simple. You would not want to move from one disaster to another, surely? Look at how different are your backgrounds.' She paused, trying to pick her words more carefully, but failing. 'He comes from a world entirely different from the one you have known.'

A twitch of annoyance crossed Mary's face. 'My father raised me t'know that 'tis people that matter, not worlds.' But she cooled as rapidly, wanting the matter over and done with. 'I am sorry t'have brought you such trouble... Y'said you wanted an end of it, and it is so.' In distraction she searched for the darning needle as the tears suddenly welled. 'Like I have told you, there is no help for it.' Her hands stopped their search and became still in her lap.

221

Agnes frowned in puzzlement. 'Are you saying the relationship is at an end?'

'I am of the Catholic faith, ma'am.' There was a flatness in the statement. Agnes, a staunch New England Protestant, was at a loss to comprehend the deeper meaning.

'I do not exactly understand you.'

Mary began another vain search for the needle as she tried to control the tremor in her voice. 'The faith decrees that marriage is forever an' unbreakable until death.' She faltered. 'If I should break my vows ... my soul would go to eternal damnation ... with the devil.' She stared down unseeingly at the washing basket, her lips trembling at having uttered the words.

Agnes's stern attitude wavered as she regarded Mary's wretchedness. 'My dear, I now see what you tell me and respect your confidence. Have you told Captain Bramwell as much?'

Mary rallied and sat stiffly upright. 'I have.'

'What did he say?'

'He said he would find a way. But he is Protestant an' not knowin' the Catholic laws.' She looked in appeal at Agnes. 'Mrs Meredith, it is done ... can we not leave it in peace?'

'I am afraid there is something I must tell you.' Agnes was embarrassed. 'Captain Bramwell has left the house and gone into quarters with his men ... Mr Meredith thought it better in the situation.'

A sudden chill ran through Mary. That she should have brought such shame and indignity on the man she loved more dearly than life!

Agnes rose, placing the letter firmly into Mary's hands. 'Please, read this as soon as you feel able, then let me know your decision ... my dear, I feel you would be wise to act upon its instruction.' In vexation at the affair, she crumpled the envelope. 'However, I shall not go back on my word regarding the McAffertys.' She left the room as quietly as she had entered.

30

Jonathan arrived at Braganza shortly before noon. Agnes had seen the dust of his approach, and went out to meet him as he drove an open carriage and pair into the yard. There was a stiffness in their salutations.

'Good morning, Mrs Meredith, I trust you are well.' He touched the peak of his cap in salute.

'Good morning, Captain Bramwell, I am. How may I help you?' She was disappointed in him and at the turn of events, though she would not say so for it was obvious enough without words. He climbed from the carriage and looked searchingly at her.

'You have spoken with Mary?'

'I have.'

'Mrs Meredith... I deeply regret the trouble I have caused you all. But this is no dalliance on my part... I am sincere in my intentions for Mary.' He glanced towards the house in hope of seeing her, but there was no sign. 'I must speak with her, ma'am.'

'Captain Bramwell ... you must know that I cannot allow you into the house.'

'I appreciated that happening, ma'am, and hired this carriage in the hope of taking Mary for a short drive away.' His voice held impatience. 'Please understand... I cannot simply leave the matter unresolved.'

'You take a great deal for granted, Captain.'

'I do not understand you, ma'am.'

'To assume that you merely had to hire a carriage, present yourself and all would be well.'

He was chastened by her tone. 'I regret your opinion of me, ma'am, for I did not mean it to be so.'

'Very well, Captain, I will accept what you say. I am given to understand that you have made a proposal of marriage to Mary. Is it so?'

He nodded firmly. 'I have asked that honour of her, ma'am.'

She regarded him with some forbearance. 'The kindest thing I can think of to reply is that you have been meagre in proper thought on the matter.'

'You mistake me, ma'am.' The words were delivered stiffly. 'I have considered the matter most carefully.'

'Captain Bramwell, you astonish me.' She spoke quietly to put her point. 'You know that Mary is married ... in no position to accept your proposal.'

'With respect, Mrs Meredith, you know as well as I that Mary's marriage is in name only. An evil affair at that.'

'Nevertheless, Captain, the girl is married, and for good or ill feels herself bound to her vows. I understand that she has told you as much.'

'She has not convinced me that is what she truly thinks, and I have come to clarify the matter.'

'Surely the subject of her faith was explained to you?'

'Her faith?' There was exasperation in his tone. 'I believe we are both aware, ma'am, of what vile fortune and indignity that ridiculous faith has led her to.' She rebuked him.

'Mary's religion is a matter concerning only herself and God.'

'I see!' His temper had become short. 'You then condone the suffering she has been subjected to at the hands of the McAffertys?'

Agnes bristled. 'I hope you will now apologise for that outrageous assertion, Captain.'

Slowly he lowered his gaze under her demanding stare. 'You are right, Mrs Meredith, it was a most outrageous outburst... I am deeply sorry.' He shuffled his feet agitatedly in the dirt. He had allowed his temper to move him from reason and give insult to this woman who had shown him and his crew so much kindness. She surely would not now allow any meeting with Mary.

'I cannot believe my conduct and too easily forget your hospitality when I was most in need.' A rueful smile came and went. 'Love has near driven me to madness ... please forgive me.' He climbed back into the carriage. 'I do not seek to excuse my behaviour, but David has told me the *Pelican* will be ready for sea much sooner than he had first thought, a few days ... I hoped to see Mary before my departure.' He had meant the words to carry weight, but they stumbled from him in a misery.

Agnes wavered in resolution as she travelled the wretchedness of his expression. The uniform was creased and heavy with dust. She felt an odd impulse to brush it clean and polish the dull buttons. 'Wait a moment, Captain.' Her tone softened. 'I shall ask Mary if she will see you. But I must remain while you are together.'

New hope came to him. 'Thank you, Mrs Meredith, thank you with all my heart.'

Any trace of demand had gone from his voice, and somehow it made Agnes pity him the more. She turned for the house, then hesitated. Pity or not, there would have to be a clear statement of her feelings to ensure no further complications.

'Captain Bramwell, I do not pretend my deep disappointment in this matter. You knew of the delicate circumstances surrounding Mary's presence here, yet chose to ignore them.' Jonathan attempted to speak, but she raised a hand to silence him. 'Mary is very young and has endured the most awful privations. I believe I am now in a position to make her life more secure. If you love her as you claim, please help me in that task.'

Wearily he looked back at her, ignorant of her meaning. Why did she not bring Mary to him instead of continuing with this lecture? 'Mrs Meredith, on my life, I would make Mary's future secure.'

Agnes persisted. 'Let me make myself clearer, Captain. Mary is a person of good nature and bearing, but inexperienced in worldly matters, a penniless, Irish, Catholic girl who would have only a disastrous marriage as testimonial to bring before

225

your father and mother.' She frowned. 'What do you imagine her reception would be?'

Jonathan hardened in defence, but chose his words with care. 'Mrs Meredith, please forgive me, but with the greatest respect I think you do Mary a disservice.' He ventured a quick smile. 'I know she would prove most able to move in any circle of society, indeed put to shame the greater majority of my friends with her elegance and erudition... My parents and sister would swiftly learn to adore her, as I do.' He paused.

'As for myself, I am full grown in my own right and ways. A man must choose his own wife, not allow his parents or any other to advise upon it ... but I should sooner die than give Mary any cause for unhappiness or regret.' He moved to placate Agnes, anxious for her goodwill. 'I do not doubt your concern for Mary, Mrs Meredith. Please believe I share your feelings.'

Agnes was anything but mollified by his words. 'I trust you do, Captain Bramwell, but we seem to be at cross-purposes in that concern.' She raised her eyebrows. 'From the way you speak it seems you mean to pursue the issue of marriage, when I understood your intention to be only that of saying farewell.' Her expression grew more severe. 'I hope you will not attempt to persuade her away from the course she is set upon.'

A sudden anger flared up in him but he fought it down. 'Mrs Meredith, I would never in any way do anything to cause Mary distress.' Damn it all. He had been too free and open. The situation must instantly be retrieved. He must not now beg the negative if he were to achieve his aim. 'You need have no worry on that score, I promise you, ma'am.'

Agnes was now in a state of indecision as she regarded Jonathan. Would he attempt to dissuade Mary from her chosen path? Or would he indeed play the gentleman as he had said? Yet he was plainly agitated, and if she refused a meeting he would only continue to seek Mary out. In any event the couple should be allowed to say a last goodbye or the issue would be bound to fester on. Far and away better to have done with it once and for all.

'I shall insist that Mary speaks with you, Captain.' Her tone

226

was firm. 'But as I have said, I cannot leave you alone together.'

Agnes sat waiting in the carriage, parked discreetly above the remoteness of Beacon Head, watching the couple as they walked some distance away, ruffled by the wind which moved in strength through the vast openness. They had not spoken on the ride out and still remained in unsure silence, wanting to hold hands but not daring to, each seeking for words that might please the other.

In a defiant effort to look her best, Mary wore a russet dress made up from a gown given her by Agnes. The wind grabbed on the fullness of it, now and again checking her progress, then pulling hard at the straw bonnet tied with lace beneath her chin. But in compensation it brought the sharp tang of the ocean, evoking memories of the headland above Killala Bay. She wished to be there with him, now, lying upon the warm grass, his arms about her, their lips in a sweet and everlasting kiss, with nothing but a skylark to bear witness to their love.

They came to a halt near the edge of the cliffs and heard the surge of the Atlantic. He looked down on the giant waves and felt at one with them as they spent their force in impotent fury against the unyielding rocks. Was this the last time he would be allowed to see her? He could not face that or he would surely go out of his mind. He must make her know how much he loved her, must convince her now to return to England with him.

He turned from the ocean and attempted to push tidy the unruly hair which blew about his face, then took her by the hand. She did not resist his gentle hold, her heartbeat growing faster as they gazed at each other in deep longing. He spoke softly, all carefully constructed thoughts and pleas gone.

'I have loved you from first sight, Mary, and shall always love you.' The wind gusted fiercely, at last winning her bonnet to send it bowling in frantic, hopping circles towards the coach where Agnes watched and waited. But Mary was oblivious to it.

'I love you an' shall always ... Jonny.' She must tell him of the letter. But not quite yet.

He caressed the hair which tumbled like a wild waterfall about her face. 'You called me Jonny ... please, always call me so, it shall be your special name for me, tell me you will.' He must speak of taking her with him, now. But he edged further from intent, fearful of rejection.

'I will, Jonny.' Her words were soft and made him more sure.

'Mary, it has been a sudden thing, this love I have for you. I have never before known the joy of it, whenever I see your dear face. The pain I have in me when you are gone from sight.'

Her smile was shy. 'It is the same for me, Jonny. I cannot believe that but a short time ago I did not even know y'walked the world, an' now ...' She faltered and he held her hand more tightly as he grew in confidence. He would win her by gentle persuasion rather than bluster.

Softly he prompted, 'And now?'

'An' now I do not recall a time when I did not know you.'

In imagination she lay in his bed, felt his caresses, knew his love, saw their children ... Why should her eternal soul be given to the devil for loving this man? A forgiving God would surely not allow such a thing. A shiver ran through her at having questioned the Almighty. She must speak of the letter. She was wrong to have encouraged Jonathan's hopes, yet had been unwilling to deny the truth of her feelings. Now, truth of another kind had been made harder to reveal.

'I have t'tell you something.'

'What is it, my love?'

'Mrs Meredith is takin' me to Boston the day after tomorrow.'

'Boston? Why would you go there?'

'T'be findin' work as a governess.'

He released her hand as if stung.

'I cannot believe what you say ... Am I gone mad?' Why had he not straightway made clear his thoughts? Now it was too late. 'Do you seek to make a worse fool of me than I already am?' The raw anger of his outburst was plucked away on the

228

wind to reach Agnes. She stirred uneasily and moved for the reins, but still waited. Better to let them blow out their storm. His fury built.

'Is it not enough I neglect my duties to follow you like a cur dog, humbling myself before you with protestations of my devotion?' His face shook with emotion. 'You dare talk to me of love, while all along you plan like a coward to run from it?'

She felt his pain, but an equal anger arose in her. 'An' you dare t'judge me without the hearin' of what else I have t'say?'

'You have said all there is to say ... madam!' He stood as a wounded animal might, teeth bared, searching for more words to hurt back, yet his eyes appealed for her reason.

But she was also wounded and closed on him without mercy. 'How would y'know that ... Captain?' She hurled the last word into his face. 'Do y'suppose I had no life before y'wrecked your stupid ship?' A pain grew within her as she cried out the words. There had been no life before his coming. Why did she scream insults at him like a common fishwife on the Sligo docks? All she wanted was to hold him close, tell him that he was her life, beg him to run with her from this place. But she could not quell her anger.

'I have been through much misery an' did not seek more!' She pointed towards Agnes. 'But for that lady I must be dead an' buried in my grave. 'Tis she got me the work so t'escape from the McAffertys.' She stopped for breath then suddenly became calmer. 'I have t'go with her.'

He did not reply, and she looked at him in puzzlement as if he should have all along been aware of her pain and true feelings. 'How could I have been knowin' your love would happen to me?' The words were gentle in appeal, damping his fury, but some time passed before he spoke in apology of his temper.

'I did not mean the cruel things I said ... you must know that.' But the bitterness remained. How could she go away? Why would she not put aside all other things to protect their love?

'You are cryin', Jonny.' She felt a stirring of compassion at his

229

vulnerability. Stubbornly he would not acknowledge the tears by brushing them away.

'I have never cried before, not even as a boy.' It was an observation made quietly, as if he were amazed at the event. Then in irritation he pulled a sleeve across his face to dismiss the weakness.

She looked at the streaks of dirt which the sleeve left behind. 'I might not be gettin' the work.' It was said on an impulse to soothe him. But it did not.

'What would that avail us?' His question was put curtly and made her sorry to have said anything as he pursued it. 'If you should go away or not, love me or not, there would still be the matter of your faith to bar our way ... tell me otherwise.' She did not answer, vexing him. 'I shall take your silence to mean you have not had a change of mind on seeking annulment.' Resignedly, he dusted his hands over the uniform jacket as though ridding himself of something unwelcome.

'So be it, now there is something I must say. The *Pelican* is almost ready.' He spoke flatly. 'I am obliged to return to England within the week.'

She felt the ground seem to give way beneath her feet and for a moment lost balance. 'So soon is it?' Weakly, the words spilled from her, all thoughts of Agnes and Boston gone from mind.

They looked at each other, brought close in their despair. 'What shall we do, Jonny?'

Gently he embraced her. 'I do not know... I only wish to God I did.' With a soft cry she put her arms about his neck and they kissed in a passion of desperation, then broke to snuggle close.

'Tell me again you love me.' His breath was warm against her neck. 'Say it now or tell me to go.'

'I love you, Jonny ... please don't be for leavin'.'

He held her closer. 'It is not my will to go from you.'

'Say then y'will not leave before I return from Boston.'

'For pity's sake! You go to work there.'

'"Tis a meeting only to see if I will suit.'

'You torment me, Mary ... what when you return?'

230

'I cannot say, Jonny. I only ask that y'give me time.'

They clung together in silence as the wind soughed about them, and a full minute passed before he spoke. 'Do you ask me to wait upon a miracle?' She hesitated only a moment. If they should part now it would be for ever. She could not bear that.

'I will tell Agnes the way I feel in my heart ... then will ask that she takes me t'see the priest t'seek forgiveness an' absolution from my vows.'

As in a languor where time and reality move in a fatigue she felt him stir at her words, watched his eyes come to hers, saw the uncertainty in his expression and heard the bewilderment in his voice.

'Are you sure?'

'I am sure, Jonny.' Her mind dwelt vaguely on what punishment would await her in the life to come and she felt fear at the thought. Then she witnessed his face grow young and radiant again as he looked into her eyes, his voice soft in adoration.

'My darling Mary ... how brave you are.'

She smiled, masking her doubts, but did not risk speech. He kissed her softly upon the forehead.

'You shame me with your courage while all I give is bluster and ranting... You are so patient with me... I swear before heaven that you shall never again be unhappy or want for anything upon this earth.'

They walked hand in hand towards the carriage, he sure in stride and expression, she unsure, yet not showing her secret thoughts to him. But as they came into view, Agnes read Mary's expression clearly enough.

31

Only recently completed on the sweat of volunteer Irish labour
and tithes, plus the unyielding and stern demands of Father
Patrick Casey, the gleaming white stone edifice of St Peter-
in-Chains dominated the high ground of Clarkstown. Within,
it was no less compelling; a richly patterned terrazzo floor
gave way to fine carpeting towards the high altar, and all
around were many superbly crafted stained-glass windows.
The high ceiling was timbered in smoothly planed oak and
interspersed with painted panels of the Creation, supported
by stone pillars which soared from between well used pews.
An impressive display of candles, flames straight as arrows,
burned upon the altar, the distinctive smell of their smoke
hanging heavily in every corner. Now and again the footsteps
of the devout, come to say evening prayer, echoed about the
place.

Mary sat with Agnes in a side pew. They had spoken little
since their arrival, now both silent in thought as they awaited
audience with the priest. Mary looked up into the eyes of the
bronze Christ. They seemed to move as the candlelight played
about them, and she imagined disapproval there. The doubts
came to plague her once more, and memories of the marriage
ceremony at Inniscourt flooded back. The dark eyes of the
selfish young priest, forcing her into vows she should never
have made. But was this, that she was about to do, any more
right? She went from the thought back to her meeting with
Jonathan. She could have done no other than what she had
promised him, surely?

A deep sigh escaped her and she attempted to close her

mind to everything save the immediate, her gaze now fixed to the corridor along which the priest would come. Agnes shifted uneasily in the pew. More used to the spartan atmosphere of the Anglican church, she was not comfortable with the pomp and grandness about her. Please God the business would soon be done with.

Mary had been adamant, her mind made up, when they had returned to Braganza from the clifftops. She would seek permission of annulment, and if it were agreed by the priest that proceedings for it could take place, return with Jonathan to England. If not, then she would go to Boston as a governess. Despite any misgivings Agnes may have nursed, she was impressed with Mary's mature attitude. The girl had made a straight issue of her problems and would see them through with no further delay, no matter the outcome. Agnes did not give any argument. When all was said and done she held no right to force the answers. It was Mary's prerogative to seek those herself, but she would at least help her in that cause.

The priest emerged from the corridor and made his way towards them, his footsteps soundless, a silver crucifix swinging gently across a long black cloak, the hem hiding his feet, making him seem to Mary as if he moved by divine miracle rather than stride. Short in stature, rotund in figure, hair greying, Father Patrick Finbar Casey was a man steeped in the Catholic faith.

Well into middle age, he had been a priest from the age of twenty in Dublin and in his years learned never to question the ways of the Church, its demands or disciplines. Yet within those strictures he was a fair and listening priest, but nobody's fool. His well-spread network of spies had kept him in full intelligence on the happenings of Mary and the McAffertys. He knew that sooner or later things would come to a head and someone would have to seek out his offices on the problem. In the event it had been the rich Protestant woman, Mrs Meredith. So be it. Naturally he would reveal nothing of his knowledge to her, for properly handled there might be political gain to be made from the encounter.

233

'Good evenin' ... Mrs Meredith, is it not?' He ignored Mary.

'Good evening. You are Father Casey?' Agnes's voice was steady. He nodded in affirmation.

'I have been expectin' you.'

Agnes indicated Mary, whose gaze was on the priest's crucifix, not wanting yet to meet his eyes. 'This is Mary.'

He kept his stare on Agnes. 'The note brought by your stable boy, Mrs Meredith. In it y'said the matter was urgent.'

'Yes. It is good of you to see us at such short notice.'

'The Lord's work never stops, Mrs Meredith.' He frowned. 'But you are not of the faith, I understand?'

'Not of the Catholic faith.'

'I see.' He frowned again. 'But y'say y'want to speak for this girl, whom I believe is a Catholic?'

'That is so.'

'Why cannot she speak for herself?' He still ignored Mary.

'I believe it might be better if I were to explain the full circumstances ... Mary may well find it too harrowing.'

'Really?' For the first time he allowed himself a glance at Mary, then returned his gaze to Agnes. 'Very well, you have my permission to do so.' He sat down within the pew but kept a yard or more distance between them. 'Proceed, if y'will.'

A half-hour elapsed before Agnes finished her story. But she decided in the telling to omit Jonathan, reasoning that it would only serve to complicate matters. In the silence which followed she could tell from the priest's expression that her words had fallen on stony ground. Yet she still hoped for advice that might secure Mary's release from Donal McAfferty.

Father Casey rose slowly, hands clasped behind him as he walked up and down in front of the altar rail, casting occasional glances at Agnes as he spoke. 'It is a terrible enough tale, Mrs Meredith, but tell me ... how d'you know it to be true?'

'Because the truth is plain there to see. Mary is the most Godfearing and honest person I have ever met ... I believe she is not capable of telling a lie.'

234

'Well now!' He regarded Mary for some moments. 'Is she not a rare person indeed t'walk the earth?' Agnes bristled under the sarcasm, but held her temper in check as the priest came to a halt at the end of the rail and addressed Mary. 'Child, if that is so, why do I not ever see you in church?'

Agnes was quick to interrupt. 'Under the circumstances it has not been possible for Mary to worship here.' She spoke appealingly.

'There was the chance she might have run across the McAffertys?' He shrugged. 'She would have come to no harm in God's house.'

Agnes did not give proper thought to her reply. 'As I have said, Mary is without deceit. She could not anyway have come to worship without a full and sincere heart...' She stopped, but her error was realised too late and the priest cut in like an arrow.

'Without a full and sincere heart, Mrs Meredith?'

She swallowed deeply, then hurried on. 'Please receive this in charity, Father Casey ... it is not a condition which will last, but I believe that what Mary has endured has turned her away from any real thought of God.' She tried to ease the statement, but only made matters worse. 'I am sure it would not be so if she were given hope.'

'God does not trade in the market place!' His fierce retort gave way to a silkily smooth question. 'But I fail t'understand you anyway, Mrs Meredith ... if the girl has turned her face from God, how then does she now see fit to plead her cause before the Church?'

Mary had writhed throughout the exchanges. Now she could stand it no longer. She rose, her tone clipped to precision. 'Father Casey ... I would have y'know that my difficulty is not visited upon the Almighty, although I have doubted Him for what has befallen me ... Now I have come t'see that my difference is not with God but His servants, and I pray He will bless and guide them in His work.' Agnes winced at the words and awaited the wrath of the priest.

To her surprise he smiled indulgently, but there was no humour in it. 'So! Y'can speak after all, Mary McAfferty? An' I see it is right what they say of you, fiery an' articulate.' His smile went. 'Thank you for prayin' for my soul an' the souls of my brother priests.' The tone was heavily sarcastic, but she was more interested that he had apparently been told of her. How much did he know of the situation?

'Y'know of me then, Father?'

He regretted the slip and went on the offensive to sidestep the question. 'I should like t'know why, when you are plainly educated, do y'let a Protestant speak for you? Is it y'seek to hide somethin'?'

She almost smiled. 'Y'will surely find I have nothin' t'hide, Father.'

The priest considered his best line of attack. Mrs Meredith would almost certainly prove to be the softer target. To spite Mary he turned again to Agnes, but Mary remained standing.

'I believe y'have taken on a rare task, Mrs Meredith.'

'And I believe it was a Christian act to do, Father Casey.'

'I see, an' what does her husband, Donal, I believe y'said his name was, what does he have t'say on the matter?'

'I would not know, I have never conversed with the man.'

'What you are sayin', Mrs Meredith, is that Mary ran away from Donal ... for whatever reason, an' that she is domiciled with you an' Mr Meredith against the wishes of her lawfully wedded husband. Am I not right in that assumption?'

'That is only the black and white of it ... Father Casey.'

'That is surely the truth of it ... Mrs Meredith.'

She was angry but her voice came evenly enough. 'I believe we are straying from the matter in hand. What I wish to know is whether or not you are able to help Mary.'

'You enquire on the annulment of marriage?'

'I do.'

'When an' where did the ceremony take place?'

Agnes looked in query at Mary. 'Do you remember the details, my dear?'

'Ma'am, I am not t'forget it for as long as I may live.' Her tone was cold. ''Twas on a Sunday, January the fifth, at Inniscourt, western Ireland.'

The priest switched his gaze to her. 'January of this year?'

236

Mary nodded. 'But it is now well into April ... that is the better part of four months. Why did you not seek advice before this time?'

'I was put straight on board the ship after the ceremony, an' did not arrive in America until March.'

Father Casey eased himself against the altar rail. He was not willing to take her on, for he saw the hostility in her eyes and had no wish to risk coming off second best in a rowdy encounter within his church. There was more spirit and ability in her than he had supposed.

'Listen t'me carefully, child. Y'have seen fit to appoint Mrs Meredith t'speak for you. Therefore I will now address only Mrs Meredith. If y'should interrupt the rest of this meetin' I will have you put from the church. However, should I need t'ask you questions y'will reply ... is that clear t'you?'

She felt triumph at his retreat. The man was frightened of her. 'As you say ... Father.'

The priest frowned then moved his attention to Agnes. 'Mrs Meredith, the McAfferty family are your tenant workers, and have been housed on your land for the better part of a month or more ... is that not so?'

'It is.' She was puzzled as to the aim of the question.

'Then Mary an' Donal lived together as man an' wife for that time, an' up to Mary runnin' away?' Mary wanted to cry out in denial. Had she not every night fought the creature off?

'Not in the true sense of man and wife ...' Agnes smoothed her hands against the pew as she selected her words with care. 'Mary had no alternative, she had tried to escape a number of times before that, but without success.'

He went stubbornly on, sure of his ground. 'Then we can take it that the marriage has been consummated?'

Agnes scowled. 'Mary was raped by her husband aboard the ship,' her voice trembled, 'while his brothers held her pinioned to the floor ... is that what you mean by consummation, Father Casey?'

'Is that so, Mrs Meredith? Well now, whether that is true or not, Mary chose t'go on living with Donal, an' I repeat, as man an' wife, after they arrived in America ... did she not?'

237

Mary screamed within. It was not the truth ... she had forever, since the night of the ship, kept herself clean and whole from the pig! But if she should speak in her own defence the priest would put her from the church. There was nothing surer. It would have to rest with Agnes, and pray to God she would succeed.

Agnes felt uncomfortable. The man was building a guilt about Mary. But the disconcerting thought came that it was damning in the logic of its construction. He repeated the question.

'Did she not go on living with him as man and wife?'

'Not of her own free will!'

'Very well, whose will was it?'

'The McAffertys kept her a virtual prisoner.'

'A prisoner? Then how ever did she manage t'get to you, Mrs Meredith?' He was enjoying his handling of the affair.

'You bewilder me with your questions. It was not a simple matter for her to escape.'

'I regret your bewilderment, but I seek only the truth.'

'Then the truth is that Mary wants annulment of the marriage. I came to you hoping for advice and understanding. Can you help the girl rid herself of this man?'

His tone was pained at her ignorance. 'Mrs Meredith ... if you were of the faith y'would not dare ask that question. In the eyes of God, Mary is married t'Donal according t'the rite of the Church, *ratum*. An' once that marriage is made *consummatum*, by even a single act of physical union, it can never be dissolved ... not even by the Pope himself.'

'I cannot believe that!' Agnes shouted the words, but he was unperturbed.

'I am sorry y'cannot, Mrs Meredith, nevertheless, I have to tell you this. The act of marriage is a holy estate between man an' woman, and in Christ, divided only by death.' He paused for just a moment before adding in grim fashion, 'Any other manner would see the perpetrator's soul go to eternal damnation ... I cannot connive with you in advice on severing this tie.'

Agnes rose to her feet. 'Connive! I wonder you dare say that in a house of God. The guilt should be placed where it best fits ... on the shoulders of the priest who forcibly married her to that creature!'

He remained unmoved under the assault. 'No priest in the Holy Roman Catholic Church could force a soul into a marriage against their will.'

Agnes fought her rising temper. She was up against a solid wall of Catholic dogma in this man. But she must keep control or lose the fight. 'The priest told Mary that if she did not agree to marry the man, then the McAffertys would not take the rest of the villagers on the ship to America. What is that if not force?'

'Mrs Meredith ... I am not able t'believe that. In any case, there would surely have been many other ships to convey them.'

'I am surprised at your ignorance of the situation in Ireland, Father Casey. But I am not here to educate you on that. Mary had lost her parents and was defenceless, her friends and neighbours were without food or money, and not a soul able or willing to help them ... if she had refused to marry, they would all have been left to die.'

'Whether that is true or not, Mrs Meredith, Mary was given free will by God. She did not have t'make her holy vows in marriage.' His words rang about Mary's head. It was as he said, she could have refused the vows.

Why had she not been more caring for herself and let the others fend for themselves? In the long run they had proved not to be worth the sacrifice. But then she remembered the kindness of Sean Dolan and hated herself for the selfishness.

Detachedly, Agnes regarded the burning candles, her mind vaguely trying to seek further words. Finally she looked up at the priest. 'Is there no higher authority with which to plead the case?' Father Casey gave a tolerant smile.

'Y'mean higher in authority than myself, Mrs Meredith?'

'With respect, Father Casey, that is what I mean.'

Reflectively he scratched his nose and thought for a few moments. 'I cannot see it would help you ... but I would not have y'go away with a poor opinion of the faith.' He took hold of the crucifix which hung from his neck and slowly rubbed it

239

to a lustre against his robes. 'The archbishop is due from Boston in two days' time. He comes t'bless the finishin' of the church. I am sure he would speak with you if y'wish it.'

Agnes tied the ribbons of the black straw bonnet more firmly beneath her chin as she made to leave. 'I would appreciate that, Father Casey. Thank you, and thank you for your time.'

Mary tightened her mouth in distaste at the mockery of the priest. Any such meeting would be time wasted, and he knew it. But she remained silent. It was finished. The Church would remain implacable, while she in her turn would keep firm the promise to Agnes and go to Boston for interview. But the priest was yet to deal his final card in the game.

Certainly, he had awaited the moment with much anticipation. 'Mrs Meredith, a word before y' go ... I did ask earlier if Mary had somethin' t'hide.' He regarded each woman in turn before continuing. 'I was thinkin' ... it may be as well, when y'talk with the archbishop, t'mention the fact of the English sea-captain.' He revelled in their embarrassment at his words. 'I would not want anyone t'be taking hold of the wrong end of the stick.' He turned about, not allowing Agnes time for reply, and walked swiftly away towards the corridor.

The eventful day had begun early for Meredith. Breakfast was a near-silent affair, attended only by Agnes and Jonathan. Aware that Meredith intended to ask Jonathan to quit the house, Agnes made an excuse and left immediately after the meal so as not to aggravate the situation.

The expulsion was expedited in a civilised style, both men painfully polite, and Jonathan did not speak in his defence until they reached the cabin to which Meredith had transported him. In the light of the conversation which followed, Meredith began to see things more clearly. If an annulment could be achieved by Mary, it would provide one answer. If not, the more realistic solution for her would be the post of governess – he had left home too early to know that the morning mail contained the letter offering an interview.

240

Meredith's first reaction was relief. Either way it seemed certain that the problem would soon be at an end. Nevertheless he thought it better for Jonathan to stay at the new quarters until the *Pelican* was ready to sail.

But as he drove the cart away from the cabin he began to meditate. Up to this moment he had thought of Mary only as a problem. But what problem had she really been? Conscience began to prick at him. The truth was that he had dwelt only on his own interests, not on the girl's sufferings. Carefully he eased on the reins, guiding the team off the dirt flats and up on to Timber Road, and within a half-hour was passing the place where he found Mary on that morning. How things had changed for him since that time, and for Agnes too. She had never properly come to terms with the death of their daughter, choosing never to discuss it. During the year just past she had become distant, taking to her own bedroom, while he, still so much in love with her, buried himself in politics and business. But since Mary's arrival he had witnessed the great change in Agnes, seen her enthusiasm for life come back and experienced the joy of her returning warmth to him.

It was late afternoon when a messenger arrived at the timberline with a note summoning him to attend an urgent meeting of the Clarkstown elite. Expecting that the scandal had become known and he was about to be dressed down and asked to resign from office, Meredith entered the council chambers with trepidation. Instead, they elected him to head off a new threat to the town. The Irish faction had made certain demands for proper recognition. They not only wanted the vote but also required that a number of their own candidates should stand for office. The city fathers would not tolerate such a happening.

Years earlier, the first Irish settlers had been made welcome. These were industrious people who had tired of the English yoke and had come with trades and life savings in prepared ambition of seeking a better life in the new world, families which quickly blended into the working and social life of the town. But there was now a growing concern, even fear, at the influx of mainly illiterate Irish who had invaded since the first

241

famine year of 1845. These had already polarised Clarkstown with their proliferation of shanty dwellings on the inland edge of town, and the regular Saturday night drunkenness and brawling. But worst of all they had brought Popery, a total anathema to the staunchly Protestant New Englanders.

To some extent, Meredith had kept the lid on any lawlessness with his liberal use of the jail, maintaining peace through the fact that the Irish were without a real leader. But that morning the previously unknown figure of Peter O'Brien had emerged, claiming the unanimous backing of the Irish and revealing himself to be the architect of the demands. Arrogantly he waved away the establishment reasoning that the majority, if not all the newcomers, still awaited official citizenship, and as such must await any entitlements. He wanted recognition now. If not, trouble would follow. O'Brien had drifted in from Boston less than three months before, and was not long in observing the wealth and prosperity of the growing town. Taking lodgings in the shanty town area, he had lain low until he sized up the situation as ripe for picking.

Then, with astute words and the generous buying of booze he had, in just a week, got himself installed as the political leader of the immigrants. In Dublin, whence he originated, he had been dubbed the Rainbow Chaser for his numerous wild schemes of one kind and another. He was also something of an actor, appearing with various groups in the city's public houses, even sometimes on the stage of lesser theatres. Of a certainty he charmed the ladies, his tall athletic figure and darkly handsome good looks leaving many a one in his trail.

But there was a sinister side to the man. He had left Dublin and gone to Cork, where he operated as a self-styled freedom fighter, heading a motley band of outlaws against the English landlords for a short time before moving to the easier task of extortion from the locals. Of a well-to-do background, he had turned into the black sheep of his family. His education was chequered and littered with expulsions from a number of good schools. Nevertheless he was a silver-tongued fellow who could talk the birds down from the trees. But above all was his talent for spellbinding oratory and rabble-rousing. There was

242

not a man better at it, and the Clarkstown establishment saw the danger in him. A reason must be found to bring the date of election forward and spike his guns before he could properly prepare. Meredith was chosen to do it, and politically, his star had never been higher than on this day.

32

Liam downed his third whisky. 'There is an old sayin'…' He stopped speaking, and stared at the remains of his evening meal while Patrick and Donal grew apprehensive, expecting another row over the food. But there was a more pressing matter on Liam's mind and he was on a devious trail to reveal it. He frowned at their lack of curiosity and repeated the words. 'Yes indeed, a very old sayin'…'

'What is it, dar, this old sayin'?' Patrick had taken the lure, and Liam visibly brightened.

'I'm glad y'asked me that, Patrick, 'tis this … if an Irishman loves y' he will die for yez. But if he hates y' he will swing for yez.' He glanced nastily at Donal. 'I trust y'are listenin' to me, 'cause it is time for the McAfferty name t'be righted!'

Donal became more attentive. 'I am that, dar, y'have heard somethin'?'

'I have, but I will right it.'

Patrick was cautious. 'What did y'hear, dar?'

'Enough gossip around the town t'set my ears burnin' wit' the shame of it, an' your man Ben Ambrose has told me more.'

Donal looked triumphantly at Patrick. 'What did I tell y'now!' He turned to his father. 'Are y' goin' t'kill him, dar?'

'I won' have t'kill the bastard, I'm fixin' for the law t'do that for us.'

Donal's face crawled with curiosity. 'How will y'fix it for the law t'kill him, dar?'

''Cause I have the brains t'figure it! Now the pair of y'shut up an' listen.'

They nodded in silent respect, and their breathing came

hard with anticipation of Liam's next words. 'The English bastard will be hung for murder!'

Donal's question was breathed out in awed reverence. 'Murder?'

Liam nodded, and watched each of his sons in turn, glorying in their reaction. Then abruptly, he changed the subject as his trail of deviousness continued. 'You boys never got t'know your grandfather, did you?' Donal was disappointed by the sudden change in tack, but knew it would earn him nothing to do other than listen.

Patrick again took the lure. 'No, dar, we were only babbies when he passed over.'

Liam beamed at him. 'Beautiful words y'use Patrick, passed over, for he is not dead. He lives in us.'

Patrick warmed to the praise. 'Y'told us the many grand tales about him, dar, how he kicked over the traces an' all.'

Liam grinned. 'Not all the tales, a great father he was t'me, feared neither man nor divvil.' He looked hard at Donal. 'An' he held the name of McAfferty in holy reverence ... he has killt men for the soilin' of it!'

Donal gulped. 'Killt men?'

'That's what I said.'

Patrick became quiet, the worried look back on him. But Donal was fascinated. 'Were these men from Inniscourt, dar?'

'They were not! My father walked Inniscourt like a giant, an' the people were in holy terror of him ... no, these men were from the north, an' had come t'live in Castlebar.'

'Who were they, dar?'

'Horse traders. They took up wit' father's young sisters, a terrible an' shameful thing altogether. They were ripe with the babbies, an' the men were not for the marryin'.'

'Jesus! What was he after doin' then?'

'He went t'visit on them with the biggest horse pistol y'could ever hope t'see ... they were still not for goin' t'the church, so he shot them both stone dead.'

'Holy Mother! Did the law not come on him?'

Liam's reply was full of scorn. 'The law? He was the law!'

'An' did he just leave them dead on the floor?'

245

Liam leaned forward over the table, and Donal could smell the whisky on his breath. 'He put great rocks about their necks an' rowed them far out to sea. No man was eejut enough t'ask questions when he returned alone.'

Donal was spellbound. 'The saints be praised for it, dar, an' what happened t'his sisters?'

'He beat them near t'death, an' ran them both out of the County Mayo. We never saw the hide nor the hair of 'em again.'

There was awe in Donal's whispered return. 'A great an' powerful man indeed.'

'He was that.' Liam had almost reached the end of his shabby trail. One more move and there would be no way of retreat left for Donal to take. 'Do y'honour his memory, son?'

'Indeed I do!' Donal nodded vigorously.

'I am glad of it, for on his deathbed he made me swear, hand on heart, that if any man brought the shame to us I would see that man done away wit'.'

Donal fidgeted under his father's stare. 'I know what you are after thinkin', dar.'

'Do y' now, an' what would that be?'

'It is the talk of the Englishman carryin' on with Mary.'

'You are not wrong, Donal. My father's ghost is hauntin' me with the shame of it.'

'But, dar, y'said the law would hang him for murder.'

'I did, but have y'not thought that there's a little matter of the fixin' of the murder t'do.'

Sweat broke out on Donal's face and he grew more uncomfortable by the second. His mind tried to grapple with the fact that he could not recall ever having had such a long conversation with his father. There had to be a bad ending to it. His voice cracked under a sudden, instinctive fear. 'How will we do that, dar?'

'With brains, Donal, with brains . . . your man Sullivan, who I will curse t'my dyin' day, is for the murderin', an' I have fixed it for the entire blame t'fall on the sailor boy.'

'I do not understand y', dar.'

'You will, Donal . . . one of the boyos repairin' the ship has

246

told me that Sullivan an' the sailor boy are havin' a private get-together tomorrow night. The booze will flow, an' the legs will be shaky for the walkin' . . . Do y'follow me, Donal?'

'I don't know, dar. Why can we not just kill the Englishman?'

'Y'have no brains, Donal. If we killt him the lawmen would be on us directly, they know what is goin' on wit' Mary an' all. They are not stupit!'

The light dawned in Donal's eyes. 'I see it now, dar.'

Liam snorted with impatience. 'I am glad of it. Now here's the way it will be. After the body is found I have a man who will put it about the town that your man an' Sullivan had the big row concernin' money for the ship repairs. He will swear on it that one thing led t'another, an' the sailor boy hit Sullivan over the head an' killt him wit' this . . .' Liam groped under the table for a moment before producing an 18-inch long, iron bar. He threw it on the table, where it landed with a loud bang to lie glinting in the glow of the lamp. 'I got it off the ship last night.'

Donal pulled his stare away from the bar. 'Will y' get Sullivan when he leaves the shindig?'

' 'Tis you who will be doin' the gettin'.'

Donal felt his stomach turn over with fear. 'Will y'not be helpin' me, dar?'

'No, nor shall Patrick. Mary is your wife, an' you get the great honour of wipin' the dirt from our name.'

Donal shook with terror as he looked away to Patrick for support, but there was none there. Donal's frantic stare went again to Liam. 'Me t'do the murderin', is it? I know nothin' of the way t'kill a man!'

Liam picked up the bar from the table and flourished it under Donal's nose. 'Put y'r weight behind this, an' your troubles are gone in the twinklin' of an eye.'

Donal looked again at the bar. Despite his fears, its squat, round ugliness fascinated him. 'Will I hit him over the head?'

'An' where else would y'hit the bloody man?'

'Dar . . . I have a desperate fear crawlin' on me, so I have. Wit' the darkness all about, how will I know when the man is dead?'

Without a word, Liam rose from his chair and crossed over

247

to a sack of vegetables which lay against the wall. Selecting a turnip, he threw it on the floor where it rolled to within a yard of Donal, then padded over to kneel beside it. 'Give me the bloody bar!'

Donal could not keep his hands from shaking as he lifted the bar from the table and handed it over. With a terrifying skill, Liam struck in sharp angles at the turnip, the vicious blows sending its pieces flying all about the room, some striking Donal and Patrick, and it seemed an eternity to them before he stopped.

With the mash dripping from his face, Liam rocked back on his heels, and almost out of breath glared up at Donal. 'That's what y'do ... y'keep hittin' ... his bloody head ... until there's nothin' left t'hit.' He stood up and banged the bar down on the table, while Donal stared at the battered remains of the turnip.

'Christ help me.' There was a pleading in his eyes as he regarded his father. 'What if somebody sees me? I'd go t'the gallows for sure.'

Liam gave a shake of the head. ''Twill be black as pitch when your man comes out.'

Whiningly, Donal pursued his argument. 'Why must it be me, dar? I've hardly killt a flea in my life.'

Liam sat down and regained his breath for a few moments. 'Because 'tis your wife who brings the shame on us.'

Fear for his life brought Donal clear of restraint. 'She does not mean that much as I'd have me neck stretched for her!' His voice grew stronger. 'Let the bloody Englishman have her. I'll find another quick enough ... sure, there's many a woman already after givin' me the glad eye in the fields, an' that's the truth of it!'

Patrick winced at the words and prepared for the wrath he knew would follow. Liam twitched in anger. 'Tell me y'are sorry for what y'have just now said.'

But Donal would not be moved. 'I have said the truth of it!'

Liam's face contorted in fury. 'Y'bloody misbegotten snake! Do y'not know what y've done? Y've reviled the name of your dear grandfather wit' your filthy tongue!' The force of the blow

248

which followed sent Donal crashing from his chair, unconscious to the floor.

'He looks bad hurt, dar, will I be pickin' him up?' Patrick moved towards his brother, but Liam checked him.

'Y'will not pick him up! Throw some water on the pig!'

Donal came chokingly back to life as the water hit his face, and Liam moved to stand over him. 'Tell me y'are sorry for what y'said.'

Donal groaned in apology and Liam gave a slow shake of the head. 'Why is it I have t'knock hell out of yez t'get any sense? Get on y'r feet an' sit down with me an' y'r brother.'

The three men sat at the table once more and Liam affected a caring tone. 'Donal, I would not get y'hung. Y'are my dear son, an' if y'had listened y'd have known y'r troubles are over.'

Donal looked up hopefully at his father. 'I am not t'do it then?'

Liam waved his hands in dismissal of the question. 'I am not for leavin' the law t'finish our man, for I once saw a judge set a fast-talkin' rogue free as the wind.' He grinned. 'No, 'tis a matter of makin' sure, an' I have the boyos for a lynchin'. With some booze down their necks, an' a few dollars in their breeches pocket, they will take him from the prison an' righteously hang the bastard.' He rubbed grubby fingers up and down the iron bar. 'I have met with a great man named O'Brien, a grand fella who will shortly be takin' this miserable little town by the scruff of the neck and gettin' us the big money and power.' His fingers gripped the bar. 'He has the use of a barn close t'the lock-up, we string your man up there ... then we are home an' dry!'

There was the faintest glimmer of hope in Donal's eyes. 'Will they be sure t'get him?'

Liam nodded, and patted Donal on the arm. 'As sure as night follows day.'

33

Awakened by the dawn light and a pounding headache from his drinking bout with Sullivan, Jonathan moved aside the blankets and lay a moment, silently vowing never to drink again. Hand to forehead he climbed from the bed and shivered as his feet touched the board floor. It was colder in the cabin than it had been in the house, and his dressing was as laboured as his thoughts. Mary was due to leave on the morning stage for Boston. He glanced at the pocket-watch which lay on the washstand. Six o'clock. She would already be gone.

It had been late on the previous afternoon when Agnes had brought Mary to see him. They did not come aboard the ship, and he joined them on the dockside where they stood in awkward silence before Agnes retreated a few paces to allow a scant privacy. He had known what Mary would say even before she spoke. He cursed softly. 'Damn the priest and the Catholic faith to hell.'

He surveyed his face in the shaving mirror. If his father could only see him at this moment. What a pitiful sight he was. Love had made him an idiot, but even now he clung to her willingness to see him again on her return from Boston.

Hands trembling slightly with the effects of the hangover, he guided the open razor under his chin, his mind moving to more immediate things. He had promised Sullivan a banker's draft for delivery today. He cursed again. 'Hell!' It meant he would have to go into Boston to see the agent when he might more easily have got the bloody man to send it by the mail coach.

He winced at the memory of his drunken vow. 'David, dear boy, I must pay you without delay. A draft shall be delivered by my own fair hands by noon. You have my word on it as a gentleman.' He frowned. When the drink was in, the wit was surely out. But he could not renege on his pledge and would now have to hire a carriage ... maybe a horse would be faster. Yes, he would go by horse.

The decision evoked memory of the day he had ridden the race against Charlotte across the downs, the heady thrill of the thoroughbreds at full stretch across the sparkling frosted grass to the Point. She had been exultant to win the wager ... but what might be her words now in his predicament? Gingerly he edged the razor about his throat and the ghost of a smile came. No doubt she would suggest that he dug more deeply with the blade.

He dismissed the thought of her as he planned his day. The price of the *Pelican*'s recovery from Blackstone Edge and its repairs was higher than estimated, and the insurers might question it. Well what if they did? They were fortunate not to be facing total loss, and the cargo had escaped damage.

His thoughts went back to Mary. Why had he not gone with her on the mail coach? He could have rightly claimed it was a business journey. But she would not have believed it, thinking he was following her. In any event there was Agnes. How completely banal the conversation would have been. He eased the razor away from his throat and looked squarely into the eyes of his reflection and murmured.

'Try not to be more ridiculous than you already are.'

His musings were brought to a halt by a sudden banging on the cabin door, making him jump. The razor cut into his throat, causing the blood to drip. 'Damn!' He dropped the razor and reached for the facecloth, holding it to the injury as he opened the door. Meredith, flanked by two peace officers, stood outside and Jonathan noted the grimness of their expressions.

'What is it, Mr Meredith?'

The reply came quietly, without feeling. 'David Sullivan has been murdered.'

251

'Murdered? I do not believe it. He was with me only last evening ... is this some jest?'

Meredith was stony-faced. 'This is no jest, Captain Bramwell, information has been laid fixing you with it. We are here to arrest you.'

Jonathan took an involuntary pace back into the room, the facecloth dropping from his hand, allowing the blood to run unchecked.

'Arrest me?'

Meredith gave a curt nod. 'I'm sure you'll be able to explain things, but you must come with us now, for your own safety.'

Jonathan rallied from the shock. 'This is a nonsense! If David has been murdered, then I am innocent of it.'

'I wouldn't know about that, but I do know there's bad feeling running through the town. David was a liked man, and there's already talk of a lynching.'

'I cannot believe this...'

Meredith interrupted in a more urgent tone. 'It's a fact, so we have to move fast.' He looked at the blood. 'How did you get in that mess?'

Still in a daze, Jonathan replied distantly, 'I cut myself shaving.'

Meredith glanced about the room and saw the bowl and razor. 'Get your coat and come with us.'

A small group of farmhands stood around as the peace officers hustled Jonathan into a prison-cart, clanging shut and locking the gate behind him. Manacled about the wrists, he gripped the bars of the cage and stood tall to meet the hostile looks. But any attempt at dignity was wrested from him when the horses were savagely whipped up, throwing him hard against the bars, and as the cart sped in a sharp circle from the yard he was hurled to the floor of the cage.

It was evening. Donal lay huddled in his bed where he had spent the day in troubled sleep, the single, ragged blanket damp with the sweat of fear. From time to time his body was

252

taken over by an uncontrollable shaking as his mind made constant return to the happenings of the previous night.

Once more he gripped the iron bar, once more he brought it down on Sullivan's head, smashing again and again at the skull as he had seen his father do at the turnip, the warm blood spurting into his face, blinding him with its stickiness. Once more he heard the clang of the bar as it hit the ground. Then the sound of his boots, the terrible running ... running and running until his lungs were bursting. The panic when he tried to scrub the blood from him at the trough. It would not leave his clothes nor be dislodged from his broken fingernails. He gagged on the sudden dryness of his mouth.

They would come and get him for sure and he would hang, eyes bulging, tongue sticking purple from the mouth and the legs jigging in the air ... as when a boy he had seen the English soldiers hang the rebel in Sligo market place. He groaned and pulled the blanket from his face, turning to look at the window as if expecting the light to give him refuge from thought. But already it was growing into a dark promise of return to the night terrors which had harried him throughout the many hours. Holy Mother of God! Make it stop ... for Christ's sake, if only he could go back and make it right.

His thoughts turned to plague him afresh, returning to the hour before he had set out to do murder, the hour in which he might have run away from it all, yes, away to Boston. He could have made his own way in the city. What did he care for the name McAfferty? What had it fetched him but the blackest of trouble? And what of Patrick, always in the clear of it, always the dar's golden boy? The voices came to haunt him again.

'Why cannot Patrick come wit' me, dar?'

'Y'have it to do alone. Me an' your brother will be puttin' ourselves about the town, an' at Murphy's bar.'

'Why would y'be doin' that?'

'Tellin' people y'are poorly abed, t'will put you many a mile from the killin' an all.'

He had been sick. 'Holy Jesus, I am mortal feared.' But there was no understanding from his father, simply a bottle of cheap whisky pushed roughly into his hands.

'Drink it! 'Twill give y'the courage of ten men.'

The alcohol had burnt his throat and made him near choke. Liam grinned at it, and handed him the iron bar which he took with fingers that trembled. His father's voice seemed to come from a far distance. 'On your feet, boy! Wait round the back of the fence where I've shown you, then come up behind your man. Use both hands now! An' keep hittin' him 'til he's a gonner.'

'Driven t'the murderin' for that cow! I wisht it was her I was hittin' over the bloody head.'

'Shut up an' mind y'make a proper job of it, then back here an' into the bed.' The last-minute plea for reprieve had fallen on ears deaf to it. 'Y'are not doin' the murderin' at all. Y'are McAfferty born an' bred, bringin' the great honour t'our name. Now go, an' show me y'have backbone!'

With a moan of anguish, Donal turned his gaze from the window and buried his head under the blanket. He had not prayed for many years but he did so now, as he had never prayed before.

34

Burning torches lit the road outside Clarkstown jail as an angry crowd, many the worse for drink, jostled and yelled for Jonathan to be brought out. In the majority were the shanty immigrants, presently faring little better in America than they had in Ireland. Around fifty or sixty of them had arrived only days ago, obliged now to live on their wits, unable to find work in the already over-manned mills or on the land. Ragged and hungry, they had been whipped into hysterical fervour by the oratory of Peter O'Brien, while his lieutenants plied them with rotgut whisky. A field stove provided soup and bread. Having been told there would soon be jobs and dollars, they were in ecstasy and prepared to follow their new-found leader clean through to hell. Some distance away, on the verandah of a grocery store, Liam stood talking with Patrick.

O'Brien detached himself from the crowd and walked over to them. He smiled, flourishing a coiled rope fashioned with a hangman's knot. 'They are in a mood to finish your fellow.'

Liam touched his forehead in respect. 'I am obliged t'you, an' will not be forgettin' the debt, Mr O'Brien.'

Theatrically, O'Brien bowed from the waist. 'My pleasure, Mr McAfferty.' He cocked his head in query. 'And why is Donal not here t'see the grand hangin'?'

Liam grinned. 'I figured you'd think it best for him t'be in his bed, where a sick man oughta be.'

Disappointment crossed O'Brien's face. One of the stars, the murderer, was missing from his production. He had looked forward to watching Donal's every expression when they hanged the prisoner. 'He would have been safe from the harm with me here.' His words were soft, but there was a lash in them.

Liam was at once apologetic. 'I am sorry, Mr O'Brien, shall I away an' get him?'

O'Brien thought a moment. 'No, there is not time.' He glanced towards the mob which had grown quieter. 'What a rabble they are.' He grimaced. 'They have not voice nor aim without their leader.' Liam chilled as the ice-blue eyes fixed on him. 'Would y'not agree, Mr McAfferty?'

Liam dredged up every last ounce of enthusiasm in reply. 'I would indeed, sir.'

O'Brien gave him a derisory look. 'Very well, let us stir them t'the hunting of the game ... do as I directed.' His smile was thin. 'Use my full name, if y'will, Mr McAfferty.'

Liam jumped from his near trance, and shouted towards the mob. 'Hold there!'

They swung as one towards him and he warmed to the feeling of power. 'Did I not just now hear our good friend an' true leader, Mr Peter O'Brien, say he saw the Englishman arguin' wit' poor Sullivan about the money for the ship repairs ... he did for him right enough!' A fresh outburst greeted this, and Liam poked an elbow into Patrick's ribs. 'Get on wit' the job, speak your piece.'

Patrick was reluctant to become involved, and his expression showed as much. But O'Brien's warning look brought him to sense, and the carefully rehearsed words came wildly from him. 'Sure enough, it is the truth! Guilty is what he is! All Englishmen are the murderin' pigs!'

The assembly ignited into new fury, and O'Brien lifted the rope high above his head, his voice coming in a hoarse scream. 'Get me the man!'

In a madness they hurled themselves at the clapboard jail, some at the windows, others at the door, in a rage of breaking glass and splintering timber. The two guards within threw aside their pistols and gave only token fight before being punched to the floor to be bound and gagged. There was a calm sureness about O'Brien as he knelt down and eased the

256

gag from one of the guards. 'I shall ask y'only the once ... who has the keys?'

With the blood running from broken teeth, the man could only mutter a reply.

'Jailer...'

'Where is he?'

The man nodded towards a brick passageway which led to the cells. 'Down there.'

A triumphant cry broke from O'Brien as he got up and made for the passageway. 'We have him!'

With howls of bravado, the dozen men who had been picked to effect the hanging surged behind their leader. The rest of the mob were left shouting and storming about the office and on the road.

Liam grabbed Patrick by the arm. 'Outside wit' you an' keep lookout. If the law comes I want t'know on the instant.'

Patrick did not move. 'We are in great trouble, dar... I'm thinkin' O'Brien is a madman... I see it in his eyes.'

Liam's reply was scathing. 'I know it, Patrick. Do not be after thinkin' I am stricken likewise!' Roughly, he pushed his son towards the broken door. 'Now get on the bloody road an' do as I told you!'

Free of the manacles, Jonathan felt no panic as he awaited the lynch mob. The jailer's intention to release him so that he might flee the crowd was past, and the man cringed against the wall, concerned solely with his own survival.

The narrow access from the passageway allowed only single file entry. O'Brien emerged from it first and smiled at Jonathan. 'I have come to hang you, Englishman.'

Jonathan regarded the man. Long black flowing cloak, broad-brimmed, floppy cap and such a strange expression ... the fellow was nothing but a playactor, he had seen many the like on the theatre stage. He would not grace the insanity with reply.

O'Brien smiled again. 'So, we will not converse. Well, soon now y'will not be able.' It did not matter any longer that Donal was not present. This fine-looking fellow was the real star of the show and would hang well off a tall horse.

257

Arms folded, O'Brien waited patiently as the hangmen began to fill the three-cell block, and within a few minutes the last man had crammed in. An odd quiet came over them at having run their quarry to earth, and in silent curiosity they stared through the bars at Jonathan. With slow deliberation he looked back at each man in turn and they lowered their eyes, unable to meet the contempt of his steady gaze – all except O'Brien and Liam.

In delight, Liam surveyed his enemy. So this was the man who had given him the trouble. A dandy indeed with his fancy uniform and gold braid, much good would they do the man now. But he was a handsome enough fella and must be worth a fortune with his own ship and all. Why, he must have the pick of all the women in the world. What in hell was he thinking of by dallying with the likes of Mary?

O'Brien watched the tumble of expressions cross Liam's face then dramatically broke the spell, punching the jailer in the stomach and taking the bunch of keys from him. For a few moments he examined them, then smiled at the terrified man.

'If you do not want t'join the Englishman's jig you had better tell me which one I should try.'

With a shaking finger the jailer pointed to one of the keys. O'Brien singled it out then motioned for two men to join him as he unlocked the cell door.

'You are going t'hell, sailor boy, and will just be in time t'have supper with the devil.'

An hour or so earlier, Ben Ambrose had carted in a load of vegetables from High Pines and witnessed the first signs of unrest outside the jail, but saw it as little more than an empty gesture. He had experienced the way lynchings were carried out in the deep South. Folk in a mind didn't gather to talk about it. They just up and did it. Anyways, Clarkstown was not hardly the place where such things happened. But the conversations which went on about him as he unloaded the cart caused him to change his mind. The man O'Brien was claimed to be behind it all, and had seemingly already promised his

258

followers that the Englishman would die on the rope that night.

Ambrose felt a mixture of guilt and fear as he drove the cart back to High Pines ... damn if he hadn't started it all up when he told Donal of the goings-on between Mary and the fella, but honest to Christ he didn't expect it would lead to this. A fist beating maybe, but not a lynching. The peace officers had laughed him out of the jail office, told him to go home and mind his business.

He pulled up at the fork which split the trail to Braganza. His hide would be on the line if something did happen to the Englishman and he was found out for his part in it. He had better get the hell to Meredith and tell him what was happening.

Having promised Agnes that he would meet her off the stage from Boston, Meredith was about to leave for the depot when he heard the cart come into the yard, quickly followed by a heavy thumping on the door.

Ambrose twirled the straw hat nervously about with hands that shook. This was a good job he had here, better not lose it with fool talk about what he had said to Donal ... just say what he had seen in town. He looked up as the door opened, blinking in the light from the oil lamp held high by Meredith.

'Ben! What in hell, have you any notion how much this fancy door cost?'

'Mighty sorry, Mr Meredith, sir, but there's bad happenin's in town.'

'What bad happenings?'

'Right bad, sir ... I'm just back from town, an' if I never saw a crowd ready to do a lynchin' then I seen one just now.'

'Hell! I might have guessed at it.' Meredith fumbled for the keys from his pocket then tossed them to Ambrose. 'Give these to Seth. Tell him to break out the guns from the armoury and rouse the sailors from the cabin, and tell Seth to make sure every man is armed and riding into town after me lickety-split.'

'Yessir! Right away, sir!'

'Then get down to the depot, Mrs Meredith and Mary are due in from Boston, take them to the lumber mill office and wait there 'til I'm through. The carriage is all set in the stables ... you understand all that?'

'Yessir!'

Meredith raced away towards the stable and within seconds rode from its doors, at full gallop for Clarkstown.

The barn was packed with a seething mass of noisy humanity, Irish to a man. Some sat on bales of straw, others perched precariously in the timber roof trusses, all agog to see the hanging of the English sea captain.

Head erect, hands tied behind him, Jonathan stood on a stack of boxes, dragged together to form a crude stage. Liam and Patrick sat close by this, the older man enjoying his moment of triumph, the younger man wishing himself elsewhere. Incongruously, O'Brien was mounted on a horse at the front of the stage. He waved, then climbed from the saddle on to the boxes and held his arms high for attention. The babble of talk died away as he pointed to Jonathan, his voice loud and full of emotion.

'The English are a terrible curse, surely sent by the devil himself t'sully the fair face of Ireland, an' make prisoners of the people.' A roar of approval from the crowd enthused him in his task. 'We have been driven from our own dear land to this place of strangers, but still we cannot find the peace. The bloody English come t'plague us, thick as fleas on a tinker's dog.' His outstretched fingers stabbed towards Jonathan. 'This is one of them!'

The mob surged forward, yelling abuse, and the horse reared in terror. O'Brien was obliged to shout long and hard to restore order. 'Hear me out! He is a murderer! I saw him strike down David Sullivan.' Uproar broke out once more, yet this time O'Brien let it continue to a natural halt.

But Jonathan was first to speak. 'You are a liar! There was no such happening!'

With a swagger, O'Brien moved to face him. 'A liar, am I?

260

Are you telling us you were happy at having to find the money t'pay for your ship's release?'

The crowd waited in silence for reply. Jonathan's mind was in a whirl. What had he said that night? He could not properly remember, damn the drink. Had he argued with David about the increase in price? Had someone been outside and overheard their talk? He recalled it as being loud. Surely to God he had not struck out? No, he remembered the pleasantries in their parting. Then how did this man know of his unease at the revised bill?

O'Brien spoke.

'Why do y'take so much time to answer, Englishman?'

'I am innocent!'

'Of course you are.'

The crowd laughed at the sarcasm, and O'Brien swung about to face them. 'On my life, I have never known the English claim t'be guilty of anythin'.' They sniggered. 'But I think we shall be gracious an' give the man a fair trial here an' now.' This was greeted with a mixture of dissent, laughter and approval.

O'Brien waved the chatter down. No one must be allowed to spoil this moment. 'We will do it in the way of the English, t'be fair an' just, with a jury an' all. And I shall be the judge.'

Most of the assembly were beginning to enjoy the rare entertainment, but Liam was anxious. The lawmen must surely have wind of happenings by now, and every moment that passed spelt danger. He dug one of his hirelings in the ribs and whispered him an instruction. The man jumped to his feet and yelled up at O'Brien.

'We came here t'hang the bastard, not t'play games! How long is this goin' t'take?'

O'Brien smiled. 'Well now, dear friend.' He took out a pocket watch and allowed it to dangle on a long chain where it turned slowly, almost touching the man's face. 'I would give it less than five minutes at the very most ... the devil grows hungry waitin' for the man.' A gale of laughter went up, and O'Brien knew he was on firm ground. Within a half-minute he had conscripted a jury to the stage.

261

'The trial will begin! An' as sure as poverty there is only the one witness.' He jabbed a finger into his chest. 'Me!' There followed loud applause and more laughter. 'You have just now heard my evidence, an' I do not want t'have to say it all over again.' He turned to address the jury.

'Now it is up to you, for we've had enough of the talkin'. Is the English bastard guilty or what?' Before they could reply, a great shout rang out from the crowd.

'Guilty!'

Hands on hips, O'Brien regarded Jonathan. 'You heard that! Now it's you for the hangin'!' He scooped up the rope from the stage, and with a deft flick sent it climbing into the air. All eyes followed its passage as it curled in a perfect arc over the central joist, and the crowd broke into wild cheers. O'Brien waved in acknowledgment, then tied the rope's end to a pillar. 'Bring him!'

A sack was pulled over Jonathan's head and he was frog-marched towards the terrified horse. A section of the crowd swung on the bridle while he was lifted with one quick heave into the saddle. Within the choking blackness of the sack, Jonathan felt the noose being slipped over his head, then the tightening of the knot, hard against the jugular. The sack was pushing into his mouth, his nose. He found it hard to breathe. He felt the writhing of the horse beneath him, heard O'Brien's final speech only vaguely, yet his mind had never been clearer. He had confidently expected rescue, but none had come. Now he was going to his death, not honourably, but at the hands of imbeciles. He would never see Mary again, never hold her, never kiss her, never make love to her ... he must make his peace with God ... would they give him time? No, they would not. Do it now! He began to pray.

Liam grinned, arms folded about him as he rocked with glee. 'What did I tell you? Your man is a gonner.' Ashen-faced, Patrick did not reply as the hysterical crowd pressed forward for a better view of the finale.

The sound of gunfire reverberated throughout the barn, volley after volley of shots smacking into the roof to send splinters of timber and showers of dust cascading on to the lynchers who cavorted around the horse. They looked towards the barn door to see a posse of five mounted men who now directed their guns to cover the hanging party. In the centre of the posse, Meredith moved his pistol to align on O'Brien, picking him out as the ringleader.

'Make one move and you're dead!' Without taking his eyes off O'Brien, he yelled at the crowd, 'Have you all gone stark raving mad? For Chrissakes! Do you know what would happen if you lynched this man? Every last one of you would hang for murder!'

The wave of fear-stricken reaction was silenced by the report of Meredith's pistol, the shot causing another shower of dust to fall. 'Shut up!'

In the prison of the sack, Jonathan could only guess what was happening, not able to hear all the words spoken, but he knew it was rescue. Be still, be calm. He tightened his legs more securely around the horse and waited.

Meredith moved his attention again to O'Brien.

'Take that noose from the prisoner's neck ... now!'

O'Brien did not move, and there was an arrogance about him. 'Your man has been found guilty of murder an' the people want t'see him swing!' Some of the mob shouted for the hanging to go ahead.

Cowering in the thick of the crowd and fearing to be seen by Meredith, Liam silently willed O'Brien to make a move... Do it. Do it now. Lash the bloody animal and it will be all over.

More voices sounded in support of O'Brien. Meredith ignored them, knowing he now held the whip hand. Yet any moves had to be made from where he sat in the saddle. The noose was tight and the horse spooked. There was no way he could get through the crowd to Jonathan, and at the same time ensure they would not carry out the lynching. He would have to gamble.

'I don't know who put you up to this, fella, but if that noose is not off by the time I count to three I shall shoot you dead where you stand.' O'Brien looked out over the silent crowd and felt his moment of glory ebbing away. Would it not be better to surrender and talk his way out? Meredith began a slow count.

'One!'

O'Brien felt the heightened beat of the pulse on his neck. What was there for him but ridicule if he did not carry out the hanging? He would be finished. Have to find a new town. Begin over again. He had no money left to do that.

'Two!'

The adrenalin pumped through his brain. The man was bluffing. He would not dare shoot, not here in front of all these people ... the day could yet be won. Distantly, he heard Meredith call out.

'Three!'

Meredith's finger began to tighten on the trigger.

A demented scream came from O'Brien, making every man's hair stand at the neck. 'Burn in hell, Englishman!'

His violent kick caught the horse on the head, and the animal whinnied with pain and terror as it reared high in the air, catapulting Jonathan from the saddle. In concert with the crack of the straightening rope came the bang of Meredith's pistol, the bullet ripping into O'Brien's forehead, tearing it wide open in a stream of blood. For a moment he lived, swaying and grinning at the jerking convulsions of his prisoner swinging before him, then crashed dead from the stage.

Pandemonium broke out, the crowd pushing mindlessly for escape from the barn, many already being trampled underfoot and crying out for help. A few men, hopeful of clemency, supported Jonathan on their shoulders, clear of the pull of the rope.

Meredith urged his mount forward and reached down to ease away the noose and sack. 'Lay him on the floor! Get water!' Quickly out of the saddle, Meredith knelt by him and looked for signs of life. Jonathan's eyes flickered open. Unable to speak, he broke into a fit of coughing while Meredith shouted in relief, 'Glory be!' He laughed shakily. 'Damned if you're not still in the land of the living.'

Just a few yards distant and careful to avoid Meredith's attention, Liam cursed O'Brien for the fateful delay. But for it, the Englishman would be dead. Yet there was still the trial. He would leave it to the law, they would make a better job of the hanging. He seized Patrick's arm. 'Come on.' They fought their way through the heaving crowd and out of the barn.

Ambrose had met the coach, but neither he nor Agnes had been able to stop Mary's headlong flight for the barn after he had revealed what was taking place. In near hysteria she fought her way through the fleeing crowd and into the building, looking wildly about for Jonathan. Suddenly she saw him.

Jonathan sat on a straw bale gingerly holding his neck. He attempted to drink water from a canteen handed him by one of the posse, but almost choked on it and through blurred vision saw Mary coming towards him. He tried to welcome her, but no sound came.

Gently, she touched his lips. 'Do not speak, Jonny.' She moved her fingers to brush the hair from his eyes while he touched her face and attempted a smile, both uncaring of the crowd who stood about them.

Meredith had been surprised at Mary's entry, but allowed the moment before moving in. 'He'll be fine ... did Ambrose not meet you?'

Mary's look was almost a scowl. Why had the man allowed any of this to happen? How could he have thought that Jonathan was capable of murder? But she would say nothing on the matter until she had learned more. Before she could answer, Ambrose entered the barn with Agnes. Meredith waved them towards him then turned back to Mary.

'I am taking the captain back to the house. He will be safer there until the trial.'

'Trial?' Mary was taken with a fury. 'For why?'

Meredith's face was set in a grim expression. 'Mary, if the man is to clear his name there has to be a trial.'

35

The day of the trial dawned with grey skies and drizzling rain. Almost a week had passed since the attempted lynching, and for Jonathan the days and nights at Braganza had been long and painful. Mary had pleaded to visit him, but he was in strict confinement to his room and allowed no visitors other than Meredith.

The initial recovery was slow, and though he had hung only briefly on the rope his injuries were severe. The neck ligaments had been torn and there were contusions about the throat and damage to the vocal chords. His voice had returned only the day previously but now held a slightly husky tone which the doctor opined would stay with him for the rest of his life. He lay on top of the bed, throat bandaged and still feeling shaky as Meredith paced nervously up and down the room.

'Do you think it wise to defend yourself? Donaldson is a good lawyer and ready to step in.'

Jonathan did not take his gaze from the ceiling. His throat ached, but the voice came strongly enough. 'I am not guilty, therefore I shall not have need of a lawyer.'

Meredith was unimpressed. 'Brendan O'Reilly is prosecuting. He's a tough nut to crack, sent more men to the gallows than you could shake a stick at.'

'He shall not send me there. I assure you of that.'

'I hope you are right.'

'Do you believe me guilty?'

'No ... no, I do not.'

'Thank you for that at least.'

Carefully, Jonathan turned his head to look at Meredith.

266

'You have not yet told me who laid the lies against me. Since I shall be on trial for my life within the hour, I believe I have a right to know.'

'I thought you knew. O'Brien claimed he saw you do it.'

Jonathan was surprised. 'The man who tried to lynch me?'

Meredith nodded. 'The same ... gave eyewitness evidence to Bert Johnson on the morning after the murder.' He looked uncomfortable as he went on. 'I tried to locate him but couldn't track him down. Then I was sworn-in to arrest you.'

'But the man is now dead, you shot him.'

Meredith grimaced. 'Had to, but I'm damned if I knew who he was at the time ... what puzzles me is why O'Brien would want you lynched, for goodness' sake. He was due to stand against me at the elections. What the judge is going to make of that worries me some.' He stopped his pacing. 'I'll tell you this much, Captain, if he had let the law run its course and given his evidence things might have been real sticky.'

Jonathan snorted in impatience. 'The man was lying.'

Thoughtfully, Meredith rocked on his heels. 'Why would he want you dead? What was his profit? Like I said, the man was aiming for high office in the town. Why would he want to go get tangled up in murder?'

Jonathan rubbed at the bandage. 'I agree, it does not seem to make any sense.'

Meredith began his pacing once more. 'The only other way I see it is that the McAffertys are behind this ... they could have plotted the whole thing with O'Brien.'

'Mr Meredith ... I will grant you the McAffertys are evil people, but I cannot see them wishing me dead.'

There was pity in Meredith's expression as he walked over to the bed. 'Love has robbed you of a brain, man! You walk around lost in a dream world.'

'I beg your pardon, sir?' Jonathan sat up, his tone stiffly formal. But Meredith was having none of it.

'Do you really suppose that no one else but us knows about you and Mary?'

'You mean her husband? But they are estranged. I cannot

think that jealousy would warrant his plotting my death ... it is quite absurd.'

'You're right, I don't think Donal gives a hoot, especially since he's been playing around with one of the field women for a month or more.'

'Then how is he my enemy?'

'It isn't Donal after you. It's his father.'

'His father? But I do not know the man, let alone have caused him harm.'

'I hope to sweet Jesus you're better at defending yourself agin O'Reilly than you are with me.' The criticism was light, but it caused Jonathan to bristle.

'I do not follow your reasoning.'

'Do you not, Captain? Well now, I'm right sorry about that.'

'Do not patronise me, sir.'

Meredith looked kindly into the defiance of Jonathan's eyes. Such a young man, not a bad bone in his body but green as new corn. O'Reilly would chop him up into little pieces and feed him to the chickens, unless he was made to see the way things were.

'Captain, I've come to know a lot about Liam McAfferty in his time here. The more I now think on that knowledge the more I am inclined to believe the worst of him.' He thrust his hands deep into his pockets. 'Together, the pair of us have made him look the complete fool, and in front of his own people. Me, for taking Mary in and keeping her here. You, for ... well now, obvious reasons and for which you are the talk of the town, and every new tale about you gets a little fancier.'

'How dare you utter such words? There is no impropriety in our relationship, nor has there ever been.'

'Not me saying the words, son, but any road you want, it comes up the same in my reckoning ... The man is after revenge.'

'If that is so, then he goes a strange way about it. Why should he murder Sullivan? It makes no sense.'

'Think, Captain. If he'd murdered you the blame would've

surely been put on him. But this way he rigged it so the law would do his dirty work, and my guess is he even fixed the lynching to make damned sure.' Jonathan pondered on the words and saw the possibility of truth there.

'If it should prove to be so, then the man is the very devil.'

'Worse, I'd say.' Meredith scratched his head. 'Somehow or another he must have had a hold on O'Brien. What exactly could it have been?'

'But how are we to prove your suspicions?'

'Don't know ... hell, I didn't even know O'Brien until after I'd shot him. I'll try to dig around some. Better get ready now, I have to take you to court for noon.'

The packed courthouse hummed with a chatter of anticipation, for such a trial as was about to take place had rarely, if ever, been witnessed by the people of Clarkstown. Rows of tight packed chairs ran clear back over the sixty-yard-long room to where the McAffertys sat deep in shadow.

Uniformed, Jonathan sat flanked by Meredith and a peace officer in an open dock at the centre of the court. The crew of the *Pelican* dominated the two front rows, and from time to time Jonathan glanced at them but they seemed to avoid his gaze. He gave a shrug. Maybe they felt embarrassment, or still thought themselves hard done by. It did not matter since he was unlikely to call on them for any evidence.

He looked around the court for sight of Mary, and suddenly she was in view, next to Agnes in one of the middle rows. Their eyes met in a warmth of reassurance but his attention was diverted when Bert Johnson, the court clerk, leaned into the dock to speak with Meredith.

'Bad news, John. Judge Lawrence has been taken sick, they've sent Verney.'

Jonathan caught Meredith's expression of concern. 'Who is Verney?' Before he could reply a tall, gaunt man in black robes emerged from a door at the front of the court.

Johnson stood back and called out, 'All stand! Judge Verney presiding!' The crowd rose with a clatter of chairs and Johnson poked his head back into the dock. 'That's Verney, a mighty hard man to please. Round the circuit they call him the hanging judge.'

Meredith twisted about to scowl at Johnson. 'For Chrissakes, Bert! This man is on trial for his life.'

Johnson looked abashed. 'Sorry, didn't mean any harm.'

Jonathan smiled politely. 'I take no offence.'

Johnson scurried away towards the judge's bench. After a brief conversation between the two, Johnson faced the court.

'The defendant will rise.'

Jonathan stood up, all eyes now on him. The judge looked him up and down. 'You are Captain Jonathan Bramwell of the merchant ship *Pelican*?'

Jonathan regarded the pale, expressionless face of the man. 'I am, sir.'

'You will address me as Your Honour.'

Jonathan nervously fingered the bandage about his neck. 'I apologise ... I am, Your Honour.'

'You stand before this court accused of the murder of one David Henry Sullivan. How do you plead?'

'Not guilty, Your Honour.'

'Who is your counsel?'

'If it pleases Your Honour, I will conduct my own defence.'

'Are you acquainted with the procedures of a court of law?'

'I have had cause to appear in the defence of various members of my crew in other parts of the world, Your Honour.'

Meredith winced at the words, while the judge frowned deeply. 'You run a lawless ship then, Captain?'

'Why no, Your Honour, the cases in question were merely drunken brawling, damage to alehouse property and the like.'

Meredith buried his face in his hands and wondered on Jonathan's state of mind. The judge leaned forward over his desk and in sharp admonition stressed the first word. 'Merely drunken brawling and damage to property. You hold the law in so little regard, then?'

Hands spread wide in appeal, Jonathan glanced at his crew. 'With respect, Your Honour, it is no more than sailors do the

270

whole world over, the release of natural spirits following long and often hazardous voyages. There is no harm in it.'

'Is there not? You obviously have low moral standards for a ship's captain.' He gave an unbelieving shake of the head. 'And now you would defend yourself on a capital charge?'

'Yes, Your Honour, since I am innocent of the charge, I have nothing to set before you but the truth.'

The judge sighed deeply. 'Captain Bramwell ... you would do well to note that your innocence, as you put it, or guilt will not be determined by you.'

'As you say, Your Honour.'

'As I say indeed!' He turned to Johnson. 'Who appears for the prosecution?'

'Brendan O'Reilly, a Clarkstown lawyer, Your Honour.'

'Clarkstown, you say? Is he by chance a friend or acquaintance of the accused?'

'I can swear they are not known to each other, Your Honour.'

'Very well, call him to make himself known.'

O'Reilly rose slowly at the usher's call. Formerly a Boston lawyer, he found himself not attuned to the pace of that city, and had retreated to the less demanding atmosphere of the small town. Fat, bald and advancing rapidly into middle age, he was well suited to the easier pickings which Clarkstown provided. Nevertheless, he was good at what he did, and had in the past steered a large number of men to the rope. In his mind this case would prove no distress in adding another to that list. His ready smile on a moon face, and the baggy, brown check suit gave him an avuncular appearance, almost comic. But they belied the inner man. He smoothed his jacket, then gave a little bow from the neck. 'May it please Your Honour, Brendan O'Reilly for the prosecution.'

The judge nodded and turned his attention to Johnson. 'Let the prisoner take the oath.'

The morning rain had given way to clear skies, and the sapping heat of early afternoon hung heavily in the courtroom. O'Reilly

271

had been skilful in his opening presentation, and now paced up and down in front of the jury box as he put Jonathan under ever-increasing pressure.

'You say you never left your cabin that night?'

'That is so.'

'We shall see. Now then, Captain, how do you come to be in Clarkstown?'

'It is common knowledge that my ship was wrecked off the coast.'

'You seem to find yourself in constant trouble, do you not?'

'You have the advantage, sir.'

'Do I? Well let me put it this way, then ... on your own admission you have an unruly crew which drags you into the courts of the wide world, then the wrecking of your ship, and now here you stand on a charge of murder most foul. Goodness knows what else will unfold about you this day.' He looked at Jonathan in a taunting fashion. 'And you so young and handsome with it.' He turned to the jury with a knowing grin. 'I'd wager you were one with the ladies, eh?' They grinned back at him.

Jonathan was rattled, and his composure slipped a little but he tried not to show it. 'The ship was becalmed and drifted on to the rocks in fog. What is more, I was not the captain at that time.'

O'Brien smiled. 'But you were the first officer, and your captain depended on you, did he not?'

The judge gave a sharp knock of the gavel. 'Mr O'Reilly, I am at a loss to know where this line of questioning is taking us.'

O'Reilly made his customary little bow. 'Your Honour, I seek to establish the fact that the accused is a liar and a criminal, well capable of murder and a man who wilfully caused the death of his captain.'

Uproar broke out in the court as some of the crew rose from their seats and began shouting protests at O'Reilly's words. The judge hit the gavel loudly against the desk as he sought to bring order, and it was some time before the court became quiet. One by one the crew wilted under the hostile stare of the judge and went silently back to their seats.

272

His tone was icy cold, and they were to be left in no doubt as to his authority, or ability. 'If another such outrage occurs I will have you all put in irons and transported to the county jail, there to be incarcerated for the prescribed period allotted for contempt of court. Do I make myself understood?' Meekly they nodded their assent, and the judge switched his wrath to the prosecutor.

'Mr O'Reilly, I think now is a good time to give you my thoughts. There is more than a hint of melodrama in your presentation, and I note your undoubted ability to incite. I trust that the path we now tread with you will lead us all to just enlightenment ... please continue.'

O'Reilly gave a polite smile. 'As you say, Your Honour.' He turned once more to Jonathan. 'Captain, I believe that Mr Anstruther was lost overboard ... do you not feel in any way responsible for that?'

'I do not. He was far from me when the ship hit the rocks.'

'Far from you? And where were you at that moment?'

'On the quarterdeck with the helmsman.'

'But surely, is that not where the captain should have been?'

'I was ordered to stay there.'

'By the captain?'

'That is so.'

'Well now.' He grinned towards the jury. 'I am only a fat landlubber with scant knowledge of the sea, but I find it odd that the master of a ship, with a crew dependent on his leadership, should put himself in mortal danger, wouldn't you say?'

'Captain Anstruther wanted to see the situation for himself.'

'Really? I would have thought that to be the task of the first officer. Am I wrong? Please answer truthfully.'

Jonathan sighed as he recalled the moment of Anstruther's obstinacy in going for'ard. 'You are not wrong.'

O'Reilly smiled in triumph. 'I know I am not wrong, Captain. Now then, your father owns the shipping line, therefore your influence over the master would have been considerable. Now I put this to your conscience, sir ... did you not

273

suggest that the late Mr Anstruther should go see for himself, while you stayed safe by the helmsman?'

A silence fell upon the court as all eyes turned to the prisoner. Liam leaned forward, ears straining for the answer. Jonathan felt his temper rise, and he fought for control of it.

'That is a wicked and unfounded statement, sir! I have told you the truth of what happened.'

O'Reilly shrugged and turned again to the jury. 'You have told me your version of the truth. What if the captain had stayed in his rightful place of command? Would it not now be you dead?' Dramatically, he swung about and stared up into the dock. 'Well, Captain?' Jonathan found himself unable to make a reply.

O'Reilly spoke more loudly. 'Answer me, Captain ... is that not so?'

Conscience came to drive reason from Jonathan. Why had he not insisted that Joseph should stay on the quarterdeck while he went to investigate? Was not at least some of O'Reilly's accusation right? He looked down into the face of the prosecutor, and his voice came wildly.

'I now wish to God it were so!'

O'Reilly pulled a large red spotted handkerchief from his pocket and mopped at his sweating brow. 'Do you really, Captain? Do you really?' Hands clasped behind his back, handkerchief trailing behind him, O'Reilly paced once more in front of the jury box. 'In trying to establish to this court just what manner of person you are, Captain Bramwell, I find myself digging ever deeper into the mud. And I am not alone in casting doubts upon your character, am I?' He looked up at Jonathan. 'Am I?'

'I do not understand you.'

'Oh, but I think you do ... you have a master's ticket? Why would not your father, the owner of the line, give you a ship of your own?'

Jonathan was surprised at the question. Where had the man got such information? His eyes scanned the crew. One of the seamen lowered his head under the accusing stare.

'Your informant has given you the wrong end of the stick,

274

sir. My father is a hard taskmaster and he thought me not yet ready for commerce. This was to have been my proving voyage.'

'I see, that is all there was to it, then?'

'That is all there was to it.'

'You are a liar, sir!'

'How dare you call me a liar?'

'Because you are one, sir! Your father, one of the leading figures in English society, and a pillar of the Church, has voiced grave doubts about you. Tell me that is not so, if you dare!'

Jonathan tried hard to remain calm under the pressure. 'I have told you that your information is not all it would seem to be. I enjoy a deep trust from my father.'

'Is that why he said you lacked discipline? That you were arrogant? Lost your temper too easily? Why, you even lost it when the ship was in mortal danger, threatening on some whim to have your crew whipped!'

'This is outrageous! I do not know how...'

O'Reilly cut across his flow of protest. 'I agree! It is outrageous!' He looked at the jury, then pointed accusingly at the dock. 'Observe how quickly the accused loses his temper.' Now focusing his full attention on Jonathan, he rocked slightly as his voice rose to a crescendo. 'That is what happened with David Sullivan, isn't it? You lost your temper when he told you that the price of the ship repairs was much higher than first estimated.'

'That is not so!'

'Yes it is! You followed him that night and murdered him with this weapon, identified as being from your own ship.'

O'Reilly picked up the iron bar from a table and grasped it with both hands, grunting with effort as he rained imagined blows in the air. 'You hit the poor man again and again about the head until he died.' With a passionate voice he addressed the court. 'Ladies and gentlemen, can you see that terrible night? Poor David Sullivan, whom we all knew and loved, suddenly attacked with this fearsome weapon.' He waved the bar once more in attacking motion. 'The skull was broken in so

275

many places it is difficult to count.' His audience moaned and shuddered. 'But it is not difficult to imagine the dying agony of the man ... the life blood spurting from so many wounds ... what a desperate way to meet your maker.'

At the back of the courtroom, Donal forced grimy knuckles into his mouth to stifle the cry which had started from him. Liam elbowed him with a savage dig. 'Y'll get us all bloody hung!'

O'Reilly had stopped his flailing, and now laid the iron bar back on the table. He looked up once more at Jonathan.

'Premeditated murder, Captain, for you planned to slip your moorings to avoid debt and escape the law. That is the truth of the matter, is it not?'

'No, it is not! I am a man of honour, wrongly accused of this crime!'

O'Reilly laboured a smile. 'So, you are a man of honour are you?'

'I endeavour to be fair and just in all my dealings.'

The prosecutor stared pointedly at Mary, then licked his lips as he glanced towards Jonathan. 'You are anything but fair and just, Captain, and your morals are lower than those of a common alley cat.' He looked away over the grim faces in the audience. 'The good people of Clarkstown took a viper to their bosom when they befriended you, Captain Bramwell.'

'You will take that back, sir!'

'Take it back? I think not ... you would have us believe that butter would not melt in your mouth, yet on this most unfortunate voyage, which has seen the deaths of your captain and David Sullivan, you have added adultery to your crimes.'

Jonathan swayed with the shock of what he knew would surely follow. Mary sought Agnes's hand, gripping it tightly as she awaited the dirtying of her love in a public and hostile arena.

Jonathan spoke with a quiet dignity. 'Mr O'Reilly, I know what you are about to say, and I appeal to your sense of propriety not to. It has no bearing on the issue now being tried in this court. It can only cause pain to the innocent, and is a

276

personal matter which can, should circumstances warrant, be easily explained if...'

O'Reilly interrupted with a wave of his arms. 'I am sure you could, as you put it, easily explain your way past the devil in hell, you fornicator! But that most damning evidence is here, present in this courtroom.'

Dramatically, he spun around on his heel to face the assembly. 'I call Mrs Donal McAfferty! Please stand, Mrs McAfferty, so that the jury may see you.'

Bravely, Mary stood up. She had not bargained for this embarrassment, but was determined to see it through. O'Reilly folded his arms and looked at her.

'You are Mrs Donal McAfferty?'

'I am.'

'Thank you, remain there please.' He smirked at Jonathan. 'I believe you know the person now standing before you?'

'We are acquainted.' The reply was stiffly formal.

A knowing look came on O'Reilly's face. 'Acquainted? Acquainted, is it? Rather more than that I think, Captain.'

'We are good friends.'

O'Reilly's smile was sarcastic. 'How easily you slide from acquaintanceship to friendship, Captain. Yet the slippery slope goes even deeper than that ... in the short time you have been in Clarkstown you have lured this woman away from her lawful and God-fearing husband, and become her lover by stealth!' The crowd broke into a babble of speculation, and chairs were knocked over as many of the spectators rose to their feet.

White with fury, Liam turned on Donal. 'Where has he got that from? Have you been openin' y'r big mouth?'

'Not me, dar! Not me f'r sure.'

Liam was almost weeping with rage. 'Our sacred an' blessed name dragged through the stinkin' mud of a stranger's country... Jesus Christ Almighty!'

The judge finally restored order, and his withering gaze scythed through the ranks of the court.

'This is a court of law, not a common circus. Just one more outburst and I will have you all thrown into the street.' He

277

addressed Mary. 'Sit down, madam!' Gratefully, she sank back to her seat as the judge switched his anger to the prosecutor.

'I have given you much rope to wander with, Mr O'Reilly. Now I warn you, get to the point before you hang yourself.'

O'Reilly was humiliated by this public dressing-down. 'As Your Honour wishes.'

The judge came at him once more. 'A word before you continue, Mr O'Reilly. I am not here to teach you your task as a lawyer, but I feel it incumbent upon me at this time to guide you. You have most certainly reached the end of the road as to the morals of the accused ... the jury must surely now be fully aware that he is not an angel freshly come from heaven.' Laughter broke out at this, but the judge failed to see any humour, and banged hard with the gavel. 'Silence in court! I have already given due warning as to your conduct.' He turned again to the prosecutor. 'Let me now hear hard evidence. Call this man O'Brien who claims to have witnessed the murder.'

O'Reilly was taken aback and he swallowed deeply, mouth opening and closing as he strove to find words.

The judge spoke with impatience. 'Are you stricken with some ailment, sir?'

The air of bafflement was still with the prosecutor as he looked towards the clerk of the court for explanation. But Johnson simply shrugged his shoulders.

Plainly shaken, all arrogance gone from him, O'Reilly looked askance at the judge.

'I thought you knew, Your Honour...'

There was acid in the reply. 'You thought I knew? I know many things, Mr O'Reilly. Would you care to particularise?'

O'Reilly dabbed the sweat from his brow. 'Mr Johnson, the clerk of the court, I thought he had told you the background of the case, Your Honour...' His voice tailed away into uneasy quiet.

The judge shifted his glare to Johnson. 'Mr Johnson, is it only within the realms of fantasy that I believe you could shed light on this affair? I trust so, for Mr O'Reilly seems to have lost his power of communication.'

Johnson fidgeted in dismay. 'Your Honour, I beg pardon for

this. I was in the belief that Mr Lawrence, who was to have judged this case, had passed his notes on to you.'

'To say I am surprised, Mr Johnson, is a gross understatement. How do you suppose a man as ill as Mr Lawrence now is would be able to do that? As clerk of the court you are most seriously at fault, for it was your task to get any notes on this case from Mr Lawrence and pass them to me!'

'I most humbly beg Your Honour's pardon.'

The judge leaned back in his chair. 'I was wrong, this is not a court, it is a common circus and I am fascinated at my patience with it. But I feel that I must very shortly experience the same manifestation as befell Saul on the road to Tarsus.' His tone changed to one of controlled fury which struck fear into prosecutor and clerk alike. 'What, exactly, are you trying to tell me?'

Johnson gulped out the reply. 'O'Brien is dead, Your Honour.'

'You are telling me that you have brought this case before me without the main witness for the prosecution?'

'I regret that is so, Your Honour.'

'Then call the next witness.'

'If it pleases Your Honour, there are no other witnesses for the prosecution.'

The judge looked slowly in turn at the two men then leaned towards the court clerk. 'Mr Johnson, I have finally arrived at the painful conclusion that you and Mr O'Reilly share the malady of insanity.' Both men lowered their heads in despair. Everyone within the courtroom had remained quiet during the interrogation of the officials, intrigued at the turn of events.

Meredith whispered to Jonathan, 'Looking good for you, Captain.' Jonathan nodded in agreement, but his face showed the strain he was under.

The judge spoke again. 'Purely as a matter of curiosity, Mr Johnson, how did Mr O'Brien meet his death?'

Johnson lifted his head and met the judge's inquiring gaze with some difficulty. 'He was shot, Your Honour.'

'Shot?'

279

'That is so, Your Honour.'

'And who shot him?'

'Our chief of police, Your Honour.'

'I see.' The judge's voice held only the thinnest veil of patience. 'The chief of police shot the only witness for the prosecution ... I will compose myself for a moment because I fear what I am further to be told.'

Meredith's voice came loud and clear from the dock. 'Excuse me, Your Honour, if you'll allow me, I'm sure I can bring this all to sense.'

The judge turned to him, a glimmer of hope in his eyes. 'If you can do that, sir, you will restore my ebbing sanity. What is your name and business in this wretched town?'

'John Meredith, Your Honour. I'm in the business of timber and farming, also I'm a city father and stipendiary police chief.'

'You are the man who shot the witness O'Brien?'

'I am, Your Honour.'

'Under what circumstances if you please, Mr Meredith?'

The better part of a half-hour had passed before Meredith completed the bizarre background of the case, during which time the judge listened with great patience and understanding.

'I am indebted to you, Mr Meredith, for a lucid, and I believe most proper explanation of the events concerning this unfortunate trial, one which should never have been brought. I thank you again, you may sit down.' He frowned at the prosecutor.

'Were you aware of all this, Mr O'Reilly?'

'Yes, Your Honour.'

'I see. You trouble me, sir, for I cannot comprehend what you hoped to achieve. I will see you in my chambers when I have finished my summing up.'

'As you wish, Your Honour.'

The judge turned away to address the jury.

'Gentlemen of the jury, I feel you must be as bemused as I at the happenings which have occurred this day, within this court. In all my long experience I have never come upon anything like it. The whole sordid affair reeks of an ill-prepared plot against the accused.' He looked carefully around the faces of the assembly. 'For reasons better known to some than others. Murder has undoubtedly been done, and it is now the duty of the Clarkstown law officers to seek out and apprehend the person, or persons responsible. There is not one shred of real evidence against the accused, and I therefore discharge him.' He turned to Jonathan.

'You are free to go, Captain Bramwell, but I would strongly advise you to choose more carefully the company you keep.' He banged the gavel hard on the desk as if to relieve his feelings. 'This court is dismissed!'

The crowd burst into instant chatter, and Mary started to rise from her seat, hoping to talk with Jonathan. Agnes realised the intent and gently restrained her. 'Not here, Mary, wait until he returns home.' She nodded in reluctant agreement and sat down, watching as Meredith shook Jonathan warmly by the hand.

'Congratulations, Captain, no bad feelings I hope.'

'There are no bad feelings, Mr Meredith.'

'I mean to make sure it ain't over for the guilty party.'

'Then I wish you good fortune in that.'

The McAffertys shuffled out of the back entrance of the building, with Donal well to the rear. There was a look of madness in Liam's eyes as he glanced at Patrick.

'I mean t'have him, son, we must not let him get away wit' the terrible shame he has brought upon us ... come on now, we cannot talk here.'

Patrick had thought the matter ended, that his father would now call a halt to the affair. But the man was hell bent on revenge. He had to be stopped before he destroyed them all.

'For pity's sake, dar, let it be! If y'do not we shall all finish up wit' ropes about our necks.'

281

Liam snarled in reply as he noisily lengthened his stride along the boardwalk.

'I've told y', he is a dead man!'

36

Bright moonlight filled the bedroom. Unable to find sleep after the tensions of the trial, Mary listened to the distant chimes of the hall clock ... three. Her mind toiled over the brief meeting with Jonathan before she had retired early to bed.

It had been a torment, Agnes sitting at the far end of the drawing room as unwanted chaperone and the conversation stilted to the extreme, both wanting to say many things but forced to deny them. He asked about her interview in Boston and she told him of how successful it was, but declined to say she would not take the offered post. He had told her that he must depart for England on the next evening tide, and she still felt the pain of his words, now wanting only his arms about her, his kisses warm on her mouth. Why would sleep not come and drown her senses from this agony?

She looked towards the window and watched the moon riding in thin wisps of silvery cloud. Was there really a God up there? If she prayed would He give her guidance? She remembered the coming visit of the archbishop from Boston. Why not go alone to see him? He would be in the church all day tomorrow. She would then. He must listen to her. But the priest had said not even the Pope himself could grant annulment. What hope then of anyone else?

With a moan of despair she turned her gaze from the window and burrowed into the blankets. But there was no escape in that darkness. Jonathan's face came clearly to her and she heard his voice begging her to return to England with him. Why could she not?

She baulked at the question which was instantly replaced by another. Why had she decided not to take the position offered her in Boston? The answer to that came readily. She could not bear to leave him and still clung to a hope that somehow the matter would resolve itself. What nonsense. How could it? The words which Jonathan had spoken on the clifftop mocked at her... 'Do you ask me to wait upon a miracle?' It was past miracles now, for this was the last night he would spend close by her. He would leave on the evening tide and she would never see him again.

The aching loneliness which plagued her made it difficult to breathe. She pulled aside the blankets and there began a battle of wills within her mind as she stared unseeing at the moon. Slowly it came into a shimmering focus, the clouds gone from it and there was no longer any fight of conscience left within her ... she must go to him now.

Jonathan was awake, reading his father's letter for at least the third time. Other correspondence littered the bedspread; Georgina had written, so had Ann, and there was a note from Charlotte. His father wrote of duty, his mother of service to the company, Ann, dear Ann, had cheered him up with promise of a wild party upon his return, while Charlotte blessed his delivery from the shipwreck and wanted to see him immediately he stepped ashore at Southampton. It all seemed to be another world, one which he wanted to be rid of but which still hung about his neck like a giant millstone.

With a grimace he gathered the letters together, placing them on the bedside table, then leaned over to lower the flame of the lamp, catching his breath as he saw Mary framed within the open door. The moonlight captured her startling beauty in a vision of silver and white, the pale nightgown clinging to the soft curves of her body, and in vivid contrast the long dark tresses, now in loose ringlets, hung almost to her waist.

'Mary ... my love.' Captivated, he spoke barely above a whisper for he had only dreamed that she might dare to visit his room. Silently, she closed the door then dropped the nightgown from her.

'Love me, Jonny ... love me an' never be for lettin' me go.'

She seemed to glide across the room and now he felt the warmth of her body against his, all uncertainty and pain going from him as he put his arms about her. They kissed in a frenzy of longing, breaking only for each to fondle the other in desire.

'Jonny, my Jonny!' Her words came like the lonely cry of a wild animal and he thrilled to them, moving his mouth about her body, caressing her breasts and she felt the hardness of him rear and pulsate against her thighs. 'Love me, Jonny, please love me.' She gloried in his gentle entry of her, wriggling tight against the throbbing warmth and ecstasy of feeling, kissing him, biting him, clawing him in an unfettered joy. She wanted never to move from him, crying out again and again in her passion, then thrusting herself into him with a wild moan of abandonment as she came to fulfilment. She felt him grow larger within her, then he was struggling to pull away.

She knew why but could not bear to be parted from him. As if her existence depended on it, she locked about him preventing his withdrawal from her, hearing his cry of passion and feeling the life seed course warmly into her. Hearts pounding, they lay still and she could feel his breath quick and warm on her neck and in her completeness knew that their child had already begun to grow within her womb. Now, no matter what, they would always be together. Intertwined, neither willing to release the other, they drifted silently into sleep.

Arms still tightly about each other, they awoke to see the first light of dawn tinge the room but made no attempt to move. 'I love you, Jonny.' She smiled in contentment. 'Our child already grows within me. I know it ... was it not grand an' beautiful in the makin'?'

He raised himself up on one elbow and smiled before kissing her softly on the lips, sure that she now intended to go with him to England. 'It was beyond any words which I may seek, my darling.'

'Tell me you will not leave for England so soon, please say y'will stay a while longer.'

He was puzzled. 'To what end, my darling? There is nothing to delay us ... we must leave this very day.'

She would not meet his eyes. 'I do not yet know if I shall be for comin' with you, Jonny.'

He drew back in astonishment. 'You are surely not still in doubt?' But he saw by her expression that it was so. 'Then why did you come to my bed and make me believe otherwise?'

She glanced towards the window where the daylight came more boldly. 'Because I could do no other.'

Some moments passed before he answered. 'You say you carry our child, surely now the only way is that you should come with me ... if you truly love me, you will say yes.'

'Never doubt my love for you, Jonny.' The words were gentle, but her manner was firm as she turned her gaze from the window. 'I go t'see the archbishop this very morning.'

'What good will that bring?' He was distraught. 'You have already seen a priest and he has said nothing can be done... How are things changed?'

'I will be goin' alone. Mrs Meredith could not speak with him as I shall.'

His reply was almost contemptuous. 'You honestly think to change their opinion?'

'I do not know on it, Jonny, only that I must try.'

'Very well, then I shall come with you.'

'Please, I must go alone.'

Annoyance crept into his voice. 'Why alone? After all our pains and privations, are we not together in this?'

'I trust we are together in everythin', but you are not of the faith, an' the archbishop would not speak with you.'

'I see, and what will you tell him?'

'Everythin', I will tell him everythin'.'

A depression settled on him. He had been so sure that all doubts were behind them and that she would return with him. 'What then will you do if this man refuses to grant you access for release?'

Slowly, she lowered her gaze and imagination took her to the time of Jonathan's departure. What then, indeed, would she do?

Would she, as so often through her mind's eye she had seen, remain on the harbour bar and wave him farewell? Or be with him, as she desired, upon the ship? She took his hands and brushed her lips against them. 'We shall know what will be before the sun goes down on this day. Be patient, Jonny.'

'Patience is a new-found thing for me, and I have difficulty with it . . . I did not ever dream there was so much pain in love.'

She held his hands more tightly. 'For me also . . . but such a sweet pain I would not be without.'

He frowned. 'Why are there so many faiths while there is only one God?'

'I have wondered on the same.'

His frown deepened. 'This archbishop might wish to know if I would change my faith.'

She shook her head. 'I would not know on that.'

'Then tell him I would, and even turn to Buddhism, or Islam, or any other if it meant that we could be together.' Despite her sorrow, she smiled at his earnestness.

'I must go now.' In brief gesture she touched his lips, then rose and made her way to the door. 'Please to wish me well.'

'I already have prayer in my heart, my love.' He was suddenly, ridiculously, sure that no matter what the Church might have to say, she would go with him. They could not now ever be parted. Not after last night. 'I will be at the ship waiting for you.'

'I know it, Jonny, an' shall come to you, no matter what.' She put on the nightgown, and as she opened the door the draught of wind brought the bouquet of her body to him. Then she was gone.

37

There was a grimly purposeful air about Donal as he left the dirt road to make his way across the fields towards Clarkstown, and his thoughts were still with the humiliation he had just suffered at the hands of Liam.

'Y'have no backbone, Donal, an' again it falls on me t'come up wit' a notion for t'finish the Englishman. You are neither use nor ornament ... never have been, never will be.' Donal had silently continued with his work, and every clump of weed sliced with the hoe was the head of his father. For what was the bloody man but a blowhard?

Liam's voice droned on, but Donal was no longer listening. The constant beatings and taunts which he had suffered from boyhood came again to him. And what was there to look forward to but more? He would surely be the goat for the rest of his life, and no escape from it. Why then should he stay here any longer? And for what? His mind turned to the previous day, when they had left the courthouse. His mouth twisted in contempt as he recalled his father's words ... 'I'll get the bastard, he's a dead man!'

The hoe struck fiercely into the thistle, and twisted deep about its roots as realisation dawned. This man, who made his life a crawling misery, who existed only on the deeds and doings of his dead, outlaw father, had no intention of killing the Englishman, not a bit of it. He talked a good tale of the murdering of men, yet had not the guts for the doing. That was the truth of it.

But he, the beaten and despised Donal McAfferty who was just now told that he was neither use nor ornament, had beaten the bloody brains from Sullivan, and could do the same to any other man. For the nightmares had gone from him, and it was surely nothing to kill any number of men after the first. He would make his dar sorry for all the beatings and bad words. In his own right he would find the sailor boy and kill him stone dead. Then go far away and make his own life.

With a wild scream he had flung the hoe into the air and run from the maize workings.

'Will I bring him back, dar?'

'No, y'will not, Patrick.' Liam had watched until Donal went from sight. 'He is gone from his mind awhile, but will surely be back ... The poor lad is not into the brains of makin' his own way.'

Donal's pace slackened, and the sweat of fear ran down his face as he walked along Main Street towards the docks. He had thought to take up a position near the *Pelican* and wait for Jonathan's appearance, even if it took the whole day. But now, in his deranged mind, it seemed that all eyes were upon him, that every man, woman and child who thronged the boardwalks knew of his deadly intent. He was about to turn and run when he saw Mary. She was no more than fifty paces away, and had not yet seen him. He turned and looked into a store window, gauging her gradual approach towards its reflection, his mind working feverishly.

There was no need for the killing ... why should he seek a revenge that would surely take him to the gallows? All he wanted was the woman. He would grab her, then take her back to High Pines. He had the right of it, for she was his wife, and God help anyone who tried to stop him.

The lust grew strong in Donal as he watched her every step close the distance between them, and the drool of anticipation trickled from his mouth. When he had the woman back in the cabin he would rip the fancy clothes from her, and then ... he blinked in disbelief as her reflection disappeared from the window. With a sharp turn of the head he looked back down

289

the street. Damn the bloody creature! She must have gone into the side road. But no bad thing. Quieter there, not so many people to get in his way. If he cut through the alley he would come out in front of her ... get on with it then, or she would be gone.

Mary was only a few yards from the church when Donal sprang from the alley to confront her.

'Well now! If it isn't herself, my dear sweet wife ... the lady high an' bloody mighty.'

The shock of his sudden appearance made her sway against the railings of the church. She looked up and down the road but it was deserted of people, and all her old fears raced back, causing her voice to tremble. 'Leave me be! I have nothin' t'say to you.'

The grin flashed briefly before his expression turned to hate. 'Have y'not? Well I have somethin' t'say t'you, y'treacherous evil bitch! I knew if I bided a while I'd come face t'face wit' you again.'

'Let me alone, I am t'see the priest an' I must not be late.'

'T'hell wit' the priest! I'm takin' y'home.'

Her words came in a hiss. 'You'll never lay hands on me again as long as y'live.'

The grin flashed once more. He was enjoying the encounter and her fear of him. 'Will I not? I betcha I don't say that t'your fancy-man sailor boy, do y'now?'

'Do not mention his name with your filthy tongue!'

He laughed. 'Me is it, filthy? You've kicked over the traces alright since the bloody Englishman landed. An' wasn't it dragged all about the court? My wife makin' me look the gossoon an' pullin' our name through the dirt. I could kick the bloody hell out of yez, an' who would blame me for the doin' of it?'

She looked at him with scorn. 'I would kill you before I'd ever let y'beat me again, an' I am not your wife, nor will I ever be. Now stand aside an' let me go into this church.'

He stepped forward and grabbed her by both arms, forcing her in a struggle towards the alley. 'No more of the bloody talkin', I'm takin' y'back, an I'm havin' my rights.' He released

290

one hand to hit her across the face. 'If y'don't stop the strugglin' I'll mount y'here an now in the churchyard.'

In terror at his threat she stopped struggling. He grinned. 'That's better now, your fancy sailor boy won't go near y'when he knows I've mounted y'again, will he now? An' this time I'll make bloody sure there's a babby in y'r belly.' They had almost reached the darkness of the alley when the voice of Father Casey came to them.

'What's going on here now? Let go that woman at once!'

Mary almost fainted with relief as she called out, 'Thank God you came, Father. Please make him let me go, he is near breakin' my arm.'

Donal kept Mary tightly in his grip as he glowered at the priest. 'She's my wife, a runaway blasphemer taken up wit' another man ... I'm after takin' her home where she belongs, an I'll thank y'not t'get in the way.'

Angrily, the priest strode over to the struggling couple. 'Do not dare speak to me in that way. Let go of her, now.'

Mary felt the grip slacken and wriggled free of Donal to run over to the priest. 'Father! I am come t'see the archbishop.' He put his arm in comfort about her shoulder while Donal spread his arms wide in appeal.

'Holy Father, she is my wife, an' her place is surely wit' me, for she made the vows t'me in the church an' all!'

'Are you Donal McAfferty?'

'Indeed I am, Father, honest an' Godfearin' t' the point of fault, an' sorely hard done by for all of it.' He bent his head in affected piety and abjection.

'Why do I not see you an' your family at church of a Sunday?'

''Tis the farm, Father, we are terrible busy.'

'Too busy to meet with God, is it?'

Donal cursed himself for the mistake. Too much of the talk, when all he wanted was the man out of the way.

'This is a stranger's land, Father, not like the old country ... they d'not give us the time t'be prayin'.'

'God makes sure He finds the time for you, Donal. So in your turn y'must find time for Him. I will expect t'see you, your

291

brother, an' your father at this church, come Sunday, an' you will all make confession. Do I make myself clear t'you?'

Donal fidgeted under the stare. Damn the bloody priest! Just when he had the woman at his mercy. Christ! Get on with it! Just tell the interfering old bugger what he wanted to hear, then get her away from him. 'Yes, Father. Forgive me for I have sinned...'

The interruption came sharply. 'Not here in the street! I will hear your confession at the proper time an' in the proper place. I will detain y'no longer. Off with y'now.'

Donal felt cornered as to his next move. He gestured towards Mary. 'An' what about her then, Father? I'm surely t'see her home.'

'Y'will not! I have the Lord's business to discuss with Mary.'

'I will wait then, so I will.'

'Donal, go back to your farm and work hard, so that y'will find more time for the Almighty.' There was a finality in the priest's command.

The thoughts buzzed about like flies in Donal's unbalanced mind. He could not be hitting the man, or he would have the whole bloody town about his neck. But he knew where she was, and she would have to leave sometime. He would away to Murphy's and have a couple of drinks, then come back. He shrugged his shoulders and walked away towards the alley, while Mary shuddered with relief.

Murphy's tavern was thronged with noisy dockers taking their midday break. But the chatter eased when Donal pushed his way through the swing doors, and all eyes were on him. Face set in grim expression, he shambled between the tables and headed for the bar. The dockers shrugged and winked knowingly at each other, then as quickly as it had eased the loud conversation broke out once more. Murphy, washing glasses behind the bar, eyed Donal with some curiosity, wondering at his appearance. The McAffertys were dirt farmers, never in the bar until late evening, and it needed no telling that there was something badly wrong with Donal.

'What'll it be?'

'Whisky, an' a glass.'

He dug into his pocket and slammed a silver dollar on the bar. Murphy placed a bottle of cheap whisky and a glass before him, picked up the dollar, and slid the change across the wet surface. Donal downed his first drink in one gulp, then poured another, which went the same way.

Murphy could contain his curiosity no longer. 'Startin' early on the drinkin' are y'not, Donal? Thought y'were busy up at the farm?'

'To bloody, roastin' hell wit' the farm, an' the Merediths.' He poured another drink, and had it halfway to his mouth when he paused. 'My dar an' Patrick ... have they been in lookin' f'r me?'

Murphy looked into the bloodshot eyes and saw madness there. 'Not t'day they haven't ... are you alright, boy?'

Donal ignored the question, and downed the drink, then turned about to stare wildly at the dockers.

'Y'all know! Don't yez? Yes y'bloody do! My cow of a wife an' the bastart Englishman!' The dockers looked back at him, and once more the chatter eased. But no one answered and they slowly returned to their talk.

Murphy grabbed the back of Donal's coat collar and swung him around. 'I want no trouble in here, so calm y'self. Your wife is your business, an' nobody else's. Sit down, an' have your drink in peace.' He released his hold on the collar, and pointed to a nearby chair.

A maudlin plea broke from Donal.

'How c'n I have the peace when every man knows I'm the eejut?'

'Shoutin' y'r mouth off will not make it better, now be a good fella an' sit y'down.'

But Donal would not be placated so easily, and his voice boomed out in threat as he swung around again to face the dockers. 'I am done wit' the talkin'! Y'll bloody see if I'm not! I'm after killin' the English bastard!' Half drunk, he swayed before his silent audience, trying hard to stare down each man in turn. But not a one took offence, for somehow he looked more pathetic than dangerous. Face bloated with drink and rage, the ragged and shrunken breeches hanging

293

above his ankles, and no stockings to the worn boots. A figure of jest.

One of the dockers laughed. 'So, you'll kill the Englishman, will y'now?'

Donal tried to focus on the man but failed. 'I will that!'

The man laughed again. 'Y'will have t'be swimmin' a long way t'do that, McAfferty!'

Donal's voice rang out above the uproar of amusement. 'What is it you are sayin' t'me?'

The docker wiped the tears of laughter from his eyes. 'Well now, I passed by his ship an hour gone, an' your man was makin' ready t'leave.'

'Is it the truth y'r tellin' me?'

'As I live an' breathe, McAfferty, your man will be off on the turn of the tide.'

Donal gripped the brass handle of the bar until his knuckles cracked and turned white. Then he saw his reflection staring back within the long mirror and was filled with a sudden self-loathing. Reviled, ridiculed, spurned, hated and with not a body to turn to for word of comfort. Had he not also killed his own mother when he had kicked and struggled his way from her in birth to this bloody world? For that was what his dar had told him often enough.

He caught his reflection again and the rage burned in him. Now all he could think of was revenge ... he might very well die fighting on this day, but by God, or the devil, he would take the Englishman with him.

Without a word he grabbed up the bottle from the bar, and ran out to the street. A babble of conversation erupted, and Murphy rebuked the man who had spoken to Donal. 'That was a damn' fool thing t'tell him! Could y'not see he is out of his mind?'

'He won't do anythin', the man is all mouth, just like the rest of his family.'

'I hope you're right, but he's a hurtin' man, and that's for sure.'

'Don't concern yourself, Murphy. He has too much whisky in him t'be able to hurt a fly.'

The talk in the bar had returned to normal when Liam walked in with Patrick. Second thoughts had come to him after Donal had left the maize workings, and in those thoughts he reasoned that there could only be trouble to follow in the wake of Donal's flight. He made straight for Murphy, who was clearing empty glasses from the tables.

'Have y'seen anythin' of Donal?'

'He's just after leavin'.'

'Was he drunk?'

Murphy was uncomfortable. 'The lad downed some whisky, but was not as I'd call drunk with it.'

'An' when he left, where was he headed?'

'Couldn't rightly say.'

A nearby docker had overheard the conversation, and he grinned drunkenly as he shouted across to Liam, 'Hey! McAfferty! I know where he's headed.'

Liam looked towards the man and there was menace in his tone. 'If y'know the truth of it, tell me, or I'll knock that clever look off your bloody face!'

The man ignored the threat, and grinned again. 'He's away t'the docks for t'kill the English captain.' He laughed. 'If he has the legs an' guts t'do it!' Liam rounded on Murphy.

'Is this eejut tellin' me a tale, or what?'

''Twas only the lad's bluster, he made threats an' all, yet I do not think...' Murphy's words trailed to a halt as Liam grabbed Patrick by the arm and strode away from the bar into the street.

The docker who had supplied the information jumped up from his chair. 'Come on now, my lads! We're surely not gonna miss this old shenanigans, are we?'

A voice called out, 'An' what about gettin' back t'work?'

The docker laughed. 'Work, is it? Sure y'have to be a right old joker, for there'll be nothin' movin' on these docks a while.' He pointed to the batwing doors which still swung after Liam's departure. 'Donal has gone t'do for the sailor boy, an' will not his father an' brother be after stoppin' him? Y'cannot want t'miss this. T'will be a circus of a thing altogether.'

With wild shouts and mocking laughter the crowd left the

295

bar and headed for the docks. Murphy looked around the deserted room for a moment then dragged off his apron and ran after them.

38

Jonathan worked his way carefully along the lower starboard
yardarm of the *Pelican*. He had gone aloft on the pretext of
examining the foot ropes, but in truth it was in hope of
catching an early glimpse of Mary. His thoughts continually
strayed to her and from time to time he glanced away for sight
of her coming, his lofty perch giving him an uninterrupted
view over the rooftops of the town to where the church lay
snuggled in the hillside.

He had become anxious. It was gone three hours since she
had left to see the archbishop, and she must soon be here.
What news would she then have? Could it be that the Church
had given its blessing? That she would be able and willing to
accompany him to England? But what would he do, come the
tide, if the issue were not settled? In agitation he turned away
and fastened his attention once more on inspection of the foot
ropes.

Sixty feet below the yardarm, Donal crouched in the shadows of a dockside warehouse and watched Jonathan's every
move. The town hall clock began to strike midday, its strident
clang startling him to more urgent thought . . . Christ! Why was
the man up there and not here on the floor where he could get
at him? But was that not it? Not a soul could help the sailor boy
up there in the rigging. It would be just the two of them. But
how would he do it? Push him off the mast? No, he might fall
with him. He needed a weapon. If only he had the iron bar.
Surely there would be one on the ship.

He looked towards the men working on deck, but not a one of
them was using such a thing. Damn every last man to buggery . . .

297

Alright then, if that's the way it was, get up there now and with his bare hands choke the bastard to death.

He stepped out of the shadows into the bright sunlight and his attention was suddenly caught by the flash of an object lying atop a coil of rope, just yards away from him. He rubbed the sweat from his eyes and strained vision to focus on it. Christ be praised!

The knife was fully a foot long from the top of its ridged bone handle to the tip of its blade and now became his only reason for being. Warily he edged against the warehouse wall until he was above the knife. One last look about him, then he swooped to clutch it tight in his hands. He stood a few moments collecting his wits, then taking a deep breath ran towards the ship's gangplank, and as swiftly was on the deck. Easing the knife carefully behind his broad leather belt, he eyed the rigging for a route which would take him to the yardarm, and had already begun to climb the mainmast shrouds when he heard a shout.

'Hey! You there!'

Donal peered down at a crewman running towards the base of the rigging. Ignoring him, he turned away, rapidly gaining height to the lower yard as the crewman began to climb in pursuit. Donal paused. The man was a nuisance, he must get rid of him. Grabbing the knife from his belt he waved it towards his pursuer. 'Get down, or I'll kill y', so help me!'

The crewman scrambled back to the deck and Donal grinned in triumph, the thoughts swinging wildly in him. Sure enough, would not his dar have to shut the big mouth if he could see him now? He felt strangely elated, for at last he was his own man ... just like the time when, only fourteen, he had run off to the Castlebar fair. He smiled in memory. There had been a terrible beating for the trip, but he had taken it without a whimper and thought only of the tinker's daughter who had lain beneath him to take away the boy and bring the man.

Grinning, he looked down at the crewman, then hawked up a mouthful of phlegm and spat it over the sailor. 'Y'show the good brains of it ... everybody wants t'go t'heaven, but nobody wants t'die. Is that not the way of it? Y'cowardly bastard!' He

298

stowed the knife in his belt, and resumed his climb as the crewman shouted out a warning to Jonathan.

'Captain! Aloft there, Captain ... can you hear me?'

But the cries were lost on the wind, and unaware of danger Jonathan lay full stretch along the yard and gazed towards the church. Donal emerged from the shrouds and fixed his gaze on the yard. The grin flickered briefly. Good! The sailor boy was facing the other way. He patted the knife handle and began to recover his breath. On the deck, crewmen were in wild commotion. Some had broken away to climb the rigging, only to be called back by the first mate.

Grant had swiftly weighed up the situation. 'You'll do no good up there! One of you double away to the captain's cabin and break out muskets ... bring one to me now!'

Liam and Patrick trotted from a side street and on to the cobbles of the dockyard. Close behind came the dockers who had vacated Murphy's tavern, their raucous cries and laughter pulling the storekeepers and shoppers in their wake. The wail of the timber mill hooter, signalling the midday break, brought the workers from the mill, and in a mass they changed course to join the crowd which closed on the ship. A runner had alerted the shanty dwellers who were now converging on the dockyard.

An armed section of the crew spilled on to the gangplank to bar any invasion of the ship, and the crowd held back at a respectful distance. Grant had meanwhile dispatched a seaman aloft in the hope of distracting Donal, but with a warning not to attempt rescue. Liam shielded his eyes against the sun and squinted into the rigging where he could just make out the figure of Jonathan, almost at the end of the yard. Shifting his gaze inboard he saw Donal climb out on to the yard. The chattering crowd watched Donal's progress, fingers pointing to call attention to his every movement.

Liam was unprepared for the emotions which now washed over him. This was his son who had become a man. No longer a knockabout object to make jest of, ridicule, or beat senseless on the whim of it, but a man of courage and purpose intent on honour. Oh, that the boy's grandfather could be stood on these docks to bear witness to it.

A gasp went up from the crowd as Donal missed his footing and only just managed to grab a hold on the jackstay. For a moment he swung freely, with nothing but air between him and a sure fall to death. Wild cheers rang out as he regained his perch on the foot ropes.

The wave of cheering reached Jonathan, and for the first time he became aware of the crowded dockside. Could it be they had come to bid him farewell? That must be it. But they were some hours early. Puzzled, he straightened up and waved in acknowledgement. The uproar of noise which greeted this caused him to smile and wave again.

''Tis not you they're cheerin', sailor boy!' The mocking call made him twist about in surprise. Donal grinned at him, the flourished knife glinting in the sun. ''Tis me they're after cheerin'... Donal McAfferty, come t'cut you to ribbons.' Sliding the knife back into his belt he began his precarious crawl along the yard.

In fascinated horror, Liam watched his son's slow progress, and conscience came to push the pride from him. What did it matter that Donal was not with the learning or the clever tongue? Good or bad he was in mortal danger up there, and had not the boy already proved himself? He grabbed at Patrick's arm. 'He has not a chance in hell, we must get him down!'

Patrick gently released his father's grasp. 'I will away t'get him, dar.'

He broke through the crowd and ran up the gangplank as the guarding crew levelled their muskets at him. Grant stepped forward to push him hard in the chest. 'Get back on the dock, or I will give the order to shoot you!' Patrick staggered under the push but came bravely back at Grant.

''Tis my brother Donal up there! Let me talk the sense in him. I can bring him down!'

'We can bring him down much faster.' Grant turned to the second mate. 'Take aim at that lunatic in the yards, and be careful not to hit the captain.'

Wilkins put the musket to his shoulder and was taking sight when Patrick hurled himself forward to send the weapon spinning away across the deck. With a curse, Grant brought the butt of his musket crashing down on Patrick's head to send him sprawling back on to the dock.

In a fury the crowd pushed in mindless movement towards the ship, trapping Liam as he attempted to reach Patrick, but a volley of gunfire brought them to a halt just a few yards from the ship, where they stood jeering at the crew. Some of the mob who were at the attempted lynching had joined the gathering and the ringleader yelled out, 'Let's be havin' some real fun of it! Untie the bloody boat!'

Within a minute the *Pelican* was free of her aft-end mooring ropes and the stern began to drift slowly from the dock. With a grinding roar, the gangplank split away, clouds of rolling dust enveloping the guards who leapt for safety from the structure as it fell away to the water.

Donal was now just twenty feet from Jonathan. The wind had freshened and plucked at the two men, threatening with every gust to rip them from their unsteady hold. Hair blowing wildly about his face, Donal sat up and wrapped his legs tight to the yard then took the knife from his belt. He was about to speak when he noticed a movement in the near rigging. The seaman sent aloft by Grant was edging his way towards them. Donal's voice came in warning. 'If y'don't want your man t'die, tell him t'go back!' Jonathan nodded.

'Get below!'

The seaman's reply was lost on the wind but he started on his descent. Donal watched him for a few moments before turning with a grin to Jonathan. 'Y'got away from the lynchin' but y'will not get away from me, sailor boy.'

Jonathan's thoughts were clear. He was in his natural element, whereas the madman who faced him was a stranger to such climbing. The chances were that he would fall before he could get near enough to use the knife. 'Mr McAfferty, you will more likely kill yourself than me. You would do better to come to sense and get back below.'

Sliding the knife between his teeth, Donal took fresh grip on the yard and lowered himself on to the foot ropes which swung chaotically as he edged nearer to Jonathan. But the ungainly boots denied him feeling or proper purchase, and suddenly he lost his footing. One leg went between yard and rope, the other swung clear, and only his strong arms stopped a fall. A howl of excitement floated up from the crowd. With a pull he was back on the yard and this time chose to crawl along it.

He stopped just three feet away from Jonathan, and sat up. Each looked at the other in open curiosity. Jonathan recalled Mary's words on the horrors she had endured at the hands of the man who now faced him, a creature barely human. Anger filled him, and for the first time in his life he had the desire to kill.

Donal felt inadequate under the steady gaze. He took the knife from his mouth and spat expertly at his target, the spittle running down Jonathan's face. 'Did y'fuck her, sailor boy?'

Jonathan wiped his sleeve across the spittle. 'You are beneath any contempt which I might offer ... do what you came to do.'

Donal's face distorted in hate as he closed both fists in tight grip on the knife and lifted it high above his head. 'Somethin' for you t'think on in hell, bastard! When I get back t'that cow she'll wish she'd never been born!' He hurled himself forward, bringing the knife down in a flashing arc.

Jonathan swung aside to avoid the assault but felt the blade rake across his chest and heard the wild scream as Donal blurred past him and away from the yard, turning over and over as he hurtled towards the deck.

A sickening thud carried clearly to Jonathan as the falling man crashed against the lower rigging to be catapulted into the narrow strip of sea which lay between ship and dock. A roar went up from the crowd, many pressing forward to watch Donal disappear beneath a flurry of foam then come up to lie still and spreadeagled on the surface, kept afloat by the buoyancy of his shirt which ballooned grotesquely from him.

Jonathan gazed down in horror, then became aware of the cutter which had been put out to arrest the ship's drift.

Slowly, the *Pelican* was being hauled in and with each passing second it threatened to pulverise Donal against the dockside... The man might still be alive.

'Ease off! He will be crushed! For God's sake ease off!' But his warning cries were lost in the uproar below, and the ship was less than fifty yards from berthing. Carefully he stood up then, taking a deep breath, dived clean away from the yard.

Half-stunned by his violent impact with the water, lungs near bursting, he hit bottom then struggled free from the deep mud to swim towards the faint light of the surface. The cheers of the crowd exploded about him as his head bobbed into view, but almost deaf from the effects of his dive, he was only dimly aware of them as he swam towards Donal.

The incoming tide was aiding the cutter's efforts and now the *Pelican* rushed broadside to the dock wall, looming above Jonathan as he put an arm around Donal's shoulders. Frantically he kicked out for the quay steps where Meredith and some of the dockers waited with ropes.

Shouts of warning filled the air as the *Pelican* rode high to come down on the men in the water. Jonathan turned his head to see the steps just a few feet away, but there was nothing he could do. The main force of the blow was taken by Donal, the hull stoving in his ribs. Jonathan felt a searing pain across his arm, almost fainting in the agony of it, and was barely conscious as Meredith dragged him on to the steps.

Both men were carried up to the level and laid out on tarpaulins. Teeth gritted against the pain, and exhausted by his efforts, Jonathan stared up into the vivid blueness of the sky, mind numbed to what was happening. The port doctor leaned over him in examination then spoke to Meredith.

'Broken arm, should be alright. Get him over to my office, I'll be there directly.' He rose to his feet. 'Got to have a look at the other man.' He walked away as Meredith and some of the dockers carried Jonathan towards the surgery.

Donal was now conscious but lay motionless under the doctor's probings while Liam and Patrick stood close by. 'Sorry, nothing I can do for him. You'd do better to get the priest ... quick as you can.'

Liam shrugged. 'Away an' get him, Patrick.' Without reply, Patrick ran to the church while Liam sank to his knees and cradled Donal's head. 'I'm desperate proud of you, son.'

Donal tried to speak, but the effort made him cough and the blood ran from his mouth to drip on the tarpaulin.

Liam comforted him. ''Twill be alright now, Patrick is away for the priest, an' we shall take y'home.'

The clatter of wheels against cobbles made Liam glance to the far side of the dock where a closed carriage came to a halt. Ambrose jumped down to open the door and Mary stepped from it with Agnes close behind. He scowled then turned his attention again to Donal. What did it matter any more what she did? Not a damn. Was not another of his sons now dying in his arms? And she the blame of it ... where in hell was the bloody priest?

The chaotic scene was a mystery to both women, but Agnes recognised one of the men from the timber mill. 'Why are you not at your work? Has there been an accident?'

He touched his cap in respect. 'Good day t'you, ma'am. Not an accident, ma'am, not as such. Donal McAfferty was havin' the arguin' with the English captain.' He swung about and pointed to the topmast of the *Pelican*. 'Up there, ma'am ... McAfferty fell into the water, an' the captain dived in t'save him. 'Twas a terrible long way t'fall ... I think the both of them are dead.'

Mary clutched Agnes in shock at the man's words. 'Dear God, do not let it be so!' Agnes put an arm about Mary's shoulder as she again questioned the man.

'Where are they?'

'Over there, ma'am.' He pointed to the warehouses. 'Stretched out on the ground.'

'Is Mr Meredith with them?'

'He is indeed, ma'am. Would you be excusin' me now? I have t'get back t'the mill.'

Agnes nodded, and the man scurried away. She was firm with Mary.

'I want you to sit in the carriage while I go to see Meredith, and find out what has happened.'

304

'Mrs Meredith, I must see for myself.'

'You are in no state to see anything. The captain will be alright, I know it ... the man was talking nonsense.'

'I must go to him, Mrs Meredith.' The words trembled from her.

Agnes insisted. 'Mary, listen to me. In view of what has already happened in this town, your appearance in front of these people can only worsen whatever has taken place here.'

She opened the carriage door. 'You would not have a riot and place us both in danger, surely?' Mary shook her head. 'Good. Now wait within. I shall return to you as soon as I have news.'

Reluctantly, Mary climbed into the carriage. Through the misted window she watched Agnes disappear into the crowd. Jonathan was somewhere out there. She must find him. But what if the crowd turned upon her as the cause of it all? It did not matter, nothing mattered but that she should be with him ... She would wait only another minute for Agnes to return.

She slumped back into the leather seating, her mind in vague recollection of the morning. Shortly after leaving Jonathan's bedroom she had slipped away from Braganza to walk the five miles into Clarkstown. But it was more like eight, forced to the backroads and woods for fear of running into the McAffertys. Yet even that was in vain. A shudder ran through her at the memory of her encounter with Donal, then bitterness at the archbishop's shattering of her hopes. Wanting only to be left to her own counsel, she had not attempted to go to the ship. Jonathan would try to persuade her to his will. It could not be that way. She alone should decide on it. Many thoughts came and went on the long walk to Braganza, but by the time the house came into sight her mind was made up. She would go with him.

The town clock struck the first hour of afternoon as she climbed from the carriage and made her way through the crowd. She felt a tug on her sleeve and turned to face a woman who pointed towards where a group of men clustered around a

305

figure lying on the ground. 'You need t'be there. He is dyin'.' The woman disappeared into the crowd. Mary caught her breath in a stifled sob and hurried forward unnoticed.

With Liam and Patrick on either side of him, Father Casey knelt beside Donal, voice droning softly in the administering of the last rites. She froze, unable to move away. The priest's murmurings came to a stop and he gave the sign of the cross. 'Donal, my son. Do you hear my voice?' Donal's lips moved, but no sound came from them.

The two law officers who stood close by shifted their feet noisily in embarrassment. With a glance of disapproval, the priest quietened their movement and took a small pewter flask of brandy from within his robes, carefully dripping some of the alcohol onto Donal's lips. 'Donal, y'will soon be with your maker. I will hear your confession.'

The brandy brought the last spark of life to the dying man. He turned his head and saw Mary, then moved his eyes towards the priest, who bent to hear the whisper. Father Casey nodded then looked across to Mary. 'He has asked you t'forgive him.'

Liam glanced up in surprise, aware for the first time of her presence. She gave a brief nod of assent to the priest, but before Liam could react, Donal's voice came with a sudden clarity and all attention turned to him.

'Bless me, Father, for I have sinned.' He coughed with the effort, and the blood ran once more from his mouth. But there was a fierce determination about him to continue. In terror he grasped at the priest's robes.

'Do not let me be goin' t'hell, Father!'

'I will not, Donal. Now make your confession, that y'may be saved.'

'I have done the terrible things ... murderin' the man Sullivan, an' knowin' of the lynchin' ... an' bein' after the murderin' of the Englishman.' His eyes took on a faraway look, then became suddenly wide and bright. 'My dar was allus a great one for the notions ... God forgive him for it.'

The light disappeared from his eyes and the life went from him. One of the law officers bent down and felt for a pulse.

'A gonner ... won' be murdering anybody else.'

Liam and Patrick exchanged glances of fear as they clambered to their feet. With his final words Donal had damned them to hang. Liam's only thoughts now were of escape and he fought to control his rising panic. 'Thank y'kindly, Father ... I am away now wit' Patrick t'fix up for the buryin' an' all.'

The law officers closed from either side, and Liam felt his wrists held in hard restraint. 'You ain't goin' any place, McAfferty. You're under arrest.' He looked across at Patrick. 'Goes for you as well, boy.'

Patrick felt a strange sense of relief. Had he not always seen this moment? It would be the gallows for the both of them now.

But the fire of hate was back in Liam as he spat at Mary. 'Y'have brought nothin' but the misery an' death t'me an mine. An' you've even now killt your fancy-man, for he'll surely die too! I curse y'both to eternal damnation!'

She looked back at him with contempt. ''Tis you will go to hell, you evil creature!' She pointed to Donal's body. 'You brought him to his death, an' God knows it!'

Head erect, she wheeled about and walked away. But the emotion of the encounter had sapped her resilience and she became disoriented within the chattering mass of onlookers. She must find Jonathan ... for pity's sake, he could not be dead! In anxiety she grabbed the arm of a bystander. 'Where have they taken the English captain?'

He indicated the far side of the docks. 'Over there, in the surgery. He's a lucky man to be alive, if you ask me, and the word is he's hurt no more than a fleabite.'

She thanked him and anxiously made her way towards the offices. Jonathan was alive, thank all of heaven, and she would soon be with him. But doubt returned. What terrible disgrace and scandal she had brought upon the man. Wrongfully imprisoned, almost lynched and then having to endure a trial ... now this murderous attack which had all but taken his life ... and poor David Sullivan too. He would be alive today if not for her. The tales must surely travel back to England, and grow fatter with every mile of the way, for the crew would not keep quiet such gossip as this would make.

How would he be able to hold up his head in the fine society? How would he properly captain a ship with all the sly remarks abounding? And what would his father have to say if she were there in England to add fire to the smoke of it? For without doubt she was the cause of it all. She stopped walking and stood uncertainly, head down in shame as the crowd thronged about her. Would it not be far better if she were now, on this instant, to go away and leave Jonathan in peace?

'You are most fortunate, Captain. A broken arm is all ... knife wound isn't much, just a scrape.' The doctor eased Jonathan's injured arm into a sling. 'But you should rest up in your cabin a while, that was some dive you took. There's bound to be some reaction from it. If you will excuse me now, I have other business to attend to.'

Meredith entered the surgery with Agnes just in time to hear the doctor's words. She ran to take Jonathan in an embrace. 'Thank God you are alive, Captain.' Before he could reply, Meredith's relief turned to angry concern.

'What in blazes got into you to do such a fool thing? You could've been killed!'

'I cannot answer that, sir ... How is the man McAfferty?'

'Dead as a doornail, and you're lucky not to be with him!'

Jonathan sighed deeply. 'I am sorry for the poor wretch. I fear that I was the cause of his death.'

'Sorry? The damned man just now made a dying confession of how he murdered David ... McAfferty an' his other son are in the lock-up for aiding and abetting ... you still sorry?'

'Is this true? Who told you of it?'

'I saw Fletcher and Stevens dragging them off, and asked them what it was all about. They told me.'

'Then it was as you suspected.'

'Bet your boots it was! Anyway it's all over now, they'll be hanged for it.'

Jonathan shivered with the effects of cold and shock. 'This has been a most terrible time. Never in all my life would I have

308

believed such an evil could happen.' His expression turned to concern. 'But where is Mary? Why is she not with you?'

Agnes answered, 'I thought it better for her to stay in the carriage, but I will fetch her now. She will be overjoyed to see you well.'

It was over a half-hour before Agnes returned to the surgery. Jonathan rose from his chair as he saw the alarm on her face.

'Mrs Meredith, what is it? Is Mary unwell?'

'She was not in the carriage and...'

Meredith interrupted. 'Don't get yourself in a state, she'll be somewhere on the dock looking for you.'

'I have searched everywhere, John, there is no sign of her.'

'Then she's probably gone back home.'

'She would not do that. It does not make sense.'

'Why does it not?'

'Because she told me this morning that she had made up her mind to go to England with Captain Bramwell.' Agnes suddenly realised that Jonathan had been unaware of the fact until this moment.

A dizziness overcame Jonathan and he slumped against the wall. Meredith helped him to a chair. 'You alright, son?'

'Thank you, sir, I will be alright in a moment.' His face brightened as he questioned Agnes. 'Is it so, Mrs Meredith? Did she really say she would return with me?'

'It is, Captain. I am sorry at having blurted it out... I had expected Mary to be here to tell you herself.'

He smiled. 'Please, do not be embarrassed, it is the most wonderful thing in the world that you tell me.'

Meredith broke in bluntly. 'Well, if it's so, why has she disappeared?'

'I believe you were right, sir, Mary will have returned to your home. All this has proved too much for her.'

Agnes shook her head. 'Mary is much stronger than you might think, Captain.'

'What are you saying, ma'am?'

'I am not sure.' She took her husband by the arm. 'John, I think we should return home at once and see if she is there.'

Meredith nodded in agreement. 'Now you're talking sense.

309

She'll be there right enough, you'll see, probably getting her things together.'

But Jonathan had caught the note of concern. 'I think I should accompany you.'

Agnes attempted a reassuring smile. 'You are not able, Captain, the doctor has said you must rest. In any case, Mary might return here and there would be no one to receive her.'

A profound exhaustion crept over him and once more he became aware of the pain. All he wanted to do in this moment was sleep, but he could not dare to. Had Mary changed her mind?

'I thank both of you for what you have done. In four hours from now the ship must sail.' His words were slurred with fatigue. 'I believe you must now know that I love Mary with all my heart ... please tell her so.' They had reached the door when he remembered the letter he had written her that morning. 'A moment, Mrs Meredith.'

He dragged the sealed envelope from his jacket. 'Please give this to Mary ... it was meant to reassure her on any last misgivings she may still have.'

Agnes took the envelope. 'I will make sure it is delivered, Captain, now rest.'

39

A weariness settled over Jonathan as he finished reading the note then placed it carefully before him on the chart desk.

'How did you come by this, Grant?'

'The doctor, sir. It had been left in his office.'

'I see.' He was brusque. 'Are you ready to give me your report on our readiness for leaving?'

'To all intents and purposes we are ready for sea, Captain.'

'Then about your business, we leave on the tide.'

Grant was plainly uncomfortable. 'With respect, sir, will you be well enough to take command? That is, I mean with...'

'Mr Grant, it is my arm which is broken, not my brain!'

'Yes sir.' He hovered in uncertainty. 'Beg pardon, sir, will there be a passenger to prepare for?' Jonathan gave a brief shake of the head. 'There will be no passenger.'

'Very well, sir, I shall prepare the crew.'

The door closed quietly behind him, and in a sudden fury Jonathan punched the note away to the deck and rose to pace about the cabin. Why would she not understand? Did their love matter so little that it should be weighed in the scales of public opinion? Once and for all he had to make her see it was not so. Wrenching open the door he strode out to the quarter-deck, almost colliding with the first mate.

'Mr Grant! Stand down the crew, we are not sailing!'

Grant was dumbfounded. 'Not sailing, sir?'

'Must I repeat myself, Mr Grant?'

'No, sir ... how long will they stand down?'

Jonathan seemed not to have heard the question. Tight-lipped, he looked away towards the town, then became calmer.

311

'Mr Grant, this was to have been my proving voyage, and I had high hopes of returning to my father's good opinions of me. But instead it has been an ill-starred journey ... Surely it cannot but get better.' He paused. 'I do not know how long my business will take, but make provision for a passenger.'

'I understand, Captain. But how shall you manage? Should I not go with you?'

'No, hold the ship at readiness for a swift departure, and mount an armed guard in the meantime. There are those who will not have forgiven recent happenings.' Without waiting for a reply, he strode quickly from the ship as Grant called after him, 'Good fortune go with you, Captain.'

'Thank you, Mr Grant, I shall need it.'

He had covered less than fifty paces towards the farrier's stable when a group of men appeared from behind a timber stack. They came to a halt just short of him, silently brandishing unlit torches from which the tar dripped on the quay. Their ringleader broke away and swaggered up to him.

'An' where would you be goin' this fine evenin', with your grand ship ready t'sail an' all?' The gang moved in rapid encirclement and Jonathan recognised them as the lynchers.

'Where I am going does not concern you. Now out of my way, or I shall have the whole crew of you arrested.'

The man laughed. 'Will y'now, an' aren't you the cocky bastard!' He pushed the torch to within a few inches of Jonathan's face. 'Your luck is gone, Englishman. We have just now watched your man Meredith leave the town, an' his peace officers must be halfway t'Boston jail wit' Liam an' Patrick.' He smirked. 'But we have sent friends t'keep them company, an' soon they will be free as the birds. Now get back aboard or we fire your ship, an' the lot of y'with it!'

Jonathan stood his ground, the tar running from the torch on to the sling about his arm. 'I shall warn you only once more ... stand aside!'

The torch was pushed hard into the injured arm. 'Shut y'r bloody mouth an' get back on the ship, or I will hit y' over the head an' drag y' there!'

312

Wincing with pain, Jonathan looked for help but the docks were now empty. 'Why are you doing this?'

'Y'know well enough. No more of the questions. Get back, an' get out or we burn y'!'

Grant had seen the incident, and as the group approached the ship, alerted the crew. He grabbed up a musket and hurried to the top of the makeshift gangplank. 'What is it, sir? What's going on?'

But before Jonathan could reply the ringleader pushed him back on to the planks. 'Do your talkin' on the ship.'

Jonathan walked Grant out of earshot of the mob. 'They threaten to torch the ship if we do not leave.'

'Shall we fire on them?'

'I think not, at least not yet.'

'The lads are game to fight, Captain.'

Jonathan wavered in his decision as he looked around the crew massed on the rail, muskets at the ready. In counter measure the ringleader lifted his arm in signal and the torches were set ablaze, the oily, black smoke swirling across the quay.

'Think on it, Englishman! Y'might be killin' some of us but y'll surely lose your ship!'

For some moments, captain and ringleader regarded each other in mutual contempt, then Jonathan turned away. 'I cannot hazard the ship, Mr Grant ... prepare to leave.'

'Aye, sir.' Angrily, he bellowed at the crew. 'Stand down your arms! All hands to seagoing stations!'

Within ten minutes the *Pelican* had cast off, and amidst roars of triumph from the mob moved slowly from the dockside, her sails cracking open as she headed downriver towards the estuary.

Agnes ran from the bedroom to see Meredith talking with Ambrose at the door. Meredith called out to her. 'Ben just had a word with one of the hands. Mary's been back here and gone.'

Ambrose piped up, 'That's so, Mrs Meredith. Seth told me as

313

how he seen her come off a cart, went in the house a while then lit off to the Timber Road.'

'How long since?'

'Figure it t'be better'n an hour, ma'am.'

'Thank you, Ben.' She looked urgently at Meredith. 'John, I must speak with you.'

Ambrose touched his forehead in salute. 'Better be off back to work, sir, gotta pick up those dry goods from town ... should I put the carriage away?'

'No, I'll take care of it.' Meredith closed the door. 'Maybe she's gone for a stroll to think things over. I wouldn't be surprised if she walked in right now.'

'You had better read this.' She handed him a sheet of paper. Meredith smoothed it out, mouthing the words slowly.

' "Dear Mr and Mrs Meredith, Forgive me. I am truly sorry for not saying a proper goodbye to you both, for you have been like a real mother and father to me." ' He cleared his throat. ' "I am to blame for all the trouble. Donal made my life a misery, but it was a bad way for him to die. Then Liam and Patrick sent to the prison. They will surely be hanged. David Sullivan would still be alive if we had not come to your town. I love Jonathan and shall forever. But I am thinking he will fare better without me. I have written him a letter and know he is well since the doctor told me so. I hope he will meet and marry a grand lady. He is a good man, deserving of happiness. I shall not forget your great kindness to me. Mary." ' Meredith lowered the note. 'Damn the McAffertys!'

'We must bring her back, John.'

'Do you suppose you can talk some sense into her?'

'I can but try.'

Agnes hurried before him to the waiting carriage. 'She will be trying to get to Boston.'

'Where else?' He smiled. 'Long as I've known the girl, she's been trying to get there. Don't worry yourself, we'll find her.'

Jonathan stood with Grant on the quarterdeck of the *Pelican* as the ship moved slowly downriver. 'Tricky waters, Mr Grant.'

'Aye, sir. I have given your orders to go with care.'

314

'Good! I do not care to suffer another shipwreck.'

'No, sir. What is our course when we clear the headland?'

'Boston. We must deliver the machinery or we shall lose the army contract. My father would not be best pleased to bear that on top of all that has happened.'

His mind returned to the note. She had said she would go to Boston. Would he try to find her? Pride said he would not, but he knew otherwise.

'Then we are for Southampton, sir?'

'With all possible speed.'

'Captain, may we speak man to man?'

'You may say what you have to.'

'Well... Me and the lads thought it a brave thing you did, diving off the yards to try and save that murdering lunatic.'

'An act of madness, more like!'

'No, sir, it took real courage. You might have been killed.' He fidgeted. 'What I really have mind to say is we did not behave proper at the shipwreck and no excuse for it...' His voice tailed away.

'What is it you are trying to say, Mr Grant?'

'Well, it was you being the owner's son and us used to the ways of Captain Anstruther ... then of a sudden you were the master, and we were fearful of your judgment.'

'Do not concern yourself, Mr Grant. I have not logged the incident, nor do I intend to take the matter further.'

'Thank you for that, sir, but it is not that we fear any punishment.'

'Then what is it?'

'That you have rightly earned our respect since that terrible time, and we are all proud to sail with you.'

'Thank you. What you have said means a great deal to me.'

Reassured, Grant pushed on. 'Captain, the men asked me to tell you not to be run out of Clarkstown on their account.'

'My business in Clarkstown is finished.'

'What I want to say is...'

The interruption was firm. 'I know what you want to say. It is not necessary to speak further.'

315

'As you say, sir.'

'Mr Grant, I appreciate your concern and cannot pretend that you are unaware of my personal life. I am also sure that you are all willing to go back and make a fight of it. But...'

'That we are, Captain!'

'Allow me to finish! I have a responsibility to you all. It would be unforgivable to hazard this ship and its crew in order to satisfy my personal desires.' He became suddenly weary. 'In any event, my father will have much to say on our return. I doubt there has been a more costly or unfortunate voyage in the whole history of this company.'

'Sir, no blame can be laid on you for that.'

'You think not? You are too kind.'

'Your father knows the way of the sea ... knows it to be a hard taskmaster.'

'We shall soon enough know what he thinks ... of that there is nothing surer.'

'He is a hard man, Captain, but he is fair, and we shall all give strong witness for you.'

'Thank you again, Mr Grant. I shall need all the help I can muster.' His thoughts returned to Mary. Why had she done this?

'You have a wife and family I believe, Mr Grant.'

'I am most happily married, sir, and with four sons who will follow me in my trade. God willing, my Margaret will be on Southampton Bar at our return.'

'Then you are to be envied.' He cleared his throat as he tried to hold his emotions. 'We should clear the straits within thirty-five minutes.'

The carriage slewed to a halt as it crested the high timberline and Meredith stared through the cloud of dust towards where the road bent away into the far valley.

'There she is!'

'Where?'

'By that log pile on the bend.'

316

She followed his pointing finger. 'I see her ... let me do the talking, if you please, John.'

Meredith smiled as he put the horses into a careful descent to the valley bottom. 'Agnes, I wouldn't have it any other way.'

Lost in thought, Mary did not hear the approaching carriage until it halted some yards behind her. Agnes jumped down and ran the short distance which separated them. 'Mary! We have been out of our minds with worry. Why are you doing this?'

'Mrs Meredith!'

'Running away will not solve the issue.'

'I am not running away!' Wearily she drew herself erect.

'Then what else would you call it?'

She did not answer, and Agnes regarded her a while before speaking in more kindly tone. 'The happenings of today have been a great shock to you, Mary. I know that. But they will pass ... now I think we should return home and talk of the future when you have had some rest.'

'I am not for comin' back, ma'am.'

'Mary, you disappoint me ... in any event, where do you think you are going?'

'I hope t'find some of my own people in Boston, then I shall obtain work.'

Agnes sighed. 'I grow more amazed, my dear. For a girl with so much intelligence, you do not use the brains you were born with. You say you love Captain Bramwell?'

'I have caused him and yourselves nothin' but trouble!'

'I see.' Agnes glanced away to where the horses munched in the grass of the clearing. Meredith shrugged as he caught her expression, and she turned again to face Mary.

'You are too stubborn and proud, my girl! At first I doubted the relationship, but no longer.' She grew more urgent. 'I believe the boy's love for you is sincere. He has suffered a testing time to prove it, and you now run from him without recourse to his feelings.'

'I am leavin' so he can find another who will give him a better life.'

317

'He wants no other, and I know it is the same for you ...
you are rid of that creature now and free to marry as you
will.'

Mary closed her eyes for a moment to shut away Agnes's
angry stare, then looked down at the forest floor. 'What
you say is right, Mrs Meredith, but other things bar our
way.'

'What other things?'

'I would shame him cruelly.'

'How would that be?'

'I am poor Irish, an' not of his religion ... with but half an
education. How could I face the great an' grand people he
walks with, and they knowin' of what has happened?'

Agnes snorted in temper. 'You are ashamed of being Irish,
then? You think the English rule the world and hold the
direction of good manners and etiquette? I am an American,
and I do not think the English are so great and grand. Neither
does the man who wants to marry you.' She suddenly remembered the envelope which Jonathan had given her. Taking it
from her pocket, she handed it to Mary.

'This is for you. Whatever the contents may be, I hope they
will bring you to sense more quickly than my efforts.'

Mary opened the envelope and tears pricked at her eyes as
she saw his handwriting for the very first time. Silently she read
the letter.

'My beloved Mary, I write this letter with thoughts of you still
sweet upon me. Fortune has not smiled upon us for these
many days, yet what matter, for we have each other and I glory
in our love.' The tears slid down her cheeks, blurring the
words. She brushed them away and read on. 'I am about to
leave for the *Pelican* – I promise you she does not really waddle
in the water, nor did I buy her with gold from the Duchess. I
will await you there. Dearest, I fear in my heart that the
archbishop will not grant you compassion. Therefore I plan to
give you this letter as soon as you come aboard. The while, I
will go about the ship as you read what I have to say. It is this.
Do not be fearful of the future, nor yet anticipate what others
may be disposed to think of us. It matters only that we are

318

together. I have my master's ticket and will obtain a position with another company. We shall have our own home in which to bring up our sons and daughters. It is right and proper that we make our own way in life without recourse to opinion or help from anyone. My life means nothing to me without you, my darling. I pray you will read my true thoughts within this letter and go with me to England. You are always in my heart. I love you, and shall forever. Jonny.'

She lifted her gaze to Agnes and was about to speak when there came the sound of a horse being hard ridden towards them. They turned to look up the road as the rider waved, kicking his mount to more effort, the dust cloud trailing high behind him. Meredith twisted about in his seat.

'What in hell! It's Ben Ambrose!'

The horse slithered to a halt in the clearing, and Ambrose tumbled from its bare back.

'It's the captain, Mr Meredith ... been run outa town!'

'Calm yourself, Ben. Who did the running?'

'Same mob 'at tried t'lynch him.'

'What happened?'

'I was gettin' the stores ... couldn't hardly believe it when I saw the ship leavin'.' He stopped and drew breath. 'Mob passed right by me ... fire torches, an' all. Laughin' fit to bust they was!'

Mary ran over to him. 'The captain, what of the captain?'

'He was right fine, not a body got hurt anyways.'

Meredith interrupted. 'Did you come straight from town?'

'Came by the ranch, sir, reckoned you'd be there ... Seth told me as how you'd lit out, goin' like the devil, he said, beggin' your pardon, sir.'

Meredith took out his pocket-watch and made a swift calculation. 'Mary, there's no time for any more talk. Make your mind up right now. Do you want to be with your man?'

Her mind cleared, and she knew in that moment that no matter the consequences she had never wanted anything more. But was it already too late? 'How can that be if he is gone?'

Meredith unhitched the reins. 'I'll take that to mean you do. Get aboard the both of you, and I'll do my best to make it so.'

In a daze of hope she climbed into the carriage while Agnes clutched at Meredith as he turned the horses.

'John, what will you do?'

'It will take him at least two hours to reach the headland. We have to get to the watchtower before then ... try and make him see us before he clears the straits!' Pulling the carriage into a tight turn, he brought the reins down in a hard crack.

It was a journey of nightmare proportions. Over an hour was spent in navigating the hazards of the timberline to cut into the opposite valley, and many times they almost came to grief. Clear of the forest they sped across the wide flatness of the plateau, horses at full stretch, carriage rocking wildly and speech made impossible. Agnes and Mary clung tightly to each other in silent prayer, only daring to look up as the pace began to slacken on the long haul up the headland towards the tower. Behind them the setting sun bathed the sky in a blaze of blood red and burnished gold, forcing the stark whiteness of the tower into vivid colour. Meredith cracked the reins in impatience, urging the horses to one last effort and they seemed to respond to his wild cry. 'Come on my beauties! ... Almost there!'

'Smooth as silk, Captain.' The helmsman steadied the wheel. 'We'll be clear of the straits in less'n a minute.'

Jonathan nodded then shouted, 'All hands! Keep a sharp lookout for rocks!'

A deep gratitude to Sullivan filled his mind as the ship moved into the shadow of the headland towering over a hundred feet to the starboard side. The shipwright had done his job well, for the *Pelican* had never handled better. But what great tragedy had been brought upon the man. Thank the Lord that at least Sullivan had left no widow to grieve for him. But there would be kin. He must set the Boston agents to search for them so they could be paid the insurance repair money.

'Straits cleared, Captain! We're in open sea!'
'Well done, Mr Grant! Get up here directly!'

The carriage lurched the last few yards up the grassy slope, skidding to a halt at the foot of the tower. Meredith leapt down and ran towards the edge of the cliff with Mary and Agnes close behind. Breathlessly they looked out over the vastness of the ocean, Mary fearful they were too late yet hoping they were not.

Meredith was first to see the ship. 'There they go!' Fully stern on to them, the *Pelican* was raising sail all round as she cleared the straits and headed for the open sea.

Meredith lowered his pointing finger. 'Too damned late! They won't see us now.'

Agnes put a comforting arm about Mary. 'I am sorry, my dear, so very sorry.'

In anger at herself, Mary looked towards the ship, its wake crimson in the deepening sunset, the vague impressions of men moving about its decks. One of them must be Jonathan, and she would not now be parted from him for want of trying.

'I will make him see me!'

Her cry hung on the air as she tore the cloak from her shoulders and swirled it in frantic circles above her head.

'Dear Lord, I love him! Please, please make him see me!'

Jonathan, face drawn with pain, leaned for support against the rail as Grant joined him on the quarterdeck. 'I am to my cabin for some rest, Mr Grant. I will return in an hour or so.'

'Aye, sir. Do you need anything?'

'Just some rest and I will be well.'

Handing his telescope to Grant, he departed to the cabin. Grant looked about the ship, then aft, as the *Pelican* began to leave the lee of the bay. Taking one last look at the headland, he muttered under his breath, 'Thanks be, we are for home.'

A sudden movement on the heights caught his eye. 'What do you make of that, Mr Abel?'

321

Both men shielded their eyes for a better view. 'Only some-body waving, Mr Grant.' He smiled. 'Likely as not the mob making sure of our leaving.' He turned back to the wheel, but Grant remained curious.

'I think not.' He raised the telescope and scanned about the cliff edge before fastening in focus on the group. 'Glory be!' He ran to the cabin to bang hard on its door. 'Captain, better come quickly!'

Jonathan wrenched open the door. 'What on earth is this commotion, Mr Grant?'

'People on the clifftop, Captain, three I make it. Looks to me like they're making signals to us!'

'Where are they?'

'Below the watchtower, sir.'

Jonathan took the telescope as they hurried to the rail. With some difficulty he trained it on the tower then lowered it to bring Meredith's face into focus, then Agnes. With a deep breath he moved it across them to see Mary waving the cloak high above her head, and his questioning words came back to him, words he had spoken when he had stood with her on that very clifftop ... *Would you have me wait upon a miracle?*'

His hand shook under the weight of the telescope and he brought it to his side. 'Put her about, Mr Grant ... I believe we shall be taking on a passenger.'

Grant smiled broadly. 'I'm glad for you, Captain, right glad ... hard o'starboard, Mr Abel! We are going about.'

The cloak fluttered from Mary's hands as she saw the ship go into a tight turn and begin to head back into shore. 'He has seen us! Did I not tell you he would?' Her voice trembled in the words as she looked up into the sky and whispered, 'Thank you, Lord, thank you for this great mercy y'have shown me.'

Agnes wept in open relief and Meredith found it hard to hold back his emotion. 'Mary, I am overjoyed it has come right for you at last.'

The *Pelican* had come to anchor, and they watched in silence as a cutter, manned by two seamen, approached the sandy beach at the foot of the cliffs while Jonathan sat upright at its stern.

Agnes dried her eyes. 'Your man is on his way. Do not keep

him waiting any longer.' She pointed. 'That way will take you down to the cove. Tread carefully now. Our hearts go with you.'

Mary turned and swept them in embrace to her. 'I owe y'both my very life an' believe the Lord chose you in the working of His miracle ... I shall never forget what you have done an' will love you forever.'

They watched her run to the path, then with a wave of farewell she was gone from their sight. Meredith put an arm about Agnes and hugged her as they watched Mary emerge on to the beach. 'Know what I think, Agnes?'

She squeezed his hand. 'Tell me, John.'

He smiled. 'Reckon it was like she said, a miracle ... never thought things would turn out this way when I picked her up on the Timber Road that morning.'

Agnes became aware of his sudden shyness, and her smile was impish. 'Like what, John?'

'You know fine well, woman. Mary brought us back together is what, and if that isn't the Almighty's doing I'll be damned.'

'John!'

'Sorry.'

She laughed, then gently took him in her arms and kissed him.

Mary stood for a moment at the foot of the cliffs, overcome with a breathless anticipation as Jonathan leapt from the cutter. For the first time she saw his injured arm and the shadows of pain about his face. An agony welled in her. He had endured so much. Why had she not been brave enough to see the rightness of their love and gone with him when he had first asked?

'Jonny! You are hurt!' She put her arms about him in tender embrace. 'I love you, Jonny, I truly love you.' She looked up into his eyes, her fingers moving gently over his bruised face. 'I shall take this hurt from you.'

'There is no hurt ... not now you are with me.' His kiss was soft on her lips, then taking her by the hand he helped her into the waiting cutter.

'Come, my love. The sorrow is past ... we are going home.'